A Maze of Glass by S. R. Hughes

https://thesrhughes.com

Published by Ritual Dark Press

Cover by GetCovers

RITUAL DARK PRESS

ISBN: 978-0-9863175-1-4 (print)
       978-0-9863175-2-1 (ebook)

Printed in the United States of America.

First Edition.

A Maze of Glass

for you

Chapter One

Keene's Falls, NY.

December, 2006.

"The mass of men lead lives of quiet desperation."

— Henry David Thoreau

Zoe lost hold.

Well-trained, physically honed and mystically enhanced, she still only weighed a hundred and thirty pounds, mostly muscle, and Omar weighed at least one-eighty and seemed unaware of his limbs, their movements, or his baseline proprioception. Freed of his human buttress, he staggered three more rambling-whispering steps before falling to his knees in the wilderness snow. Swiping handfuls of white fluff into the air, he dug at the ground. "The guts of the world churn," he panted, sweeping oak-dark hands through the blanch, "hungry for our bones."

Zoe brushed snow from her armored jacket and pants. She hazarded a glance behind them at the half-mile of forest and ski-country she'd dragged Omar through so far. In the tiny skiing village, sirens wailed; emergency lights flashed. Taking off her cap, she ran a pale hand through honey-brown hair and put it back on again. Omar, clad in blue jeans, basketball sneakers, a button-up, and a knit sweater, continued fumbling on all fours, muttering. His shoulder-length dreadlocks, bound at the back of his skull, gathered clinging pallor.

Zoe had spent her entire life on the fringes of the supernatural world, had started honing her sixth sense at fourteen and had started training for her job at sixteen. Like the vast majority of people, Omar had never undergone a legitimate paranormal experience in his life. His reaction, on the spectrum of such things, wasn't unusual.

"The night is alive, the skin of the void is the skin of the entire universe…"

The poor guy had just gone on vacation. The rental cabin the Summoner had hit belonged to a group of late twenty-somethings visiting town on a ski trip. Zoe had shown up just as the spell had triggered. She'd grabbed Omar because she'd found him on her way in. He hadn't seen much—couldn't have—but he'd seen enough.

"Come on," Zoe grunted, pulling him back upright, trying to balance him as he stagger-flailed through the snowy woods. "We're almost there."

The safehouse waited just uphill, cloaked in a camouflage of night-time wilderness.

"Teeth like lightning. Claws like gunshots…"

She wrestled him, pushing and pulling and dragging him on. "Pull yourself together. You want to go out like this?"

Omar mumbled a drool of response.

It took minutes to climb the sixty-something feet to the safehouse, but they made it before Omar's breakdown reached its barrel-bottom. Leaning him against the wall, Zoe keyed a sixteen digit alphanumeric passcode into a book-sized terminal next to the door. Omar sank, sitting. Zoe swiped her operations security card through a mag-reader. The locks disengaged.

Hauling Omar to his feet, she pushed her way inside. She let go of him once they passed the threshold, allowing him to sag and stumble out of the cabin's entryway and toward the kitchen. Shutting the door behind them, she reactivated both the technological and mystical security systems. Dense iron bolts clamped the entrance shut. A series of silent alarms and background softwares reset.

Closing her eyes, she attuned her professionally-honed sixth sense to the world around her.

The cabin's wards stood strong. No strange disturbances, sensations, or impulses of foreshadowing tugged at her awareness. She reached out farther but felt nothing. The absence of evidence didn't guarantee anything, but it put her at ease. Blinking back to the material-visual sensory input of the cabin, she released her attention.

"Shadows and light, death and time…" Omar leaned over the kitchen sink, staring at a window that wasn't really a window. Where he stared, the cabin recessed into a mountainside. He stared at a photo taken from the window of another cabin nearby, one less secret, and mystically-enhanced to appear real. "The dark eats the light the light eats the dark the dark eats the light…"

Zoe wiped sweat from her brow. She turned the oven to 500 degrees and set the microwave for five minutes. From the liquor cabinet, she procured the five oldest bottles and placed them pentacle-positioned around a silver plate next to the sink. Omar rattled more brain-break gibberish with his posture craned over the basin, staring at an enchanted photo. Trying not to listen, Zoe knocked on the fridge five times and muttered a five-syllable incantation for five repetitions. A series of unseen cogs and wheels and valves ground into motion, responding to both mechanical and magical triggers. The oven recessed into the wall and a trap door beneath it yawned into a broad set of spiraling, corrugated-steel steps.

She went to collect Omar. He thrashed and snarled at her touch, "They whisper always, *always!*" he howled, "Why!? Why can I *hear* them!?"

He flung her off of him and lunged. Half-reflexively, she bull-kicked him in the gut.

He collapsed, gagging for air.

Climbing on top of him, she pinned his legs with her knees and held his head in her hands. His arms splayed wide, jumping like fish. She whispered phrases of multi-lingual incantation, the grammar of different roots tangling together. As she felt the energy build up, she closed her eyes and focused it into a sharp spell. She imagined the tip of an ice pick. But in a good way. *Nope.* She shook off the ice-pick image and decided on the needle-tip of an adrenaline injection instead.

As Omar shivered and shook beneath her, she repeated the incantation a second time. She felt the spell take, felt her willpower grab hold of it. Zoe plucked off the last of the syllables, Korean, <<calm water,>> and drove the energy through her musculature, down her spine, along her ribs, through her humeri and carpals and phalanges and into Omar's skull.

She dove.

a million squirming nothing-something gods pulsing themselves against the skin of reality

Omar plummeted through void. Zoe plummeted in him.

She needed something real. Fast. Something that tethered Omar to the material world, the mortal-mundane, everyday one. But she didn't know Omar, didn't know anything about him. "Omar, you ever been to New York City?"

they whisper in the pores of our bone marrow they squirm through the veins

veins

subway lines

n r q w queens-bound astoria-ditmars, 7 through Sunnyside, m/r Woodside to Forest fuckin Hills

She felt the Capitalization in his thoughts. A surge of energy pulsed through her. Her lungs filled with air. Not the real ones, the dream-lungs that only existed in Omar's mind. Or did they? Magic was like that. To someone as expert as Zoe, the difference hardly mattered.

Flushing the K-Town that K-Town wants to be,

Fog swirled in from the periphery of the void. Ground opened up beneath them. *come down Roosevelt Avenue and try to be mono-lingual*, a clatter of life and the makings thereof: elevated tracks rattled as a 10-coach train howled eastward. A storefront called out 'LEARN ENGLISH.' Others announced services in Hanji, Kanji, and Cyrillic. A boba place sat next to Khan Family Pharmacies sat next to a bodega FOR RENT. A hallal cart sizzled spice in smoke and steam on the corner. "This place exists," Zoe said soothingly.

She knelt and pressed her palms to the asphalt. People stepped around her like water parting around a stone; in the memory, she didn't exist. Omar hadn't done this.

A shadow lurched from a store awning, full of sharp and violence. It quivered as if trying to peel itself away from the object casting it. The Summoner had unleashed vicious living darkness on the cabin.

Memories interrupted memories all the time. In psychic magic, stability was rare.

The shade tried to unpeel itself. It gained mass as it loosened from its anchor, becoming slowly three dimensional.

"The monster was real," she said. "But so is this place."

She felt the memory tremble, an earthquake solely-psychological.

Distantly, screams echoed down from the sky. Another, darker memory.

Zoe rushed through incantations, strained through spellcraft. She sputtered, losing her breath. Omar shouted something else. She felt him try to leave her framework; felt her body ache to split in half. She groaned, back arched, and pushed through; three more seconds, six more syllables, the spell blazing through her tendon-by-tendon...

A ward against madness.

They jerked apart in the cabin, Zoe sweat-slick, her underclothing stuck to her skin. Omar bucked a few times on the ground and went still. Zoe rolled onto her side and pushed herself back up. Panting, she pulled off her cap and tossed it aside. She ran her fingers through greasy-damp hair.

"What are you?" Omar asked, halfway up, himself.

"I'm a witch."

"What?"

"I'll explain in a..." headrush rolled through her. She balanced herself against a countertop. Inhaled. "Downstairs."

"You're a witch?"

"*Downstairs,*" she stressed, stepping away from the wall, testing her legs. "Now. Please."

"Why?"

"In case something followed us."

################

The basement contained enough supplies to last four people three weeks. Composed of two two-cot bedrooms, a simple kitchenette, a walk-in pantry and fridge, a warded office equipped with warded and encrypted internet access bounced between a dozen different mirrors and server sites around the world, two bathrooms, and a foyer, it occupied exactly eight hundred square feet. Four lockers waited in the foyer, all outfitted with multi-bolt passcode locks and all but one empty.

Zoe opened her locker and pulled out her larger gig bag. She'd taken her necessaries on patrol but had left her greater inventory behind, all cost-benefit analyzed, but now... "Omar, where are you right now?" she asked, unzipping the overstuffed rucksack.

"I don't even know..." he hovered behind her, drifted aimlessly.

"This is a safehouse. It's a house where you're safe."

"Stop talking to me like I'm a kid."

"Can you lie down on one of the beds in there?"

"Stop talking to me like—"

"I just saved your life," Zoe interrupted. "I saved your life like *ninety minutes ago*. Can you *please* lie on the bed?"

"I..." he looked away. "Yeah. Thanks."

She pulled an old cigar box from the rucksack and took it with them as they walked to the bedroom. Omar sat on the edge of one of the cots, arms folded, the dreadlocks bouquet'd behind his head iced with frost. He stared at the floor and didn't look up as she moved around the room.

"Do you know where you are, right now?" she asked.

He blinked. Stared. "We'd all rented this lodge..."

"Where?"

His Adam's apple bobbed. His hands folded over each other again and again. "Uh. North. Upstate. This little town, uh...Bloomingdale? No, Keene's Falls."

Caution tempered her relief. "Good."

"Keene's Falls," he muttered. "In the lodge. This whole group went skiing this morning but I was too hung over. Oh, fuck. Was that just this morning?"

"Omar, stay with me. Stay in the room with me, okay?"

"Did…" he gulped again. Blinked. Turned his focus from the floor to her. "Did anyone else make it out?"

(*flashes of bright red, gibberish shouts and screams as she'd pulled him out of the cabin*)

"I couldn't confirm any casualties," she answered.

"I saw what happened."

"People were certainly…injured."

He nodded, saying nothing.

She set the cigar box on a three-drawer dresser situated between the two cots. Opening it, she revealed an array of esoteric drugs and herbs, a handful of preturnatural pills, and three plastic packages filled with viscous salves. "This is medicine. Kind of."

"What 'kind of?'"

"The kind a witch carries when she thinks she might have to pull people out of monster attacks."

"You got in my head, earlier. I felt you."

"I'm a witch, it was a spell. I only did it to help you."

"But you *could* use it to hurt me?"

"That one, no. It's psychic magic but it's a warding spell, so, no, I can't hurt you that way. Do you think you can trust me for a few hours?" She pulled a sackcloth pouch from the box. Inside, a pepper-taut dreamer fruit waited in a tiny plastic bag buried in Orpheus dust. Nodding at the ingredients, she sealed it back up. "I'm going to give you a couple things to help you…stay okay. Your brain is struggling to process what you just witnessed and this will make it easier."

"Uh-huh…"

"Look, I'm going to have to trust you, too. I was hoping to dodge this, but I'm going to take something. Think of it like a magic drug or an ingestible spell, whatever. It's going to give me visions. I won't be able to do much while I'm having them."

"What, you'll be helpless?"

"I'm never helpless. But as close as I get, yeah."

"And you think I'd do something?"

"No. But you *could*. Just like I could. But since I just saved your life, I think evidence suggests that I *won't*." She plucked a fat, tightly-rolled joint from the cigar box. "This is sixth-sense stimulant, strongest when inhaled. You've smoked before?"

Omar took the joint, scoffing. "Got a light?"

"I do." Zoe smoked half a pack of cloves per day. Sometimes more, usually not. She pulled her Zippo from her jacket pocket and lit Omar's joint. Clapped the lighter closed again. "When you finish that, I'm going to give you a pill. It'll help you rest."

"You mean it'll put me under."

"Tomorrow I'll tell you anything you want to know. For tonight, I need you to trust me."

Omar smoldered through the joint without muttering more than a syllable. When she brought him the pill, he took that, too. He lost consciousness not long after, the latter drug merely a spell-enhanced dose of Ambien.

Zoe took a pinch of Orpheus dust from her sackcloth bag and positioned it under her tongue. She opened the tiny plastic baggie and pulled the dreamer fruit out by its stem. Holding the golden-hued and amber-pulsing ovoid at her lips, she hesitated. What did she want to ask the dream? What did she want to know about? Dreamer worked best when given clear direction. An avenue of exploration. "Show me the Summoner," she said. Then, again, as if telling the fruit a dark and personal secret, "Show me the Summoner."

Slipping the fruit into her mouth, she bit down. It melted to honey.

She unzipped her armored jacket but left it on. She unclipped her holster and stowed her Malleus Industries 10mm semi-automatic under her pillow, double-checking the safety. She chalked a line between the cots and muttered the words of a ward over it, setting an alarm to wake her if Omar touched the boundary. The dreamer buzzed in her brain, by then, humming sphenoidal and temporal, tickling parietal and soothingly stroking her scalp. Invisible weights hung from every eyelash, dragging her to bed. On her side, facing Omar, she put her right hand around her sidearm's grip and waited for her eyelids to curtain over her.

Poor guy. Poor wrong-place-wrong-time guy.

Something tickled between the folds of her brainmeat.

New York, NY.

April, 1997.

"The long-run is a misleading guide to current affairs; in the long-run, we are all dead."
— John Maynard Keynes

Zoe peered up at the roachden brownstone before her and sighed. A reeking crustpunk heroin-napped, sprawling the concrete steps leading up to the beefy, beater-clad bruiser at the just-ajar door. Head-sized biceps wore prison tattoos but no other needle-work marred his oil-tanned skin; no sign of track marks. Maybe he injected steroids in the ass, otherwise: cocaine.

"I'm here for Jill," Zoe said.

"You bring cash?" the man sounded like New Jersey, not just like someone *from* New Jersey, but the black-lunged tobacco-throated shore of the Hudson itself.

In 1997, Zoe didn't wear armored leather jackets. She wore an unarmored military camo jacket, oversized, and athletic pants over military surplus boots. The oxblood clutch clashed with the rest of the aesthetic but belonged to her nonetheless, as did the five hundred dollars bundled inside of it.

"That depends. Where's Jill?"

"Upstairs."

At twenty-four years of age, Zoe already had eight years of esoteric and mystical training under her belt. Eight years of martial arts and combat training, too. Only three years of professional-level para-military and law enforcement training, unfortunately, but almost doubtlessly more than the man trying to intimidate her.

Still. The situation didn't need snags.

"I'll hand over the cash soon as I see my sister."

He sniffed, wiped at his nose with the back of his thumb. He sized her up with a deep-dark gaze; she appraised him with gray-blue suspicion. He nodded. "Okay, tough lady. We'll bring her out for ya." He stepped out of the sunlight and into the dim-dark foyer of the brownstone. "Hey!" he shouted upward, "Bring down li'l Jill-Pill!"

Zoe restrained her words.

"Uh-huh," the man continued shouting. "Okay!" He turned back toward Zoe. "She'll be down in a second," he smirked, lighthearted, the pleasantry clearly cruel. "Now. The money."

Zoe revealed the rubber-banded cash from inside her clutch but didn't take it out. "When I see her."

"Sure."

Gillian Briar, Jill, was Zoe's sister. Slightly shorter and more curvaceous than Zoe, Jill was just under three years younger, had spent a week weeping over Kurt Cobain's death, and had visited four different rehabilitation centers over the prior four years. The settling of her five hundred dollar debt represented the alleged finale of her latest relapse, a promise Jill had sobbed a dozen times during their plea-filled phone call even after Zoe had already agreed to help.

Jill appeared on the stairwell woozy, somnambulant, her legs stumbling more than walking, her procession down the steps possible only through the aid of two other scrawny bodies. Her raven hair spilled in frayed tangles around her, split ends and grease, the darkness of it stark against her pallor. The two other addicts, a black boy who couldn't look at Zoe and a white woman who couldn't decide where to look at all, stopped at the threshold. Like vampires, they pulled up just short of the sunlight.

Except vampires weren't real. Not the traditional ones, at least.

"There she is," New Jersey said, grinning. "Now. Cash."

Zoe imagined throwing her pocket-hidden knife at him. She tossed the bundle of cash instead. New Jersey caught it, bending forward just-uncomfortably in the act. He glanced at her, knowing she'd made him stretch for it on purpose, and popped loose the rubber band. He made a show of counting it twice. Behind him, Jill seemed to regain her footing. She groaned. The boy wiped at his eyes. He whispered something to Jill; Jill didn't respond.

"Well, that's that, then," New Jersey nodded, satisfied. "Good luck." He gestured two-fingered toward Zoe and Jill's two ferryfolk guided her down the brownstone steps. Jill's balance quaked when they released her. Nobody said anything, nobody asked anything. Jill looped an arm across Zoe's shoulders and Zoe looped an arm around Jill's waist. The white woman and the black boy both hesitated before turning away; they both turned away. New Jersey vanished somewhere, presumably dividing money.

"I…" Jill shook. "I'm sorry."

"I know. Let's get you home." Zoe tugged on her sister and they started moving.

Jill limped and listed wayward. "Can't go home."

Sylvia Briar and Daniel Briar-Wythe had cut Gillian off after the previous relapse.

"My home," Zoe corrected. Sighing, she added, "Jill, please, can you walk?"

"I can. I'm walking."

"Not…really…" they'd only made it halfway down the block.

"I'm *walking*."

That Jill managed at all implied a descent from her high. It implied a comedown soon.

"Just hold on to me, okay?" Zoe changed tactics. She needed a cab. A cab driven by a desperate cabbie eager to flee the Lower East Side. They made it to Avenue B. Jill smelled like days of unwashed sweat and crustpunk company. Zoe pretended not to scent it whenever she inhaled. Jill stumbled while they crossed Avenue B and mumbled something about not belonging anywhere. Zoe searched traffic for anything yellow. The first cab dodged them by swerving lanes. The second one locked its doors and pretended not to notice. At Astor Place, aching from exertion and pissed off with Jill for causing all the exertion, Zoe leaned her sister against the awning of the hooded subway stairwell and sat down next to her.

"I'm sorry," Jill mused, head falling onto Zoe's shoulder.

"Yeah, well…" Zoe took a pack of cloves from her camo jacket and rapped the bottom against the heel of her left hand.

"Sorry," Jill repeated, sober enough to look awake, now, but far from sober.

"I know." Zoe took a few drags and flicked ash. More traffic passed. They sat with their backs against greened steel, people funneling up from below, the subway exit positioned on a triangle of concrete slabbed between too many streets.

Halfway through Zoe's clove, Jill broke the silence. "I can't go back to rehab."

"You have to."

"I mean I…I *can't*. Who'd pay for it?"

"I…I don't know." Trainees didn't earn much. Zoe's income barely covered her needs. The paydays all came later, in field work or tactical management.

Jill shivered against Zoe. She hiccuped, and the hiccups turned to sobs.

"We'll figure out where to come up with the money," Zoe said, looping an arm back across Jill's shoulders and hugging. "Okay?"

Jill shook her head into Zoe's neck. "It's going to kill me…"

"We'll figure it out."

A beat passed. A liminal moment.

"I have something," Jill said.

"What is it?" Concern weighted Zoe's question.

"There's a spell," Jill whispered. "I think it could…help me."

A block and a half away, Zoe noticed a handful of NYPD uniforms sharing coffees and cigarettes. "Let's get you back to my place, okay?" she squeezed Jill's shoulders and helped her stand up again. "Then we'll talk about...whatever else."

"I don't know what else to do."

"I brought tokens," Zoe said, hoping the cops didn't notice her almost wholly supporting her drained sister down the steps. "We'll just head up to my place, two stops, and we'll talk about it there. Whatever you need."

"I don't want to be *like* this anymore."

"Jill, please, please, I love you, but I need you to stay calm."

"I..."

"Just let's get home, first, okay? And then we can talk about anything you want to talk about."

################

Jill fell asleep on the train and Zoe leaned her forehead against the pane of maybe-glass between her and the steel columns whipping past outside. Jill hadn't taken to 'the life' the way she had. Jill hadn't taken to the family, either, really. Except for Zoe.

Jill's explorations into the supernatural, the bizarre and esoteric and utterly, almost entirely *secret*, trended toward depth. While most Hammer members favored practicality, efficiency and responsiveness, Jill preferred raw power and deep, profound magics, the arts and sciences that broke the rules of reality itself. That meant that if a spell existed that might help Jill kick heroin, Jill likely knew it. It also meant that if such a spell existed, it likely required time, patience, and endurance. It was likely ritual, not cantrip—it was likely the sort of the thing that happened over the course of days or weeks, not minutes or hours. And though Zoe considered herself a disciple of the practical, the efficient, the responsive, she was no fool on the measureless depths of magic's possibility...nor its sometimes-unpredictable blowback. So she knew, too, that the kind of spells that might help an addict unbind themselves from the chains of addiction were likely to be dangerous, volatile, and risky.

But, most importantly, she knew that when Jill asked, she'd say yes.

The gears churned through Zoe's skull until her meditations subsided beneath the crackle of a conductor's voice. She'd missed her stop by four or five stops, and of course the 6 went all the way up into the Bronx before it turned around again. As the train howled its way toward the 86th Street station, Zoe elbowed Jill awake. "I fell asleep, too," she lied. "Sorry. We'll turn around at the next stop."

Jill nodded, eyes dreamy-tired but not closing. "Yeah," she mumbled. "We'll turn around."

New Orleans, LA.

June, 2016.

"For every man there exists bait he cannot resist swallowing."

— *Marisha Pessl,* Night Film

Zoe crushed a cockroach underboot and flicked ash from her clove. She ground the bug into the asphalt until the cement-cells and insect-cells commingled. Taking a long drag of smoldering spice, she kept walking. Not terribly long ago, hotels rented rooms for smokers; these days, she smoked her nightfall regular while *en route* to whatever destination required her.

She'd filed her final reports on the assignment three days earlier and had received clearance and Decomp instructions that afternoon. Tomorrow, a luxury car would pull up to her hotel and ferry her to a local Malleus Industries office building. Depending on whichever other agents were wrapping up whatever other assignments in wherever other locales, she might start therapy that day. If not, the company would book her business-class to whatever city made the most sense to use as host hub for Group Therapy, an important part of Decomp.

'Decomp' abbreviated 'Decompression,' a fourteen-day, absolutely-mandatory regimen of one-on-one and group therapy, non-denominational spiritual cleansings, literal and metaphorical vaccinations, and other physiological, psychological, and mystical attendings that Malleus imagined would keep their field agents mentally sound and emotionally stable across a tenured career of professionally witnessing and disposing of 'the impossible.' But even though Decomp always felt good, even though it felt like it *worked*, Zoe couldn't think of a single veteran field agent describable as remotely mentally sound or emotionally stable. Herself, included.

Medication and talk therapy and literal magical cleansings made everything easier to deal with, but eventually the job cracked people. Because it involved a lot of victims and a lot of lying and a lot of seeing things exist that shouldn't exist and seeing things happen that should never, ever happen; seeing them happen to people they should never, ever happen to.

Another enormous roach skittered out into the middle of the sidewalk and froze. They grew 'em big in Louisiana. The state bird, some joked. It sensed Zoe's approach and fled, zipping into a pile of leaking garbage bags before Zoe could kill it.

Shrugging, Zoe finished her smoke and walked the final half-block to her hotel.

The days after the wrap of an operation always felt bitter to Zoe. They felt *empty*.

The hotel elevator took her up to the seventh floor. Her sixth sense noticed something immediately. Zoe's skin puckered, gooseflesh.

Stepping out of the elevator, she untucked her hip holster from under her armored leather jacket; unclasped it. Wrapped her hand around the ergonomic pistol grip and poised her thumb against the safety lever. She couldn't tell if the thing she felt was a threat or not.

Wasn't the uncertainty a threat in and of itself?

The sensation grew stronger as she neared the door to her room. Something waited for her. She wasn't sure of it, not in the literal sense, but she was *certain* in the figurative. A sixth sense didn't tell a person much, even one as well-honed as Zoe's. It told her that something was wrong, that something bad was happening or likely to happen or had the strong possibility of happening or had already happened recently. It made no guarantees and no references to the who, how, or why of things; it prickled and tingled with probability fields and likelihoods, hunches and instincts.

Left-handed, she drew out her room keycard and swiped it through the mag-reader. The lock LED blinked green. Half-crouched, flanking the door, she grabbed the knob and opened it just-slightly. She released the knob and the door settled barely-ajar, the only thing necessary to swing it open or shut it the barest of pushes. She waited.

"Zoe?" a familiar voice called out. "Zoe, is that you?"

"Leo?" she let go of her gun. Leonid Singh?

"I hope I haven't caught you at a bad time..." Leo had a deep, full voice, a slight British accent.

Zoe laughed, disengaging from her sixth sense. "Is there ever a 'good' time?"

"I'll stand in front of the door when you open it. My hands are up. I have some rather nice Scotch in the right one."

She opened the door, peered around the corner, and smiled.

Leonid Singh stood just a hair under six feet tall and weighed close to two hundred pounds, once mostly muscle, now increasingly not. Leo had been quite the athletic specimen as a thirty-six year old field agent, less so as a fifty-two year old consultant-to-the-Board. That night, he wore a black-tie suit, tie undone, cufflinks missing, the top two buttons of the shirt opened to reveal a gilt-chained amulet. In his right hand, he held the promised bottle of expensive Scotch. On his feet, he wore dress shoes. When Leonid was comfortable, he went barefoot.

Zoe stepped inside, closed the door, and levered the deadbolt shut. "You didn't call ahead."

"Strictly speaking, I'm not here."

Still facing the door, she tried to mask the bodywide tightening. A sixth-sense chill shivered through her. "You're not?"

"I'm not." Leo's voice carried more gravity, suddenly.

Zoe turned to face him. "How bad is it?"

"As bad as the Scotch is good."

"Then pour me a fist and let's get this started."

"My pleasure."

She followed Leo into the standard hotel bedroom; the one that served duty as a living room, dining room, kitchenette, and entertainment center all at once and in under three hundred square feet, bathroom attached. From a plastic bag of sweating ice, Leo produced a handful of cubes. He dropped two each into twin plastic cups, around the size of rocks glasses, which he filled with five fingers of Scotch. He sat on a faux-regal armchair, red and gold, and she sat on the replica mirroring it. He picked up his cup, she picked up hers. They pushed them together; plastic didn't *clink*.

"I suppose we're the last of us, now," Leo said.

"Pretty much."

"Sung-ho's dead. Tanisha's…retired. And refuses to speak to any of us."

"Valley's dead, now, too."

"Poor fellow." Leo sipped his drink. "Do you remember why we ever called him that?"

Zoe chuckled but the amusement quickly died. "I really don't. It started with Sung-ho, I think."

"He had a thing with nicknames."

"'Punjabi Bond.'" Zoe smirked.

"And the whole time, I'm Tamil."

"It doesn't have the same ring."

"It doesn't."

Her smirk disappeared. "You mind if I put something on?"

"Music?"

"Yeah."

"By all means."

Zoe crossed the room to where her old, un-WiFi-able iPod rested inlaid to a speaker system, audio-out and charging cord at the same time. She clicked through the screens and selected a playlist. Blues, mostly. Elmore James sang. The sky cried. She swirled a handsome swig of Scotch around in her mouth and pretended to care about the smoky-sweet flavor of it. Swallowed. "The bad news. What's the premise?"

"Your sister."

"My—" she choked. "My sister?"

"Gillian Briar."

"I know her fucking *name*. What about her?"

Jill had defected from Hammer/Malleus to join the Winters team in 2005. The Winters team, tracing its lineage back *mostly* through the Winters family and their rapidly-grown corporate interests, Winters-Armitage Labs, represented Malleus' head North American rival. The defection cost the Briars the very last of their political currency. Then, at some point in 2009, Jill relapsed again—not heroin, this time, but other substances, painkillers and supernatural drugs, unhealthy combinations of sixth sense stimulants and directionless dreamer and recreational psychedelics. She'd vanished from the Winters roster after a much-talked-about and ultimately-unknown conversation with Shoshanna Winters. As far as Zoe knew, nobody had tracked her since.

So she asked the pressing question: "Where?"

"You should sit down."

"*Where?*"

"There's more. The briefcase on the bed?"

"The dossier?"

"I can summarize it, but I'd have to insist you sit down."

She went to the bed. Popped the latches on the briefcase. Hesitated. With a long, quaking breath, she closed it again. Stepped away.

Joining Leo back at the table, she drained a significant amount of Scotch from her cup and didn't pretend to care how it tasted. "Don't make it cold, okay? And don't lie to me."

"I wouldn't."

"You haven't yet."

Leo ignored the implications. Staring at his drink, he explained. "Your sister has established a school for the education and development of para-normative and supernaturally-inclined adolescents."

Zoe could neither inhale nor exhale.

Leo continued: "It's small, for now, with only three known instructors and five known students all posing as a sort of large, adoptive family. But Intel-Analytics charted the models and did the math and if something like that ever reached scale…"

Zoe caught a breath, tried not to show how hard her heart beat in her chest. "She's a Column Threat."

Referring to a threat so large that it posed instability to one of the organization's primary tenets: Safety, Security, Secrecy. A threat so large it required immediate assessment and attention. A threat likely to get handled with *extreme prejudice.*

"Secrecy," Leo confirmed.

She didn't cry. She could've. She didn't. "So what's the movement?"

"It's complex. On the surface there are obvious levees against direct action, civil rights and all that. But Malleus, or rather, our specific part of Malleus—"

"It's all the same, now."

"The Advanced and Special Operations Division employs only six-point-three percent of the corporate payroll and we account for only nine-point-nine percent of its budget."

"Hammer leadership runs the board."

"There is no 'Hammer,' anymore."

"Fuck's sake..."

Organizations like theirs had to adapt to survive. Malleus had molted many carapaces before arriving at its current shape. A thousand years earlier, their group had originated from a clan of Christ-crazy witch-hunters; now it hid itself inside a para-military and security firm. The group's leadership, now referred to as the capital-B 'Board,' occupied half the chairs on the less-secret, public-facing, lower-case-b corporate board.

"In any case. The direct paths blockaded, the Board," Leo implied the capitalization with his tone, "has decided to take matters political."

"How so?"

"Redacted versions of Intel-A's report have been submitted to leadership at several other esoteric organizations."

"Who? The Belgian's people?"

Leo nodded. "The Consortium, yes. And the Temple *Beth Yetzirah.* Even the Winters family."

"Is *anyone* being left out?"

"Nobody important."

"For a school?" she balked.

"For a school."

Zoe sank low into cushion, emptying her cup. "Mr. Bond, Punjabi or otherwise, I need a refill."

"Of course." He uncorked the bottle and poured.

"How long 'til neutralization?"

"You know how long non-violent, indirect neutralization can take."

"Why are they handling this with kid's gloves?"

"Because your sister has positively identified, tracked, and recruited multiple born para-normatives and natural adepts."

Zoe's blood sharded to glass. "They're going to black bag her?"

"Whatever method she's using to locate students, our people want to know it."

"They can't black bag her. They wouldn't. Not for a school."

"Everything is still being negotiated and leveraged and measured. I'm doing everything I can to make sure *that* doesn't happen."

"This is insane. It's…" she searched for a word. "Disproportionate."

"There are a number of Board members who agree. Unfortunately, they're outvoted."

"So why tell me? If you can't pull your strings, if the Board's already decided—why?"

Leo drank. Shrugged. "Because we were all very close, once. Because in a way we still are. Because she's your sister. I don't know. Pick a card. I'm doing my best to negotiate a positive outcome for Gillian, but things look dour."

"You…you think there's something I could do."

"I owe you at least the wildly-improbable opportunity."

"Well. Thanks for that, then."

A long silence passed between them. Zoe's iPod dock played Freddie King's 'Same Old Blues.'

Leo finished his first drink, Zoe neared the end of her second. The booze flowed through her, amber ease, a false and chemical detachment warm and cozy between her and the world. Freddie King couldn't help but think. The sun used to shine. But now…?

Leo uncorked the bottle but didn't pour anything. His smile showed sadness—or, not sadness, Zoe considered, but *weariness*. "Do you remember when Sung-ho would hold those poker nights?" he asked.

"It started because you drank whenever you gambled and none of us had seen you drunk."

"I've heard the origin story, yes. And the two of you always swept the table."

"We were the best field agents in the world. You couldn't find better liars than us, back then. Hell, you couldn't find better lie detectors."

"You scored 'Best in Field,' what? Nine times over the course of your career?"

"'Over the course of my career,'" she parroted. "Like it's over."

"I don't expect it to be. But I don't imagine you'll be scoring 'Best in Field' again any time…" he trailed off.

"What, 'soon?' Or 'ever?'"

Leo chuckled. "A witch without born aptitude who can ritualize cantrips and cast spells at your speed and efficiency is an extremely rare find."

She waited for whatever line he'd rehearsed next, refusing to grant him the segue of her commentary. It wouldn't change anything, anyway.

"We haven't grown old, Zo'…but the world does stay young."

"I'm forty-four, I'm not the Crypt Keeper."

Leo looked wounded. He picked up the bottle and refreshed both drinks. "If you decide to do something stupid, there's a phone number and address on a calling card in the briefcase. Call it and I'll meet you at the address at midnight the same day. If you decide to move forward, you'll have to be very careful."

"No shit."

"It's been some years since you did anti-personnel work. Times have changed. The things we can do with technology…that even *I* can do, honestly.… There's more than just magic involved in the game, now."

"I own a smartphone."

He barely missed a beat. "Over the next nine days I have meetings in Los Angeles, Seattle, New York, and Boston. Then I'll be back in Oceanrest. If you've done your reconnaissance and your research and you still want to do this, at that point, call the number on the card. Remember, this is a process likely to take months, maybe longer. Rushing doesn't stand to benefit us."

"I'll start tomorrow. Now: *where*?"

Chapter Two

New York, NY.

June, 1997.

Checking Jill into rehab had eaten most of Zoe's savings account. Even then, they'd selected a cheap one, a place in New Jersey with a chain-link fence and a 'garden' the size of a Brooklyn bedroom. It had totaled ten thousand dollars for ninety days of service. If their parents had helped, if they'd caved to Zoe's pleas and offered to pay half, or a third, the story might have read differently. But that hadn't happened. The story read the way it read.

Zoe stopped the answering machine tape, went to the liquor cabinet, and poured herself a Scotch. She didn't usually drink, a smoker since the age of seventeen instead, but when she did, she over-did. Knowing this, she did it anyway. Lighting the day's sixth clove, she sat down at the living room table, next to the cordless phone, took a long drag and a slug of booze, and used the combined burn of these vices to smother the scream building in her lungs.

Forty-three days into her ninety-day program, Jill had somehow escaped the campus. She'd escaped by night and had disappeared somewhere along the boggy eastern coast of New Jersey. More than likely, she'd landed wherever she found her first dose.

The facility had called twelve hours earlier, and again three hours after that.

They had a strict 72-hour grace window for clients mid-relapse and Jill had already missed 36 of those hours. If she didn't return within the next 36, the facility would terminate her program due to non-compliance, as found in Section Whatever Paragraph Something of their contract. Their fee was non-refundable.

Zoe smoked her cigarette dead and refilled her drink before calling the only person she could think to call.

"Hello?" Sung-ho answered. "Zoe?"

"Yeah."

"A-ha!" Sung-ho laughed. "It works."

"What works?"

"Caller ID. It won't tell me your name, but, eh…Manhattan area code, how many people could it be?"

Zoe pretended a smile for a man who couldn't see it. "Two million, about?"

"So what's happening?" Sung-ho maintained a Seoul accent even after two decades' Americanization. Still, he wielded the vocabulary of the blues, the musical genre he fell in love with as soon as he'd heard it. "Some senior-trainee jazz got you down in the dumps? Too close to earning the wings to focus anymore?"

"It's Jill."

The amusement drained from Sung-ho's voice. "Shit. Shit! Why you didn't tell me sooner?"

"I…"

"You let me talk about Caller ID?"

"It's, um, mind-bending technology…"

"Feh. 'Technology,' maybe."

"How's Hyun-jung?"

"She's nine, she's fine. What happened with Jill?"

"We had to put her back in rehab."

"That's no good."

"Five programs in five years? It's *bad*."

Jill had started heroin the month before her sixteenth birthday. One of her friends had died, the details never having reached Zoe's ears, and Jill had taken her first dose with some of her fellow mourners. She'd been in and out of rehab ever since.

"What about one of those groups?" Sung-ho asked.

Zoe swirled a shrinking cube around an amber sea. "Like AA?"

"Why not?"

Zoe watched the ice dissolve. "She showed me a spell…"

"A spell?"

"Something that's supposed to help…people like her."

"Magic can't cure addiction," Sung-ho grouched. "Magic can't guarantee things that can't—"

"That can't be guaranteed, yeah. I know. But I don't think this is a cure, I think it's a treatment."

"You've seen it? It looks legit?"

"It looks legit. Besides, you know how smart Jill is. She wouldn't have brought it to me un-vetted."

"Jill's brilliant," Sung-ho admitted. "Right up until she gets a fix."

Zoe didn't reply to that. "And…I need a favor."

"Why else have a mentor? Shoot."

"We need a ritual space. Large, at least twice the size of my apartment, preferably secluded. It needs a bedroom with east-facing windows and a skylight that looks out at the moon. And privacy, obviously."

"You want to borrow my winter house?"

"I want to borrow your winter house."

He coughed. "This ritual messy?"

"Not terribly."

"You won't let any demons in?"

"Demons aren't real."

"'Entities we could mistake for demons.'"

"Sung…"

"You know I won't say 'no.' I'll have a copy of the keys left at a drop. Someone will get the tags to you tomorrow."

"Thanks."

"And, uh, any chance this ritual is…dangerous?"

"The last phase will be," Zoe admitted. "The rest, I dunno. It depends."

"There any Gateways?"

Most powerful rituals required some degree of isolation and all rituals required time. The shorthand 'Gateways' referred to moments during particularly isolated or uninterruptible rituals when practitioners could join or depart the casting.

"Two Gateways, forty-eight hours each. Other than that, we have to spend the entire thing in *total* solitude."

"The whole thing?"

"No outside visitors, no leaving the grounds, no nothing except during the Gateways."

Sung-ho whistled. "Wow. A recipe for stir-crazy."

Zoe had never performed a ritual that required this degree of isolation and solitude, before. She'd never performed a ritual with such strict rules regarding its Gateways and so much time spent alone, her other practitioners her only company and her other practitioners likely limited solely to her sister.

"I've been in need of some alone time, anyway," Zoe aimed for humor and fell short.

"I'll join you for the ending. Let me know when the second Gateway happens so I can come in."

"What?"

"I have plenty of PTO. It'd be nice to catch some action that wasn't just assigned to me."

"I...thanks."

"And I'll call Leo, see if he can push your final skill assessment out to the Lunar."

"Oh," Zoe balked. "I didn't even think about that."

"Ah, and that's the reason people have mentors, then. Because we are smarter than they are."

She laughed, shook her head. "Wiser, maybe."

"I said 'smarter.'" Sung-ho chuckled. Abruptly, someone shouted something in Korean in the background. Sung-ho shouted back, also in Korean. Zoe had started learning a bit, but not enough to understand the conversation. Sung-ho and Seo-yeon exchanged a few more lines in Korean, apparently across a fair distance, and Sung-ho returned. "Hyun-jung found one of my trophies," he said, urgently, rushed, "gotta go. Be safe."

"You, too."

The line died and Zoe put the handset back on the receiver. She finished her second drink, a warm buzz sloshing through her, and poured a third. Her limbs felt distant, operating at a lag from the rest of her. Staring at her reflection played across the glassy surface of the Scotch, she held her own gaze hostage. She'd need to find Jill.

Plucking the drink up from the countertop, she carried it with her to her bedroom. The drink went on a bedside table and the bed, itself, went against one wall. Zoe pulled a broad vanity away from the opposite wall into the middle of the room. Pulling her basic ritual kit from the bottom of her closet, she began chalking circles and sigils into the hardwood. Using magic while inebriated was widely considered a bad idea. Knowing this, she did it anyway.

It wasn't like anybody else was going to bother.

Sung-ho had made the great effort of loaning her a ritual space. She had to be the person who actually brought Jill to the font.

Besides, proper tracking spells took hours of ritual time. She'd sober up before she finished working.

Except she didn't.

Salem, MA.

June, 2016.

Gillian and Darnell Tims-Briar lived in a six-bedroom, three-and-a-half bath house situated on an acre of garden and lawn. Their 'friend,' Karen Woeser, rented two of the bedrooms, along with her two children, one biological and one adopted. Gillian and Darnell had three adoptees of their own. Their students ranged in age from twelve to seventeen. Of the faculty, only Darnell carried the intense sixth-sense resonance of a person born with particular abilities. Of the student body, four of the five kids carried the same general *vibe*. The one that didn't was Karen's biological son, Altan.

Malleus, ASOD, Hammer—by whatever name she called her organization, it remained the same organization—they had an entire department dedicated to tracking and predicting supernatural behaviors and movements. An entire department dedicated to finding people born with paranormal abilities and keeping tabs on them. If Jill had found four of them with the help of only two other people, that represented the kind of ultra-viable predictive methodology Intel-A might deem worth killing over in and of itself. For all Zoe knew, the school merely served as their excuse.

Crickets chirred the night. Reclined in a rental car parked behind an overgrowth of bush and brush, Zoe lowered her binoculars from her face and pursed her lips. Spell-enhanced vision made dimness out of the darkness, but so little happened that it didn't really matter. As with the beginnings of so many other cases, the first days of her latest trip mostly involved waiting.

She closed her eyes, focusing on her sixth sense.

A matryoshka of defensive wards protected the house. The wards were strong; Jill had always had a talent for protective magic. With the support of her husband, her friend, and the youngsters slowly-learning around them, they'd managed to build up a dense and substantial defense. They'd maintained it well, too. Time and mundanity decay eroded anything left unattended for very long; ritual strengthened anything regularly rehearsed. Of those three major forces governing magic's endurance, Zoe saw evidence of only one.

Still, even the strongest castle walls crumbled under siege.

Major and minor hexes, curses, and bad luck charms sizzled around the edges of the wards. Scrying spells blurred and focused, searching for possible angles of surveillance. Oneiromancers had attempted to worm their way past the house's defenses and into the skulls waiting within. Zoe estimated it would take two or three expert-level teams over a week to build up so much mysticism. With only four days under her own belt, that meant she'd showed up to the party not only outnumbered and outgunned, but late.

It didn't bode well.

Zoe's sixth sense sharped a warning through her. Something was happening. She sat up, eyes open. Squinted. Her ears burned, listening for some sound beyond insect-song and cricket-chirp. Adrenaline pulsed through her.

In the periphery of her awareness, a sixth sense struggle flared and died in seconds.

Someone had supercharged one of the spells wearing away at Jill's wards in a misguided attempt to break through. The wards won out, unraveling hours of offensive spellwork in moments. Whatever malice the aggressors had intended dissipated, gone to void before it had the chance to happen.

Zoe grabbed the chalkboard from the passenger seat and put it on her lap. With a combat knife, she drew a shallow red line across her left palm. Eyes closed, she whispered an incantation as the blood dripped onto the sigils and glyphs already chalked against the slate. She whispered it again, as quickly as she could with the grammar, and focused her intent. She wanted to follow the unraveling magic back to its source. She *needed* to.

A ritualized cantrip, the spell didn't take long to charge and cast. If Zoe had been *born* with natural magical aptitude, it would've taken her somewhere between six and twelve seconds. Since she hadn't been, it took over half a minute.

But then it *took*.

Zoe bucked in her seat, seized with impulse. Opening her eyes, she threw the chalkboard aside. She sprayed anti-bacterial medication on her left palm and wrapped it in a thin sheath of gauze. Still panting to catch her breath, she threw the rental into drive and pulled away from the shoulder.

She followed her spell-informed instincts. A vague sense of *over there* carried her through near-empty streets. She took a left, a right, a left. In her sixth sense, she felt her spell disintegrating. She pressed down on the accelerator. The rear of her car swung wide as she took a too-tight turn. She corrected flawlessly. Kept driving. The gut-level hunch about which way to turn next faded. Before it vanished completely, she found a small cluster of homes.

Turning off her headlights, she drove passed them.

A minute later, she pulled over and exited the vehicle. The summer breeze blew against warm sweat still clinging to her brow. Doubling back, she walked to the place where she'd lost the trail. Only a dozen houses remained as options. Closer than she'd thought she'd get, not as close as she'd have gotten with an extra ten or twenty seconds. Scanning the neighborhood for signs of life, she caught the bare glimpse of a cigarette cherry burning in a nearby backyard.

She crouched low and crept forward.

She tried to focus on her sixth sense with her eyes open. Generally, only people born with natural aptitude or some semi-psychic ability could handle such a multi-task, but Zoe had decades of training behind her. Fighting through an anxiety-inducing sensation that her sense of sight was *too loud*, she caught faint impressions of magic in the area. Sucking up a lungful of air, she detached from her sixth sense. She wanted more certainty in her suspicions than the sight of someone smoking in their own backyard. Crouching in a row of bushes bordering a tall fence, she closed her eyes and tried again.

Whoever had set up their operations base in the area, they'd covered it up well. Zoe felt the dissipating energy of the dying spell more sharply than anything else. It smelled like burnt ozone and tasted like liquid aluminum. Digging deeper, she found traces of other magic. They felt diffuse. Muffled.

Undoubtedly, the operating coven had built up a ward against notice, a defense against attention and investigation. Zoe would have to do something a lot more active than sixth sense meditation to confirm her enemy's location.

Opening her eyes again, she hesitated. Her pathways forward looked grim. If she broke into the house to confirm her theories, she could alert her enemies to her presence. Even if she disabled any material security systems, she could trip a ward. If she wanted to get inside the place, she'd first have to spend hours dismantling their wards against notice. After that, assuming she picked the correct house to begin with, she'd have to take apart their wards against intrusion. By the time she finished that, it would be morning and they'd find her, weak and fatigued, outside of their safehouse. Even if she somehow got inside, they'd notice their spells disrupted the next day. They'd start looking for her.

She didn't have the ops resources to handle that.

Cursing, she turned around and started back toward her rental car.

Keene's Falls, NY.

December, 2006.

Nobody knew how dreamer worked. Not even Zoe.

It oozed into the folds and wrinkles of her brain; it played symphonies along her neural filaments. She vibrated, her sense of self lost in the no-place of sleep; her frequencies aligned with frequencies unknowable, her consciousness existing in undiscoverable no-no-nowhere places; the material became immaterial, the metaphorical, dire.

The sky blackened, the fire crackled. Zoe sat on a fold-out chair and gazed into the flames. Powders and chalks painted the forest floor in symbols and sigils and glyphs. He'd warded the place—You'd warded the—She'd warded the—They'd warded the place against interlopers and performed the rites of invocation, evocation, *creation*. She was him. The Summoner. You?

Zoe paused with question but nothing stopped to answer.

Something hissed, a snake, the drawing of a sword.

Suddenly, Zoe stood elsewhere. She stood inside Omar as a terrible thing unglued itself from the walls. (S)he screamed. Everyone screamed. As (s)he ran, (s)he heard a meaty rip behind her/him, heard a sound too choked to describe as 'screaming' and too loud to describe as anything else. Everything behind her/him whirled into blender-shriek. (S)he burst through the door and fell face-first into someone's arms. "What's your name?" Zoe asked. "Omar," Zoe answered. She picked herself up, she picked him up. They ran.

Zoe stood in Sung-ho's winter home in 1997. Gillian pored over several open grimoires, the sickness and immediate withdrawal symptoms subsided, the rage tapering off—how did this connect to her current assignment?

(*every story ends the same way*)

Jill glanced up from the grimoires and Zoe was elsewhere.

She stood somewhere underground and echoing, long narrow halls leading to broad, expansive rooms. Why underground? An old stone sign read 'ALTAR' and an arrow pointed down an unlit corridor. Distantly, she heard whispers. There was always something whispering on the other side of darkness. Always, all the time. The whispers came from mouths with lips pressed against reality's skin, with tongues seeking some way in. Zoe flicked on her underbarrel flashlight and stepped farther into dark.

Pigs squealed. A death march of meat wormed down aisles framed in rusted steel. Zoe and Sung-ho fought against the press of hogs. A machine the size of a house whirred and cackled, coming for them. It carved through shrieking pigs like something starving. It cackled, coming for them. Zoe shouted something she couldn't hear. You bathe in the blood of pigs. You never wanted a slaughter. Did you want a slaughter?

a truth beneath every tale, a monster at the end of—

You grow up reading stories about wizards and warlocks, witches and *brujas* and voodoo priestesses. You grow up reading about magic. It starts the way it starts for a lot of young people—powers. Shapeshifting, maybe. Resurrecting a servile corpse, *zombi*, like the *bokor* you could be. Fireballs? Yeah. Fireballs could be cool, too.

But fantasy fiction changes (everything becomes something else eventually); the characters trend darker, grittier, and further down-at-heels. The magic gets uglier. How ugly can magic get? In the stories you find mind control but no evidence that mind control was ever used to rape anyone. Few people with mind control even exercise their terrible powers on many subservients at all. Obviously a person would start with their family. Once they got used to the control, they'd do it all the time. You grow up reading stories about wizards and warlocks, witches and *brujas* and voodoo priestesses. Ah, but then you grow up.

every story ends the same way

(*we're/they're/it's sorry, but they do*)

You grow up to read stories about people more successful than you and how they allegedly became more successful than you. You try to emulate the characters in these stories. Something about the world feels wrong, doesn't it? Every once in a while you'll be reading a news article and a strange suspicion will scratch up your innards. *This isn't the whole story. Something here is missing.* You bury these suspicions and try to emulate people more successful than you. Somehow, you are never more successful.

One night, using a TOR browser to attend an auction of grisly goods, you drunkenly buy a grimoire for half your life's savings. The math doesn't filter through your head until the next morning. Sorry, the story reads, but there are No Fucking Refunds. If things had happened differently, maybe the story would read differently but—

You grow up in debt grinding yourself to death on the cogs of a machine that wants you to work until your marrow hollows out; wants you to die as young and as cheaply as possible. Your bones ache, metaphorically. Your bones ache, literally. You spent half of your life's savings on this dusty old book, the pages legible by the blessing of the scribe's calligraphy alone, no publisher or author listed, entitled 'A Neophytes Entry into Evocation.' You spent half your life's savings on this. You wake up, wash the dishes, drink the coffee, eat a piece of toast, grab an apple, and run out the door. You work in logistics. You grind through schedules and last-minute changes and requests and bids and costs and the fuck-everybody stress of the day. You maintain a pleasant tone. You spent half your life's savings on a dusty old book.

The world erodes you. Like everyone else, you die one day at a time. Everyone says "life's a bitch and then you die" but the daily echo of it all, the deafening constant remix warbles the sentence into a thrum of its own "life's a bitch and then life's a bitch and then life's a bitch and then life's a bitch and then"

—every story ends—

One day, drunk, surrounded by stones, underground, below your apartment, you open the alleged grimoire. The first page says "Not All Can Practice Magick! — You Must Ensure Your Psychic Defenses Are Strong — First, a Test!:" and thereafter it lays out the steps of a simple 'ritual spell.' "You may need to repeat the ritual six or seven times to experience a result. If you experience no result by the eighth repetition, you are unfortunately not among the lucky few who can dabble in these divine arts. Nonetheless, we advise you keep hold of the test. One never knows about one's progeny, after all."

You piss yourself and throw up when your fifth run-through of the ritual causes a flare of bright light to sizzle in the air. The mote of blinding white hissed for two seconds, three seconds at the most, and vanished. You rolled on the floor gagging. It had worked. You'd seen it. It had worked and you'd seen it work. You vomit and laugh and vomit and laugh. You throw the pants away, take a shower, and perform the ritual again.

The world looks different, the next day.

People think all of this makes sense? Every day, waking up, washing dishes, drinking coffee, eating toast, going to work…and magic was real? How did people not know? How do people not know? Ah, there are reasons, but why would you guess them? You imagine secret organizations, shadowy government agencies snapping necks on moonless nights. You've been trained to jump to this conclusion. Why would you know the reality? Not everybody knows everything. But every story ends.

It doesn't take long. You don't know to call your sense of the supernatural your 'sixth sense' but you know you feel it growing stronger. You repeat the first page a few times. On the second attempt, that day, you throw up again but don't piss yourself. On the third, you piss yourself but don't throw up. Your fourth and fifth attempts go off without a hitch but the sixth doesn't work at all. You try over and over again but it just doesn't. You frown. You do not understand yet—if magic were a science, it would be a science. The same stimulus doesn't always provoke the same result. A science, magic isn't. *'Ain't.'*

But you experiment.

How does dreamer work?

Nobody knows.

Zoom out.

Zoe's brain buzzed, a hive. She dissolved into energy and pulsed crackle-spasmodic along a track of unknown. She saw a group of black-clad men and women shuffling into a stone-faced building. She saw the building fast-forward, growing moss. A 'For Sale' sign appeared in the grass out front. The parking lot potholed and cragged. 'Sold,' the sign updated. Scaffolding went up, renovations happened. People flitted in and out, the time-lapse accelerating to the point of pure blur. 'For Rent,' a newer, more modern sign read. Night fell.

She stood in a basement. The stone halls loomed in claustrophobic, allowing space for no more than two people to walk passed each other shoulder-to-shoulder, almost brushing. Down a dim corridor ahead, faint light aura-glowed on still more stone. Behind her, the tight hall opened into a three-way intersection. She clutched her sidearm in her hand, barrel-mounted flashlight flicked 'off.' Up ahead, dimness, an unexplored room, the laboratory scent of too much bleach. Her thumb rested against the safety lever. She moved toward the dimness and bleach scent, prepared.

What differences spanned the gap between a 'lair' and a 'sanctuary?'

She approached the threshold, every small and near-invisibly-thin hair on her body standing up static straight.

What about the differences between a 'lair' and a 'home?'

She pressed her spine against rough stonework, ready. Listening, she heard nothing from the room beyond except the buzz of electricity through bulbs.

Did a monster wait in the room beyond?

That depended on who got to define the term.

Zoe jerked awake screaming.

Chapter Three

Pittsburgh, PA.

December, 2006.

Four days after her dreamer vision, Zoe arrived in Pittsburgh with Omar in the passenger seat. Blues music yearned through the speakers.

Like a whole history of agents before her, Zoe found herself improvising around broken protocols after having done something as incredibly stupid as pulling a civilian into her assignment. Malleus had a strict procedure for such interactions, of course, but it didn't fit into her operations schedule. The prescribed four-to-six days of applied sixth sense stimulants and psychic wards she could handle on the road, but the drop-off of the 'subject' for processing, afterward, required a days' drive departure. The investigation couldn't afford it.

Instead, she'd given Omar every joint of sixth sense stimulant she found in the safehouse, built a network of psychic wards inside his mind, and told him as much of the truth as her NDA allowed. Since her NDA was a literal curse, this seemed easy enough on the surface. Unfortunately, having undergone numerous ritual adjustments to account for her career's increasingly higher-level missions, the curse allowed her a shocking amount of leeway. It only occurred to her on the third day that the curse, itself, might have allowed her to tell Omar something the Board might later need him to forget—a situation unlikely to benefit Omar.

She didn't tell him this.

Instead, she'd told him she had to keep him with her. When he'd resisted, she'd told him that she had to protect him, that the Summoner was still a threat—both lies—and that she wanted to supervise him to ensure his sixth sense inoculation worked—that part, true. And when he'd resisted that, she'd educated him about mundanity decay.

The so-called 'real' world asserted itself against magical intervention. Over time—sometimes hours, sometimes years—magic replaced itself with mundanity. Whatever the spell or supernatural event caused, the material aftermath sooner or later accrued a mundane explanation. As the supernatural energies themselves decayed, reality rewrote itself to match some inscrutable 'normalcy' audit. And after normalcy fossilized, even the strongest sixth sense in the world couldn't detect anything mystical left behind.

"Call it a law of magic," she'd told him. "Sooner or later, a normal explanation takes over. Magic covers its own tracks."

"So?" he'd asked, searching for an explanation as to how this applied to *him*.

"Calm down, okay? I'm not taking you hostage." She'd had her hands up as if that proved something. "But as mundanity sets in, it's not going to be a monster attack anymore. It's going to be a crime scene. Multiple attempted homicides, assault with a deadly weapon, maybe even murder...and when they find evidence, it's going to match a story that makes sense."

Omar had sunk back onto the cot, the explanation already clear in his mind.

"The Occam's Razor answer is that someone—or multiple someones—inside the house started slashing people. And of the obvious suspects...the guy who went missing for days afterward seems like a good place to start."

And so he'd agreed to go with her to Pittsburgh.

Why Pittsburgh?

After the dreamer vision, Zoe had rushed to write out as many images and references as she could before she forgot them all as anyone did with any dream. The act occurred partly as purposeful remembrance and partly as dreamer-guided automatic writing. Reviewing the notes after talking Omar through the first of several flashbacks, she found that one of her scribbles directed her to find 'the three river steel city.' Since the Summoner's attacks so far had concentrated in the U.S. northeast…

"You said people are born 'weird' at a rate of, uh, of one in thirteen thousand, right?" Omar asked.

"Huh?" Zoe blinked, unfocused behind the wheel. "Oh. Yeah."

"And you said it was more complicated than that?"

"Uh-huh."

"So? What makes it complicated?"

"The average changes. There are heat maps. In a lot of regions, the number trends closer to one in twenty thousand. In others, it cleaves hard the other way, closer to one in five or six thousand."

"Why?"

Zoe scanned buildings through the windshield. "Nobody really knows."

"And I'm just supposed to believe that?"

"You don't have to believe it." She shrugged with her voice. "It's true."

Like most civilians, like most Ephemeral-class assets or first-year trainees, Omar had mostly asked about possibilities and abstracts. "Are werewolves real?" "Not in the sense that you're thinking." "Are ghosts real?" "Not in the sense that you're thinking." "What about that Lovecraftian shit?" "Maybe, but, again…" "Not in the way that I'm thinking?" "Bingo."

Like most civilians, like most Ephemeral-class assets or first-year trainees, Omar had mostly asked about broad and basic topics. "How many people are…involved in your world?" "Around two million, give or take." "And nobody notices?" "Out of seven billion people? Not really." And when he'd stared at her with a face confusion-warped, she'd explained further, "It helps that, for the most part, magic isn't usually as obvious as a shadow monster. And remember…" "Most people can't witness it to begin with." "Exactly."

Driving in long, circuitous loops through the Pittsburgh metro area, Zoe scanned.

Omar shifted in his seat, angling toward her. "You know, all those numbers you've been throwing out at me…they don't add up."

"Mm-hm?"

"At one in thirteen thousand, there'd be half a million people 'born weird' living in the world today. So when you say there's two million people in your world…who else is there?"

"I wasn't born with any kind of special connection to the supernatural, no naturally occurring aptitude that anyone was aware of...but my parents were ritual practitioners. They worked to develop my sixth sense, similar to what I'm doing with you, and taught me how to attune myself to mystic and magical energies. That make sense?"

"More or less. You're saying it's less lotto-luck and more standard nepotism."

She smirked. "Pretty much."

Omar had no idea. Of the half-million born paranormatives living in the world, fewer than a quarter of them operated with any real direction or capability. Most people born with any kind of paranormal 'gift' lived their whole lives without learning how to control it. Most never even developed a full understanding of what they could do or even what they *were*. The vast majority of everyone who wielded supernatural power with any real agency had either inherited it from practitioner parents or had learned it through membership in one or another secret society. Usually both.

'Nepotism' barely grazed the surface.

"What're we looking for, anyway?" Omar asked.

"A church or..." she waited at a stoplight, rush hour traffic building as afternoon dimmed to evening. "Probably a synagogue."

"What makes you think 'synagogue?'"

"I dunno. A hunch."

(*everyone in all-black filing into the stonefaced—*)

"Well, why don't we try the library instead of driving around in circles all day?"

"The library?"

"Yeah, heard of it? Lots of books, helpful old ladies, free classes..."

"Why a library?"

"Because they have computers."

"So?"

Omar chuckled. "I guess the movies got that part right. Magic people never think about tech, huh?"

"I think about tech all the time. What's on the library computers?"

"A little thing called Google. Think of it like kind of an oracle—"

"I know what Google is."

He continued the bit anyway, "And if you feed it the right questions, it will spit out The Truth for you. If we ask the right questions, its wisdom will tell us about every synagogue in Pittsburgh."

"I know what Google is," she repeated, turning right, following the flow of traffic. She tried not to show embarrassment at not having thought of it.

"Uh-huh. So, shit, Pittsburgh Public. Let's go."

"I don't like this turn in your character."

"Why not? It seems to me like I just cracked your case." Omar grinned. "Now come on. I got a name to clear."

Zoe drummed her thoughts through her fingers on the wheel. "Sure. Just as soon as you tell me where the nearest public library is."

She tried not to think about the gentle push it took for the 'wrongfully suspected' to become a 'patsy' instead.

She still had time to deal with that.

Jersey City, NJ.

June, 1997.

Zoe's eyes fried in their sockets, hangover and sleeplessness and morning sun burning them hollow. Stepping out of the car, she uncapped a bottle of water and took a few deep gulps. Shook herself off. Lit a cigarette.

Her spells had tracked Jill to a radius of only a couple blocks. In that couple of blocks, two dozen long, narrow houses, most converted to rental properties, contained approximately two hundred and forty residents. Adjusting her shades against the day and pulling her jacket down over her Malleus-issued sidearm, she started her search with a basic heuristics scan. Places where addicts congregated together carried a certain vibe, sixth sense or otherwise, and Zoe squinted for it in the area architecture.

Killing her clove only half-finished, she headed toward a group of run-down structures cornered by a brick building 'for rent.' She sipped more water on the way, emptying the bottle and tossing it in an overflowing bin on the sidewalk. She double-checked her equipment, her purse containing a knife, two hundred dollars, and pepper spray, her holster containing a sidearm she wasn't supposed to discharge outside of training, her jacket containing arcane miscellany, and her pants pocket containing a credit card and several MTA tokens.

Getting closer to the more rundown stretch of neighborhood housing, Zoe pulled off the sidewalk down a narrow alley between two houses. Emptying a couple bones, some chalk, and a packet of Kosher salt from her jacket pockets, she began muttering the incantations underlying some basic defensive spells—wards. More of a tracker and soldier than a ward witch or a healer, Zoe's defensive magic wasn't her strong suit, but she imagined going into an unknown situation involving drug dealers and users benefited more from meager defenses than none at all.

It took her fifteen minutes to work through the basic wards she knew. It took another ten for her to recover from the exertion, leaning against one of the close-close houses and panting from labor and hangover both. Wiping viscous sweat from her brow, she pushed herself back up. Hesitated. Knelt down again.

It took another fifteen minutes for her to get her last blessing to take. When the spell crackled down her cervical spine, along her scapulae, through her pelvis, and into her feet, her hangover eased. Her senses sharpened.

She rested for another five minutes, a lone jogger passing the alley mouth as she crouched there. Then she set back out into the noon sun.

A combination of sixth-sense impulse and pure hunch brought her attention to a rundown yellow structure at the far end of the block. Beyond it, an angle of street separated it from a train yard running all the way to the Hackensack. Chain-link fence hedged in a frontage of concrete, a patch of garden, and three figures drinking around a grill. Zoe observed for several seconds before approaching, noting the lightlessness inside the house itself, the rough-shod and bent-twisted Venetian blinds blocking the windows, the front door ajar to darkness.

"This party invite-only?" she asked, approaching the fence.

A rotund white man in a polo and khakis turned a salt-pepper goatee toward her. Black-framed shades flared orange lenses over his gaze. "Depends," he said, smiling. "You bring anything to cook?"

An equally-round, older black man ambled down from the stoop. Holding a cigar, he adjusted the brim of a broad hat against the sun. "A lady like that brings her presence," he grinned. "What else does she need?"

The third guy, athletically built, racially ambiguous, kept his mouth shut. Wearing a white t-shirt over baggy jeans, he sporked mac salad into his mouth and chewed. Zoe figured the two older men as the brains, the inherent foundation of whatever business ran through the place, with the younger guy serving as their brawn.

Zoe twisted her hips, showed off the profile view that didn't include her jacket-hidden holster. "I just moved in a few days ago," she explained. "Down there."

"Well, welcome to the neighborhood, miss." Cigar said.

"Welcome," Goatee agreed. He walked up to the chain-link. "How you like your dogs cooked?"

"Black."

"Woo-wee," Goatee chuckled, opening the gate. "What a woman."

Cigar laughed along.

"I'm Dennis," Goatee said, gesturing her inside. "What's your name, neighbor?"

"Cait," she said, a name common enough to render it untraceable. "Well, Caitlin, but…"

"Cait. Got it."

She slipped through the gate between Dennis/Goatee and the fence. "Hey, I know this is kinda out of left field but my roommate went out last night and the only message I got is that she was at a house party somewhere on this street?"

Dennis glanced over at Cigar, Cigar glanced over at Macsalad.

The mood shifted.

"Your roommate?" Dennis asked, a couple feet behind her.

"Yeah. Jill."

Cigar lowered his smoke from his lips and gestured at Zoe's jacket. "What's that you got there?"

"We had a few folks over last night," Dennis said simultaneously. He chuckled again but with less humor behind it. "If we're having one of *those* nights, we just leave the door open after a while."

"Is that a goddamn *gun*?"

"Oh, yeah," Zoe said, her sixth sense sharping like a razor through her mind. Something was coming. "I always carry. A girl can't be too safe, right?"

"I'm sorry, Cait, but…we don't allow guns around the house. Would you mind just taking that off?"

Cigar's frame tightened. At the plastic white cook-out table, Macsalad coiled spring-like.

Zoe sighed. She'd screwed up too long ago to fix it, now.

She spun, slamming her purse into Dennis' head. The sports shades flew off. Pulling the purse back tight to her body, Zoe grabbed the pepper spray inside. Whirling around, she chucked the accessory at Macsalad. Macsalad caught it, tipping over the plastic white table in the process, and threw it to the ground. Zoe turned back to Dennis and unleashed a torrent of pepper spray. Dennis screamed, grabbing at his eyes, falling to his knees. Dropping the canister, Zoe went for her sidearm, unholstered it, and turned back to the scene.

Macsalad reached for a gun of his own. Cigar ran for the front door.

She sprinted for Cigar, catching up in seconds. Grabbing the back of his collar, she twisted his shouting body and spun him down the cement stoop steps. He landed tumbling, scrambling on all fours for balance. She grabbed his collar again and yanked him upright. "I'll shoot him," she snarled, already speaking before she caught Macsalad in her sight again. "I'll drop him right fucking here."

"What the fuck? What the fuck?" Hands shaking around his pistol, Macsalad repeated the same question a half-dozen times.

"What are you doing!?" Cigar choked.

With a barrel pressed against the man's spine, Zoe suddenly wondered if she'd misunderstood her situation.

"Please!" Cigar barked. "Please! What do you want!?"

"Sshhhiit," Zoe muttered.

She'd misunderstood.

So why had her sixth sense cut through her like it had?

"Who are you!?" Macsalad shouted, more terror glistening his gaze than fury. "Who the *fuck* are you!?"

A spell released inside the house. Zoe felt it charge, sizzle, and ignite in her sixth sense.

A pulse of invisible energy blasted through the area. Zoe stumbled from the force of it. Cigar went limp in her arms, halfway through asking her what she wanted again. Macsalad stopped shouting and lowered his pistol. He walked over to the grill, turned it off, and took a seat in a white plastic lawn chair. He dropped the gun on the ground, lost consciousness, and tipped over. Crashing to the concrete 'yard,' he groaned once and went silent. Deep breaths filled his ribcage.

She dropped Cigar, not quite strong enough to drag around his ample heft, and staggered for footing. Her vision swam. The magic had been strong enough to dismantle her wards. Some of it had blown through her body proper. She caught her balance just before stepping on Dennis' now-unconscious body. Holstering her weapon, she scanned the area for witnesses. Saw none. "Shit," she muttered. "*Shit.*"

"Come on," Jill lurched out of the open front door wiping vomit from her chin. "Let's go."

"Jill, what the hell?"

"Come *on!*" Jill bustled out the gate and started down the street. Days of unwashed sweat tangled her black hair, fresh injection wounds bruised her arms. Her pallor sank so sallow she looked sick.

"Jill…" Zoe hesitated for a second. Shook her head. Ran.

Jill ran out of steam at the corner and leaned panting against the brick building 'for rent.'

Grabbing her arm, Zoe pulled her away from the wall. "Don't stop *now.*"

"Ow, ow, too tight."

"Sorry." Zoe loosened her grip. She almost said something else. Didn't. "This way."

"Are you taking me back?"

"No."

"Are…" Jill panted, dazed and ragged from drug comedown and mystical exertion. Her legs gave out. Zoe caught her. After a couple lurching, spiraling strides, Jill managed to stabilize herself again. "Why—why not?"

"Just get to the car."

################

"So, where are we going?" Jill asked, breaking the long quiet that had festered in the car between Jersey City and Philadelphia.

"North Carolina."

"Why?"

"To do the ritual."

"I…" Jill stared at Zoe, blinked. "Oh."

"Whatever spell you used back there to do that to them…how long did it take?"

"I dunno." Jill pretended to care about her shoes. "Two, three hours."

"What did you take on your way out?"

Jill slouched in her seat, fiddled with her belt buckle.

"Just…dump it, please."

"What, here?"

"When we go over the Delaware," Zoe replied. "Just toss it. All of it."

"Zo', I…"

"Just fucking do it, Jill."

And Jill did.

Pittsburgh, PA.

December, 2006.

"There," Omar said, pointing through the windshield.

"That's it," she confirmed, barely a whisper.

It was the third place they'd checked on a list of only four places. Like most truly old things, it had transformed many times across the breadth of its existence. It had served as a synagogue, a church, a synagogue again. After that, it had become a house. The house expanded, the owners renovated it, and so it transformed into a five-bed-three-bath apartment. The lease allowed access to the vast yard, several parking spaces in the now-public parking lot, and the large shed outside. It forbade access to the basement or 'any other underground structures' of the property. At some point, someone had broken that part of the lease. At some point after that, they'd also stopped paying rent.

A fresh-looking eviction notice sat plastic-wrapped, framed in duct tape against the front door.

The nearby neighbors looked broken-down, too. Zoe surmised that the entire neighborhood had taken something of a downward turn in recent years. Particularly, she noticed several glassless, boarded-up window frames; cars with rusted, unfixed damage.

"I'll check it out."

"You sure?" he asked.

"Yeah. If anyone's watching the street, they'll have seen me through the window already. They might not have seen you."

"You paranoid?"

"I'm prepared." She corrected, opening the door. "I should be back in seven, eight minutes."

"Should I call for back-up if it takes longer?" Omar half-joked.

"What backup?" Then, getting it, she chuckled. "Right. Nice one."

He studied her for a moment. "How dangerous is this?"

"Somewhere between 'not at all' and 'very *very*.'" She stepped out of the car and closed the door behind her. Omar asked something but the vehicle muffled it. She crossed the street and stepped onto the building's lawn. Her boots slicked through moist grass. A sprinkle of rain and a little morning's mist clung to the leather. Her sixth sense crawled along her skin. Something was wrong about this place. She checked windows, the ones that weren't boarded up, searched for silhouettes or the hint of light off of a scope-lens; some clue of surveillance. None presented.

Reaching down, she unbuckled her holster. The apartment's front windows wore blackout curtains, blinded. Glancing overshoulder, she confirmed that Omar was, in fact, not visible from any worthwhile vantage. She stepped up onto the porch. Wood creaked underfoot.

The eviction notice dated back three weeks. She didn't know how long a tenant had to languish in non-payment to earn an eviction in Pittsburgh, Pennsylvania, but she imagined it took longer than a month. Timelines unfolded in her head, new data adding to old. The Summoner had lived here recently. Had perhaps abandoned the place. If he'd abandoned the place, he'd done it several weeks ago. At least. Why?

(*darkness and dimness, her boots scraping against the flooring of forbidden underground structures*)

Around the rear of the building, she found more blackout curtains. Nobody had looked at this place and thought 'rob it?' Nobody had seen the eviction notice and figured 'finders, keepers?' She pursed her lips. The rear of another building, this one brick, peered down on her from beyond a narrow alley. The sightlines were poor, but anyone listening would hear the glass break if she decided to enter the house via window.

Her sixth sense shivered.

Whatever awaited her inside, it wasn't good.

As if that mattered.

Drawing her sidearm from its holster, she paused.

She didn't have to break a window.

She walked over to the back door, braced herself, and bull-kicked the handle so hard it splintered free from the frame.

"Police!" she shouted, stepping inside barrel-first. "Hands up!"

Chapter Four

Salem, MA.

June, 2016.

Zoe surveilled the neighborhood for three days.

It didn't take long to figure out which house the opposing coven had rented. Anyone with real field experience could pick up on the signs within a couple days. The numerous deliveries and grocery runs had been the first clue. The particular purchases they made at the grocer, glimpsed through binoculars from half a block away, only reinforced Zoe's theory. The live chicken cinched it.

She'd only seen three people enter and exit the building. Most organizations didn't settle at three operatives for a major months-long operation. Three practitioners could pack a lot of punch, but organized groups tended to send five person teams on longer gigs for the sake of stability. A first-year trainee or anyone with Class-E intel clearance—people sometimes unkindly referred to as 'Ephemerals'—could figure that much out from basic numerology.

On the third day, just as she wondered if she'd gotten all she could get from this particular tree without shaking it, she saw a fourth agent. Tall, white, and blond, she emerged from the house wearing grays and blacks, a bright blue pendant her outfit's sole splash of color. Beneath her asymmetrical jacket, Zoe imagined she wore a kevlar vest for protection. As the woman stood on the house's stoop, Zoe's sixth sense crackled. Lowering the binoculars from her face, Zoe moved her hand toward the keys in the ignition. The woman scanned the streets.

Zoe waited.

A dirty blond man joined the woman outside the house. Zoe had seen him, before. That day, he wore a tailored button-up, sleeves halfway up his pale forearms, a bright cobalt tie, and expensive jeans. He leaned broad shoulders against the front of the house and rapped a pack of smokes against the heel of his hand. Seeing the box of cigarettes made Zoe itch. Lighting up, the man said something to the woman. The woman replied, still staring at the street.

Zoe held the keys gently at the ready.

The blond woman and the near-blond man exchanged a few more lines of unheard dialog.

The woman shrugged and went back inside. The man lingered, smoking, his head sweeping around to take in the street every few seconds. A sixth sense sensation coolly rolled along Zoe's skin. Was the man about to notice her?

He dropped the last of his cigarette and crushed it undershoe. He followed the woman back inside.

Sighing relief, Zoe started the engine. That had felt close. Pulling away from the curb, she steered her rental south. She drove a complicated route down through Lynn and almost to the marshes before turning around and driving an equally complicated route back northwest almost to the Salem Country Club. Her sixth sense settled. Once she felt sure that nobody followed her through either material or mystical means, she turned east.

She collected her thoughts as she made a driving-instructor's tour of western Salem. She turned left, left, right, left, right, right, left, right. She watched her rearview and sideview mirrors. She figured if she'd seen four agents there had to be five. Unlike with three practitioners, there was no numerological reason to have four—not if someone could afford to send five. Or seven. Or nine, if they somehow had the staff to spare.

But who did?

Nobody. Right?

Zoe parked outside of a bar and grill and exited the vehicle. Leaning against her rental, she lit a clove and smoked it down. A couple people left the squat white restaurant and a couple other people entered. Crushing the butt of her smoke underboot, she walked inside and sat at the edge of the bar. She ordered a mid-shelf bourbon and nursed it as she thought.

The team looked attached to the Belgian's 'Consortium.' They had that vibe about them—an ease bought by fat wallets and sheer power. The four Zoe had seen had all looked European in the vaguely-Aryan sense, and certainly well-dressed. That they'd hidden their magic so well implied intense training and practice; the kind of near-militancy most easily associated with the Consortium and, even moreso, her own organization, Malleus.

The Belgian and his Consortium had always had a complex relationship with Malleus.

Malleus traced its lineage back to a group of witch and monster hunters operating during the middle of the thirteenth century. Led by two born paranormatives (who ignored, and profited from, the irony of sending people to kill other born paranormatives) and a ritual practitioner, legend had it that the original group did little with their lives besides hunt monsters, destroy covens, and requisition occult goods. What records existed of those earliest days told a story of disorganization and mismanagement. By the fifteenth century, however, Malleus had become quite an efficient secret society.

The Belgian's Consortium came together during the late fifteenth century, primarily as an alliance between different magical practitioners profiteering off of the war and imperial colonization viciously exported from Europe. At the time, the few hundred members of the thing-that-became-Malleus were too busy arguing about which born paranormatives did and did not count as 'human' to notice the rise of a new mystical syndicate. When the two groups finally crossed paths in the seventeenth century, the Belgian's machinations had grown too glutted from its feast of exploitation for Malleus to simply tear them down again.

The two organizations immediately clashed around the Consortium's involvement in the slave trade, an institution that Malleus had begun decrying a scant thirty years earlier. A century of conflict followed. The groups, vastly overestimating their overall importance in the grand scheme of the world, threw numberless curses, hexes, and monsters against each other. Somehow, the majority of practitioners in leadership positions on both sides still ended up dying from old age. A lot of people lower on the ladder didn't.

At some point in the late eighteenth century, the Belgian's Consortium and the thing-that-became-Malleus realized they'd lost their footings. Other practitioners had started to find each other; competing secret societies bred wildly in every civilization's least-examined shadows. Despite the Consortium's continued involvement in the slave trade, Malleus agreed to a truce. Once the Consortium pulled out of the public slave trade in 1854, it only took two decades for the truce to become an unofficial alliance.

Did the Consortium still dabble in human trafficking? Not in any way a person could prove.

So, 'no,' as far as concerned the Board.

Malleus, ever considering itself a Knightly Order, enjoyed sneering down its nose at the Consortium's barbarism; but they coordinated with the Belgian's people more often than they confronted them. The Belgian often volunteered Consortium agents to take the lead in Malleus' less-respectable and more clandestine operations and Malleus frequently agreed. After all, the Consortium didn't have a reputation to protect.

Ha.

Zoe finished her second drink and closed her tab. She had a lot more work to do that night.

And she had to leave a message for Jill.

Pittsburgh, PA.

December, 2006.

Zoe waited in the foyer for a long time, listening. Dust danced in the dimness and spun into dark. No boards creaked, no sheets rasped against themselves; no stirring or sign of life scritched at her burning ears at all. Still, her sixth sense told her something about this place was *wrong*.

From her kit bag, an angular purse, she produced a set of chalk and bones. Kneeling at the broken door, she started working on a ward. A simple spell, it alerted her if someone else broke the indicated threshold. It took her around three minutes to cast. She used those minutes to listen for approaching sirens. She'd broken and entered, after all. She'd impersonated.

No sirens approached.

The ward sizzled through her. The muscles flanking her lumbar spine flexed; her latissimus dorsi tightened and twisted. Sweat beaded along her brow. Standing up, she wiped herself off, double-checked her sidearm's chamber and safety, and began her sweep of the floor.

Room to room she maneuvered barrel-first, checking corners, sight lines, and cover; in closets, behind curtains, under furniture. The place looked completely divorced from its history. Three bedrooms, two baths, a kitchen, a dining room, and two unclear common spaces composed the first floor. The door to the stairwell hung open, once a divider between an upstairs, two-bedroom apartment and a downstairs, three-bedroom apartment, now useless due to the single renter. She headed up.

Upstairs, she searched two unfurnished bedrooms, a small unused kitchen, and a bathroom wrecked with disorganization. She found several roaches and small insects but no sign of human occupation. Pausing for a moment at the top of the stairwell, she waited and listened again. Her sixth sense discomfort never faded. She wanted material stimuli to contextualize it.

Nothing.

She returned to the first floor. On her way to the basement door, she felt her ward shatter.

A sharp, second-long banshee blared through her head.

She pressed her spine to the wall, gripped the pistol two-handed. She edged toward an intersection, an angle of wall opening up to the shared kitchen space. Beyond that, a hallway attached to one bedroom and a bathroom, and the threshold where she'd left the ward. Crouching to use chest-high countertops for cover, she crept foot-by-foot closer to the interloper.

Heavy footfalls thunked against linoleum.

"Zoe?" Omar called out.

"Jesus," Zoe gasped, standing up from behind the kitchen counter. "Scared the shit out of me."

Omar laughed. She laughed, too, relieved.

"You were gone longer than you said, so…" he cleared his throat and dropped a backpack on the floor. She noticed the glove compartment's back-up pistol in his hand. "I thought you might want whatever's in the pack."

"Playing cavalry?" she nodded to his pistol and bent to her bag.

"I wasn't coming in here empty handed."

"Good plan." She unzipped the backpack, checked its contents. "We can use this to set up a defensive perimeter before we breach the basement."

"So now I have a gun, we're a 'we?'"

"I'll lay some basic alarm wards at the back door, the hallway next to the basement, and the basement door. I'll throw some wards on us—"

"Wards? Like the ones you, uh…"

"That I put in your head?" she offered.

He coughed. "Yeah. *Those.*"

"Exactly." Zoe started unpacking ingredients. "To save time I'm just going to throw some basic combat wards on you. I can use the opportunity to refresh mine, which I'm overdue on. I'll charge one to decelerate incoming violence—fists, bullets, whatever—and another to make us look blurry to anything trying to hurt us."

"What are we expecting here, the Spanish Inquisition?"

Zoe paused. Blinked. "Funny."

"I'm just saying. I know the—the stuff you do—"

"Magic."

"Uh-huh, the, uh, the magic…"

"It gets less weird to say it out loud the more you get used to knowing it's real."

"Well, it—the magic—it takes time."

"So?" she asked.

Omar peered back whence they came. "So you kicked down a door?"

"Nobody cares. Come on."

###############

It took much longer than expected.

The two alarm spells, one on the back door and the other on the hallway running adjacent to the basement entryway, took half an hour. And while Zoe excelled at tracking, hexes, and combat invocation, she'd never shown remarkable talent at defensive magic. After that labor, she took ten minutes to rest, drink a protein shake, and eat a handful of almonds. Omar, 'standing guard' but mostly waiting, frowned through the proceedings, bored out of his mind. He also had a protein shake and almonds for lunch.

They took turns at the first floor restroom before continuing.

"Any chance you know how to pick locks?" Zoe asked, tugging on the padlock securing the deadbolt that stapled the basement door to its threshold. Below that, a second latch lock and a knob lock also barred their subterranean access.

"Why would you think I would?" Omar asked.

"I don't, Omar. Computer nerds aren't usually the *type*. But it would be convenient."

"I don't."

"Of course not," she muttered, mostly to herself. "Okay. In my backpack there's a skeleton key and a liter bottle of water. Can you grab those while I start chalking?"

"Sure."

The locks took another hour of spellcraft to work open. Zoe strung together four spells to do it, charging them in synchrony and triggering them simultaneously. The padlock dropped to the floor, the deadbolt swung open, and the latch and knob locks disengaged at once. A hiss of windbreath pushed the door in, revealing a rough stone staircase leading down…

…to another locked door.

Finishing a meal replacement bar and her first liter of bottled water, Zoe started again. The second door looked newer, polished steel instead of old wood and iron. After another sweat-greased, laborsome hour, she had that one open, too.

More unfinished stone steps descended, bottoming out into an antechamber. Luckily, Zoe had refreshed the spell enhancing her vision more recently than she'd refreshed her wards, otherwise the darkness clouding the landing would've looked impenetrable. Still catching her breath, she started down.

At the bottom, she discovered a dusty entry hall. Rusted shelving units lined the stone wall opposite the entryway. Cobwebs mantled scores of folding chairs piled along the shelves. A single electric bulb hung from the ceiling. Zoe tugged its white-string trigger and it flickered into a fragile half-life, a glow no better than a candle's.

Omar followed. At the bottom of the stairs, he turned on the flashlight under his barrel.

"Keep it down," she whispered. When he didn't immediately understand, she added, "Point it at the ground."

He did.

The antechamber outlet branched into two directions: the unlabeled corridor to her right contained two doors on its right wall and ended somewhere beyond what her enhanced sight revealed to her; the other hallway ended in an arch over darkness and a sign built from stone reading 'ALTAR.'

Zoe waved Omar back. "We need to smoke before we go in."

"Smoke what?"

"Sixth sense uppers. For you, especially." She pressed her back to the wall and crouched down. "And when we go in, you stay behind me."

"Why?"

"Six feet or so, in case there's something in there that's…weird."

Omar searched her face for something he didn't find. "What are we expecting?"

"I dunno." She unzipped her backpack and reached inside. "Shit."

"What now?"

"We only have one joint." She considered the thing inside the tube in her hand. Frowned. "I'm running hot already. You take it."

"You sure?"

"If we see something bad in there, this will give me an edge." She held the joint his way. "But if shit really hits the fan, it'll stop *you* from losing your mind."

"Fair," Omar agreed.

She burned a clove while he sucked down the joint. Her ears rang, listening for some sign of life down in the dusty dark. For a moment she thought she heard some errant breath, a soft wheeze, but the sound didn't repeat. When Omar finished the sixth sense stimulants, she roached her clove against the rocks. "One more thing," she said, peering back around the corner. "If I say 'hold,' you hold, got it?"

"Got it."

"Okay, then. Six foot stagger, be ready to hold. I'll move on three. One…two…" She turned the corner barrel-first, still half-crouched. Pivoting as she stood, she checked her rear. No immediate threat presented itself in either direction. Swiveling back toward the stone sign reading 'ALTAR,' she walked forward slow-and-silent.

Her sixth sense tingled, prickling her skin against the squish of her sweat-soaked shirt. Her ears strained, listening so hard she could almost hear the pitched tinnitus she'd had magically healed a dozen times already.

She crept for the stone arch. Something tanged at her nostrils, a nose-wrinkling stench. She knew it but couldn't name it at first. A hospital sense-memory, a laboratory sense-memory; the stink reeked chemically.

Bleach. Disinfectants. Something else. Something formal?

Her sixth sense tugged at her brain-base, threatening flight-or-fight adrenaline.

"Hold," she whispered.

Six feet behind her, Omar held.

She waited for her mystically-enhanced eyesight to sharpen the darkness into dimness. Stone and cheap astroturf floored the room beyond, all mottled in crusty stains of red and brown. Fold-out tables and bar carts overloaded with medical equipment crowded the space, once probably a secret place of worship, a bomb shelter, some other kind of sanctuary.

Not satisfied, she reached down and turned on her under-barrel flashlight. Keeping it pointed at the floor, she padded slowly forward.

Something inside the dimness wheezed.

She froze. Waited.

Another wheeze, softer, tickled her ears.

Glancing back at Omar, she saw him itching, standing still but shifting his weight side-to-side with all the anxiety that standing still brought him. He kept his torch-beam pointed floorward but his hands shook from the effort.

She raised her eyebrows at him. He nodded.

She turned back to the dimness ahead.

It wasn't just that Omar might lose his mind. It was also a matter of processing. The more Omar witnessed, the higher clearance she'd have to argue for him to receive after debriefing. The higher clearance she'd have to argue for, the less likely the Board would grant it to Omar. He'd already need Class-E; she didn't need to push things farther.

With a deep breath, she advanced.

Something roughed against the stone floor. It rasped phlegmatic and slapped meaty appendages against the ground. Judging from the sound, Zoe figured the thing was prone or semi-prone, positioned behind a wreck of unexpected cover. Someone, perhaps the Summoner himself, had overturned an antique dining table and a dented fold-out to create a barricade. They'd thrown several chairs into the jerry-rig as well.

Something rasped and scraped behind it.

Zoe stepped through the threshold, approaching.

Whatever purpose the chamber had once served, the Summoner had renovated it into something that resembled a research lab. A risen stage and dais held what looked like a ritual space, the broad central chamber contained the pawn-shop operating theater, and the remains of a small chemistry set cluttered a long table butted up against an empty desk. Dozens of journals and notebooks sat in tall piles gathering dust.

Zoe found a desktop computer tower largely gutted. A faint magic resonance hummed across the ritual space, the last remnants of a weeks-old spell. It was too weak a signal for Zoe to infer anything from, save that the Summoner had used the space shortly before leaving. An abandoned centrifuge and various tech Zoe didn't recognize implied substantial scientific study into the supernatural. All in all, the evidence didn't tell her very much. But it told her a few things very clearly.

First, that the Summoner possessed some degree of independent wealth or, at the least, a substantial windfall. Second, that he'd studied magic for some time before seriously practicing it. And third, that he'd entirely abandoned this studio and whatever thing noised its grotesque existence inside its walls.

"Hhhhhlllll…" the groan sounded almost human.

(*a monster at the end of every*)

Another meaty slap hit the stone, another rough grind scraped along it.

Zoe thumbed off the safety and lifted the underbarrel flashlight toward the barricade.

—human skin and human parts and not all the same human—

She lowered the flashlight and gulped down a yelp of shock. She paused, controlling her breath. For half of a second she froze breakably still, afraid she'd shatter if she moved, knowing that if she moved she'd have to acknowledge what she'd seen.

"Hhhhllllllll…p…" the last sound popped, a puff of air. "P—p—p…"

She lifted the light again. The monster looked hideous and more hideous still for the implications of its life. Visually, it didn't make sense. Spines curled the wrong way and fused at angled intersections, arms jutted from cervical vertebrae and pelvic floors, legs kicked from shoulder joints and mid-backs. It flopped itself around aimless and undulous, too many lever-less limbs to navigate free from its two-penny prison.

Two of its heads knotted together, blended at a shared eye socket. Their mouths moved together, though one didn't have a lower mandible. "Huhhh-uhh-uhhh…hhhuuhh-lll…p…"

Malleus operatives, employees of the Advanced and Specialized Operations Division, all carried standardized sidearms magazines on their missions unless otherwise requested. In each mag, the first two bullets were silver, despite the rarity of silver's actual utility, and the next ten bullets came in alternating pairs of armor piercing and frangible rounds. Each extended mag lastly ended with a pair of incendiary, phosphorous, or tracer rounds, depending on the weapon's make, model, and caliber. Intel-Analytics and Tactical Strategics had come up with that particular arrangement of bullets because if shit ever really hit the fan during an op, that arrangement of bullets would kill just about anything an agent needed to kill, supernatural or otherwise.

The creature garbled humanoid shouts and groans and throatslap gibberish. It thrashed and whined as lead tunneled through it. Twelve-limbed, half of them non-functional from being folded and stuffed and bent wrongways, the monster scrambled away from its attacker and desperately sought exit from an exit-less cage. It heaved its malformed body against the barricade once, twice, three times; it stumbled backwards and flopped onto a knot of randomly twisting arms. Red-pink-green blood oozed out of it in viscous wound-drool. It kicked two legs in the air and punched a fist at the floor. It knocked its tied-together heads against the ground.

"Hlllllp…" one of its voiceboxes rasped, feeble and dying. "H-huhhh… llll…"

Zoe stepped up to the barricade and peered down at the broken-animal thing on the other side.

It didn't look like something planned. It looked like someone with moderate anatomical knowledge had sawed three corpses apart and reassembled them with the goal of eliciting terror, disgust, and trauma. The mashed-up Picasso-beast spasming and dying on the stone ground wasn't some grand construct or summoned aberration, it was a pitiful creation born crippled and alone to an underground existence.

She emptied the rest of the magazine.

The incendiary rounds sizzled but nothing burned. The scent of cooking meat filled the air. Zoe reloaded.

"Zoe!"

"Hold!"

Omar skidded through the threshold pistol-first. "Zo—"

"I said *hold*!"

"What the fuck—"

"Get out!" she turned her flashlight straight toward him, hiding the carcass with glare. "Get the *fuck* out!"

Omar backpedaled, gagging.

She thumbed the safety back into place, panting. Lowered the gun to her side.

Omar spat and retched but didn't throw up. The dry heaves echoed in the tight subterranean halls.

Turning the flashlight back to the Summoner's construct, she watched it lie still and bleeding. She watched it for almost a minute, counting heartbeats. Reasonably certain it couldn't get back up again, she walked back to the lab's entrance and peered down the hall at Omar, who sat on the dusty ground half-curled against a wall.

"You okay?" she asked.

"What was that?"

"A, uh…it's called a construct, sometimes capitalized, 'Construct.'"

"Looked like…" he grimaced, shaking his head.

"It was made from human parts but it didn't have anything like human consciousness."

"Made from human parts?" Omar echoed.

"He probably dug them out of graves. Cadaver-hunting. He built it to terrify. It's almost…it's almost like he wanted someone to see it." She glanced back at the lab behind her. "But it was frail."

Omar rested his forehead against his knees. "This is crazy."

She re-entered the lab, drifting back toward the barricade. The Construct stayed dead as she approached. "Omar?" she shouted. "There's a collection kit at the bottom of the backpack. Can you grab that?"

"Gimme a minute," he called back. "Yeah."

Waiting for Omar to return with the collection kit, she tried not think about how weak the monster had been, how killing it had felt more like putting down a sick animal than routing a dire threat. She tried not to think about how the monster was three people taken apart, stitched back together, and resuscitated mostly-mindless, essentially nonviable.

Using her underbarrel beam, she found the room's light switch.

Overhead fluorescent bulbs buzzed to life, new attachments to the ceiling. She scanned the environment, replacing one set of thoughts with another. The Summoner had performed experiments, here. What kinds? The kinds that led to cadaver-hunting and failed-Frankenstein construct-creation. Why? To build a construct? A viable one? A more powerful one? To learn summoning magic, evocation, portalcraft? To combine a construct and a summoned entity? Why?

"This it?" Omar asked, entering the room.

"Yeah," Zoe replied, retrieving the kit. "Can you do me another favor?"

"What do you need?"

"All these notebooks…just get as many of them as you can in the trunk." Opening the kit, she retrieved the collection scraper and a stoppered vial. She returned to the barricade. "And if there's anything you think we can salvage from that computer…"

"I'm, uh…I'm on it."

Stepping between toppled furniture, she peered back at Omar. "Don't look."

"Yeah, no. Didn't plan on it."

As she collected thickening grue in the glass, she tried not to think of it as 'human.'

###############

Somewhere far behind them, hours later, emergency responders tried to put out an inferno that had once been a five-bedroom rental that had once been a residential house that had once been a synagogue and a church and a synagogue. The 'underground areas' forbidden by the lease collapsed and most of the above-ground structure baked unsalvageable.

They watched the road and rarely spoke. Blues music played through the sound system on low volume. Zoe couldn't recognize the track for some reason.

(*tumbling octopod movements all human legs hands arms feet swimming across tile stone floor*)

Just before midnight, three hours after leaving Pittsburgh, Zoe pulled the car rubber-shrill-crying off the highway and into a gas station parking lot. Not even listening for Omar's inevitable question, she threw the rental into park, threw her door open, and stepped out into the sodium glare. She crossed the lot to where it curbed into grass and stepped over into the dark. Omar followed at a dozen paces, gaze constantly flitting between Zoe and the car.

She wanted to cry. No. She wanted to scream. She wanted to scream until the whole world went deaf.

The coiling thing inside of her twisted and twisted and she shook and quaked, walking out into undeveloped, winter-barren land. Once she got far out enough that nobody in the gas station could hear, she opened her mouth as wide as she could and released a single long keen. It came out uneven, neither a roar nor a wail but both.

"What was that?" Omar asked softly as she re-entered the lot.

"Therapy. Come on, we need to find a motel."

"You okay?"

She halfway laughed, climbing back into the car. "No," she said. "Never."

Chapter Five

Wilmington, NC.

June, 1997.

On the drive, Jill recounted her brief relapse.

She'd 'escaped' rehab with forty dollars and blew it within minutes on booze and two dime bags of coke; the coke dealer knew the men at the house, middle-aged types who kept deep pockets full of uppers, downers, and all-arounders for the purposes of luring college students into the building, their motivations surface-obvious; Jill found a burn-out there who had heroin and the rest of the night sizzled into spoon-oil. When Zoe's sixth-sense razored through her with warning, she'd probably felt the tail end of Jill's spell charging, not some unforeseen malice from the slimy but ultimately housebroken boys on the 'lawn.'

They made three or four u-turns before noticing the driveway, a narrow path of uphill asphalt hidden behind an angle of tall brush. In the passenger seat, Jill fidgeted, her hair sweat-coarse, her body given to occasional tremors. The first days of sobriety always went rough. Even the first hours. But Zoe knew that if Jill could struggle her way through the initial rockiness, things would smooth out.

If.

Sung-ho's winter home sat on a high, steeply-sloped hill overlooking a network of channels and creeks that all led, sooner or later, to the Atlantic Ocean, itself a twenty minute walk away. Landscaped foliage sprawled the suburban yards, obscuring the residents from each other's prying, and several rows of staggered privacy trees shielded the house from the only nearby road. Zoe could see why Sung-ho chose it, why he'd invested so much of his life's earnings into owning it. Year-round warmth and comfort, yes, but also solitude, a dawn-facing window on the topmost floor, presumably a skylight for moon viewing; all the basics a person might want for a calm, serene vacation…or for casting ritual magic.

At the end of the driveway, the engine ticked off time.

"You know…you know how they teach you in basic about supervision management?" Jill asked in a dust-dry croak.

"'Civilian intake supervision,'" Zoe corrected.

Jill didn't train for field work, her education after first year training shared little in common with Zoe's. Jill picked at her jeans. "Whatever you call it. Lockdown. I want you to do it to me."

"It doesn't work as well when the subject's in a familiar setting."

"I don't know the layout that well. Plus. You know…"

Civilian intake supervision SOP step one: escort the subject to a nearby safehouse, FOB, base-of-operations, rental room, or other transient/isolated location.

Zoe peered at Sung-ho's winter house through the windscreen.

"Anything that stops me from getting out the front door," Jill said.

Step two: isolate the subject and assess current psychological, mystical, and physiological status.

"There are a lot of doors in there," Zoe admitted. "A lot of hallways."

Step three: using the safehouse structure or other structure as perimeter, limit subject's access to the outside world.

Zoe could lock various doors throughout the house, dead-ending certain corridors, blocking certain hallways; she could turn the place into a veritable maze. She pursed her lips, thinking. She tried to conjure a blueprint from snatches of her memory.

Jill shivered, pulling her knees up into her chest. "Shit."

"If we're going to do this right, I'll have to black bag you. Blindfold you, at least. Otherwise you'll remember too much once we get inside."

"I don't feel so good."

"I'll have to keep you blindfolded until after I can finish isolation procedures. Is that okay?"

Jill nodded. Her teeth knocked rhythms through her mouth.

Step four: dose subject with sleeping pill, sixth sense stimulants, and any other necessary stabilizers. Use psychic wards and healing magic to shore up subject's psycho-spiritual defenses.

"Tonight, I'll give you something to help you sleep," Zoe said.

Step five: brief subject on whatever events required their extraction; begin basic sixth sense inoculations. If movement is necessary, convince the subject to follow. Once inoculations begin, *maintain constant supervision and/or surveillance of subject.*

"I'll blindfold you and leave you in the restroom, okay?" Zoe asked.

"Mm-hmmmm…"

"I'll load in all the supplies from the trunk and start iso procedures. It'll take, say…forty-five minutes? Sixty, tops. Then I'll take the blindfold off and bring you to your room. Is that doable?"

"I gotta…" Jill unbuckled her seatbelt and threw the door open. She tumbled from the car on all-fours and rushed for the grass. Dry-heaving, she groaned and spat and arched her back. A retch gagged out of her. Another. Nothing else. Sitting back on the asphalt, she panted, sweating. "Goddammit."

Zoe opened her glove compartment and fished a blindfold out from between two head-sized, black-fabric bags. She stepped out of the vehicle and crossed behind the trunk as she approached her sister. "Do you want to put it on?"

"Can you?"

"I…" she looked down at the blindfold in her hand. "Uh, yeah. Sure."

Still kneeling, Jill titled her head back and closed her eyes. "Thanks."

"You're sure about this?"

"Please, just…before I chicken out, okay?"

"Okay."

Zoe wrapped the cloth around Jill's head and Jill's gaze vanished in its black.

Boston, MA.

July, 2016.

Zoe checked her watch. 3:17 AM.

Boots pressed against the stall door, she folded her arms across her waist and leaned her head back against the public bathroom tile. The back-of-the-shop bathroom of a twenty-four-hour convenience store in a metropolitan area seemed as clandestine a place to meet as any. It had taken her three days to assemble the various spells and actual physical materials necessary to send the ciphered message safely to Jill, but the time and place clues she'd left as the post-cipher riddle erred on the side of obviousness.

But 3:17 AM wasn't 3:00 AM.

Had Jill not received the message, somehow? Had she failed to figure out the cipher? Had she been followed?

The door opened. Someone hesitated at the threshold.

Zoe opened her mouth, closed it. She didn't want to give herself away if someone had intercepted the message. She'd covered her own tracks well, and knew Leo had done some heavy lifting on her behalf—giving herself away so soon would come as a dramatic and embarrassing failure. But could she expect

Jill to speak first?

She pursed her lips and hovered her hand near the butt of her gun.

The person waiting eased weight from one shoe to another. Hinges squeaked.

"Jill?" Zoe asked, voice cracking.

"Zoe?" Jill answered, a whisper.

Zoe put her boots down from the door. "Oh, thank god…"

"What's going on? The past few weeks…do you know who's doing this?"

"Get in the stall next to mine. Did you bring your phone?"

Jill opened the other stall door, didn't walk in. "No, I didn't bring a phone. Why do I have to get in the stall?"

"In case someone comes in."

Jill entered the stall, locked it.

For a few seconds, neither sister spoke. Seven years had passed since they'd had regular contact, almost six since they'd had any contact at all. Once the entry theatrics passed, that long absence replaced them.

In the five silent seconds, then, Zoe's mind erupted. Questions cascaded through her like ash over Pompeii. Six years of questions, all-at-once. She hadn't prepared for that. She'd imagined the meeting like any other difficult meeting she'd had, an exchange of intel and tactics, hard dialog compromising toward hard decisions. She hadn't imagined wanting to scream and cry and throw her arms around Jill and hit Jill in the face and kiss Jill all at the same time.

When the mental volume subsided, Zoe coughed. "Where did you go?" she asked.

"Zo'…there are people following my husband to work every morning."

"I need to know."

Jill scraped shoe sole against the floor. "I went out looking for para-normatives."

"You started the school immediately?"

"No. After I met Darnell, we decided to. When I met him, he knew he had something but he didn't really know what he was or how to use it. I was just so excited to have someone I could actually talk to about everything…I sort of trained him. Mostly by accident. But then…"

"Then you kept going."

"Darnell's a natural psychic, not like the kind they warned us about in training—I've never met anyone like that—but like a surface-thoughts-and-motivations sort of psychic. You could mistake it for just being insightful if you weren't...looking for something. But even once he got a handle on being psychic..."

"You taught him ritual magic," Zoe guessed.

"He had a strong enough sixth sense, being a psychic. So, yeah. There's a hard limit to how much I can teach a psychic about being a psychic, never having been one...but magic?"

"Can I just ask...somewhere in there, during that first year after you left the Winters team and tried to go solo—"

"I didn't *try*."

"Why did you stop calling me?" The question razored out of her throat rusty. "Me and Sung-ho and Leo, we covered for you when you defected, we made sure nobody still held onto the grudge after you left Winters-Armitage, too. And at first you were so grateful. But then one day, I don't know, fourteen, fifteen months after you indie'd out of everything, you hung up the phone on your sister and you never picked it up again. Why?"

"I..." Jill trailed off. "I'm sorry."

"Just tell me. Please."

"When I realized I wanted to teach other para-normative people...I'm not a moron. I knew it would be risky. People might feel threatened by it, powerful people. And I know there are rules against it."

"So?"

"I didn't want you to have to be the person who found out what I was doing. I didn't want you to have to make that decision."

"I wouldn't have turned you in."

"I know you wouldn't have," Jill said. "And that would've been worse."

Zoe leaned her head back against the cool tile, stared at the styrofoam-textured ceiling.

"So..." Jill cleared her throat, moved around inscrutably in her stall. "Who is it out there? Malleus?"

Zoe sniffed and swallowed. Her lip quivered just-slightly. She stopped it. Took a breath. "It's everyone, Jill. It's the Belgian, it's Malleus, it's the

Temple *Beth Yetzirah*—and those are just the people I *know* about."

"I...what?" Jill balked.

"They're saying your school is a Column Threat, a danger to the Great Big Secret itself."

"No. No, that can't...it's just a school. It breaks the rules but it's still—it's a school."

"Apparently the Board has other interpretations."

"Who's leading? Who's the forward team?"

"The Belgian's people," Zoe answered.

Something squeaked from Jill's throat. Something else choked there. "They're *kids*."

Breaking gaze with the ceiling, Zoe leaned her head against the two stalls' shared wall. "I'm doing everything I can. If I can buy enough time or the situation becomes too unstable..."

"Can you do it?"

"I don't think so. I'm still one of the best, but they've got three maybe four teams working in tandem. I can buy time, sure, but until an actual exit plan takes shape..."

"What if I surrender?" Panic rode Jill's voice. "Will they let the kids go?"

Zoe explained the current terms of 'truce,' as Leo had phrased it. They read like this: the alliance of organizations aiming itself at Jill and her school would back down from further psychological and magical attacks if Jill agreed to liquidate the school, testify against Karen Woeser in front of the Arbiters and any other requested secret-society judicial authority, and allow her students to have their memories systematically altered to remove any and all references to their supernatural education. This last bit required a significant investment of resources, since even the most practiced and naturally-adept psychic witches needed to undergo months of ritual ceremony to charge such powerful spells. If it took seven practitioners seven months to work the magic, someone had to provide the necessary esoteric components, someone had to provide food, shelter, and water, someone had to pay their salaries.

And someone would do that to make these children forget.

Hearing the terms, Jill kicked the door of her stall so hard it crashed open. "Fuck them."

"Leo's working on negotiating better terms."

"And what if he can't?"

The question hung like a body.

(*a boy's body*)

Zoe swallowed. "Do you still have any way to get in touch with Shoshanna Winters?"

The Winters family had originally become noteworthy in the clandestine world of supernatural secret societies near the end of the nineteenth century. At the time, they'd worn the surname 'Winderbaum.' Like everything else that survived apocalypse, they'd molted skins. Arriving in the States, they'd settled in Oceanrest, Maine, where they opened both a pharmacy and a chemicals company. In 1974, Oskar Winters handed leadership down to his son Eli. By 1994, the Winters family had become the fourth or fifth most powerful group in their shadowy little world. In 2009, Eli Winters fell down a spiral staircase, cracked his skull open, and slipped into a coma. Now, David and Shoshanna Winters both ran the secret society and served as executives at Winters-Armitage Laboratories, a massively profitable pharmacom.

Jill had defected from Malleus to work for them, so when she left the Winters team, too, rumors bred in the wake. Rumors about Jill's exit and moreso about the unknown contents of her final conversation with Shoshanna. Zoe hoped the rumors implied a still-standing connection.

Hinges creaked as the stall door slowly shut again.

"No," Jill answered.

"They wouldn't have just *let* you leave if you didn't leave on good terms."

It had cost the entire political cache of both the Briars and the Smythes to ensure Jill a safe and costless defection, back when it had happened. Zoe felt certain that their father had died still resentful. So how had Jill performed the same feat again so gracefully?

"I left on good terms," Jill said. "I just...I don't have a way to reach out to them, anymore."

"If I could get a meeting, they might be our best bet of getting you out of here safe. But I need a meeting."

"I *know*," Jill bit off the word like a cleaver. "God, I know. Can't Leo help?"

"Maybe." Zoe knew that Leo and Shoshanna had known each other in the not-so-distant past, a time before cellphones and constant surveillance, when agents reached across enemy lines unpunished by their superiors. But that time was gone. "Even then, I'd need leverage. Something."

"If I had the leverage to save my—" Jill cut herself off. The moment stretched. "There might be one thing."

Zoe sat up. "What?"

"If you have to, if you absolutely *have* to, tell Shoshanna I told you about what David did."

"What did David do?"

"Nothing to me."

"But—"

"Your knowing or not knowing won't save my kids, Zo'." Jill stood up in her stall. "All it could do is hurt someone who really helped me. And you know that I really, really try not to do that anymore."

Zoe stood, too. "I'm sorry this is happening."

Jill opened her stall and stepped onto the bathroom tile. "Me, too."

Zoe couldn't get her arm to open the door. She hadn't seen Jill in almost six years. "Not just this, but..." she trailed off. Worked her jaw. "For everything. About everything."

On the other side of a half-inch of shaking, poorly-maintained steel, Jill took a breath. "You didn't do anything. You've only ever tried to help..."

Zoe clenched her jaw and squeezed her eyes shut. She pushed on the stall door.

The bathroom door suddenly swung in. Zoe froze.

"Is, uh...is everything okay in here?" a woman's voice asked.

"Yeah," Jill said. "Yeah, sorry. I was just...excuse me."

"Oh, sorry, yeah," the other woman muttered.

Jill left.

Zoe stood there. She opened her eyes.

The newcomer gave up on the busted second stall and moved over to the third and last.

Zoe exited. She rushed half-breathless through the store back to the sidewalk. But Jill had long-vanished by then.

Albany, NY.

December, 2006.

Switching rental cars twice in Pennsylvania and again in New York, using different credit cards belonging to different decedents for every transaction, Zoe took Omar to Albany. She rented a two bed hotel room with a cash card she bought at a corner store with money taken out of an expense account linked to a sub-contracting company that did on-site QA for Malleus' home security technology.

Field operatives did these things more out of habit than anything else. The Intel-Analytics department issued her second-hand social security numbers, stolen identities, and dead people's credit lines as a matter of procedure. She used them, too, as a matter of procedure. Like everything else, keeping secrets worked best as a ritual. The more it felt like part of someone's everyday, boring-as-hell existence, the less they even noticed they were doing it.

Zoe and Omar stayed in the hotel room for almost a week.

Over the first four days spent poring through the remains of the Summoner's journals, along with a hard drive Omar had recovered from the gutted desktop computer, they mostly learned one thing: that the Summoner had accrued a frightening volume of knowledge for an amateur. He hadn't uncovered much that needed above Class-E intel clearance but, then, he hadn't *had* Class-E intel clearance. From what they could tell, all the Summoner had had was a trio of supernatural experiences that his brain had allowed him to witness and remember. He'd built out from there. He'd built out *substantially*.

Within a year of discovering the reality of the supernatural, the Summoner had taught himself how to use basic magic. A couple years after that, he'd started building small Constructs and automatons. At some point he'd tried to introduce other people to the idea of magic's reality. It had gone poorly. Over the course of the following eighteen months, the Summoner's growing frustration—maybe even rage?—combined with his evolving mystical abilities…

Well, they'd led to the thing in the basement.

(*hhh-huuhh-uhh—*)

"… 'They must somehow profit off of keeping it secret,'" Omar read from the topmost notebook from the pile on the larger of the room's two coffee tables. "He capitalized 'They' and everything. But then, check this out: 'if we could introduce magic to a larger group of users, we could affect great change not only in our society, but in *all* societies.'"

Flipping through journal pages cross-legged on the bed, Zoe flicked her eyes up to meet his. "Bleeding hearts don't stitch corpses together."

"Oh, no, this guy's a hundred percent out of his goddamn mind," Omar said, half-chuckling. "But…well. Is he a hundred percent wrong?"

"Maybe not. But I'd say, statistically, the people using magic wouldn't generally use it to make the world a better place. I submit as evidence: people are using it and the world isn't a better place."

"But magic *could* make it better."

"So could not-magic. If we wanted to house every homeless person in America, we *could*. If we wanted to feed every hungry person, we *could*. But we *don't*. Because, collectively, people don't *want* to. Magic doesn't change that. I've spent my whole life living in this world and I can tell you with absolute fucking certainty: magic doesn't change that." She didn't know where the heat had come from, the fuel for the tirade, but it came nonetheless. "The problem isn't people having or not having magic—it isn't people having or not having any kind of tool or tech or shiny new toy—it's that people don't choose to use their tools to make the better world. They use them to kill cabins full of vacationers and build Franken-monsters in their basements."

"The right people—"

"Hey," Zoe interrupted, "what about this idea: what if there *are no right people?*"

Omar sagged back in his over-cushioned chair. "What if there are?"

"Then I hope there's someone there to stop them from going insane when they see magic for the first time in their lives."

Omar didn't reply to that.

They worked in silence for several uncomfortable minutes. Something chewed at Zoe's insides. She kept glancing up at Omar and away again. Unable to focus on the page in front of her, she tossed the notebook aside with a sigh. "I'm sorry," she said. "I'm sorry if I…"

"It's fine. Really. You're probably right. It's just…"

"What?"

"If you don't think the world can change…what's the point?"

"I never said the world couldn't change. I just said that magic didn't change it." She stood, stretching legs that suddenly ached. "There's a reason witches usually form covens, you know. Not just the 'safety in numbers' thing. It's the extra power that comes from having a group with a shared point of intent and willpower. So maybe you're the one who's right, metaphorically. Just be careful not to get the metaphor confused with the real thing."

Omar stood, too, folding away his own research. "Just so you know, I'm not feeling inspired by this guy or anything. It's *my* friends he went after, remember. I just…I know how angry he felt, finding out."

"Are you angry, Omar?"

"Fuck yes. Are you kidding me? I was *lied to.*"

"You weren't lied to. There's no unified conspiracy of silence keeping magic a secret," Zoe said, not lying except by omission. Leaving out the 'for the most part' that defined what followed, she continued, "Magic hides itself. Mundanity decay, remember? Sixth senses?"

"I know all that. But I'm still pissed."

Zoe didn't give him a reason to continue feeling pissed. No unified conspiracy existed; dozens or even scores of competing, conflicting, and occasionally collaborating conspiracies existed, instead. With another sigh, she gestured to the door, "Feel like a drink?"

Omar scowled. After a few seconds, he shook his head in concession. "Yeah. Sure."

############

A basic alarm ward jerked Zoe awake before dawn on the fifth day in the hotel. Her eyelids leapt open and her hand grabbed the butt of her sidearm beneath her pillow. Luckily she paused to take in the scene before moving.

Omar sat on the other bed, the room phone in his hand, staring at her.

She'd warded the phone but hadn't told him.

Releasing her gun, she sat up. "Omar?"

"I, uh…"

Pretending drowsiness against the adrenal surge the ward pulsed through her, she rubbed her face. "Put down the phone," she mumbled, aiming for sleep-speech.

"I need to call my mom."

"Omar." She ran her hands through her hair, tidying.

"It's been almost two weeks."

Zoe let her arms fall at her sides. She searched him for clues, trying to figure out his intent. The glassiness of his gaze and the slack in his hands persuaded her. "I have to listen in," she said, allowing the pretense of drowsiness to wear away. "In case you tell her anything sensitive."

"I just need to tell her I'm okay."

Zoe pushed herself to the edge of the mattress. With one hand on the receiver, she nodded to Omar. "Go ahead and dial. I'll disconnect it if you say something…"

"Classified?"

"Whatever. Just call."

Omar called. Someone, presumably his mother, answered. "Hey, mom," he said. "It's—oh." The voice on the other end pitched high, full of volume and worry. "I'm fine, no, I'm fine. No, it's not like that. I'm—" more shouting interrupted him. "Dennis?" he asked. "No, that's not what happened. What, the police? Mom, I'm telling you, I was there, Dennis didn't even… I can't, I—I'm with someone." The shouting stopped. A quiet question followed. "They're helping me prove I'm innocent. They...I don't know. Don't call the police. Mom, please..." he put a hand over the mic. "She's really scared. Could you talk to her?"

Zoe considered disconnecting the call. She didn't, but she considered it. Instead, she took the phone. "Hello? Mrs. Elwin-Carter?"

"And who the hell is this?" she asked. "Who the fuck kidnapped my son?"

"I'm not at liberty to say."

"Excuse me?"

"I work for a company sub-contracting with multiple federal agencies, it would violate federal law for me to give you my name."

She got a lot quieter. "Who—who are you people?"

"It is a matter of your own personal safety that you do not know." Zoe had mastered agent-voice, the tone and cadence that told civilians that they'd stepped into something they would really rather get out of. "The incident at Keene's Falls is more complicated than initial reports would make it appear. Your son is an important witness in an ongoing operation and investigation. Have the police contacted you?"

"Sometimes twice a day. They say that Omar—"

"Do not provide local law enforcement with any information. I'm sure you know that Omar is, of course, innocent. Until we can detangle the narrative and provide the necessary evidence, however, he remains at risk."

"What's going on here?"

"Just know that your son is safe. Unfortunately, I'm not at liberty to divulge any further details. We will call again in another two weeks." She hung up.

"I would've liked to talk to her more," Omar said.

"We might've been on the line too long as it was."

"You think the cops traced the call?"

"It depends on who cares about the case, how much, and how much money they have. Better to play it safe."

Omar stood up from his bed and stretched. "So...you work for the government?"

"No. I made that up. It sounds more impressive, scarier to the normal person than the truth."

Besides, she didn't tell him, all the really powerful secret societies had transitioned to the private sector, anyway.

###############

Later that day, as Omar clicked through files on a recovered hard drive attached to an internet-less laptop, Zoe saw the first piece of Class-D intel that the Summoner had figured out. Clutching Omar's shoulder, she told him to shut down the laptop and pack up.

It was a long drive to Maine.

And the Summoner was two weeks ahead of them.

Chapter Six

Wilmington, NC.

July, 1997.

Jill's withdrawal symptoms subsided after the second night. She hadn't had the time to build up enough junk in her veins to earn the shakes and sweats and retching that usually defined her early sobriety; she'd built up just enough to groan and slouch through a day and a half of faint nausea before coming through the other side.

By then, Zoe had engaged several locks and installed several more in an effort to shrink the house's overall square footage. She'd prioritized blocking window access and entry/exit points. By the time she'd finished, she'd blockaded almost half the building. The remaining square footage still doubled her apartment's.

While Jill slept through the second morning at the house, Zoe ran into town for last-minute supplies. Mostly she picked up grocery items they'd forgotten to get on the drive in.

When she returned, the ritual began.

Practitioners born with natural mystical aptitude could cast cantrips in mere seconds, often through sheer willpower and neuromuscular resources. By ritualizing these spells, many born without natural aptitude could cast them in minutes—not usually with sheer willpower, but armed with as little as a mystical focus or a piece of chalk they could use to scribble sigils and glyphs somewhere. And that magic worked well for combat prep and on-the-fly action.

But truly powerful, proper rituals took days, weeks, and even months to charge. Some took years. And they required daily attention to build and develop. They tested the practitioners' discipline and endurance. The easiest needed at least ninety minutes of labor and meditation per day; most needed far more. For this reason, most practitioners opted to perform even rituals that allowed them access to public life in relative isolation. It allowed them easier control over things that might go wrong, and anything that went wrong might cost them time and labor beyond their exhaustion.

Ritual magic also interacted with unpredictable forces. In truth, all magic did, even the seconds-long cantrips charged by born-adept witches, but ritual magic did so at a greater magnitude and for a greater duration. Small mistakes and uncontrollable variables might invite little harm one-at-a-time, but over the course of days or weeks they added up to substantial excess energy. An intelligent entity searching for a way into their world could crawl through a crack chipped out of the spell by unnoticed errors. Worse, the chaotic energy could cause unexpected side-effects in the ritual itself.

For that reason, most practitioners began a ritual with long rites of warding.

################

It took Zoe and Jill the entire first day of the ritual to finish the warding, cleansings, and other defensive magic. Sleep came easily to both sisters, that night.

The next day began the formal practice of the ritual. It required three hours of spellcraft per day from Jill and five from Zoe in the form of invocation and warding magic, along with a dash of largely-symbolic healing magic thrown in for good measure. It also required each of them to meditate for two hours per day, once under the gaze of the sun before it reached its zenith, and once under the gaze of the moon when it beamed its brightest. The first phase required a strict vegetarian diet and limited their daily intake of non-water beverages to one mug of coffee, two glasses of wine, and all the tea they could drink. Before the Gateway ended, Zoe purchased a knee-high stack of boxes stuffed with tea bags. The second phase cut the wine and coffee, a bridge to cross once they'd arrived there.

The first phase also limited Zoe's smoking habit to a mere three cloves per day. The second phase cut them, too—another bridge, hopefully un-burnt.

The cutback left her edgy. Jill seemed edgy, too, for obviously similar reasons. On the third day, over a curtly grumpy lunch, they agreed to keep their distance when possible, at least until the initial substanceless tension diminished. Jill asked Zoe to dig around the house for any grimoires or esoteric reading. Zoe agreed, if only to have something to feel frustrated about besides the decreased nicotine.

Sung-ho always kept things secreted around. Grimoires, books, scrolls, artifacts, trophies—he'd gotten into trouble more than once for pack-ratting beyond society rules. He'd gotten into trouble more than once for letting curious little Hyun-jung stumble upon his trinkets before her time, too.

Though Hammer or, now, Malleus, had nothing written in stone regarding the appropriate age for a parent to introduce a potential legacy member to the supernatural, most members waited until fourteen or fifteen. Hyun-jung was nine.

It didn't take long for Zoe to start coming up with not-so-hidden reading materials for Jill to pore over.

The fourth and fifth days passed uneventfully. Zoe pushed her first cigarette as far out from the day's beginning as she could. The ritual accounted for seven or eight hours of the day but she still spent the rest of it trapped inside. Smoking passed time.

Just before midnight on the sixth day, near the end of her third clove, Zoe wondered if the ritual reset its daily count at midnight or at dawn. At the dining table, she leaned her head back against the wall. The kitchen, abutting the ritual space, served as more or less the center of the unblockaded structure. She sat there at nights stretching out cigarettes and wine glasses, trying not to think about what she'd do during the second phase when she had neither. She puffed spice and flicked ash.

Her sixth sense shivered. She flinched, not having felt anything resembling warning or foreboding in days. True to her promise, Jill's wards had turned out to be incredibly powerful.

The silence shrill against her eardrums, Zoe stood from her chair and scanned the area. Dim yellow glow hazed down from an overhead fixture, the stove light still shone from dinner; nothing in the immediate vicinity seemed amiss. And yet...

Switching her smoke to her left hand, she edged over to the kitchen countertop and slipped a chef's knife from a wooden block. She twisted its hilt reverse-grip to make herself harder to disarm. Dread prickled through her sixth sense, a barely-there adrenal spike implying danger without obvious evidence. Frowning, she put the clove out against the granite and abandoned it there bent. Drifting through the kitchen's glow, she headed for the dimness and darkness of the hallway beyond.

She flicked the lightswitch and walked toward the end of the hall, the stairwell to the second floor.

At the bottom of the steps, she recognized a sound. A hissing, a rising and falling sibilance; the hint-subtle noise produced by muffled whispers. She crept upstairs slow and low, close to the wall. She paused at the second story landing, listening.

Around the corner to the left, a broad lounge area tightened to a small corridor leading to the bathroom. Dead ahead from the stairs, a bedroom door. Two more sat on the left side of the hall.

The sibilance seeped in from her left. She peeked out and saw nothing.

Out of the practice of daily invocation, she hadn't bothered to enhance her eyesight that morning. Scowling at her own unearned ease, she flicked on the lightswitch. Ceiling-recessed bulbs lit the area. They also gave away her movement to any presence or entity that might have made it through Jill's wards. And considering the power of the wards, she didn't like the idea of anything that might have slipped past them having that advantage.

But she needed to see.

She followed the wall on the left until it led to the four foot corridor bridging the lounge and its attached restroom. At the threshold, she waited. Peeking around the corner, she saw no light creeping out from the crack at the bottom of the bathroom door. But she heard whispers.

What did they say?

She pressed her spine against the wall, suddenly sweating. She tightened her grip on the knife.

What was a knife going to do against anything strong enough to sneak through Jill's wards?

She needed more firepower. But what?

The whispers grew louder. She took a deep breath. Held it.

"You'll never be free of this," a voice muttered from the darkness only a foot in front of her.

"Zoe?"

"Jesus!" Zoe jumped.

"Hey," Jill jumped, too, having crept up on Zoe from behind. "Hey, whoa!" she put her hands up as Zoe spun toward her. "Are you okay?"

Zoe's sixth sense calmed, threatless. No sound hissed out of the darkness. Her heart drummed in her chest. She blinked. Jill wore pajamas, loose, white and red-striped. For the first time since rehab, she'd showered. Zoe blinked again. "I, uh…I don't know."

Oceanrest, ME.

December, 2006.

Blues played through the car stereo. Howlin' Wolf watched smokestack lightning. It glowed just like…

Zoe had called Sung-ho at the end of the first day of the drive, somewhere in the stretches of snowy rural Vermont. At the end of the second day, some time in the late afternoon, she and Omar would arrive at his house. They would discuss the operation. She'd ask for Sung-ho's help. They'd worked together for over a decade before a promotion had elevated him to Tactical Management. Hopefully he'd agree.

"You still haven't told me what it is about this place got you moving like that," Omar said.

Zoe moved her jaw, unaware she'd had it clenched. She stretched her neck to a relieving *pop*. "I can't."

"Is this about, what, your NDA? Some contract?"

"I'll rephrase that: I shouldn't." She adjusted the volume. Howlin' Wolf's voice cracked. "Everything you've seen so far, everything I've told you, I can probably get you clearance to know it."

"You haven't told me who you work for, either."

"Yeah. I definitely can't get you clearance to know *that*." She wondered if that particular detail might trigger her NDA curse; if she'd start stuttering and saying other things if she tried to tell him the truth. She didn't venture to find out.

"You could just tell me and then don't put it in your report that you told me."

"That would only work until you told someone else."

"What if I didn't?" he asked.

"Sooner or later, you would."

"Fuckin'…" Omar restrained himself from saying anything else. He flicked his locs over one shoulder and leaned his head against the window. "Fine. Keep me in the dark. I'm just the motherfucker who had to watch shadows come to life two weeks ago."

They drove without speaking until the Howlin' Wolf rhythm warped into Elmore James' guitar.

"Oceanrest metro has a population a bit under two hundred thousand people," she said, her gaze never leaving the road. "Of those, we estimate at least forty and as many as sixty paranormatives—people 'born weird'— currently live in the community. It has one of the densest populations of paranormatives in the entire world and nobody knows why."

"And our guy is headed there."

"He's probably there already."

Another lull fell between them.

"Thanks," Omar said. "For telling me."

"It's better you find out now, from me, than in some class…"

"Some class?" Omar echoed.

Zoe nodded. "I'm considering recommending you for training."

A beat passed.

"I might…I might be cool with that," Omar said.

"Good."

"I mean, it's voluntary, right?"

"Mm-hmm," she grunted.

Ninety percent of all outside recruitment was voluntary.

Omar squinted but didn't ask. He settled back in his chair. "So what's the plan anyway? When we get to Oceanrest."

"My old mentor lives there. He has a ritual space, some very old and powerful foci, stuff like that," she ignored the befuddled expression twisting Omar's features, "we'll borrow some of it to perform a tracking ritual. Maybe he'll even help."

"A tracking ritual?"

"Yeah. I can use the blood from the Construct to find out who made it. From there, I can...track that person down."

"Why not just use the name on the eviction notice?"

"A name is a bank account, a social security number, *paperwork*. If the name on the eviction letter is the same name he uses in his head, in his sanctum, then maybe, but Geek Squad types like you can handle that with your buddy Google. The way I'm going to do it takes a lot more time, but I'll end up knowing where he is within a few dozen yards."

Omar squinted through the windscreen. "Uh...how much time is 'a lot more time,' exactly?"

"Depends."

"On what?"

"A lot of things. But there's good news."

"That'd be a first."

A grin tickled across her lips. "How would you like to learn some magic?"

He balked, speechless.

"That's what I thought."

################

Sung-ho lived in a two-floor colonial; robin's egg blue siding, rich crimson accents, and a backyard deck in red-timbered wood, weatherproofed. Pulling up to it for the *n*th time in her life, Zoe suddenly noticed his primary residence was smaller than his winter home in North Carolina. Turning off the engine, she hesitated at the thought, keys dangling from her fingers. Why had she suddenly remembered Sung-ho's house in North Carolina? She hadn't visited in almost five years.

"This the place?" Omar asked.

"Yeah," Zoe replied, opening her door. "The guy we're meeting will give you whatever name he wants you to call him."

"Not his real name?"

"I dunno. Maybe."

"Well, I already got his real address, so…"

"Hey, this is my mentor, okay?"

"I'm just—"

She stopped walking. "Is that going to be *okay*?"

"Yeah. Sorry, Sarge."

"Just. Be cool."

"'Be cool?'" Omar winced.

Zoe glared, speaking volumes with her gaze. She turned back toward Sung-ho's and walked up to the door.

Seo-yeon opened up.

Five-four, thin but athletic, Seo-yeon wore an easy expression and greeted Zoe with a one-armed hug. She shook Omar's hand and introduced herself by her real name. In the entry hall, they took off their shoes. From the kitchen, the first left off of the foyer's straightaway, Sung-ho shouted for them to head to his den.

"Doing dishes! Happy wife, happy life!" he explained.

Seo-yeon rolled her eyes. "But who cooked?"

"I figured," Zoe replied.

"He's been excited. It's been a while since you visited."

"I won't let on that I know."

Seo-yeon led them toward Sung-ho's den, a room near the back of the house next to the washer and dryer, its original purpose undocumented. Whatever the planner had intended, it now served as a cozy lounge for Sung-ho's visitors. Seo-yeon wished them well with a curt nod and vanished before Omar could ask whatever he'd wanted to ask her.

"She doesn't listen to business talk," Zoe said.

"Is she, uh…?"

"She's like you. Well, like *us*, technically."

"But she's not some black ops Wiccan warrior?" Omar asked.

Two chairs and a plush, crushed-velvet love seat crowded them in. A swaddling Lay-Z-Boy in cushioned brown sat behind the broad desk centering the room. Antlers that passed for a deer's at first glance curved and sharped, wall-mounted over the Lay-Z-Boy. Book shelves, file cabinets, and display cases filled the rest of the space. Standing wasn't comfortable in the confines, even with only two bodies.

Zoe sat on an armchair angled toward the desk. "I'm not Wiccan. And no. She owns a restaurant. She's got Class-E clearance, effectively D through marriage. I don't know that she knew any of this was real until they got engaged."

"And her sixth sense is…fine?" Omar still stood, staring at the door Seo-yeon had left half an inch ajar.

"She went through a lot of inoculation and basic training. A Construct built out of darkness itself could seep under the crack in her front door and she'd spit on it and ask what bills it was paying to go walking around without knocking like that."

"Huh."

"I might be exaggerating but only because I thought you'd laugh."

"Yeah…"

A bulky desktop monitor, alongside its requisite mouse and keyboard, took up most of the desk space. A plastic tower next to it sorted paperwork, 'Urgent,' 'In,' 'Out,' 'Junk.' Three piles of cigar boxes and one pile of card decks took up the remaining real estate. Looking at the clutter, Zoe could tell exactly what spot Sung-ho used to put his feet up. It was the only spot left with enough room.

Behind the desk, two enormous speakers flanked a homemade entertainment system, a record player wired into a CD player wired into an old tape deck. Sung-ho's DIY system didn't handle anything digital, yet.

Omar sat down as if uncertain of the chair.

Five minutes later, Sung-ho bustled into the room. Once battlefield-fit and now paunching into his mid-fifties, his broad, shapely shoulders tapered down to a growing bulb of belly. His shaved head gleamed under the homey overhead glow. As always, he wore a knowing smirk.

In one hand he pinched three rocks glasses together with his fingers, in the other he carried Bell's Scotch bottled for the birth of Prince William of

Wales. Slipping between the furnishings and the various shelves and displays narrowing the already-narrow room, he walked behind the desk and placed the three glasses on Zoe and Omar's side. "I started the dishes late," he said, pouring each glass halfway full. "She cooks, *whoo*, food coma."

"Uh-huh," Omar spoke as if in some kind of vague shock.

"Zoe, always a pleasure," Sung-ho set the bottle aside and picked up his drink. He gestured for her to do the same. "Next time you tell me you'll be showing up, though, maybe more than one day's notice, eh?"

"Things went a little sideways," she clinked her glass to his. "Pittsburgh didn't go as planned."

"Shocking," Sung-ho snorted. To Omar, he said, "Come on, drink up."

"Uh…"

"Right. I'm Sung-ho," Sung-ho switched his drink from right hand to left and extended his right for a shake.

"I'm Omar."

"Have a drink, Omar. It looks like you need it."

"I, uh…" Omar chuckled. "Actually, I really do."

Sung-ho sat in the giant Lay-Z-Boy. He leaned over the desk and flipped open one of the cigar boxes. "Zo'?"

"*Please*," she answered.

He handed her a tobacco-reeking cigar. Setting his drink down, he took out a polished cigar cutter. Grinning, he chopped off the end of his and offered the device to her. She took it, repeating the process.

"So," he said, "Omar, you were the guy Zoe pulled out of the attack in Keene's Falls?"

"That's me."

Sung-ho spun the box toward Omar. "Have a smoke."

"Thanks." Omar took one. Zoe handed him the clipper.

"He's been through basic intake? Inoculations?"

"The best I could do on the move," Zoe answered.

Sung-ho nodded. "Good, good. That's a good start. So," he patted himself down.

Zoe produced her Zippo, clapped it open, and lit it. She held it toward Sung-ho's cigar. "I have blood from one of the Summoner's Constructs, plus material from a ritual site."

Sung-ho puffed a couple basalt clouds and leaned back. "So you use those to single out his 'vibe' from everyone else's and then you follow that scent until it leads to your target."

"Like a goddamned bloodhound," Zoe confirmed, lighting her own cigar before holding the Zippo toward Omar.

"I'll start getting the space ready for us to use…" Sung-ho put his feet up on the only desk space still available. He leaned back, twin plumes of smoke feathering from his nostrils. "I haven't touched it since I got out of field work so we kind of turned it into storage."

Omar's brow trenched. His jaw went slack.

"I have to run an initial survey, anyway," Zoe said. "See what stands out."

"Hyun-jung's band is playing at a coffee shop tomorrow night." Sung-ho perched his drink in his lap. "So unless this tracking ritual lets a practitioner pick up and leave halfway through it, I think we'll have to start the next morning."

"What the fuck?" Omar muttered.

"We need the rest," Zoe warned.

"No, the way you two are talking about this shit…people are *dying*."

"Omar."

Omar rose from his seat; his voice rose with him. "Someone's playing a coffee shop? You're shitting me, man, come on. This *has* to take priority."

Sung-ho's everpresent smirk faded. Some of the extra thirty years that didn't usually show up on his face showed up. "Don't raise your voice," he said, steel-cool. "Sit down and enjoy your drink."

"This dude's out there *killing people*."

"Zoe, do you want to handle this or should I?"

"Excuse me?" Omar snapped.

Zoe shrugged at Sung-ho.

Sung-ho's smirk returned. "Mr. Omar, please. Your cigar's gone out."

"Listen—"

"No, you listen," Sung-ho rarely raised his voice out of anger. Excitement, sure, giddiness, yes, drunken bawdiness, of course, but rarely anger. He maintained an even tone, the carefully measured rhythm of a very patient parent talking to a child who almost understands. "This is not my assignment.

I'm doing this as a favor to my old friend," he gestured with his cigar at Zoe. "The people this man has already killed are dead. There's nothing we can do to change the past. And whatever insane thing he's planning next, it's going to take him more than two nights to do it. In the meantime," the smirk transformed into a deep, face-wrinkling scowl, "I will not miss my daughter's growing up to do someone else's job."

"Come on..." Omar sat back down.

"You might never have seen something like this before," Sung-ho continued, "but Zoe and I have. Six or seven times a year, every year, for... thirty-two years for me."

"Just eight, here," Zoe chimed in. "Five with him."

"So understand, Mr. Omar, that to us...this situation is not special."

Omar glowered. Lips pursed, he nodded.

"We'll do everything we can," Zoe reassured him. "But these things take time. And Sung-ho's doing us a huge favor."

Omar nodded again. The trenches dug around his glare and the pinching at his lips told Zoe the lie beneath. She imagined Sung-ho must have seen it, too. If he did, he didn't show it.

Sung-ho smirked, his age reversing with its shine. "Fantastic. Now, some music."

"Please not the blues," Omar muttered.

Sung-ho leaned over one arm of the Lay-Z-Boy. "I'll make you a deal. I put on the blues or I put on some *sanjo*—"

"*Sanjo*," Omar said. "Whatever the hell it is, *sanjo*."

Sung-ho glanced back at him, bobbed his head. "It's a lot of fun. Very up-tempo. Like you."

Wilmington, NC.

July, 1997.

In the kitchen that morning, Zoe found five tall spice grinders standing in a pentagram formation on top of the table. A plate sat between them. The first signs of vulgar synchronicity had presented themselves.

Synchronicities were reality-flaws and patterns of eerie coincidence that emerged around particularly powerful magic. With ritual spells, synchronicity events usually manifested either ritual patterns or metaphorical meaning; they tended to crop up around the spell's practitioners and its targets. In this case, Zoe figured the five spice grinders echoed the ritual's focus on having her, the Witness, perform her acts in sets of five repetitions. Her daily spell-work took five hours and five syllables composed her meditative mantra, "I promise my aid."

The pentagram represented strength in the mystic world, especially psychic strength, which Zoe supposed bode as well for the future as randomly-occurring mystical fallout could.

Zoe jotted a note in her thin black notebook: 'day 7: vulgar synch. 5 spice grindrs, baphomet/pentagram shape.'

On the next page she drew out a series of sigils. Pressing a palm to the page, she closed her eyes and focused. "Is the cat alive or dead?" she asked the air. The paper beneath her hand warmed. Static sizzled up the thin hairs on her neck and arms. She tuned into her sixth sense. "Is the cat alive or dead?"

The answer struck her as a flare of bright. Her sixth sense recoiled, coiled, and erupted. It followed trails of energy along every angle of the arranged spice grinders and dug through layers of reality imperceptible to the untrained mind. Burnt ozone filled Zoe's nostrils. Sucking in a lungful of air, her eyes flicked open.

The thing was harmless.

She'd thought as much, but she'd wanted to give its origins a scan anyway. Just in case.

She returned the grinders to the tall rack of their brethren and started cooking breakfast. Toast, jam, peanut butter, grapefuit juice. Twinning the meal, she set her and her sister's plates on the table and headed upstairs to get Jill.

She froze at the landing, ice-splintered.

(*you will never be free of this*)

She spun into the unlit lounge. A background-bland hiss spilled out from the bathroom hallway ahead. Zoe's sock-soft footsteps drowned out the noise. Halfway in the room, she stopped moving. Still and quiet, she listened. The sound had rhythm. The rhythms grew into syllables. Words.

Swallowing, Zoe approached. Morning felt awfully similar to night as she neared the bathroom door.

Zoe's ears burned. The noise split into multiple voices; a dialog.

"Never," a rasp crept from under the door. "*Never.*"

Zoe's pulse pounded in her temples. Her sixth sense crawled and skittered, insect legs scratching between the folds of her brain. She stood in the second floor lounge at the end of a four foot hallway ending in whispers.

Zoe knew a ward she could cast without speaking. She'd rehearsed it down to a twenty second spell on a good day. She focused on it, hands slowly shifting from one shape to another.

The doorknob twisted.

She stepped back, losing focus for one second that would cost her five more. She struggled to maintain the spell in her mind. She needed six more seconds, maybe seven…

The bathroom door swung open.

Zoe turned back toward the stairwell.

Jill stepped out of the bathroom wearing pajamas. She stared at Zoe green-eyed. Blinked. "Uh…"

Zoe turned to face her sister, cheeks warming. "I was just coming to get you. For breakfast."

"Are you okay?"

"I'm fine." Zoe's sixth-sense panic subsided. Adrenaline sweat mixed with effort-sweat, steaming her sleepwear. "It's just…nic fits."

"Oh."

"Anyway. Do you mind if I…" she gestured to the restroom behind Jill.

"Go ahead."

"Thanks."

Zoe passed Jill in the tight hall. "We had some vulgar synchronicity this morning."

Jill's shoulders tightened. She nodded, strained. "That's good."

"We can probably charge the Confessional in a couple more days."

"Great." Jill turned away, heading for the stairs. "See you down there."

Zoe watched her leave before walking into the bathroom.

As soon as the door was locked, she started searching. She reached out with her sixth sense for some sign of a presence, a malignance, an interloper, anything.

A patch of cold air hovered over the sink. Zoe stared at herself in the mirror. She reached for her reflection.

Just glass.

She sat on the toilet and buried her face in her hands. What the hell was happening?

Chapter Seven

Oceanrest, ME.

December, 2006.

After Omar and Seo-yeong had gone to sleep, Zoe and Sung-ho stayed up stinking the walls of the den with smoke and sloshing themselves tipsy on Scotch. At some point just after midnight, Hyun-jung failed to creep into the house. Sung-ho called out to her and started waving his finger, leaving the den door open as he exited the room to lecture, but the teenaged, hair-dyed girl had asked him pointedly "Dad, are you *drunk*?" and he'd burst out laughing instead. When he re-entered the den, still giggling, he shook his head. "All parents are hypocrites."

"All people," Zoe corrected.

"Mm, them, too."

Zoe didn't know why she laughed. Maybe because of the whiskey or, more likely, the pipe of weed they'd started passing.

Sung-ho lowered a match to the herb, puffed a hit, and held it. He exhaled a thin flute of smoke.

Zoe swirled her drink, leaned back in her seat. Blues played out of the massive speakers flanking Sung-ho's desk. The 8-CD changer/player below the vinyl record table contained hours of blues, 70's-era rock, Korean punk, and occasional *pansori*. Splayed back in the chair, Zoe held her glass toward the ceiling. "Is Hyun-jung…?"

"Oh, yeah. She's known for years. She'll pledge as soon as they let her."

"How old is she, now?"

"Seventeen."

"So this year?"

"Or next," Sung-ho shrugged. He sat back in the Lay-Z-Boy and adjusted the volume. R. L. Burnside's baby rode. Sung-ho bobbed his head. "Mm. They don't play it like they used to."

Zoe stared at the glassed amber in her palm. She swirled the drink. "When I first met Hyun-jung, she was…what? Five? Six?"

"You hear this guitar?" Sung-ho asked.

"Yeah, it's just…time really *passes*, doesn't it?"

Sung-ho snorted. "You think you earned Best in Field so many times by noticing case-changing details like that one?"

"Funny. But it's true. Sometimes I lose track…that I was ever eighteen or twenty-two or twenty-five. Or I forget that the past happened just as much as the present's happening. That ever happen to you?"

"No," Sung-ho said. "Sounds like something you'd get help for."

Zoe chuckled. "Yeah. Guess so."

Sung-ho put the pipe down on a pile of paperwork and pulled open two desk drawers. He sifted through them, searching for something in the semi-organized chaos. "What's your plan for your friend?" he asked.

Zoe lowered her drink and drank it. "I need to get him Class-E."

"Oooh, you're finally getting yourself an Ephemeral. You say something you weren't supposed to?"

Zoe leaned forward and balanced her empty glass on the desk-edge. "Probably. They modified my NDA when I got Charlie, again at Beta."

"They do that for everyone."

"It turns out that if I don't have a literal spell telling me what I'm supposed to say, I lose track of what civilians are allowed to hear."

Sung-ho found a pack of Lucky Strikes in his desk. Ripping another match free of his old matchbook, he lit one. He sighed out his first drag. Nodded. "You can probably swing Class-E. The Covers and Concealments guys will take care of everything else."

"I'm going to recommend him for training."

"You told him about training?"

"Yeah."

Sung-ho chortled, shaking his head. "You can't just tell civvies we can train 'em, Zo'."

"I don't know why I said it."

"Maybe you're looking for a protege. This is your stony version of a biological clock."

"Ha." Zoe stood up and retrieved the pipe from the desk. Sinking back into her chair, she didn't light it, but just held it curled in one hand. As she considered what to say next, Sung-ho pulled the bottle of Scotch from the floor and refilled their drinks.

Setting the opaque, pearlescent bottle back down, Sung-ho returned to his cigarette. "He have skillset?"

"He's good with computers. Internet stuff."

"They need that, now. Did you warn him about…" Sung-ho took his Scotch and leaned back. "Everything?"

"I don't know if he'd listen."

"Make him. You can't recommend him for training and then…" Sung-ho plucked his cigarette free from his mouth and gestured in the air with it. "You know what happens to a baby bird if mama pushes it out of the nest and it isn't ready to fly?" He spiraled the curling smoke down toward his desk and whistled a long, descending note. At its lowest pitch, he stopped it with a sharp gagging sound. "Splat!"

"Vivid," Zoe observed.

"Thank you." Sung-ho giggled, leaning back into his fold-out. "He seems like an alright guy."

"I should cut him loose. Turn him over for processing and let the C-and-C boys deal with it."

"You should," Sung-ho agreed.

Still holding the unused pipe in her left hand, Zoe reached forward with her right and collected her refilled Scotch. "If I put him up for training and he makes it…I'm going to have to…I don't know…"

"Mentor him?" Sung-ho suggested.

Zoe laughed. "I'll give him my best shot, at least."

"Well," Sung-ho sat forward, crushing his cigarette in an ashtray. "It's two AM, so either we're staying up 'til dawn or we're clocking out now. Two o'clock's my fulcrum."

"Wasn't it four?"

"I was younger, then."

"Well, I'm beat," Zoe said. "I'll take the bed."

Sung-ho stood and stretched, still holding his drink. He groaned and rolled his neck. "Yeah. Good idea." Walking around the side of the desk, he paused. Smiled. "You remember the guest room only has one bed, right?"

"Goddammit."

"See you in the morning, Zo'."

"God-motherfucking-dammit."

Bald Head, ME.

July, 2016.

The Atlantic crashed its rhythmic roar off to their left, the sunset a crystal-glitter over plunging noise. Leo walked with his hands folded behind his back, his newly-graying temples and salt-pepper beard accentuated by dye and oil, his age emphasized, his demeanor *distinguished*. People had once called him 'Punjabi Bond.' He was Tamil, but still.

They'd met for breakfast. They'd eaten at the same restaurant, seated on opposite sides from each other, watching for spies. She'd left, first, to run broader reconnaissance. Finding neither signs of successful mystical espionage nor of agent surveillance, she'd meandered her way east toward the coast. Leo had arrived shortly afterward. They'd only started speaking once they began down the curving, white stone path following the shore.

"...the current plan has the votes, unfortunately," Leo was saying, "but we've been able to tilt things slightly. There are still those on the Board who remember the oaths."

"So what have you managed to get?"

"Not much, sadly. After Jill and her husband testify against Karen to the various authorities and turn over their students for, ugh, 'processing,' both of them will be granted full immunity and pardon. Provided they agree to surveillance, of course."

"Of course," Zoe sneered. "And how is this better?"

"Her husband wasn't protected in the previous terms."

"Jesus…" Zoe rapped a pack of cloves against the heel of her hand. To their right, a field of emerald grass. To their left, a steep, rocky decline rubbling into pale, stony beach. Opening the pack, she slipped out a slender smoke. "You aren't going to ask how things are going on my end?"

"I doubt I'd like the answer."

She flicked her cigarette unnecessarily. "I guess not."

"I will ask why you called me for an extremely clandestine and allegedly urgent meeting, however."

"I need a favor." She stopped walking. "A big one."

He turned to face her, soft-eyed. "What do you need?"

"I need a meeting with Shoshanna Winters."

He blinked. "Is there anything else? Anything that the Board couldn't later argue was *treason*?"

"I know you worked with her."

"A long time ago."

Zoe fished out her Zippo and lit her clove. Took a drag. "Can you do it?"

"Zoe—"

"Can you?" she interrupted.

"The rules are stricter now than they were. The enforcement is more consistent."

"*Can* you?" She took a step toward him. "Please?"

Leo's gaze dropped to the stones beneath his polished black shoes. "I…I probably could."

"This is my sister's life."

"First, I'll issue a formal burn notice for you. Then I'll follow up with the appropriate regionals to clarify that the burn notice is merely a smokescreen, the beginnings of an embedding operation." He brought his eyes back up to meet hers; studied her face. Cleared his throat.

"Thank you," she said.

"I can arrange for its verisimilitude. It should protect you against virtually anything, assuming you don't actually get caught."

"If I get caught in the open, I won't live long enough to need protection anyway."

"What you're asking…what we're aiming to do here…it's very dangerous. Moderately dangerous for me, certainly something that would put a quick stop to my lifelong climb, and highly dangerous for you, something that might put a quick stop to your *life*." He came in close, barely whispering. "I'm up for promotion. One of the members of the Board is stepping down and I'm on the shortlist for his replacement. I could be sitting at that table by this time next year. Still, I'll do this if you tell me there are no other options."

"There are no other options," she answered.

He glanced away. Took a breath. "Any mis-steps we make could be very costly. You will have to be extremely considerate and *cautious*."

"I'm always 'cautious.'"

"No," the word came sharp as a knife. "You aren't. You're incredibly talented, intelligent, and tactical, and these things create the *illusion* of caution, but you are *not* cautious. And you should not approach the trials ahead with any kind of confidence that you are."

She peered away, feeling scolded in a way she hadn't felt in a long time. She re-lit her dead clove and puffed. "I'll die to pull this off, Leo. And if I can get Jill out of this, if I can get her family out of this, I'll die to cover for the people who helped me."

Leo chuckled. "I'm sure a great many great knights said the same thing before they met their first Inquisitor."

"Look at me, Leo. Look at my eyes."

He looked at her eyes.

"Do I look tired to you?" she asked.

He looked away.

She took another drag.

Leo sighed, hands searching for something to pretend importance about in his pockets. "Maybe when this is all over, we'll have another poker night. For old time's sakes."

"Maybe," Zoe said, the word dead before it left her mouth.

The sun rolled westward, glowing over the ocean. Leo Singh lit up auric in the early magic hour. He stared at her the way a person did when they wanted to say more but couldn't figure out the right words to say it. She stared at him similarly.

"Good luck, Zoe. I don't imagine I'll see you again until this is all over."

She nodded. "Congratulations on the promotion. Or, uh, *shubhkamna*."

"*Badhai ho*," Leo corrected. "And it's still only a nomination. But thank you."

"Yeah, *badhai ho*, then. For the nomination."

Chapter Eight

Wilmington, NC.

July, 1997.

Zoe began the day by refreshing her invocations. The spells lasted for five days on average but most agents renewed them on the third day. The inherent complexity and unpredictability of magic made it a wise practice. Nothing worked one hundred per cent of the time.

She started by chalking the sigils. She wrote in Icelandic staves, Druidic glyphs, Enochian script, even in English and Hangul. She poured her focus and energy into the shapes, transferring neuromuscular power into mystical power. Her lips formed mantras out of habit, almost unconsciously.

"I am stronger and swifter, my eyes and ears sharper, my bones unbreakable. I am stronger and swifter, my eyes and ears sharper, my bones…"

After a few minutes, the magic took. A faint static sensation crawled up Zoe's arms. With the chalk, she circled the symbols she'd drawn so far. From under her bed she withdrew a sculpture she'd commissioned after her first round of Malleus training courses. The sculptor had captured a very particular interpretation of Zoe, herself. The statue-Zoe appeared as some sort of Valkyrie, helmed and armored and wielding sword and shield, with the Malleus hammer on its chest. This figure went in the first circle, acting as a metaphorical representation and literal conduit. It would serve as a focus for the invocations that increased and protected her hearing, granted her night-sight, marginally improved her reflexes, and reinforced her bone and muscle fiber.

The defensive invocations took longer. Vodou vèvès, more Enochian, and lines of Arabic and Latin crossed the floorboards. Sweating from the neuromuscular and mystical effort, Zoe took a small break after finishing the second circle of spells to wipe her face dry. Once her heartrate slowed, she reached under the bed again and pulled out a large mason jar. Inside, a mummified cheetah paw rested in an ivory nest of hawk ribs. Its leathery grip held a black marble containing the trapped magical essence of a shadow creature.

The mason jar went in the center of the circled wards. These would make her more difficult to see, manipulate nearby threats to subtly look away from her, and slow down approaching harm.

"I am a blur in the eyes of my enemies and those who would harm me know me not. I am fast beyond catching and all arrows fall short of me. Those who hunt me become hunted. I am a blur…"

She sat between the two circles and tuned into her sixth sense. She felt the gathered energy in both spells and opened herself up to it. An over-exerted groan crawled out of her when she triggered the magic. As the invocations wove through her neuromuscular, musculoskeletal, and nervous systems, however, all the fatigue melted away.

She stood, feeling refreshed, and wiped the remaining sweat into her hair. Downstairs, she had as hearty a breakfast as the ritual allowed. She'd need it.

################

Preparations for the Confessional, the ritual's first threshold and Gateway, took two practitioners an entire day to complete. The ritual space, previously a family room with a large entertainment center, waited unfurnished save for one antique wooden table and two chairs. After breakfast, Zoe started the process of chalking and painting all the various sigils, pentacles, glyphs, and other necessary symbols around all three objects. Charging the work took over three hours. Meanwhile, Jill performed the renewals and reinforcements of all the wards and defenses they'd set up around the house.

After lunch, they joined each other in finishing the room's preparation.

The calligraphy alone took two hours. They used symbols ancient and modern from a half-dozen different practices. To increase the Confessional's potency, they even scribed short-cut deals with extra-planar entities to add more supernatural power than they could wring out of their own neuromuscular systems. They made offerings to fractal aspects of vaster intelligences, only borrowing from seldom-remembered interpretations.

The chalk, ink, and paint drying, Zoe filled offering bowls, burnt herbs, and muttered incantations. Jill set up the myriad wards and signs that would protect them from malign consciousnesses and unwanted interlopers. Sweat slimed every inch of them.

They wove together a tapestry of spells. Healing magic, mostly, with invocations for strength, endurance, and mental fortitude, a smattering of pain-killer cantrips, and a particularly esoteric method of folding the material and metaphysical together. Zoe's joints ached as she poured herself into the formation. A cramp carved its way down her left side. The muscles flanking her spine shivered and pulsed, threatening to seize.

After over five hours, they charged the last of the spells.

Zoe pushed herself up from kneeling and spun away from the chalk and paint. Stumbling on numb legs and creaking knees, she made it halfway out of the ritual space before throwing up. Her pulse rampaged in her temples. The spew slicked hardwood but luckily didn't smear any of the glyphs or sigils.

Zoe collapsed sideways into a wall and slid down.

She spat on the floor, took out her pack of smokes, and lit her first of the day. The smoldering spices covered the sharp tang living inside her mouth. They covered up the bilious stench of the mess, too. Well, almost.

Her eyes burned from the sweat that had fallen in them.

"I'll get the mop," Jill said, a gentle hand on her sweat-greased back. "You rest."

"Mm. Be careful not to wipe out any of the chalk or—"

"I know," Jill interrupted. "Trust me."

Zoe nodded. "Sorry. Thanks. Really."

"It's the least I can do."

Halfway through the clove, Zoe stood back up and snuffed it against the wall. She put the remains back in the crumpled, damp pack and put the pack back in her damp pocket. She adjusted her soaked shirt against her soaked body and stepped over the puke to get into the kitchen.

Amherst, MA.

July, 2016.

Zoe and Shoshanna met at the Emily Dickinson Museum that afternoon. Zoe almost hadn't walked in. The sight of Shoshanna's car outside, all black, windows as close to opaque as law allowed, the license plate bragging 'WA-LABS2,' had statued her on the sidewalk. The sight of Shoshanna's everpresent bodyguard, a seven-foot wall of expressionless muscle, also gave her hesitation. Shoshanna's bodyguard sent shivers through her sixth sense, not really human, not really not.

But Zoe had eventually walked in. She'd found Shoshanna in the Evergreen's lounge, studying a broad display of paintings, a black piano, and plenty of upholstered furniture.

Shoshanna wore a business suit, sleeves rolled halfway up her forearms, her skin the shade of sundarkened sand. Her hair shone voidglow in curls and tumbles down to her shoulders. Pools of veined brown glinted her gaze, considering.

"You're late," Shoshanna said.

"I almost didn't come in."

"Why not?"

"Because," Zoe admitted, shoulder to shoulder with the woman, just an inch taller, "I think it would be uncharacteristically stupid of me to trust you."

"Fair enough." Shoshanna angled herself toward Zoe. "I guess you wouldn't be interested in taking a walk, then?"

"Where to?"

"The campus. It's eerily empty over the summer."

Zoe chortled. "In broad daylight?"

"Better we talk in broad daylight than a quiet, echoing museum. I already did a sweep. I doubt anyone who wanted to spy on us could set up the means on such short notice. Not without leaving evidence."

"You haven't seen the things I've seen."

"You don't know what I've seen."

"Maybe not," Zoe allowed.

"I'd tell you about my nightmares but I'm sure you have them, too." A slight smirk perked Shoshanna's lips. "Anyway, it's up to you."

Honestly, Zoe didn't like the silent museum. She didn't like the lone ingress and Shoshanna's enormous bodyguard waiting there.

"I always wanted to visit Amherst," Zoe said. "If you're qualified to give a tour."

Shoshanna's smirk became a grin.

###############

Shoshanna proved correct. The Amherst campus seemed dissatisfied as 'abandoned,' it stretched its emptiness until its echoes accreted ghosts. Whole minutes passed on their walk without another sign of life—at least not human life. The occasional bird or squirrel zipped around the landscape, but little else. Zoe saw only a single car and a lone summer student staring at his phone as she and Shoshanna meandered the alleys and streets toward a span of emerald grass.

Ten feet behind them, Shoshanna's skin-crawl, wall-sized bodyguard followed.

"You know why I'm here," Zoe guessed, breaking the minutes-long silence.

"In general terms. You think there's something you can do to get your sister out from under...everything."

"I need an extraction team," Zoe said. "If things go far enough sideways, maybe a medical extraction team."

"You need more than that," Shoshanna replied. She carried a small purse with her left hand. "You need post-extraction support. You need your extraction to go unnoticed and, worse, unfollowed and untracked. You need somewhere to hide your refugees. You need somewhere to hide, in general. You need access to the kinds of logistics, surveillance, and magic that can keep your sister and her family safe in the mid-to-long-term."

"I'll do whatever it takes. If it comes down to my sister's life, I'll go in the front door and load them into a car. If it comes down to it, I can get her wherever I need to get her and I'll open fire on anyone or anything between points A and B."

"Even in public?"

"For Jill?"

Shoshanna stopped walking. She turned toward Zoe, something lit lambent behind her veined eyes. She examined. "You really don't care about the blowback, do you?"

"She's the only family I have left."

Shoshanna arched eyebrows. "Your mother?"

Zoe glowered in answer. Sylvia Briar was once considered among the most brilliant practitioners in the world. Now seventy four, she underwent experimental treatment for early-onset Alzheimer's maybe-or-maybe-not caused by the severe neurological stress of a lifetime spent experimenting with dark and secret arts. Zoe hadn't visited her in nearly a year.

"I understand," Shoshanna replied, voice unexpectedly soft. "You know...I have tremendous admiration for women like you. Your fearlessness. Your determination."

"I'm not here to be admired. Can — you — help?"

"It will take time."

"I can buy time. Right now it might be all I'm good for."

"I'll need at least a month."

"A month?" Zoe balked.

"Maybe longer," Shoshanna admitted. She resumed walking, leaving the sidewalk to trek across green grass. "I think it may be wise to hide this from my brother, which means I'll have to do things piecemeal, movement by movement and expense by expense. I'll need to hand-pick the extraction team and brief them personally. I'll have to figure out where I can sneak them through in terms of logistics, where I can move our refugees without them getting noticed."

"And where do they go in the immediate op?"

"We have a...facility not far from here," Shoshanna answered. "For emergency medical and ritual needs. After the immediate evacuation, I could shelter your sister and her family there."

Shoshanna's willingness made a lot more sense, all of a sudden. "A W-A facility?"

"Where else? It's not like Malleus will take her in." Shoshanna sat on a bench near the broad rear of the greenspace. Brick buildings held sentinel on the opposite streetside. "Zoe...have you considered the long-term ramifications of your success?"

Zoe stayed standing. "Like what?"

"If Leo's negotiations with your so-called 'Board' fall through and this 'Plan B' of yours succeeds...if that's somehow how events play out...what do you think happens to you, afterward?"

Zoe glanced back overshoulder, seeing nobody.

"Leo's given you an excellent cover story, but if Jill ends up getting extracted, somehow, nobody's going to doubt who made that happen. And your organization frowns on people who break orders. They especially frown on people who commit treason."

Still not looking back at Shoshanna, Zoe replied, "You're saying I should defect."

"I'm saying you'll have to."

Zoe hesitated.

"The only way Leo's cover story works is if you fail," Shoshanna pressed. "You know that."

And Zoe did know that. Some back-of-her-brain part of her had known all along. She pursed her lips. Unpursed them. Defection was so much more complicated than Shoshanna implied. Or was it? Would it really take much more time or add much more complexity to her current predicament?

Zoe peered back at Shoshanna. "Maybe. Either way, you're saying that if I can get those people out of that house, you can extract them?"

Shoshanna's gaze slid away. "Five of them."

A beat passed.

Zoe blinked. "There are eight people in that house."

Shoshanna nodded. "I can extract five."

Zoe thought about saying it. 'Jill told me what David did.' But now it seemed like a weak play, a ploy flared out by someone desperate for status. Of course, it was—it always had been—but now it *looked* like one. The tactic was impotent on its face. Not sighing out the pressure building in her chest, Zoe sat down on the bench. On the edge of her periphery, Shoshanna's bodyguard turned to face the campus. On the other edge, Shoshanna stared at the grass.

"I'm so sorry, Zoe," Shoshanna said, as if it meant anything. As if Zoe could really believe her. "It's the best I can do. Just tell Jill..."

Shoshanna trailed off, her fingers knit in her lap.

Zoe found the filter of a clove between her lips, her Zippo in her hand. Lighting up, she took the longest drag of her life. "Sure," she muttered, words twisting up in smoke. "I'll tell her."

Oceanrest, ME.

January, 2007.

It took longer than expected.

The Summoner's proficiency expanded daily. The first tracking ritual died, cut to ribbons by protective wards and counter-magic. Zoe felt it like a fist to her jaw. A couple days after that, Sung-ho's wards crackled and fried a counter-trace. Within a matter of weeks, the Summoner's knowledge of both wards and surveillance rituals had exploded. To Zoe, this suggested that either the Summoner had cut a deal with some other, greater entity, or merely played the patsy to one. Whether the other entity represented supernatural interests or just secret-society-political ones, they had no way to find out.

Omar called his mother from a payphone on Christmas. Zoe listened in on the call. Nothing exceptional happened. The day after, they got back to work in Sung-ho's basement, reworking the ritual. This time they built it to work more subtly and along more avenues, hoping to overwhelm and subdue the Summoner's wards. It worked, but the energy it sapped from the spell left them with only a general idea of the Summoner's position: somewhere on the northern end of the peninsula.

Which was a significantly larger search area than they could realistically handle.

They took New Year's Eve and New Year's Day off.

The New Year's celebrations finished and hangovers shed, Zoe drove into town to run a few errands. Malleus Industries International had started the long process of moving its North American headquarters to Oceanrest a few months earlier. A large ten-story building almost completed in downtown Oceanrest would house Malleus Industries along with a handful of other companies moving to the area. Of the ten floors, Malleus would occupy five.

Until the new headquarters formally opened, however, Malleus kept its Oceanrest offices near the less-grim western stretch of the harbor. Owing to Oceanrest's previous economic collapse, 'less-grim' felt like the most polite description. Worn-out workers loaded pallets onto commercial boats and long-haul trucks bound for destinations unknown and unimportant. A few warehouses bore decades-old visages down on concrete and boardwalk, the best-maintained among them still wearing rusted bars over dirty windows, garbed in rags of spraypaint and grime.

The eastern end of the harbor had died out and rotted. Some company or another had bought up a swath of southeastern harborspace and had allegedly started resurrecting it into a marina. Other companies had started to buy real estate in that area, as well.

The wharfs and piers and docks between the busy western end and the busy eastern end gathered gull shit and disuse. Most of the buildings lining the central harbor wore 'For Sale' or 'Condemned' signs.

The Intel-Analytics representative she met in those depressing environs shrugged. "From the name on the eviction notice we were able to figure out previous employment and bank account info, but either he's got some serious wards or he's using a fake name on paperwork because none of our people can attach anything to him mystically." The man handed her a slim manila folder. "That's everything we've pulled so far."

"Thanks," she said, trying not to sound disappointed.

The truth was that the Intel-Analytics department was understaffed for all that it did. Primarily in charge of predicting probable supernatural events, keeping tabs on known assets (including civilians with Class-E clearance), and developing more and more effective methods for finding supernaturals of all sorts, actual case work was not an Intel-A priority. It was, put bluntly, not in their job description.

So it seemed likely they'd have to wait until her tracking ritual spat out more specifics before they could make their next move. After fourteen days in Oceanrest, nine spent on the ritual, she'd expected more.

Exiting a different parking lot, much later, following a significantly more successful and mundane task, Zoe's sixth sense spiked through her. Her skin crawled. Her eyesight sharpened. A certainty reached out from her lizard brain: something bad was about to happen. She hit the brakes. In the rearview, an SUV honked at her, a crowd of people filtered in and out of the grocery store. Peering back through the windshield, she saw nothing unexpected.

She eased onto the street.

Her personal wards, unreinforced for almost a week, dispersed a tracking spell and collapsed. Her heart jumped against her sternum. Her vision narrowed and pulsed. Another car blared a horn, passing her on the right. All air evacuated her chest. Her knuckles went white around the steering wheel and—

—and two seconds later, she felt fine again. Her pulse descended and she took deep breaths to even herself out. She was fine.

Except she knew that her wards had collapsed. And she knew the Summoner had tried to use magic to track her *personally*.

Which meant he knew more than nothing about her.

She didn't like that.

And since her wards had all collapsed, he'd learned something else, too. He'd gotten some kind of ping regarding her location. Most amateur tracking spells didn't deliver much; he might've received an insight as useless as 'grocery store,' as broad as 'Oceanrest,' or as cryptic as 'closer than imagined.' Alternatively, the random chance of it all could deliver an address or even her exact geo-coordinates.

Maneuvering through traffic, she took a very long trip back to Sung-ho's house.

################

When she arrived back at the house, late afternoon hinting the beginnings of sunset, Sung-ho stood on his front porch pinching a joint. Getting out of the car, Zoe smelled it immediately: fresh rain, raw dirt, rancid meat, flower and rot. Strong sixth sense stimulants stank of potential. She walked up with plastic bags garlanding her wrists. "A little help?"

"Leave the bags here, for now."

She unbound herself. "What's up?"

"Another tracking attempt. Our wards killed it but...I don't like that he keeps trying." Sung-ho gestured to her with the joint. "We're using some dreamer, tonight. Omar and I have the ritual charged and tonight..."

"Omar just learned basic support magic. He still pukes sometimes just at *feeling* magic. He's not ready for a dreamer vision."

"Well, momma bird, there's something hungry circling our nest, so ready or not, it's fly-time."

"Sung-ho—"

"My *daughter* lives here," his voice lost all cleverness. It became a lethal thing, a thing that cuts clean and all the way through. "And a madman is closing in. So Omar is taking the dreamer."

"Fuck!" Zoe snapped, body filled with enough tension to straighten her fingers and lock her knees. Sighing herself loose, she massaged her face. "Goddammit," she muttered, running her thumb and forefinger in broad circles around her bagged eyes.

"We have to find him," Sung-ho said.

She nodded. "Yeah. We do. Hand me the joint and take in the groceries."

When Sung-ho offered the joint, she took it.

He hung his head as he carried the bags inside.

Chapter Nine

Oceanrest, ME.

January, 2007.

You practice.

The grimoire begins with a small selection of 'test' spells, ritualized cantrips subtextually meant to strengthen and inoculate your sixth sense against the physical, psychological, and spiritual trauma associated with witnessing supernatural or paranormal events as-they-really-happen. Within a few months, you can get these spells to work an average of seven out of ten castings. You do not know that this is not impressive. You also do not know that the practitioners for whom this is 'unimpressive' have all received structured, formal training. The People In the Know do not afford training to unknown nobodies such as yourself.

In this way, your expertise is quite *ab*-normal.

You practice. Even though every story ends the same way, you practice.

(*we're/they're/it's sorry, but they do*)

Nobody knew how dreamer worked. Least of all Omar. It buzzed beehive in the honeycomb of his cortex. It sang cosmic lullabies along the sinewy chords of his synaptic instrument. He vibrated at the frequency that dissolved him. He dissolved. The trillion disparate fractals of Omar splintered and danced through the no-place every-place. Zoe was in him and he was in her; she *was* him and he *was* her—they were the Summoner and so are you, practicing.

How did dreamer work?

Maybe some things are unknowable. The myriad layered infinity needs *some* mystery, after all.

You try to show other people. "No, you don't understand, I can *prove* it." The flare sizzles in the air, blinding-bright, and you've strengthened your sixth sense so much you don't even flinch at the sight. You gesture. "What?" your friend asks, clueless. "You didn't see it?" you ask. "See what?" You play it off as nothing, just a joke. Sometimes a joke is an important thing wearing the mask of unimportance.

It happens by accident. Some of that growing frustration and buried pain seeps into the spell and the flare flies into your colleague's face. She screams, flailing at it. It does no harm, unable to, and fizzles out. For seconds she stares at the wisps of silver-white smoke still illuminated even as they vanish. "What was that?" she asks. You do not know what a sixth sense is and you do not understand what lets her see it. You smile, happy to answer. She is not happy to know.

You run out of friends and colleagues to run the test on. You seek people out online.

One person seizes and foams at the mouth at the sight of the flare. It seems to you that everyone at least *notices* the spell when you fire it directly at them. You aim it at them on purpose. All of them witness it, if only for a moment. Seconds later, some remember nothing. Some take a few deep breaths and blink and simply forget, others seize and sputter, twitch and tic. During the second such incident, you try to help the woman spasming and spittle-hissing on the floor. But she doesn't need help. None of them do. Their minds reject or replace the stimuli. It just takes time.

One man starts screaming and hitting you after witnessing the flare. You push him off and throw him into the wall and when he rebounds wide-eyed he sprints back upstairs and out of the building. He screams the whole time. You don't know this, but he eventually undergoes sixty days of inpatient psychotherapy before returning to his almost-normal life. You don't know this, either: he doesn't remember you at all.

You find only two people who seem able to see and recall the flare—your colleague from weeks ago and another woman you discover through an occult forum. You don't know why. Why would you, poor thing? But you know that magic can change the world.

Turning pages deeper into the grimoire, you begin building small constructs. The magic drains you, leaves you sweat-puddled and panting, aching from head to toe, but it works. You build a rat Construct, attaching extra tails between its forelegs and giving them prehensile flexibility. As all sometimes-capitalized Constructs, it obeys. It gathers tools and supplies from around the apartment and surrounding area while you work. The ritual that gave it life took nine hours and the rat-minion survives for six days. When it dies, the added tails slowly unravel. Minutes after its death, no trace of them remains. The rat rots faster than it ought to.

You make two more.

The fourth Construct you make isn't a rat. You show it to the woman from the occult forum. She's stunned and impressed, at first. Then nervous. Her nervousness itches at you. What's to be afraid of? This is magic. This is animate flesh. Something like this could change *everything*. "Where did you get the cat?" she asks.

"Where did I get the fucking *cat*!?"

What a minuscule concern.

Everyone knew that magic had a cost. Everyone.

What is it worth to change the world? A person might as well ask what it might be worth it to save the world—*everything*. A utopia is a priceless thing. Do the ends justify the means? A question for second-generation utopians.

You can do this. Can you? You certainly believe you can.

"How?" Omar and Zoe and Sung-ho ask. "How?"

They slingshot out of your history. They drift and spin in the no-place every-place.

Fade in. EXT. ALLEYWAY, SLATE RAINY EVENING MELTING INTO NIGHT.

Behold, a pale horse, white paint scrawled on concrete. Leaking garbage bags drooled bio-color. Behind a restaurant, a sigil hummed with magic. A number of rats rove the alley, not-quite-right. They attended the sign.

Fade out.

Omar smashcut Zoe smashcut Omar smashcut—

—and where did Sung-ho go?—

(*every story*)

Jill smashed the mirror, screaming. Microsplinters chewed her knuckles red. A shard already cracked into other shards fractal-fell into the basin. Jill grabbed it. Elsewhere in the maze-like and magic-twisted house, she heard gunfire. Clutching the fractal-glass so hard it drew blood, Jill howled out of the bathroom. Would she ever be free of this? Would Zoe?

—s m a s h c u t—

What does it cost to change the world?

It costs the story a different ending, and—*we're/they're/it's sorry, but*—

—*the story might read differently if*—

(*if*)

In your dreams, a saw of teeth tore reality open. All sorts of magic spilled out, Prometheus-Pandora, undeniable and unreturnable. No take-backsies. You put your arm in the wound just to feel it. Its tongue sandpapered your skin, the scab a maw, the wound, lips. This is the thing that eats the veil.

You wondered the cost of changing the world?

Someone has to rewrite the book.

Zoe jerked awake, momentarily lost in the lunatic sensation of being and having been multiple people and things and places and times during the dreamer vision. She yelped from the overwhelm and rolled onto her side, panting. Vague commotion dopplered around her but she couldn't understand it through the vision's dissipation. Still heaving for sweet blessed air, she pulled her notebook toward her and started writing. The commotion crescendo'd, voices joining noise. She couldn't understand it, yet. Words appeared on the page. She didn't stop to read. Every good agent knew that the important thing was recording everything. Interpretation came later.

The noise sharpened, her mind-brain-soul-ego catching up to her waking body.

Her writing slowed, her tethers to the vision unraveled by urgent sound. Droplets of sweat splatted the page, blurring some of the ink. The pen hesitated. She recognized Seo-yeon shouting something in Korean. She stopped writing.

Turning, she saw Sung-ho standing up, his own notebook abandoned. He wiped sweat from his face backhanded. At the foot of the basement stairs, they'd left their sidearms in a plastic container just in case the Summoner somehow knew powerful psychic and dream arcana. Sung-ho rushed over to it speechless, grabbed his gun from inside, and started up the steps.

Dropping her pen, Zoe followed.

"Dad!" Hyun-jung called out, above. "What the *fuck is that*!?"

Zoe grabbed her pistol from the bin. Paused. Looked back.

Omar laid out on top of his sleeping bag, eyes roving behind their lids. His lips moved in rapid-fire syllables but Zoe couldn't hear anything he whispered—if he whispered anything at all—over the cavalcade clattering from upstairs. He seized, back arching, and strained against some unpleasant span of vision. A groan stretched out of him.

How strong had his sixth sense really become? How long could he stay inside a dreamer vision and safely make it back out again?

Zoe stood frozen, one foot on the basement landing and the other on the next step up. Omar's lips pressed into a line. A plaintive whine bobbed his Adam's apple.

Upstairs, something crashed to the floor. Inhuman vocal chords snarled.

Salem, MA.

July, 2016.

Zoe spent the week after her trip to Amherst running her own personal surveillance op.

The Belgian's crew clearly operated as the lead aggressors. It made sense. Watching for days through binoculars, Zoe counted a team of five. A tall, toned, blond woman seemed like the leader, maybe a particularly powerful practitioner but more likely just someone with strong organizational and leadership skills. During observation, she almost never left the house. She sent the others out instead.

Vehicles visited the Belgian's crew every couple days. One group sent their rep in a sleek black sedan, another in a hybrid Honda Civic. When these cars came, the blond woman exited the house with a broad-shouldered man as her bodyguard and held her discussions in whichever backseat appeared for her. After she returned inside, the other party drove away. This brought the total number of teams taking coordinated action against Jill to at least four. At an assumed five practitioners per team…well. The odds stretched long and thin.

After eight days spent watching, four nights sleeping in the car, Zoe left.

She needed a shower and a good night's sleep before she started the next phase of her operation.

She had to disrupt the magic targeting her sister's school. Luckily, she knew where to find the ritual space of her most aggressive opponents.

################

The property's narrow yard and short fence provided little cover for breaking and entering. Clad in all-black, bullet-resistant helmet over armored leather jacket over armor-reinforced pants, she clung to the shadows and crept to the rear of the building. Just after three in the morning, no lights shone down from the surrounding windows.

Shouldering her quick-kit to the cement stoop at the house's back door, she withdrew a set of lockpicks and unrolled them. Even with her mystically-enhanced eyesight she had to squint to see in the deep dark of the cloud-swaddled night. She'd learned, at some point, that the mundane act of picking locks took a fraction of the time it took magic to accomplish the same feat. So she'd taken lessons.

After a few searching seconds, the lock unlatched. She paused, packing the lockpicks back up. Focusing on her sixth sense, she closed her eyes and reached out. She searched for a ward, an alarm or a trap that might trigger when someone invaded their space or entered uninvited or crossed a specific threshold. Magic crackled inside the house. She couldn't feel a particular warding spell but she couldn't find certainty that one didn't wait for her, either.

She pushed the door open.

Nothing happened.

Nothing happening meant little. Most wards weren't traps. Just because she didn't feel a ward go off, and just because none of the magical effects specifically targeted or affected her, didn't prove a ward hadn't triggered. It didn't prove anything at all, except that she'd broken into her enemy's house and nothing bad had happened to her *yet*.

Crouching, she found herself in a kitchen. She maneuvered the walking space slowly, listening for movement, a footstep, a dog's huff, *something*. Even in her sixth sense she felt no jolt of warning or thrum of foreshadowing. Was it possible she'd succeeded?

She moved toward the faint resonance of built-up energy. As she approached, spells began to clarify from the vagueness.

A lot of practitioners in Zoe's realm of esoteric espionage used basements as ritual spaces. A basement represented a large chamber, private, that society demanded neither to intrude upon nor witness; a part of a building so frequently windowless that nobody ever questioned its windowlessness. It didn't surprise Zoe that a group of well-trained mystical operatives would use a rented basement for their local spellcraft.

What surprised her was what she saw when she crept through the basement door and peered down.

The sheer volume of paranormal power contained in the chamber overwhelmed her. Sixth sense panic reflexes flexed through her backbrain. She closed the basement door and pressed her spine against it, trying to bury the eight-cylinder heart-race to *run*. Swallowing, she turned her eyes upward and focused on the ceiling.

After a few seconds, she regained composure. The Belgian's crew had hidden a tremendous amount of power behind wards against attention and notice. Once her system adjusted, she felt fine.

Relying on her sight-enhancing invocations, not wanting to turn on her flashlight out of abundant caution, she descended. She controlled her sixth sense, not letting its reflexive warning alarm her but directing its attention toward the details, the accumulations and accretions of energy, the important specifics of the spells surrounding her.

Over centuries, all the numerous short-cuts discovered for numerous spells had solidified into a semi-recognizable set of sigils, items, and behaviors. Examining them closely enough could tell a practitioner what spells might hum and stir in the ozone-stink air, what loose threads of reality awaited tugging, sometimes even what trigger might set something off.

Judging from what looked *familiar enough*, Zoe estimated the Belgian's crew had set up a handful of typical wards, well-reinforced, a pair of scrying spells already weakening against their target's wards, and five major offensive rituals. She recognized the first four as variations on some she'd used, herself, during her owb anti-personnel jobs. The curses in question aimed to disrupt the sleep patterns and dream-like perceptions of the people living in Jill's house.

They affected REM cycles, nightmares, psychic-emotional discomfort, and sixth sense insights.

Zoe crumbled ash with the toe of her boot. Burnt offerings dusted the nightmare curses. Objects arranged around the sigils and glyphs shaped the way the magic manifested. Bending to investigate, Zoe found a twisted poppet wound from rough vines. It wore a broad-brimmed hat, a vine-bound ebony disc serving as the brim while a human tooth lent it a stovetop. Zoe guessed the spells aimed to cause night terrors, sleep paralysis, and hallucinations.

Actually summoning monsters into the world took effort. Summoning them from any significant distance took more. Summoning them inside someone else's home or sanctuary was nearly impossible. Giving someone hallucinations and temporary bouts of disordered sleep required a lot less, and still depleted the target's physical and psychological energy.

It took a lot of blood, sweat, and time to put someone under legitimate supernatural threat; it was far more efficient to break them down with the fear of it.

Usually, anti-personnel teams enhanced such spells with mundane reinforcement. Zoe would have to tell Jill to check around the house. Anti-personnel ops often included hallucinogenic gases pumped in through a house's HVAC systems, wall-mounted transmitters meant to vibrate surfaces at eighteen hertz, and late-night/early-morning phone calls and drive-bys meant to induce dread and disrupt a target's circadian rhythms. All very SOP.

The death curse, however, was very much *not* SOP.

Magic couldn't guarantee things like death. Few practitioners attempted true death curses in the modern age—a true death curse, the kind that later evidenced as an aneurysm or accidental death, took months or even years to charge and cast. Even then, death curses with fewer than two and a half years' of built-up magical energies failed in eighty-five percent of known cases. To truly *guarantee* someone's death through supernatural means alone, a practitioner of Zoe's level would have to invest between three and six years of ritual, each day requiring at least three hours of spellcraft. In the modern age, people mostly just shot each other.

So what Zoe saw wasn't technically a 'death curse.' It was just the closest practical thing.

It still sent a frost crisping through her blood.

She knelt for a closer look.

What most anti-personnel practitioners did instead of trying to build up real death curses, these days, was instead to create an incredibly powerful series of escalating hexes and bad luck charms. Zoe saw a score of such spells twisted and enveloped into each other, each one altering some small accretion of million-variable vectors sometimes mistaken for 'luck' to tilt a single percentage point in one direction instead of another. Linking and folding them together gave them more gravity, more strength, and broader and broader arrays of affected variables. A death curse cost years for a promise; efficiency gambled months for a very good chance.

Luckily, magic tended to be a tenuous thing, easier to destroy than to create. A person with the right training could dismantle someone else's ritual in a fraction of the time it took to charge it in the first place.

And Zoe had a lot of training.

She flexed her hands, about to get to work, and froze.

Footsteps. Overhead. Two pairs.

She clutched the grip of her sidearm and scanned the basement for cover.

"You sure you felt something?" a groggy male voice asked.

"Yes," a woman replied, sharp and awake.

"Okay, where?"

"*'Where?'* I don't know, Frank. Someone broke a perimeter ward."

"But *where*?"

"Somewhere around the perimeter!"

The groggy male, apparently Frank, grumbled. "I just thought maybe you had more specifics."

Zoe pulled her sidearm from its holster. Little cover existed in the basement; the team had cleared most of it out to make room for ritual use. A water heater and furnace boiled in a corner. She pursed her lips.

At the top of the stairs, the basement doorknob twisted.

Oceanrest, ME.

January, 2007.

Seo-yeon shouted something in Korean. Sung-ho shouted something in Korean.

Hyun-jung shouted, "There's *two* motherfuckers!"

And Zoe un-froze.

Omar shuddered on the basement floor; Zoe sprinted the stairs up to the crash of combat. She banged through the door and into the stretch of foyer connecting dining room to kitchen. In the kitchen, someone screamed. Something clattered against the tiles. Zoe spun into the room barrel-first, thumb on the safety and index finger on the trigger guard.

Seo-yeon swung a broad iron pan at a shimmering shadow in front of her. The thing moved swiftly, climbing the wall and swooping down, and Seo-yeon yelped and backpedaled, swinging wild. The shadow gained mass, clawed grooves in the cast iron as it parried a too-close blow.

Sung-ho tossed a flashlight to Hyun-jung—who wore just-back-from-a-show goth-punk merch as an outfit entire—and grabbed another from under the sink for himself. A second shadow-assassin dove at him. Sung-ho rolled to the side; the shade became solid just in time to rake claws over the ceramic he'd occupied seconds earlier.

Hyun-jung muttered a combat-drowned sentence and threw a hand to the sky. Her flashlight sparked and blew. A spinning orb of light emerged from its melting mass. The orb, crackling, settled in Hyun-jung's palm. She crushed it with a quick flex of her hand.

Slants and shafts of blinding bright seared away every shadow in the room.

The twin shades howled, forced to take material form as all darkness died. One of them singed and burned, wobbling in noiseless pain.

Zoe hadn't known that Hyun-jung was a born witch. The realization froze her for a second. She'd only met a couple born-paranormatives in her entire life. Or…well, apparently more than she'd thought…

The uninjured creature darted toward Hyun-jung. Zoe opened fire. Bullets speared through the shade as it rushed its prey. Where exit wounds guttered out, swirls of void lightlessness flickered through the air. Hyun-jung back-pedaled, hands and lips moving, maybe casting a cantrip that her natural aptitude allowed her to cast in two or three seconds. Except she only had one or two.

Zoe moved to intercept.

Sung-ho spun the beam of the under-sink flashlight toward the monster. A sound like steam hissing out of a lobster's shell shrilled the air. The shade stumbled, slowing. It didn't appreciate direct light. The move bought Hyun-jung enough time to finish her cantrip, a ward humming around her. Zoe continued on her collision course with the monster but resumed firing.

Patches of darkness scabbed its wounds closed but new ones opened up. Shuddering from pain, a sibilant keen wailing out of it, it twisted toward Zoe and rushed the foyer. Zoe caught the monster, trying to tackle it. Somehow it got its heft under her arms in the second-long grapple and lifted her off the floor.

She pressed her gunbarrel against the thing's back and finished emptying the mag.

It died a few steps later, dropping Zoe hard on her spine, its body already wisping away as it went limp on top of her.

She remembered the wounded one. Reaching for her—

She'd forgotten her spare mag in the basement. Pushing the shrinking weight of the disintegrating creature off of her, she spun toward—

The staggered, injured creature crashed into her as it went for the unlit foyer. Her nose didn't break from the impact but a jet of blood spurt out of her face and a stream followed. She rolled over, springing up. In her periphery, Sung-ho glanced it with the direct beam of his flashlight.

But the thing was already gone.

The surviving shade de-materialized in the dimness, its existence a shadow among less-dark shadows. It swam through the mail slot and vanished into the night. The scent of its light-charred flesh lingered.

Zoe took a moment. Blood ran down her lips and trickled off of her chin. The monster she'd killed unspooled in sifts of lightlessness, its mass dwindling before her eyes. She peered over at Sung-ho, who brought her a tea towel.

"I've got things covered up here," he told her.

Nodding, Zoe rushed back down to the basement.

Omar shuddered on his sleeping bag. His muscles twitched and shivered, his face crawled with tics and sputters. He hissed. His fingers kinked at the knuckles; his eyes bulged beneath their lids.

Zoe ran for him.

His spine arched, his sternum lifting skywards. "Eats — the — veil!" Omar shouted.

Dropping her pistol somewhere, she fell to her knees at his side.

"Tear-rip, pull curtain, behold, every story!"

Zoe's heart skipped a beat.

Omar collapsed back to the cushioned bedroll, shuddering, grinding his teeth.

Zoe grabbed his face, his temples under her fingers. Thick dark-red drops splashed his forehead as her nosebleed slowed.

She started whispering. She lost syllabic rhythm for a second, so much exertion catching up to her, and heaved a throat-tearing gasp to catch up again. She imagined the needletip of an adrenaline syringe. She almost reached <<calm water>> but—

Chapter Ten

Salem, MA.

July, 2016.

Zoe focused on the magic, tried to push her will into and through it. The door at the top of the staircase swung open. Sweat dripped from Zoe's face. She struggled to keep her breath quiet. Closing her eyes, she brought her sixth sense to the fore. She needed to feel the threads of the magic. At the basement threshold, a woman spoke: "So? You're so sure it's a false alarm, you go first."

"You think they'd go straight to the basement?" the apparently-Frank asked.

"Why else break in?"

"And you're sure you felt something?"

"Can you *check*?"

The hesitance and argument only lasted seconds, but Zoe had found herself in an economy where seconds mattered. Her lungs burned. She took a deep breath, straining for control. Her sixth sense brushed up against the shape of the spell she needed to access. She dug in. A cramp sliced up her left flank, knots twisted and tightened around her hips. Gritting her teeth, she strangled a groan.

Heavy footfalls began their descent.

Zoe lurched forward, veins bulging. Tears rimmed her eyes from sheer effort. She swallowed gooey spit down a cracked-sand throat. Took a strangled breath. Pushing her willpower out, she dug into the sigil beneath her knees. She wrapped herself in threads of magic.

It felt like the spell took. She was too dizzy to be sure.

Blinking away a sea of headrush, Zoe saw Frank at the bottom of the stairs. He was shorter than he sounded—maybe five seven, around Zoe's height —but wore the shaped, taut musculature of someone familiar with intense physical training. Dirty blond haired and blue-eyed, he wore pajama pants, a tanktop, and a kevlar vest. A pendant draped at his clavicle hummed with some kind of enchantment. Zoe couldn't tell what.

She recognized Frank from her surveillance — the bodyguard for the woman in charge. Which told her who Lacey was, too.

Frank squinted around the basement. "Hit the lights, yeah?"

"Invoke nightsight."

"Nobody's here." Frank turned for the stairs.

The light flicked on. Darkness glowed to dimness, the few living bulbs buzzing through the last of their filaments.

Frank nodded, grunting, and turned back to the basement. He carried a 9mm machine pistol, not of Malleus make. Zoe grasped her own sidearm's grip, not sure where Frank had stowed his before that moment, not sure how he'd gotten his hands on it so quickly.

As Frank stepped cautiously into the ritual space, the tall, blond, blue-eyed Lacey followed. Appropriately paranoid for the goings-on, she wore a knife-resistant bodysuit under a kevlar vest. Zoe's sixth sense picked up magic around her, probably wards.

"See?" Frank said. "Nothing."

"A sweep, Frank. Just in case."

"Lacey..." Frank trailed off. "Fine." He approached the furnace, the water heater. The shadows behind it.

Zoe took a deep breath, index finger on the trigger guard.

Frank turned away.

Lacey, also suddenly-armed, walked along the far wall. Lowering her machine pistol to her side, she frowned back at the stairwell. "Okay. Maybe the basement's clear. We should still do a floor-by-floor."

"If it turns out you were just having a bad dream…"

"Hold it."

Lacey approached the furnace, the heater, a series of wards and seals, an old toolbox squatting next to the stairwell. She swept her gunsights across the area. Zoe kept one hand pressed to the floor and the other wrapped around the grip of her sidearm. She held a breath.

"Yeah?" Frank grunted.

Lacey squinted. Hovered. Stepped back. "Nothing. Let's go wake the others."

"Fine." Frank turned away, working his jaw as he scanned the basement again. "For the record, I just think—"

"Shut up," Lacey interrupted. "We're doing a floor-by-floor."

"Whatever you say."

"And contact B team," Lacey added, throwing a look over her shoulder at the dim corner where Zoe hid. "Tell them we might have interference."

"First thing in the morning."

They ascended, the basement door closing in their wake.

Zoe sat back, collapsed into a wall, and buried her sweat-slick face in her palms.

Close.

Too close.

She stood on shaky legs. Tapping into the property's wards against outside notice had drained her near empty. Folding part of the spell around her body as a shield against Frank and Lacey had exhausted her further. Bracing herself left-handed against a wall, she waited for the headrush to pass. Took a few breaths. Pushed off.

She smudged some of the chalk around the largest curse, the jerry-rigged 'death curse,' but didn't have energy to do more than cost them a couple of hours of work. At the top of the steps, she stopped. Left hand on the doorknob, right hand gripping her pistol, she listened. She heard movement muffled through the second floor, grumbling voices, closets opening…

Did anyone wait on the first floor?

Nobody she heard.

Through the door, around the corner, a kitchen, a laundry room, a mudroom, a back door. Through that, a screen door, a fence—the screen door snapped shut. Zoe jumped the fence and stumbled landing. She whirled and caught her balance. In the house behind her, movement reoriented her way. Her gait uneven from exhaustion, she raced across a yard. Shouts echoed from behind.

Zoe sprinted jaggedly across the street into another yard. Through that, over another fence, across another street, and she turned left at the face of a four-floor brick apartment building. She slowed unevenly to a walk. Her muscles shivered. She braced herself against the brick facade of a sandwich shop. She hacked and coughed and spat up a phlegmatic smoker's hock.

Wiping her lips backhanded, she turned the corner and stuck close to the buildings. Commercial structures gave way to residential ones again. When a car engine purred toward her, she sank away from the street lights and into one of the recesses between two homes. Crouched in the night, she waited with her gun drawn.

A car passed, its windows too dark to show passengers.

The waiting stretched on. Zoe's breath slowed; her heart rate normalized. Her body ached, sore and tired.

The same car passed again, heading the other way.

The waiting *stretched*.

Zoe holstered her gun, wiped sweat-slick palms against her jacket, and unholstered her gun again. Breath broadened her habit-choked lungs. She stood, thighs burning, and crept back up along the side of one house.

She waited.

For a long time, nothing happened.

Still shaky with adrenaline, she ached her way back onto the sidewalk. She gave the street lights a wide berth even as deep-night black brightened to pre-dawn purple. No matter how many wrong turns and double-backs she made, she couldn't shake the sense of being watched. She spent two hours searing her legs around the pseudo-suburban sprawl waiting for a counterattack that never came.

Once the purple sky brightened lilac, Zoe headed back toward her newest rental, casting periodic glances overshoulder.

She lit a clove and put it out again. Dawn leaked over the horizon.

She had to get to those people.

How?

Wilmington, NC.

July, 1997.

Silver-white bright shafted in from the skylight. The air hummed with magic, so much energy sizzling in the room that even the numbest sixth-sense would recognize it. Her wrists bound with silk, the real restraints mystic in nature, Jill sat on the Confessor's end of the table. Wearing an executioner's hood and the closest thing they had to 'traditional armour' (a Kevlar vest), Zoe stood behind the armchair on the opposite side.

On the table between them waited a voice recorder, mystically enhanced and backed-up with scrying spells, a blade hopefully-imbued with Jill's will, and a light leather whip.

"Your next sin," Zoe insisted.

A drop of sweat rolled down Jill's slick face. Jill pursed her lips, squeezed her eyes against tears.

"Your next sin," Zoe repeated.

"Ninety-four," Jill said, voice attenuate from the extended ceremony. "I think it was August."

Zoe remembered this but said nothing.

Jill swallowed, rolled her neck. She picked her bound hands up from the table and wiped some of the accumulated dampness from her face. "It was…"

Jill trailed off.

Zoe unfolded her arms, gripped the back the unoccupied chair, and banged its back legs against the hardwood. Jill jumped but didn't speak. Zoe slammed the chairlegs down again, the loud clamor echoing for microseconds afterward.

"It was—it was…uh…when I ran away. The worst time, I guess."

Zoe released the chair, neither confirming nor denying.

Jill stared at the table. "It's when I…I took mom's amulet and dad's bank card and…and your trophies…"

"Look at me," Zoe said.

Jill brought her glassy gaze up. Coughed. "Uh. So I withdrew a couple hundred dollars and I…I sold the rest of it. I was gone, I don't know how long…"

Nine days, Zoe didn't mention. Nine terrifying, up-all-night, crying days. Nine days of not knowing.

"I'm so sorry," Jill garbled. "I just couldn't get away. I couldn't get out."

Zoe waited for the rest of the story. For the sake of the ritual, she couldn't accept any apologies until after the Confessor had 'fully described' the 'sin.' Leaving the armchair behind, she stepped over to the table itself and assessed the selection of ceremonial objects.

"I'll finish, I'll finish," Jill said.

Zoe nodded but stayed at the table's edge. She folded her hands behind her back.

"I…spent all the money. Mostly on junk. Booze and coke but mostly just…and at some point I sold the bank card. I told the guy I'd just swiped it off of someone. I was already running out of everything and I…I called you but when you answered I just hung up."

Three times, Zoe didn't correct. Jill had called three times in that or similar fashion.

"I don't—I can't—"

Zoe unfolded her hands. "The whole thing."

"The guy I sold the card to, he couldn't use it, obviously, so…so…I don't know how he found me me, but he did. I was sleeping in a tent in Tompkins. He didn't even open the thing, he just took it down with me still inside it and started kicking." Jill gulped, throat flexing with restraint. "I couldn't breathe. I didn't know what was happening, I just…I was trying to claw my way out of the tent, I was trying to scream—I don't even remember if I could or not. I thought I was going to die. I thought he was going to rape me. I thought…"

Jill paused, breath coming in short, fast inhalations.

"When you're ready, continue," Zoe instructed.

"I don't know how long it went on like that. Not long, I guess…but it felt like shrieking fucking forever. Then suddenly he was shouting for help, too, and I was tangled up in the tent trying to free myself. This woman, I mean this real Alphabet City *butch*, was hitting the guy with a baseball bat. Bright pink buzzcut, septum piercing, tattoos, big-ass keyring, the whole thing. And the guy was on the ground trying to crawl away and she kept shouting at him 'how you like it, how you like it, how you like it.'" A faint smile weakly twitched across Jill's lips. "After she was…done, I guess…she came over and helped me up. She knew a nurse who could come take a look at me. I went to her apartment. She told me to wait for her."

"And…?"

"She was gone a while. I thought, you know, I thought she just wanted to fuck me or whatever. Or I told myself that. I didn't know this woman, I didn't know her friends…but I know those weren't the real reasons that I…that I…"

Zoe rested a hand on the thick grip of the whip.

"I'm telling it," Jill said. "Okay? Fuck. I'm telling it."

Zoe nodded.

"I started to feel sick. But I was out of money. So."

"Say it."

"So I swiped her shit and ran, okay? I stole her VHS player, some cash, some weed I found…and I just walked out. It all added up to maybe a hundred bucks but it was a hundred bucks I didn't have. I didn't even spend it all before I called you. I just…I didn't want to be the person who did what I did. But I was. I am." Tears threatened Jill's eyes. "And then you took me to the pawn where I'd sold all her shit and you helped me buy most of it back and when I gave it to her she just looked at me like I was…nothing. She said 'thanks, now get the fuck out of my neighborhood.'"

Zoe released the whip.

"But I was back in her neighborhood two months after getting out of rehab because I—because I—'cause I-I-I—" Jill seized, back arching into her seat. She gagged, choking on the syllable. She slammed her bound fists against the table. "Nnnnn. Nnnnn."

Zoe walked quickly behind Jill's chair, steadying it as Jill thrashed. She reached out and placed her hands on either side of Jill's head, making sure she made contact with the temples. She'd only done this twice outside of a classroom.

"Never," Jill spat, gray spittle spraying her lips. "*Never*."

Zoe muttered the multi-lingual words of the spell. Her muscles twisted and knotted, her tendons strained. Magic built up through her every fiber, hungry for resources. Sweat flopped her brow and slicked her back. Her words slowed, separated by ragged pants. She barely managed the last syllables, Korean, <<calm water,>> before a sharp spasm ran down her right leg and nearly dropped her to the floor. Jill seized, arching back, maw yawning as a descending pitch roughed and graveled. "You'll never be free," the new-yet-familiar voice snarled. "Never!"

Zoe held tight. She muttered the incantation again, her heart rate climbing, pulse thrumming engine-loud. She formed the magic in her mind, a cool pulse inward, her will becoming fascia over Jill's, buttressing. The syllables gooey with drymouth, she reached the end of the incantation again, <<calm water.>> Her shoulder hitched, her scapulae drove toward her spine. A groan rattled out of her.

The spell took.

"Never!" Jill screamed, her voice now the same raspy, gravely lowness as the haunting whispers...

Zoe dove, crashing her consciousness into Jill's.

Oceanrest, ME.

January, 2007.

—but Omar jerked awake, flinging Zoe's arms aside.

He rolled over and spewed a hiccup of vomit; ejecta like toast popping out of a toaster. A single *hurk* flexed through him and it was over. He panted two ragged breaths and threw himself over onto his other side, grabbing for pen and pad.

"Are you okay?" Zoe wiped red from her nose onto the back of her hand.

"Shhh, shhh, shhh," Omar hushed, scribbling notes.

Zoe sat on the floor, weight buttressed up on one arm. Panting dryly through her open mouth, she finally brought the tea towel to her face.

Movement and multi-lingual conversation filtered down from upstairs. Footsteps ran the foyer and muffled into distance. More tracked toward the back porch. Zoe's breathing steadied. Omar scribbled and scrawled. He tore a page loose and threw it aside, already onto the next.

"The man behind the curtain is magic," Omar whispered. "The man behind the curtain is magic…"

Sung-ho descended the stairs. "He okay?"

"I think so…"

Sung-ho regarded Omar's rapid auto-writing coolly. As Zoe squeezed her nose with the tea towel, Sung-ho said, "Hyun-jung is fetching my shooting practice targets from the attic. We'll need weed and whiskey, at least."

"The Hunter S. cover up?"

Sung-ho gave a single, curt nod.

Zoe grinned. "It's fun to have fun. Better to have a convenient excuse for gunfire."

Sung-ho replied with a smirk.

Omar stopped writing. He stared at the page in front of him.

"Omar?" Zoe asked.

"Where…where am I?" Omar sank back on his knees, genuflective. "Who—what?"

"Tell me about your mother," Zoe said.

"What?" Omar echoed. "Who?"

"Your mom, Omar. Tell me about your mom."

"What about her?"

"What was your favorite Christmas present?" Sung-ho prompted.

Omar laughed, shaking.

Zoe slowly lowered the stained rag from her face. "Tell us."

"It's just…" Omar licked his lips, chuckled. Shook his head. "When I was a kid, my mom got me a Sega Saturn and a copy of this game called *Panzer Dragoon Saga*. I must've played that shit twenty or thirty times—and it wasn't a short game."

Sung-ho and Zoe exchanged a glance.

"Uh…how long was it?" Zoe asked.

"Four disks?" Omar estimated. "I think. Four. And you know the worst part? I scratched the last disk before I finished my first play-through. I scratched it just exactly right so I couldn't watch the last cinematic. So I went into the game like twenty times, beat the last boss twenty times, and saw the *beginning* of the final cinematic *twenty times*. And then the system would restart. I'd be watching this villager chilling in a pottery shop and this huge shadow would pass over him—my dragon—and before the camera cut to…whatever came next, I dunno…I guess I always assumed the next shot would be me like flying the dragon to…wherever. I think I was rescuing some alien chick? And…"

Zoe and Sung-ho stared, eyebrows raised.

Omar's breathing slowed. His body stopped shaking. "Well," he muttered. "That's embarrassing…"

"At least you're out of the vision state," Zoe offered.

Sung-ho coughed gruffly. "Zoe. Weed and whiskey, very quickly."

"I'll be right there."

"Omar, you rest," Sung-ho said. "It looks like your first dreamer vision was… intense."

Omar nodded, rubbing sweat away from his nose and eyes.

################

Outside, floodlights blaring down on target practice caricatures and broad green lawn and the dim, farthest reaches of the adjacent property, Zoe and Sung-ho sat in Adirondack chairs with their discharged sidearms cooling on a table between them. They drank Macallan, four fingers, one rock each. Their joint stood in the ashtray like a grave marker.

No sirens had ever arrived.

Sung-ho had lived in Oceanrest, barring assignment transit, for twenty-six years. Most of the neighbors had already hated him, met him, and forgiven him. He had the easy humor and glinting grin of an easily likable man. More importantly: once somebody participated in the fun, themselves, they tended to make allowances for it.

Maybe nobody had called the police or maybe the police just hadn't come. Either way.

"He attacked my house," Sung-ho said, breaking a seconds-long silence. "He knows where we are."

"He does."

Sung-ho refilled his drink and settled the glass on the broad arm of the Adirondack. He peered out to where the floodlights revealed shot-up caricatures. "I need you to call your sister."

Puffing back the cherry on her clove, Zoe snapped her Zippo shut.

"Mm-hmm."

(*every story*)

(*you'll never be free of this*)

"I need her to ward my family before I send them somewhere safe. And if this guy's as good as he seems, we'll need her to disrupt whatever other spells he's working on."

"I'll call her." Zoe stood. She flicked ash. "What is he trying to do, do you think?"

Sung-ho shifted in his seat, shrugging. "Who knows? Maybe the man doesn't know, himself."

The night wind breezed softly.

Chapter Eleven

Wilmington, NC.

July, 1997.

every story ends the same way—

Jill plummeted through chaos and Zoe plummeted after. Zoe struggled to grab onto something, a memory or a thought or a place, something material that attached Jill back to the world outside the spell—but she'd mostly practiced this in a controlled setting and suddenly everything whipped passed them so quickly she couldn't pull sense out of any of it.

—we're sorry, but they do—

Threads of tar-like black criss-crossed the bottomless plummet. They dripped in oil and viscera rotted to liquescence. Shapes twitched and waited in the dark, million-eyed and hungry. Jill landed on a string of sticky sable and twisted around.

A spiderleg dropped from the darkness and speared her.

"Help!" Jill screamed.

Not a spiderleg, though. A mess of old syringes taped together, the needle tip of the last one eighteen inches long and circumferenced wrist-thick. It slammed through Jill's shoulder as Jill screamed again. Zoe tried to maneuver the sticky-tacky web toward her. Jill kicked and thrashed, trying to pull her shoulder away from the syringe.

The syringe-limb retracted.

Zoe leapt. Her hands found Jill's ankles. The extra weight drew a throat-tearing shriek from Jill.

And then—

In a high school history class not long before Jonathan's funeral and so not long before Jill's first dose of heroin, Jill raised her hand. "Excuse me, but what kind of psycho piles rocks on a guy until he dies?"

"While now we understand that witches aren't real," the teacher said, sitting on a broad desk in front of the chalkboard, "back then, they were believed to exist. They were believed to be monstrous agents of Satan."

"So?"

The teacher's eyelids fluttered. "What?"

"Geraldo Rivera would probably think I'm an agent of Satan—are you gonna hang me?"

"Obviously not, but that's largely because of our modern perspective."

"I guess what I'm really asking is…what crimes did they commit? Like what did Margaret Jones do besides screw up at work and hang out with her cat too much?"

"Again, *from our perspective*, that's probably what happened. But back then, she'd been accused of witchcraft, which means she could have done any number of things."

Jill snorted. "Drain the life from her patients with her 'withering touch?'"

"If you believe in witchcraft, maybe."

"So they didn't have any charges against her unless she was a witch?"

The teacher nodded. "Yes."

"And their proof that she was a witch was that she did these things they couldn't charge her with?"

"Essentially."

"Okay. And was anyone ever accused of being a *good* witch?"

"I don't think so."

"So a witch was by necessity a sinister or evil thing to be?"

The teacher laughed. "Again, we're still fundamentally talking about people who *believed in witches*. Although, Gillian, your point does bring me to today's in-class activity…"

every story

(*never*)

Tumbling again, Zoe caught a strand of slick gross and pulled herself back onto the web. A lacquered, voidglowing platform grew from the bundling. She stepped up onto it. In the unclear distance, Jill stood facing a mirror, her back to Zoe. From the darkness overhead, four syringe-limbs jabbed into Jill's upper back at regular intervals, taking turns.

"What you are is always more important than who you are," Jill snarled at the mirror. "Ask anyone. It's humankind. Remember Jonathan? Who was he? *What*. Was is gone, whoever lived in it corpsed over into nothing. Jonathan's nothing."

Zoe hesitated. She hardly remembered Jonathan. She hadn't known him very well. Zoe, three years Jill's senior, had never shared social circles with her sister. Not until after Malleus, anyway. Zoe hadn't been around when Jonathan had been important to Jill.

But she remembered Jill crying when he'd killed himself. If her investigative timelines proved correct, Jill's first injection happened only weeks after Jonathan's funeral.

"You'll never be free of this," Jill growled. "Never. You're a what, first. You thing. 'Witch.' If nobody else looks for a 'who' or sees a 'who' then how do you know that you have one? Maybe you don't. Maybe under the surface there's nothing. Maybe, under everything, there's just *me*."

"Jill?" Zoe's voice cracked. She stood ten feet from her sister, hesitant.

"Fuckhole. Witchcunt. Cold as a hot pair of tits, look at you. Thou shalt not suffer a slut to love."

Zoe kept walking. She wished for her satchel of tricks, her on-the-go cantrips, her gun.

"You're a what-thing until you're nothing, corpse. Just meat to verb."

Only six feet behind Jill, Zoe started whispering an incantation.

"You want to change the world?" Jill pouted at her reflection. "Boo-hoo. You can't. Go ahead, try. But the world's going to break your jaw and rape you. And when it's finished beating and fucking you into the ground, it'll leave you there, crushed, until the rats get hungry."

Zoe imagined layers of magic folding in on themselves into a knife. Her parched throat lost a syllable in the incantation and she paused. Swallowed. Picked up again. She dropped into a sprinter's stance, focusing her energy.

"The world wins," Jill said. "The world always wins. Why hurt yourself so much trying to fight it? There's such a better way to go."

Jill pulled a syringe out of the mirror. The four spider-syringe-limbs stopped jabbing her, their bloodied needletips hovering. Elsewhere in the darkness around them, more needles clattered their bits together giddily.

"Just rest for a little while," Jill said. "Worst case scenario, you won't have to feel it when the world does it rough."

Zoe felt another memory bulb up from the ground beneath her. Shards of it cut through the black webbing. The mirror reformed into a vanity, the one Jill had used in high school. The web began unraveling, bit by bit becoming Gillian's high school bedroom.

The first time she'd used? No, Zoe knew that grim tale.

The first time she'd used alone? Maybe.

She couldn't risk things going deeper.

Zoe exploded from the sprinter's stance, the last syllable of the spell leaving her lips in a pant. The energy focused, the spell hewn, Zoe rushed at Jill from behind. Syringe-in-hand, Jill turned with wide eyes—too slowly. Zoe crash-tackled into her, sprawling them both through the strange void transitioning memories.

Zoe triggered her spell. The nightmares, dreams, and memories clouding Jill's mind split apart. Moonlight spilled through the broadening gaps. She pulled.

The air reeked of ozone and static-sizzle-burnt with energy. Zoe bucked back from Jill's chair and slammed into the opposite wall. With a shout, Jill rocked onto her side, the chair legs snapping all at the same time. The table jumped a few inches in the air and landed again. The ozone stench clung dusty inside of Zoe's nostrils as she pushed herself back up.

The Confessional seemed charged.

"Jill?" Zoe asked.

Jill spat a gray chunk of meatlike goo onto the floor. Mostly the shade of dusted cinder, veins of white and black marbled it. A viscous, similarly-shaded liquid followed, first in a sharp puke of vomitus and then in a drool.

"Jill?" Zoe repeated, standing now. "*Jill?*"

"Ugh…" Jill groaned, wiping at her spew-stained face with her bound hands. She spat more. "Is the Confessional ready?"

"I think so. Yeah."

"Could you untie me?"

"Jill…we have to talk."

"What?" Jill jerked in the broken chair, scraping it against the hardwood floor.

"Whatever that was…it's in the spell, now. The whole ritual."

"Zoe…"

"It felt dangerous."

"Please."

Zoe managed her way to Jill's collapsed chair and starting working on the binds wrapping Jill's waist. "We don't know what that thing's capable of. We don't even know what it *is*."

"Zoe."

Working to unravel the knots tying Jill's wrists, Zoe sighed. "*What?*"

"We *know* what it is."

"You mean how it's a whispering vomit-monster living in your…" she trailed off.

"In my head." Jill confirmed.

Zoe stopped untying, the realization leaving her with nothing left. "Oh."

"You didn't think it would go down without a fight, did you?"

Oceanrest, ME.

January, 2007.

The next day, while they waited for Jill, they reviewed the notes they'd scribbled out after their dreamer visions.

Zoe's:
adrift / a / drift / a / rift
doesn't this world feel flat to you?
it is (every story)
the eyes are not there — yet —
peel back the lids, hold the head steady, we'll show them
(the same ending)
rift / Breach / rip / tear / Veil / I've heard the whispers /
eater of the
Pandora's box
forever

Sung-ho's [marked where translated]:
[from Hangeul] *waiting around the city*
digital triggering fuses
someone shouting "fire" in crowded
[in English] *abattoir-terroirs here is a fallow*
(story)
you'll smell it first you smell it first you smelled it ffff
a torch handing down
in the long-term
[from Hangeul] *legacy is struggle*
[in English] *when you smell it pause.*

…and Omar's:
the plan is a higher power than the mind that made it.

Beyond Omar's single sentence, he'd written only one other thing… albeit many, many times. A series of numbers repeated themselves endlessly across two pages. Zoe and Sung-ho agreed that they looked *familiar*, but they couldn't quite place how. And if the core tracking spell they'd imbued into the dreamer vision had churned out any immediately useful intel, Zoe and Sung-ho couldn't find it in *their* writing.

"Hold on," Omar said, standing up from the semi-circle they'd formed around the notes. "Can I use your computer?"

"For what?" Sung-ho asked.

"I want to plug the numbers into a search engine."

Sung-ho shrugged. "Use my daughter's."

"Uh…"

"Just blame me and do it."

"Uh, okay…" Omar took one of the eerily-identical pages of integer scrawl and took them upstairs. A short, stilted conversation muffled through the floor, unintelligible.

"You have eyes-only stuff on your desktop?" Zoe asked.

Sung-ho snorted. "Sure."

"Porn?"

"Passwords," Sung-ho replied. "They don't do a lot if you give them out to people."

Zoe rattled the papers around. She tapped part of Sung-ho's. "Whatever you smell first, you better tell me about it."

"Oh, sure. I'll just yell stuff out as I scent it."

"I hate dreamer visions."

They fell to a comfortable silence, examining and re-examining the contextless prophecies they'd managed to scribble out before forgetting them. After they'd passed their pages between themselves for several uninspired and unsuccessful minutes, Omar returned. He carried a handful of print-outs in one hand.

"They were coordinates," he told them from the landing. "They led to an address."

"And?" Sung-ho pressed.

"It's a slaughterhouse. The state shut it down in ninety-nine and it stayed shut. It's about twenty miles northwest from here."

Sung-ho stood. Cleared his throat. Said, "Shit."

"Shit?" Omar repeated. "Are you kidding me? I found him! He's there!"

"Yeah. Which is bad news." Sung-ho met Omar at the stairwell landing. Leaning across the other man, he shouted upstairs, "Yeobo!?"

Seo-yeon appeared at the top of the steps. <<Yes?>> she asked in Korean.

The couple held a brief conversation that rapidly outpaced Zoe's ability to translate the language she still struggled to master. At the end of the half-minute exchange, Seo-yeon nodded. Whatever Sung-ho had asked, she answered in English. "Yeah. The Ashers owned it."

"Shit," Zoe muttered.

"Who?" Omar asked. "Who are the Ashers?"

"Thank you, darling." Sung-ho grinned at his wife as she walked away.

"Who are the Ashers?" Omar repeated.

"They *were* one of the most powerful families in the supernatural world," Zoe filled in, standing herself. "But they're all dead, now. Every last Asher to sprout from the family tree since they planted it in Oceanrest in the eighteenth century."

"Like...someone killed them?"

Zoe rolled her neck, finding an ache in her shoulder. "They died from heart attacks, strokes, car crashes, shootings, stabbings, homicides and suicides…the whole gamut, really. They just all did it within a three year period. Almost seven hundred total descendants spread across five continents."

"Holy fuck." Omar stepped deeper into the basement. "Was this—was this some kind of conspiracy shit?"

"No. At least, not that we know about. Just…" something popped relief in her neck. She sighed. "We deal with forces we barely understand. Some we *don't* understand; maybe even some we *can't*. Sometimes that leads to volatile results."

"'Seven hundred people' volatile?"

"If only we knew all the answers, eh?" Sung-ho chimed in. "But we don't. What we *do* know is that the Ashers were knee-deep in kooky-spooky shit. If they owned the slaughterhouse, they probably used it for something besides profit."

"If the Summoner knows how to tap into leftover energies or old spells, that might explain how he's throwing so much at us so quickly," Zoe said.

"Wait, wait, wait, didn't you say that all that stuff fades away?" Omar asked. "Mundanity decay, right?"

"Oh, it fades, for sure, but if there's enough of it built up over a long enough time…especially if it's blood magic…"

"Blood magic?"

"We don't have time to explain *everything*," Sung-ho waved the question away. "I'm more worried about this Summoner having a history of building constructs and *summoning* things. Leftover magic, sure, bad news, but how many skeletons do you think he can dig up, there? How much rebar? What rusted steel?"

"He'd have a lot of material," Zoe admitted.

"And no witnesses," Sung-ho added.

"Whatever he builds or summons could survive for a long time that far away from notice."

"So we agree, then. This is a trap."

Zoe nodded. "Seems like."

"How!?" Omar balked. "We learned it from a *vision*. I had to run shit through a *computer*!"

"Nobody knows how dreamer works," Zoe said, the words feeling somehow too-too-familiar spilling off of her tongue. "Or what, exactly, it does to us. Or if it has agenda. Why does it show us what it shows us? Why does it take us where it does? Why give us these visions, these phrases, this building?"

"We asked for it," Omar answered.

"The Summoner's there, I don't doubt that. But a place with at least a dozen mass-graves, enough scrap and leftover junk to build a Construct out of sharp, rusted steel? Do we think we're just going to waltz in?"

Omar opened his mouth. Closed it.

"When my sister gets here, she can help us with this."

Almost on cue, the doorbell rang.

Chapter Twelve

Oceanrest, ME.

January, 2007.

It took two days for Jill to assemble piecemeal wards for Hyun-jung and Seo-yeon. Jill had to visit the house several times, completing the spells in sections. She worked at Winters-Armitage Laboratories, in the Special Research Division headed by Shoshanna Winters. And while Malleus' corporate umbrella didn't compete with Winters-Armitage, the two secret societies living inside the corporations did. Technically, Jill wasn't supposed to help them without special permission. She did so in pseudo-secret, under-the-radar, perhaps suspected by Shoshanna but not questioned about it.

Thus, it took two days.

At that point, Hyun-jung and Seo-yeon went to stay vaguely *elsewhere*. Jill's wards proved powerful. Testing them with a weaker version of the tracking spell they'd used against the Summoner, Zoe and Sung-ho found themselves rapidly overwhelmed, all the will and energy they'd pooled and collected over hours of labor almost instantly dismantled by the defenses Jill had built. The exertion left them burnt out, a whole day lost to a field performance test. At least Sung-ho's family seemed safe.

Zoe, Omar, and Sung-ho took shifts sleeping. Another attack didn't come.

Throughout that week, both Jill and Zoe drove long circuits through Oceanrest. Separately, they marked locations where their sixth senses had picked up trace impressions of mysticism or supernatural influence around the city. They planned to compare notes when they met again.

Two days after Sung-ho's family drove off, Jill joined Zoe's ragtag team at the house for the weekend. Jill had bolstered her own wards against notice and observation to the point that she felt confident in her privacy. Or at least in the notion that, if or when someone violated that privacy, her wards would alert her.

And they did.

#################

Zoe jumped awake, adrenalized by Jill's sudden shouts.

"Everyone up!" Jill yelled, a singleton stampede in the hall. "Something's coming!"

Already on her feet, Zoe bent down to grab a bullet- and knife-resistant vest. She slung it over her tanktop and grabbed her holster. As Omar rolled off the opposite side of the mattress, she yanked the holster over her left shoulder and rushed out of the guest room. She didn't wait for Omar to finish gearing up. They didn't have time.

In the hallway, sheets tangled out of Hyun-jung's room in the wake of Jill's rush. On the other end of the corridor, a pajama'd Jill slammed a fist against the master bedroom's door. Before Zoe woke up enough to speak, Sung-ho answered Jill's knock, already armored. "What's up?" he asked.

"I don't know yet," Jill answered, panting more from nightmare than exertion. "Something triggered the wards."

"Eh, shit."

"Kitchen," Zoe said, still shaking off the last of her sleep.

They sprinted downstairs, Omar only seconds behind, and rushed to the kitchen. Someone turned on the overheads. Omar had a heavy utility flashlight. Zoe and Sung-ho held their sidearms low, fingers over trigger guards, thumbs poised on safety levers. Gathered there, they waited.

Their breaths echoed in the deep-night silence.

A phone rang.

For a moment, all they did was look at each other. They hesitated in unison.

Then the phone rang again and they surged for Sung-ho's office in unison, too.

They crowded the small space. Zoe and Omar hung back as much as they could, sticking by the door. Jill sat cross-legged between the twinned armchairs and managed a shard of chalk from a pajama-pant pocket. She dulled it against the hardwood as Sung-ho walked behind his desk, opened a drawer, and unraveled a heavy, antique handset from a long, tangled wire.

"You got the wrong number, sorry," Sung-ho dismissed.

Someone replied on the other end of the line, inaudible.

Zoe's armhair stood on end. A static-cling sensation rippled along her skin.

Jill tapped into an earlier spell and added an improvised, cantrip-level element before triggering it.

"Like I said, wrong number."

The reply came out louder, this time.

"What did you say?" Sung-ho asked.

Jill's mouth moved but it wasn't her voice that spoke. "I know you're watching me," the Summoner said, voice modulated technologically. The words didn't quite align with Jill's lips. "Now you know I'm watching you."

"Uh-huh. So?"

A pause. Uncertainty?

"Who do you work for?" the Summoner/Jill asked.

Sung-ho barked a laugh. "Oh, baby, you *are* green."

"Do you not think I can find your family?"

The air changed with Sung-ho's expression. "Do you not think we can find you?"

"Why are you doing this?"

"Well, first of all, you're a murderer—"

"People need to know!" the Summoner shouted through Jill's strained throat.

Sung-ho leaned against the rear wall next to a massive speaker. "Magic can't fix the world."

"It can. If people like you weren't keeping it a secret."

A hint of smirk pricked at Sung-ho's lips. "You don't even know who we are."

"I know who *you* are, Mr. Park. I know the name of your wife. Your kid."

Sung-ho's jaw flexed.

Zoe's hand balled into a white-knuckled fist.

As the Summoner continued, Jill's head lolled around to face Sung-ho. "Look, I—I don't want to hurt you. I don't want to hurt anyone."

Sung-ho snorted.

Jill's throat bobbed. The Summoner picked back up. "I don't *want* to, but I am *willing* to. People only see magic when it's pointed at them. I tried everything else."

(*a shadow unpeeling itself from a wall*)

Heat seethed through Zoe's veins.

Jill's jaw bobbed and the Summoner spoke. "People have to know. I've seen incredible things—impossible things."

(*a squirm of fumbling limbs*)

"You have, too."

(*hh—lllllp—*)

"You know nothing has to be the way that it is. You *know* it. And I know that you know it. And how do you know that and just let things…stay the way they are?"

(*a noise that came out of her, neither a roar nor a wail but both*)

"I hate to tell you this, kid, but you killed those people for nothing," Sung-ho said. "None of the witnesses remember seeing anything magical or mysterious. They just saw blood."

A long second passed. Zoe's hands hurt.

"Who the fuck do you work for?" the Summoner growled.

"Take a wild guess."

"Go to hell."

The call ended. Jill lurched forward, gagging. She choked and arched her back. After a few seconds, she spat out a hock of gooey saliva and shakily stood back up.

When Zoe unballed her hands, her forearms ached. Bright red grooves marked her palms where her nails had broken skin.

Sung-ho stared at the viscous film spattering his rug. "You okay?" he asked.

"Uh-huh," Jill answered hoarsely.

"You get it?" he asked.

"I got it," she said.

Salem, MA.

August, 2016.

Salem wasn't a night-life town. It had its bars and late-night establishments, its last-call drunks and after-party nocturnes, but in the main, few lurkers inhabited the pre-dawn hours. Even at its wildest, Salem wasn't New York or even Boston—and it sure as hell wasn't New Orleans. Driving back to her rental just before midnight, Zoe saw few pedestrians and fewer vehicles.

Until.

Five minutes out from the rental, a shade-windowed sedan passed her on the street. As she traveled west, it traveled east. A semi-opaque shield hid the front license plate. As it drove by, a sixth sense surge pulsed through her. Rapid-fire images flashed ominously through her mind, a dozen bad endings overlapping each other at the speed of chemistry. Forcing herself to focus through the adrenaline rush, Zoe brought her gaze to the rearview mirror and caught the last two digits on the rear plate.

The last digit on the plate had read '0' and something about that didn't settle with her. Something she'd once known about Massachusetts plates that she didn't know anymore.

Twenty minutes later, pulled over on the shoulder of another street several miles from her newest rental, Zoe rested her forehead against the steering wheel. She wanted to call Sung-ho. Nobody else in her life had ever been Sung-ho. This made sense, intellectually; it broke her, emotionally.

She wanted to call Sung-ho but Sung-ho no longer received calls. The dead rarely did.

Still, deep in the shadowed corridors of her airtight neural compound, a name and number existed that she still recalled by rote. And if any situation needed her to set aside her own bullshit and make the call, this was it.

It still took her five minutes to dial.

Oceanrest, ME.

January, 2007.

Even armed with the psychic impression Jill had assembled while diving into the shrieking chaos of the phone line, it would have taken at least a week to dismantle the Summoner's city-wide ritual. And a week they didn't have. They had four days, Zoe figured, and that was at best.

So they moved forward with a much blunter and sloppier sabotage.

They didn't need to take the spells apart, *per se*, they just needed the spells not to work. By disrupting the individual ritual sites and disconnecting them from each other, they could feasibly render the Summoner's grand work non-functional over a span of around forty-eight hours. All they had to do was *be careful*.

Practitioners stitched their spells together from patchworks, using esoteric reference to thread in outside energies and directing them with focus and will to set up a desired effect. Unraveling the network of ritual sites the Summoner had created without knowing his planned endgame required meticulous examination, a slow-going precision, and an amount of romanticized guess-work that Zoe tried not to think about.

Because screwing up a spell didn't stop the accrual of paranormal energy. Eventually, all the sizzle-static charge the Summoner had pulled in from other dimensions or collective unconsciousnesses or through his own neuromuscular metabolism had to go *somewhere*. Either the spell would trigger and, totally disrupted, it would behave in a chaotic, unpredictable, and dangerous fashion, doing things the Summoner hadn't intended and that they wouldn't know—or it wouldn't trigger, and all the power built up over weeks of ritual would slowly seep out into the mundane world. High strangeness would abound.

So the work had to be painstaking.

Frazzling the summoning circles proved the easiest task. Little existed that a person of the Summoner's skill could pull forth that Zoe and Sung-ho hadn't dealt with a half-dozen times already. They read right through the symbols and signs and knew exactly what to do. The spells designed to rapidly assemble Constructs were more difficult. None of them knew much about that particular arcanum, not even Jill, and the Summoner hadn't left the construction materials at any of his ritual sites.

Omar, keeping watch in the car at the intersection between asphalt and dirt road above, thumbed through the Summoner's notes in search of answers. Through a dense thicket of naked deciduous and needly coniferous below, Zoe, Jill, and Sung-ho worked around a years-abandoned campground; one of the Summoner's seven ritual sites spread across the peninsula. Zoe sketched approximations of the Summoner's sigils in a notebook, notating what she knew and what she didn't. Jill sat on an age-grayed picnic table, legs folded, eyes swimming beneath their lids. Sung-ho paced the perimeter, flicking the butt of a cigarette he only puffed to keep lit, trying to figure out the practical methodology of a madman.

"Besides the basic alarms Jill shut off before we came in here, the guy doesn't have any wards."

"Hmm?" Zoe turned to face Sung-ho, having stared thoughtlessly at an unrecognizable glyph for several seconds before he spoke.

"No wards against notice, no wards against investigation, no wards against scrying…just some voodoo-tripwires and a defense against intrusion so weak we barely noticed it."

"He wants people to see," Zoe said.

"So nix the ward against outside notice, he still should've had the others."

"Wards don't seem to be his particular expertise. We don't call him 'the Warder.'"

"But he's got wards up around the slaughterhouse," Sung-ho replied. "He must. Otherwise we wouldn't need a dreamer vision to find the place."

Zoe set her notebook aside. "What are you thinking?"

"I'm trying to figure out what *he's* thinking. He hides the slaughterhouse and leaves his whole ritual open to be found. He's got seven sites spread out across the whole banana, which means he's put in the blood, sweat, and tears — a minimum of twenty-one hours per week on the ritual, plus whatever he's doing at the slaughterhouse. Why leave it open? I put twenty-one hours of work a week into something, four, five weeks, I'd hide it. I'd hide it from my *wife*."

Zoe stood from the matted grass and dirt where she'd sat sketching. "It's occurred to me that he might not even care."

"So you tell me now?"

"Well, he wants people to see magic, right? Obviously he doesn't understand what a sixth sense really is or how it works or how most people react to it — he just wants them to *see*. So he sets up the rituals, a bunch of summoned creatures and monsters and whatever else, and a dozen bizarro Constructs, besides, and points them at Oceanrest. If it works, he thinks, maybe an undeniable number of people will see monsters. If it doesn't…well, maybe by now he's figured out that taking a spell apart takes a lot more time than just screwing it up. And maybe he figures that'll be our move. And when we catch him at the slaughterhouse, and maybe he knows we will, maybe he'll have a way to trigger the ritual from there. All that energy floods through the area but now that we've wrecked everything up it doesn't have anything guiding it."

Sung-ho puffed his cigarette back to life. "So maybe it rips open a Breach."

"Exactly."

"If that's his plan…" Sung-ho pinched the cigarette between thumb and forefinger, "…then it's a dumb one."

"All of his plans have been dumb, so far," Zoe replied. "Why would he switch it up, now?"

A sixth-sense surge bristled through the vicinity. A plunging fight/flight urge clutched at Zoe's heart. She reached reflexively for her sidearm but stopped herself before loosing it. The ominous crackle-throb pulled her gaze to Jill. As the sudden rush dissipated, Jill's eyes opened.

"There's something else here," she said, unfolding herself from the picnic table. Frozen sweat crystallized through the locks of her long black hair. She stumbled when she tried to walk and steadied herself.

"What's up?" Zoe asked.

"Something," Jill's answer carried all the authority of something considered clearly self-explanatory. "One of the cabins."

Jill started to run but didn't make it far. Zoe caught her sister by the arm before she fell.

"Headrush," Jill muttered. It took a couple seconds before she straightened out. "Sorry. There's something in one of the cabins, something we missed. Over there," she pointed to two slouched, gray structures, once lodges, tree-speared and splintered.

They approached, Sung-ho taking point, Zoe close behind. They drew sidearms, safeties on, and lit underbarrel flashlights. Jill hung back, unarmed. In the static-skied late-afternoon, the wilderness shadows swaddled the cabins thickly.

Inside, shafts of light plunged through the prevailing darkness. Young trees and younger saplings had breached the sinking floor, the tallest of which pressed branches through the sagging ceiling to seek the sky. Their flashlight beams tracked over toppled bunk beds, rusted frames, abandoned mattresses twitching with insects. The farther depths of the derelict lodge were blockaded, inaccessible.

Zoe's boot found a clump of cobwebs. A collection of empty bottles glinted nearby.

Someone had cleaned.

Straining to keep her eyes open, she took a deep breath and attuned herself to her sixth sense.

Before she could get any real information, Sung-ho gestured her toward him. "Here," he whispered.

She let her sixth sense stick to the background and joined her mentor in the center of the rotten floor. His torch-beam lit a bulbous, wired object; a simple sigil beneath it. It took Zoe's brain a fraction of a second to put all the pieces together and recognize the thing as a bomb. An Improvised Explosive Device.

"Well," Zoe muttered. "That's not good…"

And then something *click-click-click'*ed from the darkness.

Chapter Thirteen

Wilmington, NC.

July, 1997.

Time dilated in the ritual's second phase. On a vegetarian diet without any booze or nicotine and limited to only two cups of coffee per day, Zoe felt the hours expand like Big Bang fallout. The minutes unraveled at the fringes of the observable, every second somehow several seconds long. Itchy and prickly and nauseous, nauseous especially during those first few nic-fit shouting-match days, Zoe felt suspended, adrift on some temporal derivative as x approached infinity.

She'd only thrown up twice. That put her ahead of Jill on the scoreboard, at least.

The ritual work expanded, too. Zoe's five hour labors groaned into seven. The increased exertion sustained over longer hours left her queasy and frail. She needed a cigarette. If she had a cigarette, she introduced more instability into the spell. So far, she'd only thrown up twice. She'd had zero cigarettes.

The work expanded...

The second phase required more collaboration. The practitioners—Jill and Zoe—performed their morning meditations together, facing the dawn, and ate both breakfast and dinner as a group. In this case, a pair. A week into the second phase, their commingling withdrawals and frustrations had already revealed themselves in armor and claw, fights snarled over issues as stupid as undercooked pasta. Why?

Because Jill needed a fix and Zoe needed a cigarette and the dark, gravelly-voiced thing whispering in the walls needed them to need those things.

"You will never be free of this."

(*never*)

(*never never never*)

During the Gateway between the Confessional and the second phase, the Proclamation, Zoe had taken the car into town for supplies. On the drive back, she'd stopped at a gas station to refill the tank. She'd walked inside almost without thinking and ordered a pack of Djarum almost without thinking. She'd paid for the gas and started driving back. Window open, filter between her lips, she'd barely stopped the lighter before she puffed. She'd snapped the Zippo shut and tossed the smoke. The rest of the pack had followed.

(*never*)

On the ninth day of the second phase, the Proclamation building slowly-but-surely toward its climax, Zoe stalked smoke-less upstairs to fetch Jill for lunch. Approaching Jill's door, she felt an increase in the magic crackling in the air—a sixth sense sensation bristling against the skin of her ear-drums—and hesitated. "Jill?"

"Hold on!"

Zoe frowned, no longer nauseous from not smoking but plagued by the dual diseases of post-quitting lethargy and a leprosy of patience. She grabbed Jill's doorknob, twisted, and pulled. A mystic force held it fast. "Are you kidding me?"

"One sec!"

Zoe yanked on the door again. The spell fastening it to the threshold weakened, magic not an especially strong force. It opened on the third tug, flinging Zoe back with sheer inertia. Zoe caught herself and stomped into Jill's room. "What are you—"

Jill froze mid-movement. Several illusions glowed in the air, illustrations glimmering and hovering like sci-fi holograms. Five books also floated, untethered from gravity by more magic. Another dozen books and grimoires strew the floor, half-circling a lap-table overpiled with notes. "I was...

researching."

"How many spells are you flinging around in here!?"

"They're tiny. Nobody's here who can notice them, anyway."

"The spell is already *infested* with what sounds like every dark and self-loathing impulse you've ever had—why would you take even the *smallest* risk of destabilizing what little stability we have?" Zoe barreled over every interruption Jill made, giving no quarter for more than a single syllable. "What if that thing *wins*?"

"I'm sorry. I was just…I found something in Sung-ho's collection and I think I'm onto a proof, a new way to reinforce—"

"You're risking this entire ritual for fucking *academia*?"

The illuso-grams fritzed and died. The books fell broken-backed to the floor. "I'm sorry," Jill said, "I'm sorry, I just…"

"You 'want to know,' right?" Zoe didn't bother to fight the sarcasm thickening her tone.

"There's nothing else to do here!" Jill shouted.

"And how do you think *I* feel!?" Zoe shouted back.

"Fuck!" Jill kicked her bedframe to little effect.

Zoe wrangled control over her volume. "Shit. Goddammit. Why were you doing this?"

"It…" Jill stopped shouting, turned away, and took a deep breath. "It helps me organize things."

"Could you try just pinning things to the walls? Draw it out by hand, tape it up?"

"I'm not the best calligrapher."

"And I'm not a substance use counselor!" Zoe threw up her hands. "But here we are."

Jill opened her mouth to yell. Her nostrils flared, her eyes widened. She paused. Backed down. "I'm…okay. I'll try pinning things up."

"Like band posters."

Jill shook her head, arms folding. "Sure."

"Look, I'm sorry I barged in and I'm sorry for…I don't know, for yelling, I guess. But we have to be really careful with how and when we use magic in this house. We can't risk anything. I mean *anything*. Okay?"

"I said yeah."

"You said 'sure.' With attitude."

"Jesus. I'm trying to find something to do that isn't…"

Zoe pinched the bridge of her nose. "I know."

Jill sat sharply on the edge of the mattress. "How are we going to make it through this? It's, what, two more weeks until the Proclamation?"

"We'll make it because we have to."

Jill pressed the heels of her hands into her eye sockets and leaned her elbows into her thighs.

"Look, we're in too deep to turn back now. You said so yourself. So… let's have lunch, okay?"

"Yeah," Jill answered. "Lunch."

"I'll go set the table or…something." Zoe stepped backward out of the room. She hesitated, wanting to say something else but not sure what it was. Turning away, she followed the long hallway past another bedroom (two bunkbeds), the lounge with attached bathroom, and down the stairs. At the first floor landing, before heading into the kitchen, a shot of pure cold blew through her. She braced herself, waiting.

The temperature dove. Zoe shivered.

"Hey, you," a friendly voice called out from the kitchen. "Take a load off."

Zoe crossed the threshold. Afternoon sunlight shafted in from the windows. The eat-in kitchen was exactly the way she'd left it. Except.

Except for a pack of cloves on the eat-in table.

The temperature returned to normal, the sensation more sixth-sense than material anyway.

Zoe picked up the pack and carried it over to the sink. She turned on the faucet and flicked the switch that set the garbage disposal to roaring and gurgling. She fed the cloves to the shrieking teeth of it. Blades jammed and jittered as they chopped through the box. The disposal roared. Tobacco and spice flew everywhere. Breathless for a reason she couldn't name, Zoe yanked out the half-chewed remains and started tearing them apart with her hands. She tore soggy cigarettes into pieces and threw the clumps into the steel-screaming noise.

Afterward, she stood over the sink, panting.

She turned off the garbage disposal.

the story might read differently if

"Zo'?" Jill asked.

"Sorry. I, uh. I found some rotten food."

"Already?"

Zoe pushed away from the sink and turned to face her sister. "Yeah. Anyway. Lunch. What do you feel like?"

Oceanrest, ME.

January, 2007.

The click-click-clicking clarified into a centipede scuttle. The monster crawled out of the darkness. Despite its mostly metal manufacture, it virtually *squirmed*. A body of oil drums and trash cans rattled along on meticulously-articulated, uncountable steel legs. Six mantid arms, razor-sharp, pivoted up from modular shoulder joints irregularly spaced along its torso. Animated by hours of ritual magic and Frankenstein sci-fi, it drove toward them.

Like all of the Summoner's previous Constructs, it proved scarier in appearance than in combat. The supernatural binds holding the thing together unraveled after a half-dozen bullets, barely making it close enough to Zoe and Sung-ho to take a single, inches-short swing. It collapsed on the cement floor and jerked away, rolling onto its side before going still. When the last vestiges of magic dissipated, the Construct broke into pieces.

"Huh," Sung-ho grunted, approaching the rusted carcass. He nudged it with his shoe. Nothing happened. "Scared me there for a second."

"Yeah," Zoe said. "He builds them like that."

Sung-ho gave the thing a harder kick. The drums and cans racketed along the floor. The monster didn't look like anything more than trash, now.

"So what do we do about that?" Sung-ho asked, indicating the bomb.

"We'll have to disarm it."

"Plus any others he left lying around."

"You think he's got a ward or something to alert him to tampering?"

Sung-ho shrugged. "I dunno. He's not my assignment." He turned to her. "What do you think?"

"I think he's a big fan of the movie *Saw*."

"What?"

"It doesn't matter," Zoe said. "We should get Jill in here to deep-dive the thing."

Peeking outside, Zoe saw Omar driving downhill toward them, Jill in the passenger seat. They seemed panicked until Zoe stepped out of the cabin and waved to them. The car stopped a couple yards from the sagging structure and Jill and Omar got out.

"What happened?" Jill asked.

"We killed a Construct," Zoe answered, turning back inside. "But the bomb is the real problem."

"The what?" Omar came around the hood of the vehicle and stalled.

Zoe peered back briefly. "Come on. We have a new plan to figure out."

It took Jill just over an hour to finish the mystic, metaphysic, and supernatural assessment of the IED. While they waited, Sung-ho smoked Lucky Strikes and examined the physical object with Omar. Zoe burned cloves, standing at the sagging cabin's ragged threshold and scanning their surroundings for any approaching threats. Her lungs ached by the end of the waiting.

"Zo'," Sung-ho got her attention. He pointed his half-smoked Lucky at Jill, who bent forward, straight-armed, her palms on the floor, panting. "She's done."

Zoe re-entered the cabin.

Jill cleared her throat, spat, and sat up. She wiped her mouth backhanded. "Water?"

Sung-ho offered one of several bottles they'd unloaded from the car.

Jill took a few sips before speaking. "It's all pretty basic stuff. He had a ward against notice—probably why we overlooked it, at first—and some minor protective wards. It felt like he tried to jerry-rig a spell to trigger the fuse if someone tried to defuse it, but he doesn't know enough to do anything remotely that powerful."

"So what's that mean?" Omar asked.

"Maybe he rushed through this part," Jill guessed. "I don't know. But the magic around the bomb is so weak it's almost a waste of time to disperse it."

"So what do we do?"

Everyone got the kind of quiet they got when they all knew the answer and didn't want to say it.

Zoe cleared her throat. Even she usually didn't smoke this much — her vocal chords felt raw. "Well," she began, the last reedy rasp cracking free of her. "We need to split into two teams. Me and Sung-ho will take the slaughterhouse, you and Jill will handle the...the bombs."

Omar balked. "What?"

Zoe glanced between Sung-ho and Jill but of course neither of them chimed in. "Me and Sung-ho have the most combat training. Jill can make sure the target's rituals don't do anything crazy while she helps you—"

"Helps me *what*?" Omar pressed.

"Helps you defuse the IEDs. The basic parts and schematics of which we'll draw out based on this one."

Omar blinked. "You want me to defuse a fucking bomb?"

"Think of it like disassembling a motherboard—"

"I will abso-fucking-lutely *not*."

"Omar."

"Look, I get it, I'm in this, now, whatever, and I know I'm a suspect or a person-of-interest in all that shit in Keene's Falls, but now you're asking.... This isn't a computer, it's a *bomb*. I fuck up, I'm *dead*."

Sung-ho opened his mouth; closed it when Zoe took a creak-wood step forward.

"Omar," she said. "I understand your fear. Believe me, I do. Because if any of us fuck up on this, we're dead, too. The Summoner's not going to work his magic from an undefended location. There'll be Constructs. Traps, maybe. Other bombs, land mines, guns...if I make the wrong move out there, I'm not coming back. Ditto Sung-ho. We're all taking a chance, here. And it's like you said, you're in this, now."

Omar pursed his lips and creased his brow. His eyes narrowed. Zoe watched him tongue words around in his mouth; watched him swallow them.

It crossed her mind he might make noises to suggest taking his chances with the police. That he might say something about getting out. And if he did, it crossed her mind that she'd have to tell him that of course they couldn't let him do that at this point.

And then what?

A wire-tight tension relaxed out of her when he nodded. "Fine, then. Let's see what this thing looks like."

Swallowing a sigh of relief, Zoe knelt with the other three and picked up a flashlight.

Wilmington, NC.

August, 1997.

What did people *do* all day?

What did people do with their hands?

Zoe itched like fever. The initial physical symptoms had seemed bad enough. Going from seven per day down to three per day had seemed bad enough. Going from three to zero? It felt impossible. Even in the first week of August, fourteen days after the First Confessional, somewhere between six and nine days before the Proclamation, it felt threadworn, unrealistic, tenuous as a single molecular chain encountering hostile forces. The nic fits and heightened frustration lingered on even after the last queasy symptoms of physical withdrawal died out.

And, increasingly, the boredom.

She paced. A small TV played a re-run of a re-run of a re-run, the screen occasionally fritzing and snowing as a natural but inexplicable response to prolonged exposure to magic. She turned the volume up but couldn't care about what any of the characters said or did. She paced. In the kitchen, she finished leftover dinner—more salad, now wilted.

She flicked the butt of her cigarette.

Wait.

She flicked—

Wait.

She stared at the slim black clove between her fingers. She felt something brewing in her head. Her mind blanked, her zen the calm before an apocalyptic storm. Her Zippo felt heavier in her pocket. Had she even put it in her pocket that morning? And where had the clove come from?

(*never*)

She dropped the smokestick to the tile and stomped it dead. When she picked up her shoe, nothing remained.

Her pocket felt light. She hadn't put her Zippo in it, that morning. Why would she have?

Laugh-track roared from the small kitchen television. Something sang along Zoe's sixth sense as she turned to face it.

Silent static disruptions crawled up the visage of a black-and-white TV show. A man with a slender mic addressed a cackling audience. "You know what the funniest thing is?" he asked, the picture warping and melting more and more with every word. "They do it to themselves!" And the audience howled. The footage blurred and fizzled. It burned away until a tarry darkness filled the screen. A low, gravel-churned voice rumbled out. "All I have to do is remind them that the poison *exists*…"

Zoe's arms shook. She realized she'd grabbed the sides of the television; she squeezed the frame so hard it hurt her fingers. Her breath came in ash-hot blasts. She was going to rip the thing out of the wall and smash it.

But she didn't. Jill screamed before she could.

Chapter Fourteen

Boston, MA.

August, 2016.

Omar and Zoe held the embrace for a long time. The car Omar had stepped out of with his kit bag had pulled away seconds earlier. People passed them on the sidewalk, at least one of them noticing. Still, they held on.

"I'm sorry," she whispered, not knowing what else to say after so many months.

"It wasn't your fault," he soothed.

She hadn't always been as good a mentor as Sung-ho had been.

"It wouldn't've happened if I hadn't fucked up…"

He pulled away from her just enough to hold eye contact, his endless pools and her gray-blue shallows. "Everyone fucks up," he said. "You still pulled me out in one piece."

"It's less impressive when I'm the one who put you in the shit to begin with."

His lips parted, not quite a smirk but not quite *not*, either. "Funny."

They drifted away from each other inch by inch. "What?"

"I know you're talking about New Mexico, but I was just thinking…it'll be ten years this winter. When we met."

She chuckled. The near-laughter eased some of the aching tension bundled along her spine. "I guess I really *am* the one who put you in the shit. I'm sorry for that, too."

"Don't be. It made my life." Omar used a rolling suitcase as a general gig kit, a 'tactical' cross-body pack for proper runs. A laptop bag hung from one shoulder, unexplained. He tilted the case to roll. "Besides, if I was holding a grudge, I wouldn't've been on the plane."

They walked down Boylston toward the Public Garden and Commons. Zoe chose the rendezvous point for its clamor; a place too busy for them to stand out. "Thanks, by the way," Zoe said.

"Thank me when we win." A smirk slanted brightness through his lips. "So. You mentioned active opposition?"

"I think it's the Belgian's people. They burned my last rental."

"They *burned* it?"

"Not literally. They compromised it."

"I was kidding," Omar said. "Sounds like they got a head start on us."

"They do."

"So what's the plan to come back on 'em?"

"I'm still…collating. Right now all I know for sure is that I can't do this on my own. Even with everything Jill and her people are doing inside the house…there are too many fronts to fight on."

They waited at a crosswalk. Omar rolled his neck. Something popped and he noised that it felt *good*. "Well," he said, after, as they began walking again, "that's just a numbers game. You think the Belgian's crew is on point?"

"I'm sure they are."

"So we start from there."

She stopped walking. He went on a few more paces before stopping, himself. He turned toward her, his face lined with questions.

"I was so scared you wouldn't show up," she admitted. "Or that I'd be waiting here and someone else from ASOD would…"

He drew in close to her. "What? Black-bag you?"

She didn't answer.

He put his free hand on her arm. It felt familiar; comfortable in way Zoe hadn't felt in a long time. "Why in the world would I do that?"

"It just…. Thank you."

A phone rang. One of the several burners cluttered at the bottom of her purse. Digging through gig supplies, a spare magazine, foundation, a snack bar, and a water bottle, she found the clatter of devices and starting feeling for a vibration. When she pulled the right one out, she frowned at the encrypted label markered across its back.

It was the number she'd given Jill.

Pulling away from Omar, she hand-signaled him to wait. She leaned against a column outside of a clothing store. "Jill?" she asked, answering the call.

"Something bad's coming," Jill said.

"I know."

"No, you don't. Darnell's a *psychic*."

"It doesn't work like that."

"You think I don't know how it 'works?'" Jill almost snarled. "It's been keeping him up, waking him up all night. Hitting him at work. His sixth sense is going crazy."

"There are a lot of spells targeting you, right now. Psychic attacks, dream magic, astral—"

"He *knows*," she spat the word like a curse. "Goddammit. Can't you just believe me?"

"I do. I do," Zoe soothed.

Omar watched, brow rucked.

"The kids are so scared," Jill whispered. "Someone follows Darnell to work some mornings. Sometimes I think someone follows us to the grocery store."

"Eat more delivery. Use more sick days."

"Like it's that easy."

"I'm putting things together," Zoe said. She didn't even know if she was lying or not.

"They're going to win."

Zoe changed tactics. "You and Darnell and Karen, use any sick days or PTO you've got. Anything you can do to limit interaction with the outside world. Keep reinforcing any wards and defenses you have. Next time you go to the grocery store, stock up."

"We can't just *wait*."

"Anything else you do will expose you to attack."

"So let them attack me."

Anger roughed Zoe's voice, "No! Goddammit, stop!"

"What!?"

"I can't—" (*lose you*), "I—I just…you're the best witch in that house. If you go down, if something happens, who's going to protect everyone else?"

"Darnell's a psychic and Karen—"

"This is their plan working," Zoe interrupted, feeling steel and sturdy again. "Take a step back and take a breath and think about it. This is part of how their plan works."

"Attrition," Jill agreed. "They grind us out."

"They want you to break down. They want you to do something severe and risky."

A brief silence lulled on Jill's end of the line. Jill broke it by clearing her throat. "We have to get the kids out of here," she whispered. "Tell me you get that."

"I do. And I'm putting together an extraction plan." Zoe waited for Jill to interrupt, but Jill didn't. Zoe considered her words before continuing. "I need to neutralize some of the more powerful spells targeting your school and handle some of the more intense surveillance. I just need to figure out how to get you from Point A to Point B without…anything happening."

"How soon?" Jill asked.

"Three or four weeks."

"Goddammit, Zo'…"

"It's the best I can do. And in the meantime, I'll do everything I can. Everything."

And who knew, maybe she even could.

"I'm sorry, I…" Jill sighed, the breath expressing too many emotions at once. "I'm just sorry. I thought I was out of that world but I guess nobody ever is and…and I just don't want all these other people to get hurt because of me. I don't want these *children* to get hurt."

"We'll do everything we can to stop that from happening. Just please… do whatever you can to stay inside."

"I love you, Zo'."

"I love you, too."

The call disconnected.

Omar hovered close to her. Some other time, years ago, he might've pulled her to him. But this wasn't that time, anymore. "It sounds like we have a lot of work to do."

Zoe sniffled and wiped backhanded at her nose. "You have no idea."

"Then let's get somewhere secure so you can give me one."

Wilmington, NC.

August, 1997.

Jill screamed again. Something heavy crashed against the floor upstairs.

In Zoe's hands, the TV turned off. She staggered back from it like a winded boxer.

She ran.

Every light in the house flickered and buzzed, flashing shadows on the walls. Whispers pressed up from the floorboards, too many overlapping phrases for any of them to make sense and all sharing a single voice. Zoe hammered the stairs up to the lounge on the left and passed it, passed two other bedroom doors, and crashed into Jill's.

"Jill!?" she shouted, rebounding from impact.

Jill shrieked and cried. Another heavy something slammed against the hardwood.

Zoe twisted the knob and put her shoulder into the door. No magic held it fast—it blew open and she plowed into the room, unbalanced from sheer momentum. It took her a couple clumsy strides to slow down.

Jill curled up behind a barricade of overturned furniture in the far corner of the room. In the center, painted symbols and Kosher salt formed a seal. Zoe felt a layer of wards crackling dome-like up from the seal's perimeter. In the center of it all, a small bag of heroin, a spoon, a rubber hose, and a butane lighter waited.

Jill's screams stopped, reduced to sobs. She shook, rattling her bones.

"What happened?" Zoe asked.

Jill gagged on a sob. Spat it out. "I can't live like this..."

"What happened?" Zoe repeated.

"What do you *think*?"

(*you know what the funniest thing is?*)

Zoe knelt on the other side of the busted-furniture barricade. "It was just a trick."

"I couldn't open the door. It wasn't locked I just couldn't open it. It wouldn't open."

"It's okay, now. I'm here."

"I just. I don't get it. How do people do it? *How*?"

Zoe felt like she'd missed part of the conversation. "Do...what?"

"How do people wake up and this is the world we live in? How do people look around for more than five minutes and not want all of this to go away?"

The junk in the middle of Jill's salt-circle bubbled and melted, oozing into a splat of tarry black. Zoe wondered, if she'd bound and sealed the pack of cloves she'd thrown down the garbage disposal, would it have become viscous, vantablack ejecta, too?

She blinked. Answering Jill, she said, "I don't know."

"I keep having this dream..." Jill had stopped sobbing and now just sounded tired. "And I keep thinking back, remembering. Jonathan didn't really kill himself, you know."

Zoe froze. "What?"

"It's the world. All the pressure and the pain people put you through not even on purpose but just because nobody cares, or just because they can. We know magic, Zo'...we should be able to save someone."

"You couldn't have done anything."

"Then who could've!?" Jill stood all-at-once with the words.

Zoe leapt up out of instinct. Hesitated. "I...I don't know."

"Everyone says that to everyone else until nobody has to be accountable. People were *monstrous* to him. So many people treated him like so much shit and all of them are still out there just living their lives telling themselves there was nothing anybody could have done. But they piled on the rocks, they piled on the rocks until the rocks fucking crushed him."

(*what kind of psycho piles rocks on*)

(*today's in-class activity*)

Zoe didn't know what to say. Maybe there wasn't anything.

"I don't want to be here, anymore," Jill whispered. Furniture scraped hardwood as she pushed her way through her makeshift barricade. "Here needs to be different or I need to be somewhere else, but I can't...I just can't."

"Yeah, well. Too bad."

"Jesus. Could you please *not*?"

"I—I'm sorry. I sounded like dad for a second."

"You did," Jill confirmed.

A beat passed.

Jill continued, "Have I ever said...I think Sung-ho's been a good, you know, a good influence for you?"

Zoe chuckled. "Yeah, you've said it. In front of dad."

Jill's face shrank into a pucker of surprise. "Oh shit. Was I...?"

"You were."

"Oh."

Zoe shrugged. "Fuck him." Paused. "You're my only sister, you know."

"Uh...yeah?"

"Just. You can't leave me alone with these psychos."

Jill laughed. "I won't. I just—"

"It's fine. You're not wrong. About the world, I mean." An overturned bookshelf groaned as Zoe turned it upright. "Maybe...maybe you can start some of your research again, if it helps. *After* Sung-ho gets here."

Jill shifted uncomfortably, foot to foot. "You're sure?"

"After Sung-ho," Zoe repeated. "But, yeah. I'm sure. Now," she turned to her sister with an almost-real smile painted on her face, "care to give me a hand? Something really tore this place apart."

Oceanrest, ME.

January, 2007.

Zoe couldn't sleep. She rarely could in the lead-up to a run. Everyone knew how much a good night's sleep helped a witch in the field but nobody knew how to stop adrenaline. And so, hours after everyone else had punched the clock, she sat in Sung-ho's den nursing a double-whiskey and trying to smoke herself into rest-adjacent catatonia.

Leaning back in the cozy vastness of Sung-ho's chair, she listened to Blind Willie Johnson wonder about the Soul of a Man. Halfway through the night's second joint, she blew smoke at the ceiling.

"Zoe?" Omar asked, just outside the door.

"Yeah. Come in."

He walked in wearing pajamas and slippers.

"Couldn't sleep?" Zoe exhaled smoke into the haze.

"Something like that."

"Have a seat. You want a smoke?" Zoe took her feet off the desk and sat up. She'd rolled another joint but hadn't gotten around to smoking it.

"Sure." Omar sat, taking the joint when Zoe offered it. "So…

tomorrow."

"Tomorrow," Zoe echoed.

"What happens if something goes wrong?"

Zoe set her own joint along the edge of the ashtray. She picked her Zippo up from the mess, cracked it, flicked the flint, and held the flame over the desk toward Omar. As he leaned in, she spoke. "That depends on which thing goes wrong."

He took a small puff and eased back into the chair. "What happens if I die?"

She clapped the Zippo shut. "You probably won't. The bombs are simple, the spells around them, weak."

"But *what if?*"

Was that what kept her awake, too?

She cleared her throat. "There are protocols for that kind of thing. Scripts. As soon as the…" she almost said 'company,' but stopped herself. "As soon as the society knows there's an active casualty, they'll send an emergency anti-personnel team. There won't be anyone with the skill that me or Sung-ho have, but there'll be six of them and they'll have orders to kill the Summoner on sight. Another agent, someone like me, will disassemble any remaining magic and re-stage the deaths to match mundanity decay. Whatever doesn't raise questions."

"What happens with my mom?"

"Someone who *looks* federal will show up at her door and tell her you died serving your country or your community or something like that. They'll say that because of the *special role* you played, she's eligible for a lifelong stipend."

"Hush money."

Zoe shrugged. "Still spends. Two hundred dollars a week until the day she dies."

Omar nodded. Took another hit.

Zoe plucked her joint back up from the edge of the ashtray. "I have news, by the way."

"For who?"

"Me and Sung-ho talked to a friend of ours. Someone higher up. We found out just after dinner — you've been granted Class-E intel clearance. And if you're still interested in this fucked up little shadow-world of ours, we can get you into training."

"So when do I start?"

Zoe noised an amused 'hm.' "I didn't think you were in a joking mood."

"I'm not," Omar confirmed.

"Give it some thought. Once you're about a year into training, there's no way back out again."

"Back out of what?"

"All of it. *Any* of it. The magic, the monsters metaphorical and otherwise…once you sign on, you sign on to everything. The assignments, the hierarchy, the politics. Everything. And once you're far enough in, they won't let you leave."

Omar stared for a second, watching. Then he blinked. Leaned forward. "I'm already in. I went to a ski lodge with some friends and fucking shadow-monsters attacked us. I almost lost my mind, almost lost it in a way I never thought I could. And now I'm a suspect in the attack because nobody remembers or believes in shadow-monsters. So how am I not already 'in?'"

"This is different."

"Damn right it is. The difference is, people like you know what's coming. And how to fight it."

Zoe re-lit the joint and took a shallow puff. "This life…it's a maze of glass. Once you're sure that magic exists, you can't be sure of anything else ever. When is a car crash just a car crash, after all? And when is it the result of an accretion of hexes and curses, probability fields micro-adjusted until one of them became inevitable? Because once mundanity sets in, the end result looks the same. So we're all locked into this little world where reality itself is uncertain, where we can't really tell the difference between the walls and the floor and the ceiling, where we can't see a dead end straight ahead of us unless the light hits it just right. Sometimes people get cancer and sometimes cancer is incurably vicious, but the right magic can *give* someone incurable cancer. It's a lot of work and really not worth it, but it's possible. Knowing that means that I always have to wonder. Realistically, I'll rarely ever know. So I just keep my hands out and try not to get too far from the walls, in case I lose them, and I pray I never need to sprint because when something really chases you in the maze, if you really have to run, sooner or later you'll hit a dead end, another pane of glass you couldn't see because the light didn't hit it the right way…and by the time you realize you've crashed face-first through a dead-end of slivered glass, the shards of your fuck-up will already have shred the skin from your bones."

Omar took a long drag. A slight smirk found its way onto his face. "You worked on that for a long time, huh?"

Zoe let herself chuckle. "I did, yeah."

"Why?"

"I don't know. I guess…nobody ever warned me. I never really even had a choice."

"I'm sorry to hear that," he said. "I really am. But from where I'm sitting, man, I'm already in the maze. I know the shit exists; I'll know it for the rest of my life. And if the cost of learning how to deal with it is having someone remind me that I'm locked in, once in a while, that's a price I'm willing to pay."

For a few seconds they sat in silence, hazy the air between them.

Zoe cleared her throat. "Alright, then. If you still feel that way after the run, I'll send them your answer."

"Thank you."

Maybe it was Omar's earnest tone, the sincerity of his words; maybe it was the cannabis haze and warmglow lighting of Sung-ho's office; maybe it was the weeks spent in constant proximity — it was something, in any case — but as Zoe lifted the joint to her lips for another hit, she suddenly realized that Omar was surprisingly *handsome*. Attractive in a way she hadn't noticed previously. The cherry burnt back almost to her fingertips and she held her breath for a long moment before exhaling. She coughed harshly, twice, and crushed the roach in the ashtray. "I'm not high enough for this," she muttered.

"You're telling me," Omar replied.

She laughed, shaking her head, and didn't correct him. Picking through the crowded desktop, she instead asked, "Where did I put the damn papers?"

Chapter Fifteen

Wilmington, NC.

August, 1997.

According to the grimoire, the Proclamation was the easiest part of the ritual.

Zoe prayed that held true.

They'd started preparations three days after they'd put Jill's bedroom back together. Jill reinforced the old wards and put up new ones. She handled routine summonings and banishments, inviting nearby interlopers in, sealing them, and flinging them off into nowhere again. Zoe worked on the Proclamation itself, a massive series of interlocked invocation and psychic spells allegedly meant to strengthen them for the final phase of the ritual.

On the bright side, preparing for the Proclamation took time. It was labor-intensive. The work left them with only a few, exhausted minutes per day to itch and fiend.

They put the finishing touches on the preparation at dusk, after their dinner and before their nightly meditations. They rested.

Before the moon reached its zenith, before it shone its brightest, they regrouped in the ritual space. Jill sat cross-legged in the center of a salt sigil.

Between the granular angles, dozens of smaller glyphs rested in white paint. Jill peered up through the skylight. The curtain of the cosmos seemed to roil and warp beyond the lunar glow.

Across the room, Zoe stood in a similar protective circle, parallel to Jill, before a makeshift altar (a music stand) which held the open grimoire. "Are you ready?" she asked.

"I am prepared," Jill replied, still staring at the moon.

Immediately, voices began whispering under the floorboards. The shadows thrown by lit candelabra shivered and stalked. The electric light spilling in from the open door flickered. The dimness surrounding the threshold pulsed and quivered.

"Are you prepared to seek that within yourself that drives you toward damnation?" Zoe read the words from the book.

"I seek the counsel of my fellow practitioners and make plea to the secret and sacred energies of this world for strength." Jill intoned, bathed in moonlight.

"Speak the names of your most scabrous flaws, speak the names of the wounds that carved them into you."

"I am selfish, tired, and easily hurt. I lash out. I lie and steal. I hurt people without even thinking about it. My wounds are the very knives of this world, its cruelty without reason."

"Where did your downfall begin?" Zoe asked.

"After Jonathan killed himself, some of his older friends invited me over to their apartment. They were doing heroin, mostly just snorting it at the time, and I wasn't sure but they wouldn't stop asking me if I wanted to do it and I knew they wouldn't stop until my answer was 'yes' so I did it. And I loved it. And I have been finding it at all costs ever since."

The electric light flickered and buzzed. The candelabra flared. Shadows unstuck themselves from the angled darkness. They moved sinuously around the room's perimeter, stalking, waiting. Magic crackled in the air. A faint scent of hot ozone tickled Zoe's nose.

"Do you commit to mastering yourself?" Zoe asked.

"I seek the counsel of my fellow practitioners. I make a plea to the secret and sacred energies of the universe. I commit to discipline and meditation, I commit to the first step and the second. I will master myself."

"As above, so below," Zoe said.

"As above, so below," Jill repeated.

A tremor shuddered through the floor. The sky behind the moon changed. The air grew humid with potential. Every tiny hair on Zoe's body straightened out. A scab of darkness reached across the door to the room and blocked out the electric glow from beyond. "What are the first vows of your transfiguration?"

"I have control of my thoughts. I seek the counsel of my fellow practitioners and the strength of the secret and sacred energies. I will banish my temptation and soothe my anguish. Through my thoughts, I control my actions. I will maintain the clarity of my vessel. I will master myself."

"As above, so below," Zoe said.

"As above, so below."

The shades charged at them from the room perimeter.

Their claws bled blurry black and their teeth sputtered gray dimness. Thirteen of them stampeded from the dancing dark, all of them twist-contorting around light and shadow. They stopped just a foot away from the salt circles, six on Zoe and seven on Jill. They held ranks in perfect circumference, hissing and whispering in other people's voices.

"You'll never be free of this," one of them snarled.

"Never."

Zoe gasped at the suddenness of their movement. The momentary panic affected the ritual, her strength and fearlessness a part of the magic. The ward keeping the shades at bay weakened, a scratch in its surface.

"We can do this," Jill whispered, staring solely at Zoe.

Zoe swallowed, nodded. She braced herself against the music stand, focused on the grimoire. "As your fellow practitioner," she cleared her throat, worried her voice might break, "I promise you my guidance and my counsel. May the secret and sacred energies connect us always."

"I lean upon your strength as I confront my weaknesses and wounds. As above, so below."

The candelabra flared. The shades snarled and rasped. A pack of cloves appeared on the music stand.

Zoe stepped back.

Salt crunched beneath her boot heel. She froze. The shades lurched forward several inches all-at-once. A long hiss breathed up from the floorboards. The air reeked of burning ozone. Energy hummed through the walls. A phlegmatic snicker rolled through the room.

No pack of cigarettes waited on the music stand. Only the grimoire, open.

"As above, so below," Zoe repeated.

Jill disappeared. In the blink of an eye, gone.

The candelabra all went out. An unnatural light bathed Zoe, glowing up from the circumference of her protective circle. As she stared breathless and wide-eyed across the room, Jill's circle started glowing, too. In the center of the angled lines, a lunchbox opened to a bag of crumbled heroin, a butane lighter, a spoon.

Jill had disappeared. Zoe stared.

All around her, shades snickered and snarled. They rasped and whispered in voices not their own.

"We know *magic*, Zo'," one of them muttered. "We should be able to save someone."

"Never," another snapped. "*Never.*"

Zoe pulled the clove from between her lips (how had it gotten there?) and dropped it to the floor. From her pocket, she withdrew the Zippo she hadn't put there that morning. She hinged open the top.

Would the little flame keep the monsters away?

She pursed her lips, breathing hard. Sweat rolled down her forehead.

She had to cross the room. Didn't she? Of course she did. Because her fearlessness was part of the magic.

And these things scared her.

Unless it was a trap. But her thinking it was a trap might be a trap in and of itself. She squeezed the real-not-real lighter. Only a dozen feet stewed in the darkness between her ward and Jill's. She could make that. Couldn't she?

The flint sparked. She squeezed her eyelids shut. Inhaled.

Oceanrest, ME.

January, 2007.

The old slaughterhouse sat three miles northwest of the Asher farmstead proper, itself five miles northwest from Squatter City, itself eight miles northeast of Sung-ho's house—as the crow flew, at least. As the car drove, the path somewhat longer, it took Zoe and Sung-ho just under forty-five minutes to make the trip. They parked in the afternoon sun a mile north of the abattoir and approached from there on foot.

Wilderness held dominion. Civilization had abandoned the region northwest of Highway-1 and the dense Hancock county forests had seized it. Angled deciduous trunks and conifer needles spiked the earth, and tangles of bush and brush garlanded the ground. Winter whited all of it, burying the pine greens and dusting over the rest of the naked branches. Tall, dead grass poked up from the snow and bent back down to it again.

They found an old hiking trail near the potholed backroad they'd parked on and followed it half the distance to the slaughterhouse, their boots crunching ice with every step. From there, they trudged through ankle- and sometimes shin-deep snow until they saw it.

Little remained of the old Asher slaughterhouse. Time and the elements had pulled the perimeter fence apart, strangling boards of wood and rusted steel with branches and ivy.

Descending the gentle slope toward the abattoir, they pulled ventilated facemasks over their noses and mouths. The masks filtered air, reducing the potential effectiveness of any biological or gas-based attacks, including those of a mystical nature; they also minimized whatever stench might still linger in that ancient derelict of death. Even so, the sense-enhancing invocations they'd undertaken that morning gave Zoe enough scent and sixth-sense to pick up traces of senescence and fear.

Most of the animal guiding rails were gone, leaving only spans of white between the different herding and slaughtering structures, all of which sagged and rubbled, demolished by a decade of untended Maine winters. They approached slow and low, eyes wide and sweeping, invocation-enhanced, ears prickling, invocation- and mil-tech earbud-enhanced. The helmet shielding the rear and top of Zoe's head swamped with humidity, hot sweat bristling on the back of her neck.

"No movement," Sung-ho said.

"Let's advance there," Zoe gestured to the half-splintered building farthest from them. "Clear our way to the interior."

Sung-ho bobbed his head. "Advance."

They moved along the wreck of the perimeter toward the far corner. The wind pushed something rusted; a metal groan echoed out from inside. Zoe's sixth-sense pulsed a steady stream of adrenaline through her veins. A threat lurked nearby, waiting. Somewhere.

"Hold." Sung-ho grabbed her arm.

"What?"

"Hold," he repeated, almost inaudible. He squinted, scanning the wreck ahead. Muffled through his mask, he sniffed. He unholstered his sidearm. "It's too bright with the snow."

Zoe's skin crawled with sixth-sense instinct. She unholstered her pistol, too. "Let's advance. We're in the open, here."

"No. Wait."

"Why?"

(*you'll smell it first you smell it first you*)

"Just…" Sung-ho trailed off.

Something stirred in the shadows of the half-collapsed building ahead. A sheet of white dusted free as a mutated silhouette huffed and shrugged itself up from the ground. Slowly, Sung-ho let go of Zoe's arm. Zoe thumbed off her pistol's safety lever. The Construct, whatever it was, hoofed at the dirt and snorted. It shuffled in the dimness, hidden less by the dark than by the brightness glaring off the snow.

"We should have requisitioned bigger guns," Zoe whispered.

"You should have said something yesterday," Sung-ho muttered back.

Armory requisitions processed quickly for active-assignment agents, they just hadn't filed one. There'd been too much else going on.

"Are you guys alright out there?" Jill's voice whispered through the mil-tech earbuds.

Zoe pressed the helmet mechanism to transmit her mic. "Shh."

Jill shushed.

"Change course?" Zoe suggested.

Sung-ho raised his eyebrows. From their position crouched in brush-cover, both of them could see only a yawning, dangerous span of property between themselves and the slaughterhouse proper. Little protection existed if the monsters started multiplying. Worse, assuming the Summoner expected some kind of attack or raid, he could easily watch their approach across the open space.

"Okay, so there's no other course. What's *your* idea?"

Sung-ho grinned, opening his cross-body gig kit. "I left a spare mag out of the kit so I could fit a grenade, instead."

"You brought a grenade?"

He shrugged.

She'd switched a spare mag out, too. Jill had given her a vial of glossy black movement, a swirling something caught inside. Inked glyphs and sigils covered its surface in four stacks. Jill had told her only to use it if the Summoner somehow got the upper hand.

The monster hoofed the ground and snorted, again. Its unclear mass edged closer to the light. Zoe estimated it at eight feet tall, eight feet long, and five feet wide, front- and top-heavy. When it neared the edge of its shelter, it sniffed. The sound echoed. Zoe frowned. How?

But when it nosed into the sun, the answer became obvious. It hadn't been an echo. It had been a dozen different snouts scenting not-quite-simultaneously.

An unclear number of boar and swine corpses made up the creature's face, piled up and speared together, outfitted with rebar tusks. A steel skeleton supported their heft, itself armed with four jabbing, cattle-prod arms. Below, a grinding mass of cow legs steered the beast.

It reeked. Magic had given it life but not enough. Already, strips of skin hung loose from the thing, and some of the regenerated carcasses already bloated with gas. The livelier ones gnawed and gnashed at the air hungrily.

They'd renewed their invocations that morning. All the spells bolstering their stamina, speed, reflexes, endurance, and even their hearing and eyesight buzzed at their most optimal. Jill and Sung-ho had handled basic defensive wards, magic that reduced the velocities and impact forces of incoming damage, another giving them a blurred appearance to anyone or anything that saw them. It all gave them a distinct advantage.

It made them think, move, and react more quickly than normal. But it didn't make them superheroes. It didn't make them geniuses or Olympians.

The monster huffed again, stepping into the light. It scented the air and searched for a source with half-gone, rot-melting eyes.

Sung-ho took a bright cylinder from his kit and grabbed a pin at the top.

"Thermite?" Zoe asked.

"From work," he affirmed, winking.

"Wait."

He waited.

"After we hit the big fucker, there'll be smaller ones. We'll have to fight our way inside. And if that thing doesn't go down fast enough, it'll—"

Zoe had more to say but the beast noticed them, then, and its centipedal swarm of cow legs stampeded their way.

Chapter Sixteen

Oceanrest, ME.

January, 2007.

The grenade exploded on descent, spraying napalm all over the charging beast.

As gelatinous burn sizzled through enlivened corpses, Zoe and Sung-ho leapt from the overgrown brush. They stayed close to the mess of tangle and nettle, the gnarled twigs and reaching branches obscured by the snow. The monster kept coming, the livelier corpses composing its body squealing and cooking. The longer-dead ones merely huffed air through decomposed throats, the flame-bright ooze eating through skin to gas and putrescence.

From their position on the other side of the foliage, Zoe and Sung-ho opened fire.

For the most part, Constructs died. Architectural damage that immobilized them worked fastest and best, but when uncountable cow legs served as the monster's locomotion, disabling it seemed unlikely. Luckily, magic seemed to understand that anything existing could be made to not-exist through methods of force, so most Constructs usually died after extreme enough applications of violence.

Some particularly powerful outliers, however, operated as functionally-unkillable, often with no exterior feature to differentiate them from more mortal opponents. So when her first, fourteen-round, extended mag ejected from her sidearm, Zoe decided she didn't have enough intel to continue an offensive. "Advance!" she shouted.

Some of the cow legs and rebar-tusks tangled in the brush. The monster shook itself, burning and squealing and still shifting its weight back and forth, breaking free. Drips of napalm singed through winter-dry tangles. Cattle prods shocked the air. Pigs shrieked.

"Come on!" She grabbed Sung-ho's arm and turned.

More mutant figures clambered up from the ground in uneven drifts of snow. Most looked small, two or three animals workshopped together, but several stood man-sized, animated scarecrows and sackcloth-bodies stuffed with meat.

A dozen such monsters rose up and shuffled around the field between them and the slaughterhouse.

Zoe slapped in her first backup mag. She had two, plus Jill's vial-of-something and a combat knife. Sung-ho also had two, but what else?

"Break left," Sung-ho said.

Pigs screamed and boars huffed. Pork-smoke and corpse-stink billowed the air. Brush snapped, hooves stomped.

They raced toward the slaughterhouse through ankle-deep snow. Zoe estimated the span at thirty meters, thirty open meters across poor terrain. She dodged around a remnant of steel fence and something lunged at her from her glare-blind periphery. Recognizing only that it was *not Sung-ho*, she fired four bullets into the center mass of the thing and spun back toward the abattoir.

A gunshot blasted the snow a foot ahead of her. She broke left. A second shot patted somewhere behind her. Her thighs burned. "Shooter!" she shouted— or screamed—the difference no longer certain. "Dead ahead!"

"Here!" Sung-ho shout-screamed back.

She banked according to echolocation. Another shot blew through brush-cover ahead of her. Back behind her, the pigs grew quieter and the groan of the monster's mass snapping free of its tangles grew louder. A rifle-crack thundered. It didn't hit her but she didn't know if it hit anything else. A burst of small-arms fire chattered ahead of her and she ran toward it.

She found Sung-ho crouched behind a pile of rust-wrecked parts, reloading.

"Down to one," he said, wiping sweat from his face. "This fucking helmet…"

The humidity slimed her, too. Her hair felt like a bundle of grease slathered against her scalp. "He's got sights…not sure where…"

"We can't stay here forever."

Crouching next to him, she squinted through bright white toward the next piece of cover. There wasn't much. Another twelve meters ahead she saw the ramped entryway to the slaughterhouse, the alley they'd once marched animals through to their deaths. "I think we have to make another rush, a sprint straight at it."

Sung-ho squinted with her. "Goddammit."

"On three?"

"Mm."

"One…two…"

They didn't pause for target assessment, they just ran. Something lunged at Zoe and she fired another four rounds, shoved it away, and kept running. A rifle-shot struck the ground ahead of them and they broke away from each other. Zoe slowed fractionally to give Sung-ho a lead. A bullet blew through the air in front of her and she renewed her pace.

The Summoner must have lost his line of sight, at that point. No further rifle-fire followed them.

But cow hooves did.

"Faster!" Zoe shouted.

Something lunged at Sung-ho with a cow's head and stilt-legs, buzzsaw-armed. Sung-ho ducked the swinging blades and shouldered the Construct aside. It stumbled and re-oriented but he'd already dawn sights. He opened fire and Zoe followed suit. They each put four bullets into the thing and it went down. Ahead, another grotesquery blocked them from the slaughterhouse entrance.

Without hesitation, they both turned their pistols toward it.

It lunged at them, a coiled-wire skeleton and eight wriggling limbs tipped with automatic carving tools. Garlands of meat and fused parts gave it a torso and joints. They aimed for the center mass of the thing, hoping the repeating combination of armor piercing and frangible rounds would shred it apart.

And they did, but not before the thing had reached Sung-ho. Two blades notched slender gaps in the side of his helmet and several more carved ribbons of fiber from his armor. Sung-ho pushed himself back. Zoe didn't see any blood.

Before the monster could do more harm, it stumbled backward and fell to pieces.

Zoe ejected her spent mag. "You okay?"

"Fine!" Sung-ho ran for the entrance, limping.

The cow hooves thundered, now. Too close.

They hadn't seen it through the snowglare, but a barricade of plywood shored the entryway. Pulling a loose corner wide, Sung-ho crouched and peered within. Zoe caught up and glanced behind them. The charred and still-bubbling monster-Construct teetered toward them. It had lost some of its legs but didn't seem to care. "In, in!"

Sung-ho rolled inside. Zoe followed.

Inside the dim-dark building, rows of steel fence guided them toward assembly-line machinery. Without scanning for more than basic terrain, Zoe grabbed Sung-ho's arm and hauled him with her. They rushed through the guideways. Behind them, the rebar-tusked monster crashed through the plywood.

It didn't slow down.

Screaming, Zoe sprinted. Her legs ached, molten and collapsing. Her shoulder clipped a gap in the steel fence and she let go of Sung-ho. She spun toward him but he gestured for her to keep moving. Blurry, behind him, the monster crashed through sections of fence and knocked over barricades, pursuing.

She *sprinted*.

She lost balance, bounced against a rusted piece of fence, rebounded from more steel on the opposite side, and swallowed ragged gut-filling gulps of air as the monster barreled through architecture like a bull through paper walls. She fell to her hands and knees. Sung-ho caught up. He shouted something she didn't hear over the keening racket of the Construct rampaging through the rusted maze toward them.

Sung-ho had her halfway to her feet when the monster stopped moving.

The reeking behemoth had speared itself to death; broken rails and shards of barricade gored through it, chunks of fence skewered it. Many of its load-bearing cow legs had snapped or broken in the chase. The near-magma thermite had seared and melted its top portion into a stink of charred and rancid meat.

It heaved one final *whuff* of rotten air, pushed itself forward one more foot, and went limp. The cow legs splintered beneath the platform. The porcine carcasses composing its body tumbled and sloughed loose from each other. One of the rebar tusks, machine-sharpened and grimed with blood, pointed at Zoe from only a yard away.

"Keep moving," Sung-ho panted, helping her the rest of the way to her feet. "Before it starts to *really* smell."

Zoe slapped in her spare mag. Nodded.

They moved. The guidelanes narrowed to an assembly line killing floor. They followed the murderous alley to an unlit intersection, their invocations making the boarded-up darkness visible. Mold, fungi, and dust plastered every surface. The abandoned slaughterhouse had already begun its transformation, fruiting a new environment through its dereliction, becoming the thing it would one day become.

(*everything becomes something else eventually*)

"Team B?" Zoe asked.

"At site four. I'm getting tired but the magic's nothing I can't handle. There is another problem…"

"This bomb," Omar's voice piped in, "it doesn't look like the others."

She glanced over at Sung-ho. Sung-ho nodded.

She said, "If it comes down to it, leave."

"What?" he asked.

"Like you said, this isn't your job. If the risk gets too high, bail."

A long pause. She felt Omar thinking.

"We're going quiet," she said. "Over."

The intersection split the structure into two wings. Ahead, the continued butcher's alley led to faint outlines of maybe-lockers; to the right, scores of unused meathooks dangled from the ceiling, a wire-fenced window peered across bright white snow, and another left turn led…somewhere.

Toward the Summoner, in any case.

They conversed with gestures. They decided that Zoe would turn right and move through the span of meathooks, that she'd take the next intersection and find out where it led. Sung-ho would take the avenue straight-ahead, through a hundred forgotten years of slaughter to the lockers and whatever else waited beyond them. If more Constructs guarded the halls, they'd keep track of each other through echolocation, gunfire and radio chatter.

They split up.

Wilmington, NC.

August, 1997.

The music stand hit the floor as Zoe sprinted past it, eyes shut. She leapt over a table and prayed she landed where she'd hoped to land. She didn't open her eyes to check. All around her, snarls and hisses filled the air. Claws raked at her clothes, tearing fabric. Shallow cuts peeled skin from her sides. She dropped the real-not-real Zippo and dove forward.

She landed in salt. And then—

She fell. Darkness surrounded her. Wind whipped past her ears. Her hair danced away from her scalp. She put an arm out ahead of her as if that would stop her from splattering all over the place whenever her terminal velocity suddenly ceased.

She landed, didn't explode, and rolled onto her side. Black floor, black walls, black ceiling. She barely saw a foot in front of her. All around: lightlessness.

"Help!" Jill shouted, her voice a directionless echo through unknown halls.

Zoe crashed into a wall. The stonework came to life, squirming wetly into a limb. It lashed out, all claws, and barely missed. Zoe felt the breeze of it against her nose. She stumbled backwards. She had mystically-enhanced sight and she couldn't *see*.

"Help!" Jill cried again. Her voice sounded more ragged, now.

Zoe held up the Zippo—which she remembered dropping but somehow still had—and moved through the dimness. Ink rolled down the walls. Her shoes squicked over slick ground. Even with the flame, eyesight-invocation be damned, she saw only four feet ahead.

"The world wins," a gravelly rasp insisted. "The world always wins."

"We have magic," an ovular, inhuman head oozed out of the wall next to Zoe; Its Jill-like voice made her jump. The visage wore neither eyes nor nose, only a gaping mouth of layered fangs and angled incisors. Its bloated, purple tongue pulsed between green gums. "We should be able to save someone."

"Never," an echo invited Zoe deeper into the labyrinth. "*Never.*"

(*every story*)

"Oh my god, help!" Jill shrieked, closer now.

"Under the surface there's nothing," the gravelly voice taunted. "Under everything there's just *me*!"

Zoe moved forward, breath coming hard and hot through her nose. Loud, too. The Zippo flame wavered. It glowed along the viscous dripping rocks, the damp everything. Stone bubbled tar-like, eyes and fingers and mouths bobbing to the surface and sinking down again. Zoe came to a four-way intersection and froze, ears burning.

"Come on, Jill, one more shout..."

She waited. It worried her that she didn't hear anything.

Something roughed against the earthen floor behind her. She spun around, the Zippo almost going out with the sudden motion. Squinting into the four feet of visibility she had, she saw nothing. Darkness moved against darkness. Another roughness echoed out. Her palms moistened with sweat. Beads of it drooled down her face.

She couldn't get Jill out of there if she didn't move.

She had to *move*.

Which way?

The thing scraping toward her found its footing—or whatever method it used for locomotion. It lunged at her from the darkness and it, itself, was so dark that she could barely understand its shape. She threw an arm up against a shelf-like limb, blocking its descent toward her, and drove a kick into whatever approximated the monster's center mass. It slid backward, semi-gelatinous. She spun away and fled.

A tremor shook the labyrinth. Stones tumbled from the ceiling. Several crashed on Zoe's shoulders, on her back—a small one cracked off the top of her head before tumbling away. The Zippo went out and she crashed into a wall, rebounded, and kept running. Limbs lashed out from all sides. They clawed her kevlar down to the shirt; ripped the fabric down to her skin. Thin cuts trickled claret.

"Jill!" she called out. "Jill, where are you!?"

The ground fell away beneath her. It tumbled into a rockslide. Zoe leapt away from it and flew into—

She stood in front of the music stand. The ritual space crawled with shadows. On the other side of the room, Jill's sigil lay ruined, salt sprayed all over the floor. A creature exactly Jill's shape but seemingly constructed from sizzling viscous *something* bore down over Jill, skin dripping off of its hands. Its always-sloughing-never-gone fingers found Jill's throat and slowly wrapped around.

Zoe blinked, breathless from everything that had or hadn't just happened.

"The world always wins," a shade whispered, behind her.

Her hand shook around the Zippo that wasn't really there.

She didn't look.

Jill roused on the floor. She kicked, seeing her inky-tar clone craned over her. Jill punched at the Jill-clone Manifestation's sides while the Manifestation remained stolid and still. Zoe saw Jill's blows weaken one by one...

"Always," the shade echoed, its cold-as-corpses breath against the back of Zoe's neck.

Jill tried to buck against the dark-mirror reflection of herself but got nowhere.

Zoe pushed aside the music stand and charged.

A chorus of shrieks rose up around her. A whirlwind of appendages whipped out from the dark. She dove for the Manifestation's sizzling flesh. Cloth ripped from skin ripped from muscle; shots of anguish sliced her back like a dozen starving whips. She screamed, crashing into the Manifestation. Their bodies plunged into a sigil and—

Zoe rocked back, still standing in front of the grimoire.

Across the room, Jill sat folded in her protective circle.

Both of them panted, sweaty and breathless, clothes soaked. Distant, near-phantom pains ached along Zoe's back and sides, wounds that hadn't really happened but, in a way, also had. The sensation dissipated quickly.

Zoe blinked, searched for her place on the page. "I promise to you my strength and my counsel. I vow to buttress you and carry you, I vow to lend my aid whenever and always. I steel myself to this will. As above, so below."

Jill wiped sheets of sweat from her brow. "As above, so below," she whispered.

All the interlocking spells of the Proclamation triggered. Invocations and psychic wards fused through their bones. Blessings electrified them. Good luck charms, spiritual protections, and physical power; a dozen spells wormed through them all at once. The candelabra flared.

The magic reached its apex. The mysticism fused with them.

So much energy thrummed through the room, editing reality, that it lifted Zoe off the ground. She floated with her toes just an inch above the floor.

The Proclamation took. It activated, infused them, and settled.

Zoe landed gently back on the ground. "Whew, okay," she muttered, wiping sweat backhanded from her brow. "Not so bad, after all. Right?"

Jill chuckled, too drained for real laughter.

Then all the lights went out at once and all the windows shattered.

Oceanrest, ME.

January, 2007.

Zoe crept across the slaughterhouse floor, eyes roving constantly. Muffled by structure and distance, she heard Sung-ho fire several rounds elsewhere in the building.

"Constructs present," Sung-ho whispered through her earbud.

Lips pursed, she moved up to the next intersection. Across from her, a wire-fenced window looked out on the open span of rough terrain they'd crossed earlier. The Summoner had probably taken his potshots at them from somewhere along the hallway to her left…

Pressing her back against the wall, she listened.

Something scraped steel-on-cement just a few feet away. It huffed inhumanly.

Zoe took the turn gun-first.

A rust-toothed bear trap gaped in front of her—even with her invocations, she didn't notice it soon enough to stop her momentum. But, thanks to her invocations, she noticed it soon enough to jump over it.

She landed two feet from another of the Summoner's monstrous

Constructs. A servo-mounted pig's head stared at her with cataracted eyes. Its mechanical body whirred; two jerry-rigged arm-blades slashed at the air. Zoe strafed sideways as the Construct sawed toward her. The uneven edges tore at her leather jacket and bit into the armor beneath. Shreds and flakes of material trailed Zoe as she made distance. When she turned around, she fired four bullets into its center mass, an under-servo vat squelching with wires and rancid meat.

The bullet-resistant shielding encasing the Construct's innards warped around the first three bullets and cracked at the fourth. Shards flaked away from a growing gap; softmeat unfolded like a ribbon from the wound. Mixed oil and blood oozed out. The sawing blade-arms jerked unevenly, ninety degrees one way, ninety degrees another, never completing a swing. A pitched mechanical whir mixed with irregular snoutish huffs. It lurched toward Zoe again, undeterred.

Zoe easily backed away from its clumsy shuffle. Watching it move, she noticed its nub-like legs, its top-heavy design. As it spasmed toward her, weapons only half-mobile, she put two more rounds into its meat-wire vat and charged. She put her shoulder into the thing and it fell. One of its saw-arms chewed at the top of her boot but didn't even cut through to her shin guard. She stepped back, panting. It lashed around on the floor, bleeding, until one of its arms snapped into the waiting bear trap.

The thing went still.

Somewhere in the distance, Sung-ho fired four more rounds.

A rifle returned fire.

Zoe spun. Froze. Almost stepped in another bear trap.

Catching her suddenly-gone breath, she crept around the rusted teeth and kept moving.

"I can't—I can't do this," Omar crackled in her ear.

"So bail," she whispered back.

"I just—"

"*Bail*," she stressed, not-quite-whispering. "And keep comms silent."

She muted the relay, entering another room she couldn't figure out the use of, a vast chamber with a clutch of small offices in one corner. She searched her surroundings for another threat. Found nothing.

Another exchange of bullets echoed through the walls, louder.

She spun toward the noise and picked up pace.

A living scarecrow lunged out of the darkness toward her. She threw her shoulder into it as it came and they rebounded from each other. The scarecrow pinwheeled from the momentum and rushed back toward her. Zoe squeezed the trigger and four gunshots roared. Tufts of hay and sinewy organ-meat burst out of the Construct.

It closed distance in an instant and slashed at her with one clawed hand, raking leather and armor and skin. Zoe felt the sting of blood meeting air in narrow scratches across her chest. She backpedaled, making space to raise her pistol, and the scarecrow swung again. It missed as she leapt back, caught in its own momentum.

Zoe set her sights and fired. Lead shred the scarecrow, scouring ichor and stuffing from its innards. The Construct fell to its knees, half its legs unraveling. It lifted one clawed hand feebly toward her and collapsed.

Two bullets left. She had two bullets left. Which meant—

"Drop the gun!" someone shouted in the distance. Someone not Sung-ho. "Now! Now!"

She ran as quickly as she could. The smoking caught up to her. All the earlier exertion, the combat, the demands all the invocations put on her body—it all caught up. A cramp sliced through her side. Her gait destabilized.

"I said put down the fucking gun!"

The voice sounded meters away, through one wall.

She rushed down the hallway, searching for a way through. A few yards ahead, a dead Construct began to dissipate and collapse in the center of an intersection. Steadying herself against the wall, she fumbled at her kit, moved as quickly as the breathlessness and the cramp allowed.

Even closer, now: "Five! Four!—"

Chapter Seventeen

Wilmington, NC.

September, 1997.

Nothing happened after the power surge. The bulbs all blew, the windows exploded shardly outward—but nothing else happened. The next morning, Zoe felt the Gateway open.

The Gateway only lasted for two days, so they acted quickly.

They didn't have time to repair all the glass, of course, so they bought plywood and two-by-fours and nailed up barricades at all the broken windows. They bought panicked-people volumes of canned and frozen goods—their diet for the next nine days purely vegetarian and most produce being spoilable—and stocked up on paper goods, flashlight batteries, candles (votive and otherwise), and other essential miscellany. By the time they'd finished the various chores, shopping trips, and errands required to continue the ritual, thirty-six of the Gateway's forty-eight hours had passed.

Sung-ho pulled into the driveway just before dinner. He drove a wood-paneled station wagon, the back compartment stuffed with briefcases and storage tubs. As he stepped out, the sunset shining off the bristles of his recently-shaved scalp, he peered at the boarded-up windows and adjusted his sunglasses.

Put his hands on his khaki, utility-shorted hips.

Zoe descended the steps from the front entrance to the driveway. "I'll cover the damages."

"What exactly, uh…happened?"

"The shaved head looks great."

Sung-ho had worn long locks, side-swept, and a rough goatee, once upon a time. Sometime after Gillian's second stint in rehab, however, he'd started developing a bald spot. Never one for half-measures, Sung-ho confirmed his situation and took a razor to the whole thing.

"Thanks," he said. "But, ah, again…what happened?"

"The ritual turned out to be more dangerous than we thought."

"Hum me the tune."

"I might've made a small mistake very early on, tracking Jill after… getting extremely drunk. I'm not sure if it impacted the ritual directly, but there've been other small things. And Jill's made a few mistakes, too."

"Hmmm, yes, it's clear to me now how all of my windows broke. Many small mistakes."

Zoe continued as if the sarcasm hadn't registered. "There's a manifestation in the spell, some material or semi-material extrusion of Jill's… trauma. We ran into it a few nights ago during the end of the second phase, the Proclamation, and we managed to activate all the magic anyway. But then the windows exploded."

"And is there a particular *reason* somewhere in all that jazz?"

Zoe peered back at the house behind her, the numerous plywood sheets patching its dozen eyes. "I assume so. But I don't know it."

"That's a bad sign."

Zoe cleared her throat. "Were you able to deal with the dietary bullshit?"

"I haven't had a drink in a week, a smoke in three or four days…"

"Coffee?"

Sung-ho shrugged. "Eh."

"It's a rough quit."

"Everything is." He sighed, turned back toward the station wagon. "Come on, help me unpack. You owe me for the windows."

Salem, MA.

August, 2016.

They'd spent a few days searching the town for signs of larger matrices at work. Darnell's dark premonition had Zoe on edge, whether she admitted it or not. And if the Powers-That-Were planned to dismantle Jill's school through nonviolent means, they'd need powerful magic to do it; not just a handful of rental sites scrawled with glyphs and runes but a considerable circuit of interlocked mysticism.

It hadn't taken long to find the first clues. The Belgian's crew, aided by Malleus and presumably everyone else Zoe had noticed in town besides the Winters team, had set up a vast network of spells all over Salem and even into Peabody, Beverly, and Clifton. In five days, Zoe and Omar uncovered six ritual sites, with evidence suggesting several more.

Even then, haunted by a psychic's suggestion, she wondered, too, if the paranoia owed itself to opposition forces. It didn't take a psychic to foresee dark days and terrible traumas ahead for the school and its constituents, but perhaps Darnell's frenetic insistence pointed at something else. Maybe it illustrated the extremes to which the enemy's campaign of psychological warfare had already succeeded.

(*there are no enemies anymore*)

Still, they knew they had to disrupt or neutralize the major matrices if they wanted to save Jill.

So before they had time to develop a plan, they already had tasks to accomplish.

Zoe watched their latest target through binoculars, waiting for the sky to fade into dusk. Prepared practitioners favored certain times of day for spellcraft —the rumored 'witching hour' from two to four in the morning, the dawn and dusk of every day, and whatever hour it was when the sun hit its zenith or the moon shone its brightest. With so many people building up so many spells, Zoe imagined they worked in shifts. She hoped to spy on whoever showed up to tend to the rituals before moving in to disrupt them.

But she wasn't going to wait until two in the morning, if it came to that.

Her mind wandering, it occurred to her that she'd never known anyone who'd died in the field, before. Few people did, on the whole, but the anxiety that she *might* made the odds feel worthy of re-examination. Most agents switched to a desk job in their forties or fifties and retired in their sixties and died from the same things everyone else died from. More of them died from suicide than the gen pop, but that grim statistic applied to every industry that specialized in horror.

Valley had killed himself in 2011. He'd left a note—something about something he'd done on a job, a price he'd been willing to pay at the time but, then, after years of having to remember it…

And Sung-ho had died from a heart attack owed to decades of smoking and drinking and burning out his adrenal gland on a hundred dangerous jobs. It had been his second heart attack, the first having been relatively minor. It had happened two years ago.

It made sense, intellectually. Emotionally, it felt cosmically unfair that someone as grandiose as Sung-ho had died from a fucking heart attack.

It also would have felt cosmically unfair if some monster or egomaniacal sorcerer had deprived Hyun-jung of a father, Seo-yeon of a husband.

Some people lived so iconically that any death at all seemed unfair; any ending, unsatisfactory.

"Not him," she'd wanted to tell the universe. "He's never supposed to go."

But, of course, sooner or later, everyone went.

every story ends the same way

As dusk darkened to night, she lowered the binoculars. She wanted a cigarette very badly but couldn't risk the cherry glowing through the black curtain of night. Dropping the binocs into her kit, she checked the rest of her inventory: two spare mags, a set of lockpicks, and a satchel of esoteric materia she planned to use to enhance the upcoming sabotage.

They'd hidden their work well. Two cemeteries backed up against an arc of parkland flanked by forested suburbs. Nearby, a school campus waded a soccer field into a thicket of brush, a swath of untended land skirting the park. Near the water, a copse of trees and foliage hid the ritual site, itself. Zoe headed that way.

People forgot about their own myopia all the time. The tucked-away sprawl of brush surrounding the ritual space grew only six hundred feet from a residential street. But who saw six hundred feet? In the darkness, it didn't take long to lose a person. Sometimes they stayed lost.

Overhead, a drone whirred near-inaudibly. It drew long paths across the night, flying low over the graveyards and parkland, avoiding the suburban streets.

Zoe crept into the copse of trees and tangled bush hiding the ritual site. She found an offering bowl, a brazier, a handful of broken rune sticks, and a pile of burnt bones and ivory shards. The opposition had stayed away from spells that required sigils or glyphs, they'd avoided making any long-term markings. The defensiveness implied knowledge.

It implied that they'd known someone would show up to screw with things.

Zoe reached for her holster, cerebral judgment and sixth-sense impulse reaching the same conclusion at nearly the same time.

"Freeze," a male voice growled. A voice she knew as 'Frank.' "Put your hands up. Nice and slow."

Oceanrest, ME.

January, 2007.

Removed from its foam-block protection, the vial thrummed with magic. Cold enough to hurt Zoe's fingers, the seethe of shadows within seemed to leach all warmth from her body.

"Three!" the Summoner shouted.

"The S-S-S-Summoner," Zoe whispered, teeth chattering.

"Two!"

A full-body wrench drove Zoe to her knees as she activated Jill's spell. Headrush curled ink through her vision. She threw the vial and it shattered.

The whole world slowed down.

The thing that unspooled from the broken glass, whatever Jill had summoned and bound with her magic, Zoe felt It more than she saw It.

It moved like sci-fi *something*, a liqui-metal or nano-cloud, a tide of grayshade momentum. It had no limbs; It had hundreds of limbs. Roiling like ball-lightning, It slid faster-than-mortal around the corner and into the next room, the room where the Summoner pointed a rifle at a bullet-less Sung-ho. In Zoe's sixth sense she felt It roll over the Summoner even as his lips oh'd and his trigger finger flexed; she felt It thread Itself around him at the speed of dark. It didn't know what a gun was and so It threw the gun away. It knew arms, though. It knew legs.

It rose up, lifting the Summoner skyward until the man had no more fight than a limp puppet, and It flexed.

The grinding, snapping *crunch* of so many bones simultaneously breaking bolted Zoe's consciousness back into the material. The overwhelming sensation put her on her knees. She almost dropped her gun, reflexively reaching for her guts. A rhythmic *whoosh* filled her ears, the only sound she heard until the Summoner's screams rose above it.

Back on her feet, she holstered her pistol and followed the cries.

The creature had already dissipated back to whatever nether realm or dark plane Jill had coaxed it from; only a faint scent of ozone and a vague sixth-sense dread remained. On the floor of the large chamber, the Summoner shrieked and bucked, three of his four limbs splayed and folded wrongly around him. Neither his ankles nor his knees aligned and it looked like both of his hips had dislocated. His one working arm, wounded and sprain-inflamed, clutched at his ribs.

"Shut up," Sung-ho muttered, retrieving the Summoner's rifle.

The Summoner's volume dwindled. He whimpered and panted, shivering in shock as Zoe approached.

"Just do it," he sputtered as she knelt next to him. "Just fucking do it."

Ignoring the raw-throated rasp, Zoe peered back at Sung-ho. "We need to do some kind of healing spell."

Usually when management wanted a subject 'dead or alive,' they preferred 'alive.' Or at least they preferred to make the final decision themselves.

Slinging the unloaded long-gun over his shoulder, Sung-ho grunted. "Never really my forte…"

"Anything's better than nothing," Zoe said.

Inside their kits, they carried basic mystic-medical field supplies, healing salves and minor spell ingredients. Emptying her pack's last compartment, Zoe started chalking sigils on the ground.

"Who are you?" the Summoner groaned, pallor paling. "Who do you work for?"

"If I told you anything, it'd be a lie," she answered absentmindedly.

"How—how can you know magic and keep it a secret?"

Sung-ho joined them. "Nothing external?"

The salves needed blood or plasma to work.

"Doesn't look like."

"Hm."

"Don't you get it?" The Summoner panted. "Magic changes everything. *Everything.*" He lunged with his workable hand and grabbed her jacket. "It changes the whole world."

She shrugged him off. "Don't fucking touch me."

"We can do *anything.*"

"Magic's been here this whole time and the world is still the way it is. Magic doesn't make people better the same way cellphones don't make people better. It's just a tool."

"Not enough people know—"

"They can't. Most people can't remember paranormative experiences, or remembering them is traumatizing. The average person either forgets or goes insane."

"I had plans. I could've—"

"You had plans to bomb some buildings and summon monsters."

"Everyone sees magic when it's pointed at them!"

Zoe laughed. "For a second, sure. Then they forget. Or they go crazy. And your amateur, half-cocked psychic defenses weren't going to stop that. All you were going to do was hurt a lot of people. All you did, already, was hurt a lot of people."

He reached for her again and Sung-ho grabbed his wound-bloated forearm. Sung-ho leveraged the multi-joint sprain until the Summoner's groan shrank to a whimper. "She said don't touch."

"Who are you people?" the Summoner asked.

Zoe poured a line of amaranth seeds through an angled section of glyph. She sprinkled dried heather and tansy flowers in symmetrical arrangements around the amaranth line. Peering at the heap of man just feet away from her, she sighed. Said, "I literally can't tell you and it honestly doesn't matter."

The Summoner's teeth stopped chattering. "So what happens now?"

"Now, we use a spell to make sure you don't die in front of us. And then

I think we'll pick up some dinner."

"Are you—are you detaining me?"

"No. My job was just to neutralize you."

"So why heal me? Just finish it."

A single 'ha' barked out of her. "We did. This spell isn't to get you back on your feet, it's to stop you from bleeding out until someone else decides what to do with you. If you think you can crawl out of here on one half-busted arm, go ahead and do it. But five minutes from now, me and him are putting this place as far in the past as we can. You included."

"You're—you're leaving me here?"

"Like I said, my job is done."

"So what the fuck happens next?" Volume and panic re-entered his voice.

"Next," Sung-ho replied, "you shut up before I have to take off one of my sweaty, bloody old socks and gag you with it."

"Please," the Summoner whispered. "Please…"

Zoe placed her hands on either side of the chalked sigil and closed her eyes.

Good healing witches didn't come cheap. Few born-adepts existed and the ritualized cantrips required extensive training. Most Malleus agents knew enough to patch a gunshot or repair some skewered organs, emergency-use spells intended to meet catastrophic circumstances, but the complex web of wounds Zoe expected to find inside the Summoner's bone-splintered body…

Well. Magic couldn't guarantee things that couldn't be guaranteed, anyway.

Zoe and Sung-ho muttered multi-lingual prayers and phrases, channeling their half-spent neuromuscular energy and the material ingredients into the magic. Sweat swamped them. Zoe forgot their winter surroundings through the heat and exertion. Hunger gnashed at her innards. Exhaustion ached her joints.

Between them, it took just over a minute to charge the spell. By then, blood speckled the Summoner's lips and his words had turned to wheezes. A sixth-sense static hummed, a faint scent of ozone tanged the air. The odor changed, searing flat and burning, when Zoe and Sung-ho activated the magic.

It pulsed through the Summoner's body as a wave of warmth. Zoe and Sung-ho guided it toward the pooling claret and shredded fibers, the places where shards of broken bone had severed important systems. But the damage overwhelmed their abilities. Pushing the spell through the Summoner, trying to use its energy to fuse softmeat and muscle back together, it drained them.

The kickback laid Zoe out on the floor, a feverish sweat painting her heavy. Rolling onto her side to spit up a palmful of sick, she felt her muscles creak and groan. The electric crackle had subsided. The undercurrent of ozone stank, burnt. Her vision danced with phantasms and multi-hue geometry.

Slowly, she got her feet back under her and pushed herself back up.

A growth of flora surrounded the Summoner, tiny clovers and inch-tall plant-life that had risen up and dried out over the course of the cast. Even seconds later, the wind had already started dusting the evidence away.

"He won't bleed out," Sung-ho muttered, still seated, massaging his temples.

"Not anytime soon," Zoe agreed, dry-throated.

"Sepsis?"

"Maybe." Zoe shrugged.

"What?" the Summoner's voice, though quiet, had returned.

Sung-ho stood with a groan. He put a hand on his lower back. "Goddammit."

"You pull something?"

"You smirking?" Sung-ho replied.

"Not at all," she said, smirking as much as her exhaustion allowed. "Let's get out of here."

As she and Sung-ho headed back toward the exit, Zoe assessed their wounds. Nothing appeared severe. A good night's sleep and the little salve they had should do the trick. If not, the rest would hopefully give them enough energy to handle another healing spell the next day.

"Wait!" The Summoner shouted behind them. "*Wait!*"

Only a few yards ahead of the prone figure, Zoe turned back around to face him. "What *now*?"

"Please, I—I just wanted to change the world."

"Look at me."

And he did.

"I don't care," she said.

And then they left.

Chapter Eighteen

Salem, MA.

August, 2016.

"Yeah, that's right. Hands up, real slow."

Zoe took a deep breath, spread her fingers wide, and one-inch-at-a-time lifted her arms overhead. Nearby, the commercial drone hovered, out of sight. Ahead of her, burnt offerings and leftover magic, a river blackened by the lightless skies. Behind her, an automatic pistol, a blond-haired, blue-eyed enforcer working for the most powerful and sinister man alive.

"Who do you work for?" Frank asked.

"Nobody."

A suburban street waited silently only six hundred feet away. Nobody dozing through their pre-sleep routines knew what happened at such distance, but they'd hear the gun chatter if Frank pulled the trigger. She knew he could do so only once.

So she knew she could afford to push him a little.

"You think you're clever?" Frank took a step, sole scraping rock and hard dirt. "Think you're the only one who knows how to track?"

He paused as if waiting for a response.

She didn't provide one.

He continued, "At first I really did think Lacey was having nightmares. She's paranoid, been working for the boss too long to keep her head straight. But then...someone had tapped into our magic. And it made sense, seeing as how someone's been tampering with our operations all over Salem."

She wondered if his sight-enhancing invocation was more powerfully laid than her vision-blurring ward.

"So," Frank said. "How big's your team? Three people, four?"

"Just me."

Frank snorted. "Sure."

"If I'm not alone, where's my cover?" she asked.

"Hey," Frank wasn't talking to her, but to someone on the other end of a mic, a radio, a cellphone. "You guys find the rest of 'em, yet?"

Zoe relaxed her shoulders, let her elbows and knees soften. Frank's answer came unheard—not over a radio but through some other piece of tech. Maybe even through some psychic method.

"I think you've got a guy in the graveyard and someone else on the drone," Frank replied. "Maybe a fourth on the other side of the river, if you're smart."

"Maybe," Zoe said.

"But the ritual site's got canopy cover from above, tree cover from the bank, and..." Frank trailed off, catching himself.

"It's a good spot. Exactly where I would have gone."

"Good for you. Now, slowly, put your hands behind your back."

She had to admit, they'd accounted for everything. Almost.

She stretched her arms behind her back. "What about the school?"

Nearby, a high school backed up to a stretch of barely-maintained forest. Crossing the rough, occasionally hazardous terrain made for a difficult approach, but still *an* approach. Assuming an appropriate distraction—such as a witch showing up to degrade and disrupt their spells.

The forestation edging up to the riverside also provided a great hideaway for someone to operate a drone.

"The school?" Frank echoed.

Foliage rustled from twenty feet behind Zoe.

She ducked and banked left. Frank lifted his pistol but didn't fire. "She's running," he said, talking to his earpiece again.

When he turned to give chase, Frank ran face-first into the butt of Omar's pistol. Frank shouted once before Omar grabbed his collar. Omar slammed his pistol-grip into Frank's temple and the latter dropped like a man hanged. "Okay," Omar said, "grab his feet. We gotta get him back to the school before anyone else shows up."

Zoe grabbed Frank's ankles.

Wilmington, NC.

September, 1997.

The final phase of the ritual happened in nine day cycles. If the Confrontation didn't trigger on the ninth day, another two day Gateway would open and the process would start again. But in the best case scenario, it only took nine grueling, ascetic, laborsome days to complete. The asceticism extended to a complete refrain from all caffeine, alcohol, cigarettes, cannabis, any and all substances that may alter the mental state, sex of any kind, masturbation or other self-pleasure, any beverage besides water (lemon wedge possible), and any food not derived from plant matter.

And the labor?

It went like this:

At dawn, Zoe and Jill awoke and meditated on concepts of beginnings, resurrections, and other related metaphorical notions. They considered the day's destruction of night and night's destruction of day. They meditated on the topic of relapse.

For breakfast, all practitioners (Zoe, Jill, Sung-ho) gathered for a meal. They shared greetings and well-wishes before the meal, ate the meal without speaking a single syllable, and continued talking after setting the dishes aside.

After breakfast, Zoe and Sung-ho worked on building the Confrontation itself. They folded numerous invocations into each other. They arranged good luck charms and minor protections around the ritual space.

Meanwhile, Jill continued to fortify the perimeter and its various ingresses and egresses. She summoned potential interlopers into complicated seals and banished them from the procession to follow. She built up the wards protecting the house, shielding it from notice and preventing supernatural break-ins.

The practitioners met for lunch, speaking both before and after the meal but eating, again, in silence.

After lunch, Jill returned to her room for further meditation and self-counsel.

Zoe and Sung-ho checked all the boards blockading the windows.

They had a break until sunset.

At sunset, the practitioners met in the ritual space and meditated on cycles, behaviors, and their own failings. They spent sixty minutes self-assessing. After this, the trio continued working up the interlocking spells of the Confrontation. The work lasted up until dinner.

They ate dinner according the same rules as every other meal.

After dinner, under the moonlight, Zoe and Sung-ho listened to Jill talk. Jill talked about relapse and resurrection, about nights that destroyed days and days that destroyed, about her behaviors and her cycles and all of her failings. Once the moon reached its brightest, the ritual allowed Zoe and Sung-ho six sentences each to advise, counsel, and buttress Jill.

After that, they were allowed to do whatever they wanted. But even by the end of the first night, what they wanted was to sleep.

They all had caffeine headaches and Zoe still had lingering nic fits. Sung-ho, freshly quit of a lifelong fondness for coffee, threw up once on the first day. He managed through the second day in a grump, a walking underbreath mutter. By the morning of the third day, things had settled somewhat. As much as they could in a house full of itchy, physically uncomfortable, and utterly exhausted witches.

The third day also went according to plan. As did the fourth. Until.

After dinner, under the moonlight, Zoe and Sung-ho listened to Jill talk.

Jill talked about relapse and resurrection, about nights that destroyed days, about all of her failings. Jill stared at the floor in front of her, cross-legged, seated on a sigil. "When mom and dad kicked me out, for a while I guess I thought, I dunno, maybe the world was supposed to eat me. I let a lot of bad people into my life and hurt a lot of other good ones and now I think—or I wonder—whether I did it subconsciously."

They still had nine minutes until the moon shone its brightest.

Jill coughed. "I think I did. I wanted to—to—to—" she stuttered. She froze. She reached for her throat and gagged. Her eyes bulged, emeralds drowned in milk. Something rattled wheezy and phlegmatic in her windpipe. Something crawled around beneath her skin.

Zoe lurched forward and Sung-ho put an arm out to stop her. He gestured her to 'wait.'

Jill leaned forward and planted her hands on the ground. She sucked air, burped, sucked air, burped. Sweat flopped her brow and scarlet flushed her face. "Mmm," she groaned. "Mmmhmmnnnn!"

Zoe pursed her lips, coiled. Sung-ho kept his arm out straight.

Jill's visage writhed as if a civilization of slender worms frenzied beneath it. "Hh—hhuuhh!"

Electronic feedback shrieked through the air. The unnatural sound dopplered and faded, echoed and overlapped itself. Zoe grabbed her ears and Sung-ho dropped his arm, grimacing. The candelabra burned bright, hot flames dancing higher and higher. The flat, chemical stench of burnt ozone stank everywhere.

Jill puked up a ball of hairy brown-yellow vomitus. Every vein in her body bulged.

"The sun screams butane down on a sea of sizzling black tar!" Jill wailed. Another skin seemed to jerk and stab out from beneath her own. "The waves bubble, they seethe up to eat the shores."

Zoe had a hand over her mouth; every muscle in her body tightened.

Sung-ho stared at her in warning.

"There is a war going on behind things," Jill shouted. "Beneath them! Every story ends the same way. In the long run," she arched her back, lifting herself up until she howled at the ceiling. "The seas eat the shores, the skies choke, the land blisters, this world is track marks and hollow cheeks. There's a war going on in every story."

Zoe could've cried. One hand clamped over her tight-shut lips, joints aching with the want to *act*, she felt the impulse crawl up her neck and across her scalp, felt it tingle in her sinuses. She could've. But she didn't.

Sung-ho held onto her other arm, grip weak from the day's efforts. They'd seen things like this in cases of possession or infestations of psychic or semi-psychic entities—rare fringe occurrences so improbable that most agents didn't train to deal with them, anymore. But as a byproduct of a ritual spell? Never.

Jill shot to her tip-toes, standing rigid as a nailed-up scarecrow. "The sun is a spoonhead sizzling, the seas boil black tar, my veins, every story, a war, above and below, macro as micro as macro as apocalypse. Don't you get it, yet? Under everything there's just *me*!"

A high banshee pitch flayed the crackling air.

Sung-ho removed his hand, bracing for action. Zoe settled into her crouch, ready.

Jill collapsed.

She hit the floor limp. A static-colored drool oozed out of one side of her mouth. For five seconds that felt like five years, Jill neither blinked nor breathed.

Then she screamed, curling up fetal inside her sigil.

The alarm clock announced the moon's brightest moment. Sung-ho slapped it off.

"I'm so sorry," Zoe said.

But Jill just kept crying.

Salem, MA.

September, 2016.

Zoe had to give it to him: Frank didn't squawk for three whole days.

Omar played the good cop and she played the bad one. They'd performed the routine dozens of times. They had it down to an art. Alas, not a science.

Zoe's job felt easier than usual. It *was* easier. With invocations reinforcing her knuckles, she broke Frank's cheekbone. After Omar 'cooled her off,' she went through ten minutes of healing magic to un-break it. It still bruised and swelled, but the structural integrity of his skull remained intact.

She'd given him a few cracks, knocked his brain around its casement a bit, but she didn't torture him. Mostly because she knew torture didn't work. Virtually all intel gathered through torture turned out incorrect, random spoutings made up to stop the pain. The blows were largely performance. It gave Omar something to step in and stop. It created the illusion that Omar cared about Frank's life any more than Zoe did.

Between the carrot and the stick, the carrot delivered the results. The stick just made the carrot more palatable.

After three days of keeping Frank locked in a utility closet in the basement of a Malleus safehouse, Omar found Zoe in the standard safehouse bedroom and leaned against the doorframe. "He's talking."

"What's he saying?" she asked, reclined on a cot, reviewing their schedule of counter-casting, spell degradation, interrogation, and, somehow, self-subsistence.

"Nothing we don't already know. He's with the Belgian's people."

"Better to have it confirmed."

"Not by much," Omar replied. "I acted appropriately surprised and shit, pretended like the name-drop had some kind of effect on me...he's already offered me a lot of money to get him out of here."

Zoe set aside her binder of spreadsheets and notes. "So you're in. We just need to leverage some actual intel out of him."

"Take the lead, pig."

Zoe grinned as she stood.

###############

Down the hall from the utility closet, Zoe took out a dictaphone and held it to her lips. "John Doe interrogation session number nine," she said. "John Doe has agreed to start answering questions from me, lead interrogator," for the future 'cover,' if Omar needed it, "Zoe Briar."

They opened the door. Frank faced the rear of the closet, hedged in by steel shelving units, hands bound into fists, with three rolls of duct tape wrapping him to his chair. The chair, itself, was one of the typical low-budget office varieties with fabric upholstery and wheels that kinda-worked but also didn't.

"I already saw your faces," Frank said. "So you might as well turn me around."

"I heard you wanted to talk," Zoe replied.

"So let's talk face-to-face."

"You work for the Belgian."

"Heard of him?"

Zoe crossed the floor behind Frank. Took out a buffed cigarette case and her Zippo. "Has he heard of you?" The question hung. She continued, "You're on a team led by an agent working on assignment for a handler who answers to some secret society middle-manager who maybe shook your hand once. If I put a bullet in the back of your head today the only thing the Belgian will remember about you will be a red line in his ledger at the end of the year."

Frank chewed on that for a while. Eventually, he said, "I need protection."

A snort of laughter ripped out of her. Opening the chrome case, she withdrew a slender black clove. Snapped the case shut. Tapping the top with the butt of the cigarette, she asked, "Was my threat not direct enough?"

"Maybe the Belgian doesn't know my face, but if I squawk to some two-bit like you, you better believe my name travels up the ladder real quick. So what, you'll shoot me in the head? If I rat, the Belgian'll do the same thing. Except he won't stop with just me."

"Yeah, I heard he's a real Soze, 'your parents and your parents' friends,' et cetera." She placed the filter between her lips and sparked the Zippo. Lit up, puffed, and pocketed the lighter. "Maybe I'll start with some questions. How many teams are coordinating on this? How many eyes are on the house, itself? Where are other ritual sites?"

Frank tried vainly to turn his head enough to see her. He cranked his neck both ways before settling his gaze dead ahead again. "You really have no idea the shit you have stepped in, do you?"

"Enlighten me."

Frank shook his head. "You stupid bitch."

She sizzled the cherry against the back of his neck. He rocked and howled, the thick wrap of tape straining as he wrestled to break free. When the burning stopped, she returned the filter to her lips, dug her Zippo back out of her pocket, and re-lit the clove. In an herbal haze, she said, "Start again."

Frank panted, sweaty with pain.

"I noticed the Winters people hanging back," Zoe offered. "Like maybe they're not sure what side they're on, yet. And you guys and Malleus are on point, obviously. But there are other operatives in play."

Frank gulped. "No shit."

"How many? Who are they? Where are their ritual sites? Who's watching the house?" She repeated the questions with dull indifference, a performed boredom.

"If you don't know those answers by now, you're already fucked."

"Frank, if I'm already fucked, I'm gonna have to kill you." She took a long drag and blew a silver-gray stream over the top of the man's head. "So think of a better answer before I finish smoking."

Frank didn't reply immediately.

Zoe smoked. The cherry crawled raggedly toward the filter. A barely-there haze blurred the room by the time she snuffed the clove against the wall. Replacing the cigarette with her sidearm, she stepped up behind Frank. Thumbed off the safety lever, thumbed back the hammer, and waited.

But not for very long.

She pressed the barrel against the base of Frank's skull, took a breath, and squeezed the trigger.

The hammer fell on an empty chamber.

"Five!" Frank shouted, jerking forward. "Five teams!"

Zoe took out a mag and slapped it in. "Who?"

"Us, Malleus, the Temple, those Solar Dynasty li'l shits...even the weirdo vegan tree-fuckers from old Ireland showed up. And who do you work for?"

"How many people watch the house?"

"You can't send me back with nothing. He'll kill my whole family."

Zoe lowered the gun next to Frank's ear and fired a bullet into the wall in front of him. It sounded like mortarfire in the tight space. Zoe's morning invocations shielded her eardrums from the noise. Frank hadn't performed his for days. He screamed, head straining to escape the damage that had already happened.

"What!?" Zoe yelled.

Frank howled, thrashing in his chair.

"How — many — people — watch — the house?" Zoe shouted each syllable straight into Frank's working ear.

"Fuck!" he cried, still struggling. "Shit!"

She waited for him to quiet down. Waited for him to stop fighting and slouch into a panting heap. It took longer than she'd expected. When he finally gave up and collapsed, she took a deep, audible breath. "Maybe I won't kill you," she said. "Maybe I'll stuff dreamer in your mouth and force you to give yourself visions of Dachau or the Rwandan genocide or the trans-Atlantic slave trade. Maybe that'll work faster than this."

"You can't."

"I can. I *shouldn't*. But I can. It's a lot harder than killing you but I think it's more likely to get me results."

"You'll be burned from every organization in the world."

She snorted. "How, Frankie? How do you think they'd ever even find out?"

The door to the room flew open. Omar, fake-panting, ran through the threshold. "I—Did I hear a gunshot!?"

"He's fine," Zoe answered, playing the part. "At least, well. For now."

"We can't just treat prisoners—"

"We *shouldn't*." Zoe repeated her earlier correction. "And if you get him to answer my goddamned questions, we won't have to."

"Can we...talk about this?"

Zoe sighed. She levered her sidearm's safety back into place and followed Omar back out of the closet. Omar closed the door behind them and she turned off the dictaphone. They walked back to the safehouse common area before speaking again.

"You set him?" Omar asked.

"I did what I could. Definitely gave him a scare."

"What's the angle?"

"Tell him you can protect him and his family. Maybe offer some kind of defection deal. Hem and haw and all that, but...offer him some version of the things he wants."

"Toned down for realism," Omar added. "Got it."

"We need as much as possible about surveillance on Jill's house. All types."

"Oh, weird, I was going to ask him about his election hot-takes."

"Omar."

"We've had the same objective for days, Zo'. I know what I'm looking for."

"Right. Sorry." She took a breath, trying to release the tight thing in her chest. "So then he's all yours."

And when Omar walked back in alone, Frank told him everything.

Chapter Nineteen

Oceanrest, ME.

August, 2007.

The police never picked up the Summoner. The case trailed off.

The story read like this: the Summoner, real name Tyler King Bennett, and at least one as-yet-unknown accomplice murdered four men and five women across five different crime scenes. Perhaps the accomplice was one of the kids at the rental cabin, but evidence didn't point to anyone in particular. Everyone felt certain that the Summoner, now a known entity, would rear his hideous visage once again, and when he did, the badges would swarm.

Of course, Zoe knew better. Zoe knew that, realistically, either Malleus had spirited the Summoner away to what was essentially a black site, or the man had died from complications of his wounds. There were other possible endings, especially given the reality-bending nature of magic, but those two were the most likely.

The story didn't end, it just unraveled. It went on as the world did.

(*life's a bitch and then life's a bitch and then life's a*)

The people who needed answers would invent the answers they needed. Sooner or later, already or eventually, the Summoner would rot in some unmarked grave, a closed case never officially closed.

Maybe the story would end differently if it read differently, but the story read the way it read.

Omar left the bomb but the bomb never went off. None of them went off.

After, he went through the various NDA procedures. It took four days for all the interlocked hexes and curses and corporate paperwork to process, but after that, he walked out with Delta clearance. He went back home to visit his mother and consider what the future held for him.

Zoe went back to New York City. She went on assignments in Montana and Louisiana before Omar got back to her with an answer. Some time in late July, Omar sent a ciphered message to Zoe through an email address attached to a random-numbers domain. Zoe forwarded the decrypted message to Sung-ho and Leonid Singh.

They granted Omar's mother Class-E intel clearance.

Omar's first series of courses started the last week of August. So, the Friday before, Zoe found herself parking a rental car in Sung-ho's driveway. They had all gathered there to celebrate Omar's going-forward. The sight of the place, the one-car garage, Sung-ho's car parked outside of it, Leo's behind that —it displaced her from time. It reminded her of not-so-long-ago days, before Leo and Sung-ho got their respective promotions, when they'd celebrate their respective successes with regular parties, when they'd meet between gigs to catch up over drinks or coffee or both. Years had passed since then, but not so many as it felt.

She withdrew the keys from the ignition. She was still standing next to her vehicle when Omar's arrived.

He parked behind her and emerged smiling. Freshly-renewed dreadlocks fell to his shoulders. A trimmed beard sandpapered his face. He wore a tailored suit, three-piece and gray, with a purple tie as a slash of color down his chest. "I look good, right?"

"Right," she answered, back in the right year again. And he did. "How's it feel?"

"Weird," he replied.

"Yeah. That doesn't go away. Ready?"

"As I'll ever be."

###############

The Parks had installed a deck. It reminded Zoe of the one they had at their summer home in Wilmington. A different set of memories stirred in her guts. She swallowed them down. Climbing the few steps to join the rest of the crew, she re-introduced Omar.

"Leo," Leo said, last, extending a hand.

"Nice to meet you, Leo. You got a last name?"

"When you have the proper clearance, I do." Leo's bright grin sliced through a bristling beard.

Omar laughed. "Okay, okay. I see that."

Sung-ho stubbed out a cigarette. "You get the right clearance when you graduate. It's not *real* intel. You want a drink?"

"Sure. What's good?"

"Everything I buy is good," Sung-ho answered. "But the bottle closest to me is a Macallan eighteen-year single malt Highland Scotch."

"Any ice?" Omar asked.

"Not in an eighteen-year single malt, no." Sung-ho poured from the bottle into a clear plastic cup. Halfway full, he handed it to Omar. "Zoe?"

She blinked. "Hm?"

"Scotch?"

"Yeah." She unglued her feet and walked to the rest of them.

"Please, sit. 'Take a load off,' as they say." Leo swirled his own drink around his own plastic cup. Sipped. "Share some war stories with the new recruit."

Among the circle of chairs surrounding the square, glass table, two waited empty, one next to Leo and the other next to Sung-ho. She sat next to Sung-ho. "Scotch me."

Sung-ho poured. Between the drinks served so far, they'd halfway emptied the bottle.

Omar sat in the last remaining seat. "So...is Zoe as big a deal as it seems like?"

"A sufficiently large fish in a relatively small pond, indeed she is," Leo answered. Turning to Sung-ho, he asked, "How many times did you and Zo' earn Best in Field?"

After her extensive training, Sung-ho's mentorship had extended into Zoe's early field work. They'd run assignments together for over five years before his desk job had appeared. They'd earned top organizational decorations in four of those years.

Sung-ho smacked his tongue against the roof of his mouth. "We're not here to brag. We're here to get tipsy and high and tell Omar old stories and shoot guns at cartoon caricatures until the cops show up to fine me again."

Leo didn't literally roll his eyes, but the twist of his facial expression— and a slight tic in his right eyebrow—achieved the same effect. "Suffice it to say, Omar, that you're in very good hands. I expect Zoe will be a mentor unmatched by any other."

"Hey!"

"Present company excluded, of course."

And Zoe had really wanted to be.

She really had.

Salem, MA.

September, 2016.

Among other things, Frank told them the approximate locations of the two largest supporting teams — the agents from the Druidic Order and those from the Temple *Beth Yetzirah*. The Druids, generally the less dangerous of the two, had laid camp somewhere in the untended wild-growth south of Salem Woods and west of Eagles Hill. Armed with proximal intel about their location, Zoe and Omar found the specifics in under forty-eight hours. Preparations began immediately.

Jill relented in her constant stewardship of her house's wards and defenses to help develop offensive tools. She'd had her misgivings, Darnell's recent visions especially, but the possibility of removing one of the parties aligned against her laid them to rest. Eight days after Frank's capture, Jill met Zoe in the bathroom of another 24-hour convenience store just outside of Boston and pushed a gym bag full of artifacts and enchanted objects between the stalls. The tchotchkes inside contained spells to disrupt and redirect the druids' mystical workings, to wither and drain their invocations and abilities, and one particular glass sphereoid, foam-packed, to hold a writhing, smoldering, multi-hue light, which Jill called a 'chaos bomb' with deadly seriousness. The 'chaos bomb' served as the centerpiece of their counter-assault. Jill didn't describe exactly what it did, but she assured Zoe that it would 'do enough.'

They'd left the convenience store separately. The sound of the door swinging shut had put something heavy behind Zoe's sternum. It had taken her a long time to stand up.

While Jill had labored to create their offense, Zoe and Omar had worked the spellcraft to get them inside the druids' camp to begin with. Natural stealth wouldn't cut it. They'd ritualized a series of cantrips and invocations to create the spell. When triggered, it would silence all noise they made, render them invisible, and obscure them from alarm and perimeter wards. It carried a significant neuromuscular demand to keep running, but they didn't plan to need it for longer than eight or ten seconds. With their combined enchanting skills far inferior to Jill's, it took Zoe and Omar seven sweaty hours to inlay the effect into two breakable wax seals even after the days spent in ritual.

They gave themselves one day to resume their regular tampering with the wide matrix of magic criss-crossing Salem and another to recharge.

On the tenth night after capturing Frank, Zoe and Omar drove up to where the road went over the Forest River and parked about a hundred yards away from a golf range. In the lightless late, they unpacked their kits from the trunk of the rental and double-checked their armor and armaments. Zoe carried the chaos bomb, still foam-padded, in a blanket-cushioned backpack. Everything else, plus her two spare mags, went into the tac-pack.

They headed east.

################

Magic was most effective from a distance, using spells assembled, charged, and triggered from places the opposition couldn't find. Ideally, a practitioner on the offense knew the proximate geographic locale of their targets and their targets knew nothing about them. But affecting things at any great distance required extreme neuromuscular expense, plus access to the proper items and ingredients, and added significant time to the rituals. Thus the who's-who reunion of so many shadowy organizations in Salem simultaneously. The threat of armed agents kept Jill and her school in a predictable physical location; the vast network of spells targeting them benefited both from the proximity of the armed agents fueling them and from the stillness and predictability of the school's physical location.

In the asymmetry of the conflict, Zoe, Omar, and Jill lacked the resources to compete. If the situation became more symmetrical, however… Well. It bought time. Time for Shoshanna Winters to assemble the med-evac team. Time for Zoe to figure out how to transport the members of Jill's school that Shoshanna couldn't. Time, in any case. And they needed it.

In their run on the Druidic Order, Zoe and Omar planned to use the governing guidelines on the other end of magic's spectrum — it was more powerful up close. More powerful and easier to aim.

"They were active. Recently." Omar noted. From their position on the uneven hill above, they could see a bonfire crackling between the Druidic structures. It looked on its ebb, once an inferno now sinking into ember.

"They may still have a patrol up," Zoe surmised.

Practitioners of the Druidic Order were generally masters of healing and invocation arcana. More than any other organization, they knew the mystical forces tethered to the natural world, the human body, and the growth, modification, and renewal of both. These masteries maintained their standing in the underground world of the supernatural. Magical healing was always a desired asset, and thus lucrative to both trade- and spy-craft, while powerful invokers could bolster the physical senses and abilities of themselves and their fellow practitioners to superhuman levels. An adept invoker with enough time could grant night-sight to an entire coven, possibly with up to double the range of the same invocation affecting Zoe and Omar.

In short, a druid on patrol might see thirty feet to their fifteen, might hear noises in lower decibel ranges than they could, and might swing a fist with almost twice as much force and doubly-reinforced bone strength.

But they couldn't risk using their carefully-crafted stealth spell until they knew where the druids kept their ritual space.

So they slowly, quietly, carefully crept downhill toward the camp.

Wilmington, NC.

September, 1997.

They pushed through.

After Jill's 'vision'—or 'incident'—she started presenting symptoms of withdrawal again. So far out from her last binge and even further from her last long-term burn-out, the recurrence seemed impossible. Medically, at least. But sometimes magic looked like that. Sometimes magic looked like sallow-sick pallor and hollowed cheeks, like shivers and quakes and hours of rollercoaster nausea. Jill did her best to fight through her daily labors, anyway.

Three days after the incident and only two before the Confrontation proper, Zoe heard muffled moans and shuffling scrapes from Jill's room. Creeping out of bed, she padded down the hall to Jill's door. "Jill?" she asked, knuckles poised to knock but hesitant.

"Zoe?" came the weak reply.

"Are you…are you okay in there?"

"I really need help."

"May I come in?"

"Yes, please, yes…"

The ward sealing the lock released and Zoe pushed her way into the room. A skeleton splayed the floor by the bed, surrounded by notebooks and hardbacks. It took a moment for Zoe to recognize Jill through the crawling, bone-white skin, the sweat-crusted hair, coarse and thin, angling from her scalp like broken stalks.

Zoe rushed over to her. "What happened?"

"Had to throw up," Jill rolled her head vaguely. Zoe saw a glistening spew of yellow bile and clear fluid pooled by the bedside table. Seeing it made her notice its sharp, sour stink. "And I fell over."

"I'm so sorry."

"Zo'…"

"Let me help you up."

"I can't do this. Look at me. You know I can't."

"I know you *can*."

"I'm dying!" Jill snapped. "Fuck."

"I'm here for you."

"Not all the time."

"Two days. Please, *please*, can you do two days?"

"I'm throwing up nothing. It's over."

"No."

"Please," Jill whispered. "Please just help me get back in bed."

Zoe cradled her sister, withered into a collection of sharp angles and hardened corners, as best she could. "I can help. I'll stay up tonight and stitch together some invocations and wards, what little healing magic I know…I can prop you up until it's over."

Jill fluttered her eyelids. Blinked. "You'd do that?"

Zoe forced a chuckle through her throat. In her arms, Jill felt like bone and paper. "I'm pretty sure I literally swore to something like it just a week ago."

"Has it only been a week?" The haze clouding Jill's gaze suggested legitimate confusion.

Zoe could've cried, but she didn't. She smiled. "Well…nine days. Including the Gateway."

"Time crawls," Jill said, joking and not.

Jill groaned like weathered steel as Zoe helped her stand. Buttressed, she moaned and creaked her way to the bed. Beneath the blankets she looked even narrower. Curled up, she shivered. Zoe thought she almost heard Jill's bones clacking together. Still, six minutes later, Jill's breath steadied and her shaking stopped.

Zoe crept back to her own bedroom to gather her supplies. She began the spellcraft as soon as she returned.

Jill's condition called for more than basic morning invocations. It called for spells more powerful and longer lasting. Jill needed increased endurance and stamina not for twenty-four hours, but for at least sixty. Jill needed dulled pain receptors not for an intense, hour-long raid but for days of mundane exhaustion. And while Zoe knew a handful of quick-and-dirty combat healing rituals, she didn't know much about cleansing a person's blood of toxins or bolstering a naturally-failing organ. She did her best. Stringing the single spells into a concentrated matrix increased their overall efficiency, but that work, too, took time and focus and effort.

Zoe stopped funneling her energy into the spellcraft when confusion and dizziness started blanking her mind. She stopped because she repeated the same step of the same spell three times and still couldn't get it to take. Breathing hard and feeling embarrassingly frail, she pushed herself away from the symbols and glyphs and ashes and miscellany littering the floor. She used a tipped-over stack of books to help her stand back up.

After the day's labor and the night's extra credit, she couldn't think straight. Her mind felt simultaneously chaotic-cluttered and serenity-empty. Remembering why she'd stood up to begin with, she leaned against a wall and closed her eyes.

When she triggered the matrix she almost lost consciousness. Her eyelids fluttered and she collapsed to her knees, but the bang of her joints against the hardwood sent her straight back up, yelping, wide-awake. She cursed, massaging the bones. Her face burning, she gritted her teeth and ground them against a surge of other shouts.

The spell took.

She hobbled away from the wall and maneuvered the room to the exit. She left her stuff behind. She didn't have the strength to pick it up.

Still snarling in the hallway, she took out a clove, lit it with her Zippo, and took a puff. Her hands shook; her tendons ached even to hold those. She exhaled. Took a second puff.

Froze.

Exhaled.

And realized that she hadn't put her Zippo in her pocket that morning and that she hadn't bought a pack of cigarettes in weeks. Dashing the cherry against the wall until the whole black stick broke apart to the filter, Zoe knew it was already too late. She stood for a long time in the dark corridor waiting for everything to collapse.

Nothing happened.

At least, not yet.

Chapter Twenty

Salem, MA.

September, 2016.

Zoe and Omar stopped before reaching the perimeter of the druid camp. They'd seen no evidence to indicate they'd tripped any wards, yet, but at some point they would. They'd need to use their stealth spell before they did, and they needed to know where the druids kept their ritual space before that.

A dozen feet from the approximate perimeter of the wilderness outpost, they broke into a wide arc around the exterior. They searched for some sixth sense sign of gathered magic while doing their best to remain aware of possible patrols. Wards against notice and investigation clouded their minds, obscuring mystical materia. Zoe squinted as if it would help. It didn't.

But something else might...

She gestured for Omar to hold.

Omar raised his eyebrows in response.

She signed for him to watch her. When he mouthed 'why?' she signed it again.

Before he pressed any further, she settled into the brush, closed her eyes, and attuned herself to her sixth sense. With a deep breath, she sank deeper into her supernatural awareness. With another, her awareness drifted away from her physical body. She felt her sixth sense spread out; she felt it *reach*.

Mystical noise and esoteric distortion warped everything around them. A painful pitch rang out inside of her as she tried to focus through it. She pushed out. Tried to feel some large accretion of energy beyond all the static.

She rocked back, suddenly in her body again. The wards had won out. Nothing short of a full scrying spell would tell them anything exact.

"It's not close," she whispered, regretting her voice instantly.

Omar nodded, helping her off the ground and back into a crouch.

The tents, shacks, and tree-houses the druids had built formed a crescent in the small valley-like dip. The dying bonfire smoked at the center. Zoe supposed it made tactical sense to keep the ritual space near the same spot. The druids would have good sight lines from all angles and intruders would have to cross a lot of ground, much of it warded and probably trapped. And during initial surveillance, neither she nor Omar had found good vantage to examine the centermost building...

Zoe caught Omar's eye again and signed for them to make a run for the bonfire.

Omar had about the same idea.

They removed the enchanted wax seals from their kits. Simultaneously, they snapped the seals in half.

It was a complex matrix of spells; they were not excellent enchanters.

The magic hit Zoe like a fist, doubling her over. She lost her breath in that first second, as the weave of spells wrapped around her. When it came back, it came back hard. She started sweating before she even moved. Walking felt like jogging with a low grade fever.

When they crossed the wards protecting the perimeter, she had her wits about her enough not to immediately lose consciousness. The headrush that crashed over her as the stealth magic crackled against the Druidic defenses tripped her. The drain of the silencing spell as it quieted the twig-snap brush-crunch of her stumble made her groan. Covering up the groan had its own minor cost.

After a couple seconds, she regained enough composure to reorient herself. She tried to run for the embered bonfire but her legs fought back. She moved as quickly as she could with so many reality-hacking spells riding her neuromuscular systems.

The dying flames glinted against glass.

A greenhouse. How? It didn't matter.

Zoe crossed another ward on approach. The magic enveloping her seized. A cramp jolted up her right thigh, over her hip, into her core. The stealth matrix overcame the defenses. The exertion tunneled Zoe's vision. Blurs of black and purple glittered across everything. Nausea curdled in her guts. Her heart pounded.

She reached the door and braced herself against it. Heaving for air, already gagging on nothing, she couldn't keep the magic running long enough to pick the lock. Stepping away, she fought to clear her head.

The door silently imploded. Zoe saw Omar flashing into visibility as he stumbled through the threshold. Zoe's own mystical matrix collapsed moments later as she limped into the same structure and closed the entrance behind them. She fell to the floor with her back against it.

The entire ordeal had lasted fewer than ten seconds and had left both of them coughing, sputtering, and panting on the ground.

"Okay," Zoe muttered half a minute later, once she felt well enough to speak. "Okay..."

The room took shape in her sixth sense before any of the others. Spellcraft hummed densely in the air, ozone odor and static-kinetic-potential crackle. Weeks of pooled supernatural energy surrounded them — maybe months.

"Okay," Zoe said a third time. "Now the easy part..."

Omar managed a chuckle.

Triggering the magic in the enchanted objects Jill had given them, they dug into the Druidic spells.

Disrupting ritual was easier than developing it. A minute of sabotage often required ten to twelve minutes of spellcraft to address. Armed with Jill's intra-magickal spells, they siphoned and dwindled gathered supernatural energy from the rituals and used them to alter the rituals themselves. They didn't need to make particularly large alterations to make an impact. A practitioner layered intent into their spellcraft, and without their presence to anchor that intent, it was an easy thing to monkey-wrench. In spell matrices, taking out a single cantrip destabilized the whole structure. Between the two of them, they could easily set the Druidic coven back by days.

But 'days' wasn't the goal. Thus, Zoe supposed, the so-called 'chaos bomb.'

"You think anyone noticed anything yet?" Omar asked, crouched near three small trees twined together, wiping his brow.

Zoe poked her head between green plant shoots to press her eyes to the glass-paned wall. At this range, one member of the Druidic coven or another would feel their interference eventually. But "Not yet," Zoe replied.

Lights lanced over the horizon before she could look away.

"Hold on," she muttered. "Something's happening out there."

Omar crept over to her, pushing brush aside for a clear look.

Headlights crested the rise to the camp's north. An ATV rumbled down the slope toward the druid encampment. It carried one driver and two passengers. Zoe felt a vague recognition even in the dim-dark night.

"This change the plan?" Omar asked.

"I don't know yet," she whispered.

An oil lamp rose to glow inside a ghillie-camouflaged tree-house built along the boughs of a broad elm. The ATV slowed to a stop a few yards from the bole. Zoe couldn't make out any details; at such distance, even with the diffuse light, her night-sight revealed only silhouettes and shadows.

But she still recognized the woman who rose from the back seat to pull off her helmet.

"Start getting the bomb ready," Zoe said, still staring outside.

"That the 'Lacey' Frank talked about?" Omar asked, already pulling a piece of chalk and a narrow container of salt from his pack.

"Yeah. The Belgian's rep on the run, operations supervisor."

"Pretty late for a meeting..."

Zoe watched as a man wearing body armor and a bear pelt leapt down from the tree-house to meet Lacey. Lacey's new bodyguard, the smoking man Zoe had originally seen weeks earlier, hovered nearby, scanning. Lacey and the pelt-mantled druid held a conversation on the edge of the lampglow. After a minute, a second druid approached, armored and furred. Moments later, the bear-clad man gestured toward the greenhouse.

"Shit." Zoe reached for her sidearm. "They're coming."

Omar dripped with sweat. He looked ill. "It's ready."

Lacey, along with her bodyguards and the two druids, vanished in the swath of darkness between the distant tent-glow and the edge of her night-sight.

Dropping her pistol, she dropped to hands and knees in the salt circle across from Omar and leaned her head against his. She placed her hands symmetrically around the pentacle, the tips of her middle fingers touching the tips of Omar's. Together, they took a breath and closed their eyes.

The bomb went off.

Wilmington, NC.

September, 1997.

Zoe hadn't told Jill or Sung-ho about the clove. They'd gone too far to turn back.

So, almost two days after the single drag she'd taken in violation of the ritual's rules, they performed the Confrontation anyway.

So much energy bristled around them that it gave the air weight, humidity—the ritual space felt like a steam room without steam. A sheath of cloud-cover obscured the moon from the skylight and dozens of candles and candelabra danced in the dimness. A resonant hum vibrated through the floor, a sensation tingling more in their sixth senses than in their bones.

They'd finished most of the Confrontation already. They'd summoned, bound, and banished a score of entities—most, but not all, metaphorical—and they'd reinforced the wards and invocations wired through their bodies and the architecture around them. On the second day of the Confrontation, they'd laid out the intricate matrices of sigils, glyphs, and spellcraft illustrated in the grimoire. The morning of the third day, Sung-ho and Zoe added a number of back-up measures. At dusk of the third day, the Confrontation began in earnest.

Zoe and Sung-ho wore light, combat-ready armor over their everyday clothes. Jill wore a bullet- and knife-resistant vest over a once-white, sweat-yellowed robe. Zoe and Sung-ho carried their gig kits and wore their sidearms in holsters. Jill had a collection of pouches filled with ingredients for relatively quick magic. None of them had been born with natural aptitude, so even the shortest spells took sixteen or twenty seconds to cast—seconds they'd likely lose if anything tipped sideways—but what else could they do?

"I am not the person I was," Jill panted from inside a nest of concentric salt circles, wards, and seals. A half-empty, liter water bottle waited next to her, one of her skeletal hands wrapped around it. Sweat greased her skin. "I reforged myself through the fire of my failures. I resurrect myself as a conscious choice, a decision, a deed. I dedicate myself to transfiguration and transcendence. As above, so below."

"As above, so below," Zoe and Sung-ho chorused.

Over the next several minutes, Jill recounted the harms she'd caused and committed as best she could recall them. She did this frankly and honestly, a practice honed during the Confessional and Jill's subsequent meditations. As she spoke, the shadows dancing 'round the candle flames shivered and thickened. They gained a kind of mass, the light no longer strong enough to dissipate them on its own. Beneath the floorboards, whispers rose.

"I am not the person I was," Jill repeated, voice slowed by concern. She uncapped the water bottle and took a gulp. Swallowed. "I reforged myself…" she peered from the twisting shadows over to Zoe. Zoe nodded and Jill continued the incantation. "…through the fire of my failures. I resurrect—"

The whispers under the floor blurred into a hiss. The air crackled around them. A shower of taps and scratches drummed in from the walls, a noise like an endless army of clawed *somethings* scaling and scaling the house but somehow never reaching the roof.

Jill took a quivering breath. "I resurrect myself myself as a conscious choice, a decision, a deed. I dedicate myself to transfig—"

Jill's body arched and spasmed. A gush of bubbling, brown-yellow fluid burst out of her mouth. A second flue followed. Jill lurched forward on hands-and-knees, spine rounding, and flexed through a third rush of vomit. The viscous gross rolled over circles of Kosher salt and pooled across the floor.

Zoe and Sung-ho leapt to their feet. They glanced at each other, at Jill, at each other again. The grimoire hadn't mentioned anything like this. She watched

Jill, waiting for some sign or signal to clarify her next act, and Jill stared back with bulging, bloodshot eyes and ejecta clinging to her nostrils.

"I'm sorry," Jill whispered. A fourth bout of vomit spilled out of her. "I'm so, s-so sorry…"

An arm jolted up from the viscous pool as if breaching the surface of a lake. A second arm followed. Clawed and five-fingered, draped in garlands of puke and froth and skinned in heroin residue, they braced themselves against the floor, and some terrible thing began to pull itself out of the sick and into their world.

Salem, MA.

September, 2016.

Zoe hadn't known what she'd expected from Jill's description. 'Chaos bomb.' Of course, triggering the magic told her everything — or almost everything — but it had already detonated before her brain processed the information.

The chaos bomb unleashed all the supernatural energy in the greenhouse at once. It tangled up every spell, siphoned all the diffuse mysticism humming ozone in the air, and exploded. The sudden eruption overpowered every ward, every defense, and even mundanity decay itself. It ripped a hole in reality.

Jill's bomb tore open a Breach.

Disoriented from the non-physical explosion and sixth-sense overstimulation, Zoe dizzily sank to the floor. She reached for her sidearm, vision blurring, and barely got a grip on it before Omar pulled her to her feet.

"Come on," he mumbled, chin grueled with vomit. "Gotta move."

A Breach was like a wound in reality, and every semi-real, unreal, supernatural entity searching for a way to wriggle even the thinnest dripping tendril into the world sniffed them out like hunting sharks.

Holding onto each other for balance, Zoe and Omar stumble-tripped through the hydroponic foliage, hoping for a back door.

Behind them, through a near-invisible slit in space-time *materia terra*, a serpentine rattle followed a long hiss. Outside the greenhouse, gas lamps, fae-fire, and light-bulbs flared on; people awoke with a shouting clatter. Supernatural fallout expanded from the Breach, minor blessings and curses, random mystical effects, and, somehow, already, monsters.

They found a back door. Somewhere in the camp, the first gunshots pierced the night.

Cold air seared Zoe's eyes wide. Separating from Omar, she twisted toward a series of shouts. Two druids spilled out of a nearby tent holding rifles. One of them caught Zoe in his periphery and turned. She fired first. The bullet barely grazed the man as he dove for cover. Zoe kept squeezing the trigger anyway, noise and violence as a warning to keep distance.

She and Omar walk-jogged unevenly toward the treeline as she laid down the suppressing fire. When her pistol ejected its spent mag, Omar took over, firing bullets blindly into the chaos behind them while Zoe reloaded.

A couple seconds of return-fire pitted the dirt and splintered bark inches from them but quickly ceased. Whatever had rushed out of the Breach in the half-minute since they'd opened it required significant and immediate attention. An unreal shriek scoured the air to confirm her suspicion.

Too exhausted to run, they moved as quickly as they could.

When Omar moved to reload, Zoe turned to face the scene. Most of the action happened too far away for her night-sight to make out. Walking backwards, she rattled off bullets anyway, just in case.

Over and down a steep hill, they reached denser forestation before Zoe finished slapping in her last magazine.

################

In the adrenal whirlwind following the run, Zoe lost track of how it started.

An hour of seething paranoia had passed in the car, weaving circuitous routes of counter-surveillance evasiveness through the sprawling suburbs. When they'd gotten back to their rented ranch house, all that unease melted into a high-strung euphoria, a giddy *holy shit we did it*, and in that rush she'd grabbed Omar and pressed her mouth against his. After a moment's shock, Omar had kissed her back.

Her heart—

She laughed into his teeth. He grinned. Still laughing, she kissed him again, bit his lower lip, pulled just slightly, and let go. Chuckled. Wrapped an arm around his waist and up to the dense musculature of his middle back.

The house barely existed around them.

They took turns leading each other through wherever to the bedroom. Armor hit the floor, then shirts, then pants. Omar only managed to peel off one sock before Zoe grabbed him again. She put him against the wall and he lowered his face to meet hers. A simultaneous breath escaped them as their tongues met.

She ran her fingertips down his sides, brushing against the numerous feather-thin scars that healing magic had made out of massive wounds. Her body owned its own fair share, a lifetime of life-threatening injuries mystically reduced to slender arcs of barely-raised skin. Some of hers had dates tattooed above them—the only tattoos she had—and she didn't even remember them all.

But when Omar touched her she didn't just feel it on the surface. She felt it layers deeper, almost like something in her sixth sense, as if her scars crusted a mantle of broken, sharded glass and the warmth of his palms fused it whole and smoothed it out again.

She climbed him with her mouth, her teeth, her tongue, all the way up to his jaw line. "Now. Please."

"Fuck, Zoe…"

She pulled him to the edge of the mattress and, with one arm wrapped around her back, he lowered her down. Her mind went blissfully blank as he tied back his dreadlocks. Against her inner thigh she felt warm breath, then lips. Her eyes closed half-reflexively as he kissed his way down. His hands gripped her hips.

Chapter Twenty One

Wilmington, NC.

September, 1997.

It looked like Jill if Jill had skin the shade of heroin dust and wore slops of tar and grease as clothing. It looked like Jill if some crazed sorcerer had taken Jill and stretched her out, if someone had elongated her five-foot-four frame into a warped six-foot-five. It looked like Jill if Jill had clawed fingers and all-white eyes and hair that bubbled and sizzled and fell out in gobs on the floor.

(*underneath everything there's just—*)

Zoe and Sung-ho drew their sidearms and—

All the candles and candelabra went out. In the distant rest of the house, Zoe heard light bulbs bursting. Everything plunged to darkness, night sight invocations giving them the barest six-foot dim of awareness. Muzzle flares strobed the room as Zoe and Sung-ho opened fire. In the microsecond flashes, Zoe saw this newborn Manifestation haul her sister to her feet.

"Hold!" Zoe shouted, grabbing Sung-ho's arm and pushing it down.

Sung-ho didn't need further explanation. He followed the movement of his arm back to the floor, kneeling, and pressed his palms against the sigil-painted hardwood. His lips moved in inaudible syllables.

Zoe charged. If she could press the barrel of her gun against the monster maybe she could—

The plan died before any part of it hatched. In the second between seeing the creature hoisting her sister up and reaching the place where it had happened, the Manifestation had disappeared. It had melted into the floor and walls and taken Jill with It.

"We got a problem!" she shouted. She spun around to return to Sung-ho and found the Manifestation standing feet away.

Drops of diamorphine and oozing tar dripped off of It. Standing so close, Zoe noticed a pinprick of pupil and iris in the vast milky sclera of its gaze. Needletips and razors edged its fingers.

It stepped forward and she stepped back. With a breath, she brought her sidearm to bear and opened fire.

The first two bullets blew through the Manifestation and—

It bled into the darkness too fast to see.

Sung-ho finished the invocation. A surge of energy filled Zoe, sizzling between muscle fibers and along tendon and ligament. Mystic reinforcement buttressed her bones and wired her together.

"It's too dark," Sung-ho said, wiping sweat from his brow with the back of his gunhand. "We need flashlights."

"Where are they?" Zoe asked.

Sung-ho paused. "I—I don't know."

"We have to move. Jill's somewhere inside the spell."

"This wasn't in the book..." Sung-ho scanned the room, grip tightening on his sidearm. "We should take a moment to assess."

"Help!" Jill screamed, muffled by distance. Something crashed upstairs.

"We'll assess as we move," Sung-ho said.

But Zoe had already started moving as quickly as her night-sight allowed.

As soon as she entered the kitchen, the Manifestation attacked. It emerged from the dimness itself, slammed into her side, and threw her against the eat-in table. The force of the blow sent a crack running through the wood and sucked all the air out of Zoe's body. Rebounding, she twisted toward the blow and found nothing.

Sung-ho entered the room only a few seconds behind her. "You okay?"

he asked.

"Mm," she grunted.

Clawed hands reached out from the walls as they moved. Ropes like slender tentacles unfurled from the ceiling and grasped for them. Everything oozed a foamy, cooked-heroin brown.

They kept low to the ground and moved for the stairway up.

As they approached the steps, a body dropped down. A young teenage boy's neck snapped. His feet dangled. Zoe and Sung-ho jerked back.

"We're inside the spell," Sung-ho said.

"Completely immersed," Zoe confirmed.

They moved around the gently swinging corpse and climbed.

"Be careful," Sung-ho advised. "Don't break formation."

At the second-floor landing, voices hissed out of the lightless lounge.

"You will never be free of this," one whispered.

"*Never.*"

Sung-ho made the gesture to hold. He squinted over his gun-sights at the darkness.

Zoe's heart pulsed in her head.

"Neeevvvveeerrrr." The dusty croak emerged from the nothing inches in front of Sung-ho's barrel.

Sung-ho braced himself.

"Help!" Jill screamed. A series of harsh slaps followed. "Help me, please!"

"Sung-ho…"

"One second!"

"Help, somebody! Zoe! Please!" It sounded like whips biting flesh, steel coils slicing air…

Zoe broke formation.

She threw open the door to Jill's room and ran through without looking.

Soles sucked slop as she moved. Everything in the room had melted into surrealist ink. She sludged through tar. "Help!" the Manifestation shouted in a voice close enough to Jill's to pass at a distance, Its back to Zoe, sizzle-flesh shoulders hitching in faux-sorrow. "Help, please!"

Zoe tried to change her momentum, to turn around.

Too late.

Sung-ho yelled the first syllable of her name before the door slammed shut.

The Manifestation's faked despair churned into phlegmatic laughter. "Haven't you figured it out, yet? Under everything there's just *me*."

It charged. Zoe opened fire with her sidearm—assuming it was still even real. Gunfire thunder overwhelmed all other sound. The Manifestation's movement eclipsed all other sight. When they met, Zoe remembered the first time a major wave had tumbled her into offshore darkness.

Salem, MA.

September, 2016.

The Druidic Order pulled out of the operation three days after the run. They'd sealed the Breach, packed up their camp, and vanished. The area their greenhouse had occupied looked as if nothing had ever been there at all. It was possible that nothing had been.

With the retreat of an entire coven, those remaining had started acting more aggressively. More cars drove by Jill's house at night, more phone calls rang in with silence on the other end. Nightmares conjured from oneiromancy haunted the household. But the opposition had also started to spread itself thin. Their plan involved five major, global organizations, but with the Winters team hanging back and the Druidic Order fleeing the scene, they had fewer practitioners working the sites. It gave Zoe and Omar an advantage of time.

Shoshanna Winters only needed another week to assemble and hide the extraction. That secured five of Jill's eight family members. And Zoe had started working on ideas for securing the last three…

Listening to the steady throb of Omar's heart as he slept, her mind quietly tinkered with possibilities.

It would be easy to set them loose, but too risky. Even if Omar could fab a new identity for her, and she didn't know that he could, and even if she used a falsified credit line to get Karen, Altan, and Batu into another country, sooner or later someone would find them. To truly protect them, Zoe needed to figure out a political solution. She needed them to end up under the guardianship of at least a mid-level secret society.

Or maybe, if she could get them out of country, maybe-just-maybe that would buy Shoshanna the kind of time needed to hide another three people.

Her eyelids drooped. She fell cozily asleep before thinking through a plan.

When her eyelids clicked back open, a cool warning pulsed through her limbic system.

"Something breached the perimeter wards," she whispered, knowing Omar had awoken too.

"I felt it," he confirmed.

They moved slowly, at first, listening. Zoe pulled on a tanktop, a thin kevlar vest, and her armored jacket. Her holstered sidearm went around her waist. In the strained quiet, she could hear Omar's every movement. As Zoe pulled pants over her bare legs, a loud, structural tearing howled through the air.

Gun drawn, Zoe bolted into the hallway.

At the entryway to the second-floor apartment, a hulking golem stood holding the entire front door, framed in the bent, twisted threshold.

Zoe had never seen a golem in the field, before. Allegedly, only a dozen existed, almost all created by the hands of the six leaders of the Temple *Beth Yetzirah*. Extraordinarily difficult to kill, even by supernatural standards, and built to exert tremendous violence in defense of those under-defended, golems primarily acted in protective or custodial roles. The notion that the Temple would send one all the way to North America in an offensive capacity seemed so crazy it gave Zoe momentary pause at seeing the creature. *It couldn't be*, she thought. But her sixth sense already knew and the other five quickly verified that, of course, it was.

And, of course, she *had* seen one before. She just hadn't known it.

Nearly seven feet tall, dead gray skin garbed in cheap athletic sweats, Its distant gaze and set jaw betrayed no expression. Staring past her, It dropped the apartment door dully to the floor and stepped inside.

Zoe opened fire.

The researchers who had developed the munitions loadout for Malleus sidearm magazines had done so in an attempt to address the broadest possible range of supernatural threats. Golems did not fall in that range. Bullets alone would not stop such a creature. But they slowed It down.

Lead pierced Its gray flesh to meet mud, dirt, and stone beneath. Still, each violent impact exerted its forces of physics; the golem twisted and stumbled Its way forward foot by foot.

"Bedroom window!" Zoe shouted overshoulder.

"On it!" Omar replied, already whipping around.

Zoe slammed the door shut behind them and overturned an end-table against it. Omar put three bullets through the window, picked up his half-unpacked suitcase, and hurled it crashing into the night air. Holstering her pistol, Zoe scooped her purse and gig kit up from the floor and flung them over her shoulder. One of her burner phones started ringing.

Omar turned away from the outdoor breeze and ran for his laptop case. He grabbed it just as the golem yanked the door effortlessly off its hinges and tossed it aside. Fumbling between the overshoulder strap and his pistol, Omar squeezed off a trio of poorly-aimed shots.

Zoe reached the shattered window, the twenty-something feet to the ground. "Now!"

Omar ran as the gray-faced hulk recovered. He took the jump, tuck-and-rolled, and sprang up. Zoe followed only a microsecond later. The roll protected her from injury but the impact still hurt. Even invocation-enhanced, her ankles groaned and flared as she stood back up. Above, the whole bed-frame, including mattress and boxspring, smashed the rest of the glass from the window-frame and sagged away.

The burner phone stopped ringing. It started again a second later.

Omar pulled the car up along the sidewalk as the golem tossed the bed-frame aside and stepped out into the air. The ground sank where It landed. Zoe grabbed the passenger-side door as It straightened up. She threw herself into the vehicle already shouting, "Go! Go!"

The engine roared. The car jerked forward just as the golem reached it, Its hand falling only inches short.

They sped into the night. They headed toward Salem Woods, a large enough expanse of forestry to lose themselves in. And if they cut through it the right way, it let them out close to Jill's house…

Zoe fumbled through tangled straps to unzip her purse. Inside, a phone rang. She dug through the once-organized clutter until she found the four burners at the bottom of the bag. As Omar took them away from streetlights and toward wilder dark, she found the right device and yanked it loose. For a second, Jill's number flashed on the screen. Then it vanished.

Zoe called back.

Jill answered immediately. "Oh my god, he's dead—"

"Who?" Zoe asked. "What happened?"

Another woman wailed in the background. Karen Woeser?

"Karen's s—her—*our*—Altan. Altan. Altan," Jill kept stammering. "I—I found him. I tried…"

"The ambulance is on its way!" Darnell shouted somewhere in the chaos. "Come on! There has to be a spell. Something!"

"I tried the fucking spell!" Karen screamed.

"I should've been working the wards. I should've been… I built a bomb instead of working on the wards."

"What happened?" Zoe whispered.

From the background, Karen Woeser's strained shrieks provided an answer.

"I should've been working the wards," Jill mumble-sobbed. "Oh, my god…"

"Jill—"

"Not again," Jill's words spilled senselessly across the line. "Not again, please, not again…"

Zoe forgot about the car and the world passing around them. She dropped the phone; Jill's murmurs and Karen's cries crackled together over the line.

"What happened?" Omar asked.

"Karen Woeser's son just killed himself," she answered flatly.

Chapter Twenty Two

Salem, MA.

September, 2016.

Everything slowed down after the suicide.

At least, everything *seemed* to slow down. But Zoe knew better. The withdrawal of immediate surveillance and on-site operatives from Jill's school and neighborhood was little better than a lampshade. The global charter technically forbade murder and so all active aggressors had to make a show of recoiling at the results of their own ongoing actions. Even the Belgian had to pretend contrition out of etiquette.

Nobody wanted to look like they were parading over a corpse. Especially when they were.

The reality was that Altan Woeser's suicide was proof that the campaign was working. All the psychic magic, dream magic, illusion magic, all the pressure of late night phone calls, of surveillance both obvious and occulted— nobody had ever planned to storm the school with guns and handcuffs. The plan had looked like this all along.

Nobody had needed to kill Earnest Hemingway, either. They just needed not to follow him. They didn't follow him right up until he put a gun to his head and disappeared.

So while Malleus and the Belgian reined in their more visible and aggressive efforts, they doubled down on everything else. They only tucked away the things that might grab attention from a regulatory *grigori* or an everyday detective.

Zoe and Omar had also retreated. The golem had set them back. The apartment became a crime scene, the payment method they'd used to rent the space on the cloud BnB software lost along with the associated identity and all the materials they'd unpacked before the attack. The golem, itself, also represented a threat. They couldn't match it in combat and any mystical efforts to dismantle, paralyze, or banish it required more time and labor than they could afford. So they fell back to the safehouse.

It didn't take much more than a good night's sleep for Zoe to come to terms with the situation.

It no longer mattered that Shoshanna couldn't take everyone. It no longer mattered that Zoe didn't have a plan to rescue anyone else. Getting anyone out was better than getting nobody out, and those were the only options she had left.

################

A ninety minute drive from the safehouse, Zoe sat in the parking lot of a convenience store with a burner phone against her ear. "…Jill won't leave before the funeral," she said. "Two days from now."

"Then the evacuation team will be ready that night," Shoshanna Winters replied.

"How long will they stay ready?"

"I can give you a twelve-hour window."

"I need forty-eight."

A beat passed.

"Why?" Shoshanna asked.

"The extraction's going to be compromised."

"How so?"

Zoe watched a couple enter the store; a slouched man smoked a cigarette outside. "I've been sabotaging rituals for weeks. I've seen the spellwork. As soon as they step outside of that house and all the wards protecting it, opposition makes its move."

Another pause.

"I—I'll do the best I can," Shoshanna replied.

Zoe frowned. "What does that mean?" she asked, already knowing the expression usually meant nothing.

"I want Jill out of there—well, not just as much as you do, but…I do. I really do. But all of this has to be hidden until it's done. You know that." As Shoshanna spoke, Zoe restrained her words. "My own brother doesn't even know what I'm doing, not in any way that matters," Shoshanna continued. "I can't leave a team waiting out in the open."

"They're going to move on the funeral. Whatever they do, we'll need time to react and reorganize."

"Then stop your sister from going to it."

"How?"

Shoshanna sighed. "The team will wait as long as they can."

"And how long is that?" Zoe pressed.

"I don't know," Shoshanna said. "Just get your passengers there as soon as possible."

"I need—"

"It's the best I can do," Shoshanna interrupted. "I'm sorry."

The line went dead. Zoe wanted to throw the phone, smash the screen, just break it somehow. Turning it off, she slipped it back into her kit and zipped the kit closed. The evac team would wait as long as they could for a party of five. Nevermind that Jill's family still numbered seven.

Starting the engine, Zoe scanned the area. A man smoked. A couple stood in the checkout line.

She pulled out of the lot and began the drive back to the safehouse.

###############

She found Omar in the bunks, headphones on, hands dancing across his laptop keyboard. When she threw her kit on the floor, he took out an earbud. "What's up?" he asked.

"We have a tight window. No more than twenty-four hours."

"We knew that was a probability."

She hadn't told him about the five-passenger limit. She hadn't told Jill, either.

She cleared her throat. "Frank making any noise?"

"Not that I heard." Omar pointed to his remaining earbud.

"Right." Zoe nodded. "I'll be right back." She hesitated at the exit. "Can I just ask…what are you working on that's so important on that thing? You're not running an assignment or something, are you?"

Omar chuckled. "No, nothing like that."

"Then what?"

"I'd, uh, rather not say. It's kind of embarrassing."

"What?"

"It's a side-project. Something I've been working on."

"Which is…?"

"Fan-fiction," Omar deadpanned.

"Fan-fiction?"

"I said I didn't want to talk about it."

Her eyes sharped, examining him. She couldn't press him too hard. The only questions he could throw out to caltrop hers didn't have answers she wanted to give, either. "Alright, then, I guess. Uh. Good luck with it."

She walked the length of the safehouse to the room where they kept Frank. She entered with her pistol drawn, the heavy door clunking closed behind her. Frank faced the far wall, arms and legs bound with a chair's, waist wrapped in bike-locked extension cords. She stood behind him, waiting.

"Hello?" Frank's voice carried an uncertainty earned through days of mind-altering solitude.

"What's going to happen when those people leave that house?"

"Or what? You'll hit me in the head again?"

She pointed the barrel at the back of his head but kept her finger on the trigger guard.

Seconds passed.

"Or *what*?" Frank repeated. "You're the bad cop. Tell me."

She didn't answer. She weighed the decision. Frank might still have answers; she and Omar might coax one or two of them out of him. But in interrogating him, they'd revealed too much of themselves. Sooner or later, she'd probably have to kill him anyway.

Maybe if he realized that, too, his desperation for survival would yield intel worth knowing.

After a while, a slight tremor developed in her hands from holding the gun aloft and she let the barely-there quake rattle the finer steel parts of the pistol. Anywhere other than a quiet room, a person wouldn't have heard the noise. But Frank did.

"So it's come down like that," he said.

She pursed her lips, still silent.

"Well, then." He coughed. "Would you believe I don't know?"

"No."

"I don't."

"Why not?"

"Do you have any idea how many rituals and ritual matrices and little cantrips are all pointed at those people? Do you know how many ops are running on this?"

She strengthened her grip.

Frank rolled his head from side to side as if trying to see her. When he couldn't, he bowed forward. "I couldn't tell you what will land, but something will. Probably a few things. And I've been locked down here too long to know what any of the final details look like."

"Who is the death curse pointed at?"

"Which one?" He paused after asking, hesitant with thought. "Right. You mean the one in the basement."

"If you give me a name and I believe you, I walk out of this room right now."

"You let me live?"

"I let you live."

He sat up again. "The last I knew...it was Darnell Tims-Briar."

"Not the primary?"

"No. The secondaries only. Everyone wants the primary taken alive.

Well, you know."

"Black-bagged."

"Yeah. You know."

She lowered the pistol to her side and walked out of the room. She let him live.

For now.

a house unreal and dark.

September, 1997.

Zoe stumbled into a funeral home. Or the Manifestation's interpretation of a funeral home.

She didn't need to ask whose funeral. She didn't stop to gawk at the mourners whose own flesh already hung in strips from their rotting bodies. (*reverence the dead whose mourners too shall soon be—)(—you, too, soon—*) She followed the trail of blood and heroin and tar and grease down the only hallway that mattered.

"Are you with the party for Jo—"

Zoe brushed past the thing with the suit and the half-missing face and entered—

—a vast hanging nothing. Or not nothing, but the optical illusion thereof, a combination of black paint and forced perspective that gave Zoe vertigo. She stood, not having realized she'd fallen to all fours, and spun around to search for her quarry.

Sung-ho sat tied to a chair. The Manifestation had already worked through his armor and his shirt. Sung-ho's abdomen glistened with blood, no single wound deep enough to draw much but the dozens of barely-a-scrape scratches adding up to a lot.

"Drink?" the Manifestation asked, holding out a rocks glass of Scotch.

"No," Sung-ho muttered.

The Manifestation drank the booze and threw the glass into the side of Sung-ho's head. It shattered, small shards slivering his scalp.

Zoe rushed at—

She stumbled into a funeral home. Body bags hung from the ceiling. Muffled voices sobbed pleas from within; occasional jerks and jumps implied the victims could still move. She held her maybe-real gun close to her body and searched for an exit. As she scanned the vicinity she realized thick, knotted rope tethered the bags to the ceiling. Or, rather, they hanged the bodies that the bags draped over...

Zoe had only been inside of four spells, before. She'd run dozens of scenarios and 'field simulations,' but she lacked hands-on experience. She wanted to ask Sung-ho what to do next but the Manifestation had already separated them.

She heard the hinge-creak of a Zippo opening right next to her. One of the zippered black pods began to smolder. The thing (*boy*) inside it thrashed, choking on its own strangled cries. Yards away, another began the same process. A miasma of reeking smoke and gagging keens oppressed all. Zoe inched between burning, begging blurs with squinted, aching eyes. The stink of charring flesh clung to the back of her throat.

A slosh dampened her boot-soles. Hot liquid poured in from the unseen edges of the chamber. Heroin, of course. Zoe didn't even glance down to acknowledge the development until the bubbling froth rose to her ankles. And kept rising.

She tried to remember how to manipulate the magic from its insides. It had something to do with leveraging the psychic relationship between the practitioners and the liminal reality of the spell. If she could harness her own sense of faith and shape her desire into a tool, maybe she could force the Manifestation's realm to give her an exit. The sort of spellcraft witches used to approximate the abilities of true psychics and mediums wasn't Zoe's strong suit, but given a minute to focus—

One of the burning black bulbs burst open. A heap of rag-tangled bones sloughed into the rising heroin tide. Zoe jumped at the suddenness and sound.

The hot dark liquid sputtered around her knees. As far as she could see, flaming beacons marked an endless billow of choking smog.

Something rose up from the bubbling pool.

"Oh, no. No, no, no," Zoe choked.

Those were the bones of a boy. Those were the bones of a boy sinewed together by strands of tar and needletips. Rivulets of heroin rolled off of it as it pushed itself up from the drown.

Backing away, Zoe pointed her sidearm at the undead creature. The pool sloshed halfway up to her shins. Somewhere in the blinding fumes, another bag unloaded its innards with a splash — and another. Zoe squeezed the trigger and with a ear-ringing bark the creature (*boy*) collapsed into the rising tide.

Moments later, it emerged again. An uneven bullet hole widened one of its vacant eye sockets. It reached toward her with small phalanges tar-tendon'd. A wheeze of air passed through its hollowness, indistinguishable from the earlier whimpers. It lurched forward, skeletal hand outstretched.

Zoe backed away farther; the hot, cooking heroin reached up passed her knees. Her grip shivered; the small metal pieces inside her maybe-imaginary pistol rattled. Or at least they did in the Manifestation's projected reality.

"Stay away," she said, barely whispering, talking to a skull emptied of anything that could respond. She thumbed the hammer back on her sidearm unnecessarily. "Don't make me do this," and this time she wasn't talking to the child's skeleton, "Please don't make me do this."

The tide barely slowed the skeleton — it passed through the small rib cage like water through a sieve. As the hot, bubbling wet soaked up to Zoe's navel and slowed her like molasses, the outreached claw only accelerated. She fired another bullet and the bones sank beneath the brown again.

She had to remember how to affect the spell. She had to find a way out. She had to—

A body bag thrashed and leapt as she backed into it. She jumped aside, yelping. It swung by its noose, the body within struggling to reach her. Stepping away, she fought to calm her breathing. She reminded herself that relatively few witches had ever actually died while inside a spell. Before the comforting thought left her head, her brain made an unbidden and pithy response: few wasn't zero.

Something clicked. Zoe engaged her sixth sense. Focused on the idea of an exit; a door leading back to Sung-ho. Taking a deep breath, standing still as the flood kept building, she funneled her willpower into an act of psychic magic. By aligning her will with the spell's, and using her standing as one of the ritual's principals, she could force such a thing to exist. Though whether she'd even see her way out through the miasmic fog, she didn't know.

A hand grabbed her right ankle. Losing concentration, she pointed the barrel of her gun toward the heroin bubbling up to her waist and squeezed the trigger. Nothing happened. At some point during her efforts, she'd accidentally submerged the pistol. Dripping wet, it didn't fire. She reflexively squeezed the trigger two more times before the realization caught up to her. "Fuck!" she screamed, hurling her sidearm into the smog.

Another hand grabbed her right thigh. Another, her left…

Then came the teeth.

Groaning with pain, Zoe plunged her arm beneath the seethe and found what felt like the base of a skull. The bones jerked as the thing gnawed at her leg. Beneath the concave curve, she found the knobs of twisted vertebrae. Gripping tightly, she pulled. She pried the mouth free of her and kept pulling until the cervical spine snapped apart from the thoracic. She let the head drift away.

Another skeleton erupted from the heroin and landed on her left arm. Its mandibles chomped at her neck, missing by less than an inch. She spun, trying to get a grip on the thing, and managed to get her hand around *something*. The pool rose higher, climbing her ribs even as she wrestled the five-foot-five skeleton of a sixteen year old boy off of her side. It fell halfway into the swirling sizzle and she stomped its spine until two vertebrae separated.

More figures waded toward her. Not only the tall skeletons of a replicated sixteen year old, but of younger children, too. Some stood only a couple feet above the tide. She turned to keep moving but another rattle of living bones crashed into her legs.

She went under. Everything collapsed into thrashing.

It wasn't just whole skeletons attacking her. Some of the monsters were mere torso, others arms alone. They were frail and breakable, but none stayed dead and they more than outnumbered her. Tumbling through hot heroin, she grabbed the spine of her latest assailant and wrenched on it until it broke. She flung it slow-motion into the swallowing blindness only a foot from her burning eyes. A seethe of ivory emerged in response.

She kicked and twisted, trying to free herself of all the reaching, clawing phalanges and gnashing mandibles. Gravity lost all meaning in that dark, weightless sea. Her lungs blazed wildfire in her chest. The undead caught up to her. Their bites broke apart her armor and tore through fabric to her skin. She ripped the skull from a half-bodied monster and threw it at an approaching silhouette. Even as she did, another bite sent a shock up her leg.

What did they want? Meat? Blood?

Life?

She had to breathe. Which way was up?

Before she could get her bearings, another swarm of bone overwhelmed her. So many dead boys swam their yellowed hollowness toward her that they truly resembled a school of fish. Piranhas. As hungry as death.

And she needed to breathe.

Chapter Twenty Three

Salem, MA.

September, 2016.

They'd used the vehicles to pool risk. Jill, who didn't seem like a target for the various heavy hexes and life-risking curses around town, rode with the children. Karen and Darnell, both already targeted, rode with each other. Omar tailed Jill and Zoe tailed Karen and Darnell. They spaced themselves out in traffic, with Omar hanging back slightly *in the event*. It was the best way to make sure none of the kids got hurt.

To make sure no *more* of the kids got hurt, at least.

The route they drove took them mostly through sagging suburbia; all same-looking houses, fences, and trees. The low skyline gave them broad sight-lines. They passed a grocery store positioned at a bizarre intersection, a criss-cross of curved suburban streets.

Everything en route to the cemetery looked vaguely familiar to Zoe. The whole of Salem shivered with deja vu.

As they drew closer, Darnell slowed down. He swerved onto a road shoulder, parked, unparked, and pulled away. Zoe felt it, too, though even her finely honed sixth sense paled in comparison to a psychic's. All the deja vu familiarity crystallized into actual recognition. Her sixth sense shrieked.

She didn't just *feel* familiarity—she knew this place. She knew it well. She'd surveilled it.

(*two cemeteries backed up against an arc of parkland*)

"Something's happening here," Zoe told her headset.

"We'll be there in five," Omar replied through an earbud.

She felt energy in the air. It was the sort of sensation normal people rarely but occasionally experienced, the instinctive sense of an oncoming storm, of something rippling through electro-magnetic fields, detectable but only unconsciously. The breeze blowing through the dashboard vents carried a faint, real-and-not-real scent of heating ozone.

The attack. But what was it?

(*once you're sure that magic exists you can't be sure of anything else ever*)

"Guys?" Zoe asked.

"Three minutes, gaining."

They approached another tangled knot of strange intersection and she saw them. Standing on the sidewalk, Lacey and two other members of the Belgian's crew scanned the area. Zoe saw them see Darnell's car as it rolled forward, obeying the speed limit.

Someone in a heavy four-wheel-drive box didn't see their light turn red. They didn't obey the speed limit.

The four-wheel hammered Darnell's sedan from the passenger side and sent the thing spinning. Another car shrieked rubber too late to make a difference—the brakes dipped the hood and slammed it under Darnell's. The car flipped and rolled. More cars swerved and banked, one more colliding with Darnell's and two more colliding with each other. Ozone and rubber stink filled the intersection. Horns howled, steel crunched, glass shattered. Zoe yanked up on her emergency brake, barely avoiding the pile-up.

In the moments after the accident, everything went silent. The strewn vehicles wore streaks of blood. Nothing moved behind the airbags. Karen's forearm sat in the sunlit open.

(*when is a car crash just a car crash after all and when is it the result of*)

People started screaming. They screamed at each other, at themselves, into phones, into nothing. They screamed just at having witnessed what had happened.

Through the screaming bystanders, Zoe saw them: Lacey and the Belgian's crew. Their mouths hung agape, lips trying for words that didn't come out. Even they hadn't expected something this bad. But the effect was more surprise than empathy or regret, and when a black SUV pulled around the disaster and stopped in front of them, they all got inside.

Zoe released the emergency brake, threw the car in drive, and hit the gas.

a house unreal and dark.

September, 1997.

Deep in a hadal, opioid darkness, Zoe thrashed in a melee of bones. The swimming dead never stopped coming. They multiplied, two attackers replacing every one that Zoe dispatched; and even the bare parts of her broken foes returned to her. Her throat seized around the need to breathe. Her lungs sizzled like phosphorous. As scratching claws and digging teeth found the flesh beneath her armor, her every movement slowed and drooped. Her senses drifted away.

A final trail of bubbles floated out of her nostrils.

Her mouth opened reflexively. Inevitably, she inhaled.

A spew of vileness surged out of her gullet. Soaked and shivering, Zoe scrambled across a plunging blackness on hands and knees. Vertigo knotted her guts. She couldn't breathe. Coughs and burps croaked out of her. Every inhalation came as a gagged heave. Another upchuck spilled from her lips, the yellow-brown of rotted egg yolks. Her pruned fingers splashed through acidic vomit. Tears streaked through the grime covering her face. A score of small wounds stung her everywhere.

"Smoke?" the Manifestation asked like a growl.

A clove appeared between her sick-stained lips.

The Manifestation's fingers elongated with a sickly creak and offered a rust-mottled Zippo.

Zoe spat out the cigarette. Its slenderness tumbled toward the sense-defying floor. Watching it land amid the illusory depth churned her emptied stomach. With a sputter of bilious spit, she collapsed. Her arms gave out and her legs slid away. Her eyelids fluttered. She squeezed them shut to block out the spiraling optical illusion below.

She heard Sung-ho shout, "Stay away from her!"

And the Manifestation replied, "Or you'll do what?"

Zoe tried to push herself up but couldn't. She felt the Manifestation put one foot on her back and press her down. Another foot found her elbow. She gritted her teeth but made no sound.

The Manifestation's long, spider-leg claws sliced through all the remaining armor and fabric protecting her back. Protecting her spine.

"We know you can't kill us." Sung-ho said. "We're no two-bit, street corner amateurs, here."

Fingernails like boxcutters delicately tickled Zoe's back, climbing from pelvis to skull. Its voice sounded too-too-similar to Jill's. "Not all of you, no. But there may be enough fuck-up in this ritual to give me the leverage to leave one of you paralyzed. Why assume I'd pick my own vehicle?"

Sung-ho chuckled. "You're bluffing. We were by-the-book. Every note."

Zoe felt sick. She couldn't speak. If she opened her mouth she'd vomit until it wore away her teeth.

"Zoe didn't tell you?" the Manifestation cooed. "All those hours of meditation and conversation, all the vulnerability and honesty inherent in the spell, all of that and she couldn't rouse *the spine* to confess?"

Zoe spat up a taste of liquid ashes.

"Zo'?" Sung-ho's question hung like a dead boy.

The sharp, sharp claws tracked the thinnest trails of blood into Zoe's skin. She pursed her lips to silence a whimper. The Manifestation continued, "But I'll make a deal. I'll stop hurting her as soon as you start helping me."

The cuts felt so soft they only hurt seconds after happening.

"Have a drink," the Manifestation said. "A smoke. Hash, weed, Lucky Strikes…I'll hand you anything you want. Ask me to feed it to you and she doesn't even have to have a scar."

"Empower you? And you'll let us live?" Sung-ho snorted. "Please."

"Do you think I *want* to kill you?" the Manifestation asked. The cutting stopped. The Manifestation had shaved off a single layer of epidermis. The air seethed and howled across Zoe's back. "Do you think I *want* to paralyze Zoe? Just because I can? Sung-ho, I'm telling you that I'm going to make you watch and listen as I flay your friend, and all you have to do to avoid that is to ask me for a drink. Just *ask*."

Sung-ho didn't reply. Zoe heard his rising blood pressure steam in his breath. She tried to get her arms back under her but the Manifestation had too much weight on the right elbow.

"What about you?" the Manifestation's face suddenly nuzzled into the side of Zoe's head. "Don't *you* want to make it stop?"

She did. Everything hurt. Everything hurt and she didn't have the strength to fight anymore.

She unstuck her jaw. "Where's Jill?"

The Manifestation laughed, lowly at first, growing louder as Its neck retracted and lifted its lips from Zoe's ears. "Where do you think you *are*, Zo'?"

This time It didn't just sound like Jill, It had Jill's voice, the pitch-perfect and seemingly-authentic article.

Zoe strained to move. A renewed inferno scorched her back. Her muscles groaned. Her elbow twisted. She buckled.

The Manifestation stepped off of her. Zoe flexed her right hand.

With a hard kick, the Manifestation rolled her face-up. The floor clung to her searing dermis like a million pinpoint needles. She screamed. Her every sense became flash-blind anguish. She writhed in some reflexive attempt to escape it but this only made it worse. Her eyes shot open. The vertiginous dark grabbed her guts. Through the dizzying nausea and agony, she tried to focus on the Manifestation as It slunk sinuously away from her and toward the chair-bound Sung-ho.

"Do you have any idea how lucky you are?" It asked in her sister's voice. "Such a shitty dad and the world just handed you an extra one. I didn't get that—*Jill* didn't. We got a half-present mentor who barely even cared about our numerous absences."

"Jill," Zoe groaned. "Where's Jill?"

The Manifestation stopped behind Sung-ho's chair. Sung-ho strained against ropes of tar and leather. He balled up his fist when the Manifestation tried to overlay its razorbladed claws on top of his fingers. "Have you ever watched somebody die? Of course you have. But you probably knew it. The way people die around the two of you, everything's definitive. Bullets and blood, hexes and wards, magickal cancer…you see both the process and its result. Jonathan just hung himself one day. The process was so slow it was almost invisible. They only added one rock at a time…" It lowered Its melting Jill-face to Sung-ho's ear. "Open your hand," It whispered.

Sung-ho braced himself but said nothing.

"Alright, then. Don't." And the Manifestation dug into the back of Sung-ho's fist with Its razored claws and opened trenches between his bones. Decades of training couldn't stop his scream; his mouth warped and widened and a sharp, piercing wail spiked out. Redness slicked his arm in seconds. Strips of meat drooped and tangled from his butchered appendage.

"Stop!" Zoe shouted.

"Smoke?" It asked, suddenly standing close, a lit Zippo in Its hand.

Zoe's lower lip quivered beneath the weight of a clove.

"Just ask," It said, "and all three of you can wake up back in the ritual space. So you failed. People fail every day. Is success at this one ritual really worth the pain?"

Her back had scabbed into a tight, thin sheet. She could taste the clove even through the gross of her mouth. Sung-ho gritted his teeth, tears twinkling down his face.

With a shaking hand, Zoe withdrew the cigarette. Stared at it. "I—"

"Fuck you," the Manifestation muttered. A roil of bubbles swam up Its facial features.

Zoe blinked. "What?"

"I said—I said—" the Manifestation's eyes rolled. It shuddered and spasmed, joints jerking in ways that should have broken them but didn't. The Zippo fell from Its grip, evaporating before it hit the floor.

Zoe didn't know what to do.

A pale hand burst out of the Manifestation's chest, clutching a shard of shattered mirror. With the jagged edge of the glass it sawed its way down the Manifestation's torso, spilling slops of white organs and black blood.

Jill sliced and clawed her way out of the Manifestation's half-hollowed body. Falling free, she collapsed forward, soaked slick in a mottled mess of fluids. Spitting and panting, she shuffled around on all fours to face the Manifestation.

"I said '*fuck* you.'"

Salem, MA.

September, 2016.

Sirens rose up in the distance. The Belgian's coven drove their getaway SUV northwestward, away from the scene of the pile-up and the two cemeteries and their own gruesome handiwork. Zoe swerved around the wreck and followed.

"What the fuck happened!?" Omar shouted in her ear.

"Start the fucking evac *now*!"

"What—why!?"

"Just do it!" She ripped the earbud free and tossed it. The engine snarled. She swerved into the oncoming lane to pass someone, swerved back, and blared her horn at the truck she'd almost crashed into. She caught up to the SUV in twelve seconds.

More shouting crackled through the earpiece. She ignored it.

Moving halfway back into the oncoming lane, she pulled up alongside the SUV and jerked her steering wheel sharply. Her car crashed tilted into theirs. Her sideview mirror fractured apart. The SUV swerved, overcorrected, and overcorrected again. Gaining speed, Zoe swung the rear of her car into the front of theirs. They spun, tires keening. Zoe hit the brakes as she spun, too, not wanting to lose them.

Horns roared. Both vehicles almost collided with traffic.

They recovered first, heading down a side street. Zoe followed, catching another horn blare from whomever she'd almost hit.

The road deteriorated beneath them. Asphalt cracked and potholed until the whole stretch became half-rubble. Another graveyard appeared up ahead on the left, fenced in. On the right, a row of rundown houses kept nearly no windows open to face the dead.

Zoe rode up on the sidewalk. The engine gnashed and growled, bringing her back alongside the SUV.

This time she didn't let up. She slammed her car into theirs and kept the wheel turned in and the accelerator on the floor. Stuck together by inertia and violent stubbornness, they crashed through the wrought iron fence and jumped and bucked over crumbling tombstones. The grave markers exacted their revenge even as they broke apart, splintering chassis and smashing windscreen, tearing up the undersides of both vehicles. Finally, the SUV crumpled against a broad-bole'd tree. Zoe's car slid, two tires popped, axles demolished, until it came to a stop against a tall tower of white stone, totaled. She unbuckled her seat belt, pushed her door open, and sagged out into the grass.

She'd gotten cut up in the rush. Bright red blood trickled down one side of her face and thinner tributaries curled around her left arm. Her bones ached from the shuddering, rumbling chassis and the half-dozen jumping impacts, and numberless bruises swelled their promises across her skin. Groaning, she reached back into the car and grabbed her submachine gun.

She didn't wait for signs of life. As soon as she had her feet under her, she levered off the safety and squeezed the trigger.

Approaching the crumpled SUV, she emptied the first mag in a series of three- to five-round bursts. She fired through the windshield, the front passenger door, and the passenger window. Ejecting the first mag, she grabbed a replacement from her tac pack and reloaded. Crimson sprays slicked the interior of the vehicle. Airbags sagged, burst apart. Whoever sat in the passenger seat slumped over motionless.

Her wards and invocations started burning out. She couldn't salvage the defense against attention. The invocation that slightly muffled noises around her shattered within seconds. The ward protecting her hearing strained. Zoe stumbled, a headrush dizzying her as the magic siphoned its demands from her neuromuscular systems.

Moving toward the rear of the vehicle, Zoe poured most of the second magazine through the rear passenger-side door, the rear windscreen, and the trunk. She didn't bother counting bullets or managing bursts; she rattled off rounds until the recoil jumped her aim and stopped just long enough to realign her sights. The chamber dry-fired as she reached the driver's side of the wreck.

The door hung open, blood drooling over the interior. Reloading, Zoe searched the area.

Lacey crawled through the grass just a few yards away. Considering the compound fracture spiking through one of her legs, she'd made it pretty far. With only three functional limbs, gore-streaked and panting, she wouldn't make it much farther.

Lacey must have heard Zoe's approach because she turned over when Zoe got close. "Wait," she said, holding up a hand as if the meat of her palm could really protect the meat of her face. "Wait, please, you don't know what—"

Zoe shot her in the forehead.

When Lacey went limp on the grass, Zoe fired four more times. Lacey's skull was a broken bowl spilling.

The sirens multiplied, screaming doom.

A sudden surge of vomit filled Zoe's throat. She caught it in her mouth and palm, smearing chunks of it around her lips and chin as she swallowed the rest. Her heart hammered her ribs into broken stones. She couldn't breathe. She had to make sure to contain the vomit. Her DNA tracked back to yet another person who wasn't really her, but fabbing a DNA background was expensive and time consuming. She had to make sure.

She'd had to make sure.

She stumbled over a tombstone and caught herself halfway to the ground. A couple stray plops of ejecta tumbled into the grass. Straightening out, she peered over at her demolished car. The distant sirens grew closer. Dizziness swirled around her; she felt herself detaching from the physical world.

Omar's sedan rolled up along one of the no-car cemetery thoroughfares. The man himself spilled out in a run, reaching for Zoe yards before he could touch her. "We gotta go!" he shouted, sprinting. "We gotta—" He slowed, face twisting, lips curled open in shock. "What the—what the fuck did you *do*?"

Zoe stared at him, answerless.

Chapter Twenty Four

a house unreal and dark.

September, 1997.

The Manifestation's long, gaping wound wormed itself shut. The spilled organmeat melted into the vertiginous black floor.

"I really didn't think you had it in you," It said.

"You have no idea what I'm capable of," Jill replied.

"I know *exactly* what you're capable of — I've watched you every day since the month before you turned sixteen."

"I am ninety-nine days clean." Jill's voice boomed with the sentence. It rolled in from every angle of the void. "I transform myself. I fall and I rise. I create who I am. You have no power, here."

"As above, so below," Sung-ho croaked.

"As above, so below," Zoe echoed, still on her hands and knees.

The Manifestation shivered. It jerked through reality and blink-fast *appeared* in front of Jill. It grabbed Jill's hand and wrenched until the wrist bent wrong-ways and Jill twisted to a kneel with a shout.

"You think you're powerful?" It asked, Its voice a sizzle and hiss. "I bend you. You've been ninety-nine days in fortressed isolation. The world's still waiting for you outside, and it's hungry. It always is."

Jill panted against the growing bulb of pain in her wrist. She threw the palm of her uninjured hand in Sung-ho's direction and all his bindings released at once. He fell forward, dizzy with pain and bloodloss, and clambered away from the chair.

The Manifestation's skin oozed. Tendrils drooped out of It, skinny, sinewy tentacles that reached for Jill's bent, kneeling form. "The world wins," It muttered. "It will cut you and slice you up and needle you."

"The world wins…" Jill chuckled. "Sure. Then the sun wins and then some black hole wins and then heat death wins."

"I will take every part of you. I will eat you like the earth will eat your bones."

Zoe stood. "I promise you my strength and counsel. I vow to buttress you and carry you. I steel myself to this will."

"As above, so below," Sung-ho managed, not yet standing, himself.

"As above, so below," Zoe repeated, hoarse and half-whispered.

Jill opened her mouth but no sound emerged. Dozens of slender appendages wrapped her throat, squeezing. The Manifestation no longer merely had a hold of Jill, It had started growing over her. "You will drown in me," the Manifestation purred. "You will sink to the bottom of the deepest trench."

Zoe braced herself. Took a breath. And ran, roaring with pain, into the Manifestation. She barely made the distance before anguish and exhaustion overtook her. Her sprint slowed to a stagger as she crashed into the unreal thing. She stumbled, somehow tangled in Its impossible flesh. She couldn't win. She'd already emptied her tank.

But she bought Jill a second.

"As above, so below."

A hideous shriek ripped apart the air. Zoe tumbled and spun through a directionless nowhere.

"This won't be the end," the Manifestation growled from everywhere. "I'll always be waiting here. You know I'll find my pinprick way back into you again."

"And now I know that I can push you out," Jill replied, the voice of the sky.

"Sooner or later I will have you."

"I don't care. You don't have me, now."

################

They jolted awake in the ritual space, morning sun spilling down from the skylight.

Sung-ho screamed rolling onto his side. His hand wasn't completely destroyed—not in the literal, material world—but some of the damage had transferred over. Gashes and cuts bled brightly against his skin, none too deep but all deep enough.

Zoe tried not to mirror Sung-ho's volume, her back wet red and burning pain, and pushed herself up onto all fours. It hurt scream-worthy but she knew that Sung-ho's wounds required more immediate attention. She choked on her own voice, crawling across the floor.

Hobbling to her feet, her breaks becoming sprains and her sprains becoming aching inflammation, Jill went for the nearby first aid kit and the pack of esoteric salves they'd readied for the ritual. Still hobbling, she navigated the dozen or so feet over the course of seconds. She wrapped Sung-ho's hand in bandage and began muttering a healing spell.

For natural adepts, minor or moderate healing could take very little time to apply. For people without the natural-born talents, including everyone in the room, it took minutes to address anything of need. Even with their injuries diminished by the transition from the mystic to the material, it took almost an hour for Jill to attend to their wounds. In the exertion, Jill threw up twice and worsened her own damages. After they'd stopped groaning and grunting and panting, Sung-ho and Zoe returned the favor as best they could.

Bandaged and healed beyond the need for medical attention, the trio sat in the ritual space for a long time afterward, not knowing what to do or say next.

"Even with the salves and the spells, it might take a day or so for everything to heal," Jill said.

Zoe and Sung-ho nodded.

"I, uh..." Jill swallowed. "Thank you. I know I've said it, before, but just...thank you."

"Any time," Zoe replied. Her throat felt like a decades-dry gulch.

Sung-ho flexed and clenched his hand. Flexed and clenched. "Feels tight."

"It will for a while."

"Huh."

"Well."

"Well," Sung-ho agreed.

"What now?" Zoe asked.

"I...don't know," Jill admitted.

Zoe nodded. "I'll do anything I can to help."

Sung-ho stood up, stretching. "But first, I need everyone to help me un-barricade my house."

Salem, MA.

September, 2016.

Zoe stared at the laptop screen. Freckles of blood and vomit dried to her slack face.

"They don't talk about the maze at the Academy," Omar said, standing by the door. "None of the spy shit, really. Those first few years, all I heard was 'killing monsters,' 'saving lives,' all that 'Three Keystone Columns' bullshit. 'Safety, Secrecy, Security.' You were the only person around me talking about the org like maybe we weren't the good guys."

She stared.

He'd put together a hell of a backup plan.

Stepping away from the wall, he opened her cigarette holder and withdrew two cloves. When he offered one to Zoe, she took it without glancing up from the screen. He picked up her Zippo from its spot on the mattress next to her. He lit her cigarette first, then his own. After a long drag, she blew a stream of silver smoke at the laptop.

He fumed his own silvery billow and cleared his throat. "Before you pulled me up to partner with you, they put me with this old white guy. Real rumpled dude. *Old.* And *tired.*" He returned to the bunk-room threshold. "A couple months before I started running gigs with you, they sent us on my first anti-personnel run."

The cuts on her lips gooed plasma, scabbing over.

"It was scary how smooth it went. Everything according to plan. It was some coven, low-level hedge-type shit, but one of them was born adept. They'd done some minor summoning, manifestations...nothing important. But Intel-A reported they'd also started buying a lot of bomb-making supplies. Orders came down to neutralize. Dead or alive, all of them...except the born adept. They wanted her alive *one hundred percent.* Anyway. It was mostly psychic and oneiric magic. Not my strong suit, but it worked. After a week and a half, one of the practitioners went nuts. He shot one of the other coven members. Me and the old man intervened immediately, sidearms and silencers, had the whole coven dead or unconscious in under a minute. The born adept put up a fight, wounded both of us before we got her down and zip-tied..."

He trailed off. Puffed. Flicked ash from the cherry of his cigarette.

"Sorry," he continued. "What happened...that wasn't the point. We stayed in some motel before Decomp, some cheap nowhere shit-hole...I was wondering what Intel-A thought the coven had planned that made the gig an organization issue instead of a police problem. The old man laughed so hard he snorted. Said, 'what made it an organization issue was that they had something the organization wanted.' He told me some Druid off-shoot was probably hoping to win over the whole coven and we probably just got the jump 'cause we found something to use as leverage. Most of the coven ends up dead or in prison, we snatch the born adept to re-educate at some black site, the Druids take another lump, Malleus tallies another win. For all we knew, someone in Malleus swiped one of the practitioner's identities and made the bomb-making purchases, themselves. All the stolen identities us field agents burn through? We have the tools to do it." Irony flattened his chuckle. "You were right. We can't be sure of anything ever. Welcome to the fuckin' maze."

All she had to do was hit 'Enter.' The keystroke would start the program and Omar would sweep Jill and the children off into hiding. She wanted to ask how he planned to dodge the inevitable blowback. Her fingertip hesitating over the key, she wanted to ask how he planned to dodge the inevitable blowback.

So why wasn't she asking?

"When you called me, I thought I saw a dead end coming. From my angle, the light hit it just right. You, out here, running the most asymmetrical op I ever heard of? All you had time to do was slow 'em down. Even with my help we were never gonna do better than that. So it seemed to me that someone somewhere had somehow written out your ending already."

She didn't ask because she had a nauseous hunch about the answer.

"So I wasn't lying when I told you it was fan fiction. I just wrote a new ending. Maybe one that pulls you back from the glass wall ahead of you."

And all she had to do was…

She hit 'Enter.' A scroll of data started running down the screen, hundreds of credit and debit cards linked to scores of accounts linked to dozens of stolen identities all making purchases. She took a seconds-stretching, lung-searing drag on her clove. Coughed a fume free of her throat. "Done," she croaked.

Omar nodded. "I'll get to it, then."

After he left the room, Zoe didn't see him again for a long, long time.

Chapter Twenty Five

Wilmington, NC.

September, 1997.

The weekend after the ritual, Sung-ho invited everyone to the summer house. The Park family arrived first, of course, on Thursday, with a nine-year-old Hyun-jung buried in a fantasy novel. Leo arrived Friday morning, a case of mid-range whiskey in his trunk, and Tanisha followed that afternoon, fresh from Decomp after a run in Texas. Valley, a gargantuan white guy with bright blond hair whose real name Zoe could never remember, arrived last, after sunset on Friday when everyone else—except for Jill and Hyun-jung—had already started drinking. Valley didn't drink anymore, for reasons unexplained, but he did smoke weed. Sung-ho clarified that the smoking of anything, weed or otherwise, would only happen on the deck and in his den.

Daniel Briar-Smythe, their father, never made an appearance. For their mother's part, Sylvia Briar projected a multi-sensory pseudo-hologram of herself into the kitchen. Whatever she'd used to fuel the complicated arrangement of spells to make it happen, she'd only given enough fuel to keep things stable for six minutes. Sylvia hugged both of her daughters—extra labor spent to make her illusion tactile—and congratulated Jill on pulling off such a difficult and dangerous spell.

Sylvia offered to move Jill into a small guest house on her property in Short Hills. "I don't mean any offense," she'd said, "I'm just not sure Manhattan is a good place for you, right now."

Jill's face had fallen, but she'd nodded. "Yeah. Maybe not."

Nobody else knew how to reply. The moment passed. The celebration continued.

Night went on. Seo-yeon managed to get Hyun-jung to bed with minimal help from her husband. Everyone drank until buzz became sloppiness; everyone excepting Valley and Jill, at least. Even Leo imbibed more than usual, never quite becoming drunk but veering broadly in that direction.

At some point between one and three in the morning, as the party began its natural decline, Zoe walked through one of the halls she'd barricaded for the purposes of the ritual and passed through a glass door onto the deck. Behind her, Tanisha and Leo laughed at something. Ahead of her, Sung-ho sat alone on a lawn chair, a scotch in his healing hand and a cigar in his other. He turned slightly as she approached, revealing the moon reflected in sunglasses.

"You're just wearing those to make me ask why," she observed, sipping her own mid-range bourbon.

"Pffft," Sung-ho snorted in reply, turning back to peer at the trees, the sky, the moon.

Zoe walked up to one of the other five empty lawn chairs lining the railing of the deck. "This seat taken?"

"You think I'm out here partying with ghosts? Go ahead, sit."

She sat, leaning back. "How do you feel?"

"Eh, my hand still hurts. You?"

"Back still hurts. Other than that…"

"Other than that, I feel *good*," Sung-ho said.

Zoe followed Sung-ho's shaded gaze out to the night. Insects chirred and sang in the woods. The moon glimmered between skinny clouds. Swirling her bourbon in its glass, she took a deep breath and sank into her seat. Her mind wandered back to the Manifestation's trap, the way Jill had found the strength within the spell and within herself to take control of things. With Jill having over one hundred days clean, Zoe wondered if she should give up smoking, at least. The nic fits had subsided and the lingering impulses had weakened almost beyond notice.

She didn't, of course. But she wondered about it.

Sung-ho puffed the cigar cherry back to life and exhaled rings of smoke. Chasing the cigar with the scotch, he angled his face to look at Zoe over the rim of his sunglasses. "Want to know what's up with these shades?"

Zoe laughed. "I get the feeling you want to tell me."

Sung-ho smirked. "It's 'cause the future's so bright."

Zoe laughed again.

But nothing stayed bright forever. Just as nothing stayed dark.

Oceanrest, ME.

October, 2016.

Leonid Singh's primary residence was a two-floor penthouse a mere ten minute walk from Malleus' North American Headquarters in Oceanrest, Maine. Despite numerous layers of security, getting inside had been easy for Zoe. She'd taken the time since leaving Salem to ritualize, reinforce, and empower her invocations. She wore a ward against notice, a ward against attention, and a ward against investigation. She appeared as a blur of shadow and static on CCTV. Nobody had laid inquiry on her in the lobby or at the elevators.

Once on Singh's floor, Zoe hacked the penthouse pin-pad and picked the proper door locks. Walking into the foyer, she almost removed her shoes out of habit. Stopped herself. Locked the door behind her. At the boundary of the entryway, her sixth sense spiked. Focusing on the stimulus, she found a powerful defensive spell at the threshold. A ward against intruders. Something that hadn't applied to her at any previous visit.

It would take the rest of the night to work around the spell, so she didn't. She passed through it and felt it rip her own wards apart in an eye-blink. It diminished her invocations, too, virtually neutralizing all the advantages she'd spent days building up. Not too far away, it alerted Leo that someone had entered his penthouse uninvited. Somehow she doubted that he'd send in either police or agency personnel without finding out more.

It felt otherworldly, entering Leo's home with nobody there to greet her. She felt like a ghost prowling its empty halls.

Beyond the entry hall, a kitchen rose up on her left, a living room ahead of her. Dark curtains half-lidded floor-to-ceiling windows. Turning right, she followed a wall passed a powder room to a stairwell. Beyond the stairwell, a guest bedroom, attached bath, waited. She'd slept there at least a dozen times.

She ascended the stairs.

She crept through the penthouse's dim second floor until she reached Leo's home office. He'd left it unlocked. Just inside, on a small end-table near the door, she found an old .mp3 player plugged into an old charger-speaker system. She clicked the device awake. Leo had been listening to a blues playlist.

At a volume loud enough to hear from the stairway landing and quiet enough not to hear from below, Freddie King sang the *Same Old Blues*.

Zoe lowered herself into one of the two blood-red leather chairs angled at the broad executive desk dominating the space. On the round table between them, she set down her lockpicks and the device she'd used to trick the pin-pad. She pulled her pistol and suppressor from her tac-pack and threaded them together.

Leo entered not long after, looking alarmed but not surprised when he turned on the lights to find Zoe waiting.

It all looked like clouds to Freddie.

"Sit down," she said, gesturing with the suppressor to the chair behind the desk.

Leo sighed. Still, he did as she'd told him. "I don't imagine you'd tell me whether or not you planned to kill me?"

"Leo…"

"What? Did the question wound your honor?"

In truth, the first several iterations she'd imagined *had* involved his death. But he hadn't been the one to orchestrate anything, he was just the closest guy she knew. "The plan is not to hurt you *unless*," she answered.

His shoulders dropped. His posture relaxed. "So, then…what do you want?"

She wanted to scream at him. She didn't. Cleared her throat, instead. "This isn't about what I want. It's about what's going to happen next, whether anybody wants it or not. But before I get to that, I need to ask a few questions."

He looked at her with sternness unbecoming a hostage.

"Like I said, *unless*."

"What do you want to know?" he asked.

"Why did you send me into that?"

"I didn't."

"Come on."

Another sigh; he looked away. "I'm on your side, Zoe. I always have been. I was presented with an impossible situation. The movement against Jill's school was enormous — almost every major organization with active operatives in the Americas had interests involved."

"So why did you send me in?"

"I didn't," he repeated. "I gave you the intel and you went ahead. I helped wherever I could."

"You gave me a cover story that only worked if I failed."

"Because the odds were that you would."

She lost her breath for a moment. Recovered. "And now that Jill's MIA?"

"Officially, she isn't. Some people believe we have her in our custody, more believe the Winterses have her in *their* custody. I've added some weight to the second theory, in part to redirect the Belgian's fury, and in part because it dove-tails so easily into your cover story."

"What was your plan?"

"I didn't have one. By the time the news about Jill had reached me, things already looked grim. I gave you the intel and a cover story as a shield. If you failed, you were already covered. If you succeeded, you'd either need to truly defect or you'd spend the rest of your life in various degrees of hiding."

"Both situations that left your hands ostensibly clean," Zoe assessed.

"As long as Shoshanna Winters didn't go to anyone on the Board with what she knew."

"Which wouldn't work in her interest anyway."

"Indeed not. And, now, what she knows gives her significant leverage over yours truly. Leverage she's already begun to manipulate."

"But that was always a possible outcome," Zoe said. "Likely, even. As soon as you put the two of us in touch."

Leo nodded, adding nothing.

"And what about Omar?" she asked.

"He's an AWOL operative missing since the end of his last Decomp cycle, or so goes the story. A story I've had to maintain at some effort, given the loose ends the two of you left behind."

"A story you can't maintain forever."

"Unless Jill somehow appears in either our custody or the Winterses', and soon, *none* of this can be maintained forever. Or even for another month."

"How many people are looking for her?"

An amused huff noised out of him. "Not many, yet. A few operatives from us, a few from Winters-Armitage. Everyone in Intel-A with Beta clearance, to no effect. I assume Omar wrote the software?"

Zoe didn't answer.

Leo nodded again. "Train tickets, plane tickets, bus tickets…purchases at multiple gas stations and parking garages, tiny little companies in half the cities in the nation…he overwhelmed us with possible paths. One of my mentees is an analyst in Intel-A…they told me they'd thought they'd found something when they noticed a pattern of security glitches and hacks, but even that turned out to be a false lead. Your partner vanished in a 'net-wide noise of his own creation. You must be proud."

She wasn't. But she still said, "Something like that."

"I assume he didn't tell you where he was actually going?"

"He didn't," she confirmed. She chewed on the next one, something she didn't need to know but wanted to. Eventually she asked, "How did anyone manage to bring in a golem?"

"You opened a Breach," Leo answered. "You opened a Breach and took the Druidic Order off the board. The Temple assumed its operatives were next in line and they weren't going to give up their seat at the negotiations."

She wanted to ask another question but she'd already figured out the rest of the answers. She wanted something more. She wasn't sure what.

Leo broke the long silence. "So…what happens next?"

Zoe lowered the gun-barrel. "Your office phone is going to ring soon. It'll probably be Omar, but on the off-chance it's Jill, don't be surprised. They'll have an offer. I'm not sure exactly what it'll be, but what I expect is…" she paused. She needed a breath. "What I expect is, they'll offer Jill's conditional surrender. She'll want her kids left alone for the rest of their lives. She'll want to end up at a W-A facility instead of a Malleus black site. And…"

"And she'll want a story written that covers you and Omar," Leo surmised.

"Yeah."

"Then I suppose that is that." Reaching into a desk drawer, Leo produced a black rotary phone and placed it next to his computer keyboard. He folded his hands, waiting. "Before it rings…I want you to know I'm sorry, Zoe. I truly am."

"Yeah. Me, too."

Chapter Twenty Six

the note she left.

[decrypted & deciphered]

Zo'—

I'm sorry. I tried. When I agreed to do this, I almost thought I really could.

I never belonged in this world, anyway. It's too cruel — too content in its cruelty. The fact that I made it this far, I owe it to you and Darnell. I know Sung-ho helped but I was never close to him the way you were. It was all you and D.

I miss him so much, Zo'.

I miss all of them so much. I just can't keep missing, anymore.

Before anything else, I want to thank you. Thank you for everything you did — for me and, even more, for my children. I don't know where they are and I can't find them through any method. Which probably means about the same for the people you helped shield them from. And even though I'm locked in here, knowing that they're not... well, it won't stop what I'm going to do next, but it means a lot. So thank you. Thank you forever.

Do you remember when you first pledged to Hammer? Or whatever it was called back then, or whatever they like to call it now? Dad was so proud of you. He got us drunk on champagne even though we were both underage. He cooked a whole three course dinner. Even mom liked it, ever the discerning consumer...

I always think about the look on his face that day when I think about the look on his face the first time he sent me to rehab.

My best friend hanged himself. My best friend hanged himself and heroin was the thing I stumbled into because I didn't have the coping mechanisms to process that. I just wanted to stop hurting. I wanted to disappear. And I did.

I got lost out there.

Maybe I still am.

But after that summer — '97 I think? — I never did heroin again. I fell into a couple other holes, I know you know that, but never heroin. And I'm proud of that, I guess, because even in recovery you'd be surprised how often I knew where to get some. Or maybe you wouldn't be surprised : it was always. Within a few months of living anywhere, I *always* knew where to get some.

And I never did. So maybe that's something.

Darnell was lost, too, when we met. He'd figured out he had some kind of psychic *thing* going on but mostly all it did was scare him. He didn't know how to turn it on or off, how to tuck it into the back of his mind or bring it to the fore, he didn't know *anything*. It ran him down. On our fifth or sixth date I was over at his house and his sixth sense overwhelmed him. He tried to write it off as a panic attack and told me to take a rain check on the date. Then something clicked, maybe he picked up some random thought I was having or had some momentary slice of unlikely insight, but he looked at me and asked, "You know?" so I asked, "Know what?" and then he pointed to his head and I said "Oh, that, yeah. I know."

Our daughter is a born paranormative, a 'natural adept.' We knew it before we finished the adoption process. We didn't want her to spend half of her life afraid of herself, barely knowing what she was, so we taught her. Not long after, a friend of mine from my days at Winters-Armitage joined us along with her own son. She'd left the org on pretty good terms, the Winterses a bit more lenient about quitting a job than Hammer ever was...

I guess you know what happened after that.

Now Karen is dead and Darnell is dead and I'm...

I'm here. Same-day after groggy same-day. Breakfast, pills, lunch, interrogation, pills, dinner, therapy, pills, sleep. Tomorrow, tomorrow, tomorrow.

Haven't I been trapped here, before? Change the pills to powder, give the orderlies different outfits... new cage, same bars.

I love you, Zoe. Everything you've done for me, for my kids... I thank you forever and I love you *forever*. But I can't stay here, anymore.

Just remember: under all the cases and assignments and gigs, under all the Intel-A reports and personnel dossiers and operations, under everything, there's just me. There's just people like me.

May the secret and sacred energies connect us always,

Jill.

New York, NY.

October, 2019.

"The long-run is a misleading guide to current affairs; in the
long-run, we are all dead."
— *John Maynard Keynes*

every story ends the same way: every story ends.
(*nothing ever really ends*)

Zoe, forty-seven years old, sat back against the same greened steel hood
above the Astor Place station that she'd sat back against at twenty-four. She was
the dangerous kind of drunk a person only became when they needed booze as
an excuse to weep and sob and scream. She had a switchblade, a can of pepper
spray, and a half-empty bottle of whiskey on her. She felt ready to use any or all
of it.

Twenty years had passed. How had twenty years passed? Astor Place was a fucking Chase Bank now. When had that happened? How hadn't she noticed?

The NYU kids had manifested their destinies all across Alphabet City and had reached Avenue C before their wave broke and crashed back again. Tompkins Square still played host to a revue of indigents, but the streets and avenues ran more rampant with cops than crust-punks. At some point, she guessed she'd stopped leaving Murray Hill. Everything had changed, unobserved. How? And *why*?

Jill had killed herself.

The story read like this: during her lucid hours, Jill realized that the frequent visitors who came during her non-lucid states were Malleus agents. Medical staff, employed by the Winters-Armitage corporation, dismissed her subsequent paranoia as a further symptom of her alleged psychosis. Jill didn't want to talk to Malleus, didn't want to tell them whatever they wanted to know, and so she'd spent her lucidity working on a spell. Nobody in the company knew how long it had taken. One day, a nurse walked into the room to discover Gillian Briar freed from her restraints and hanged with a bedsheet.

The psych facility specifically selected bedsheets that lacked the tensile strength to break the cervical vertebrae. They weren't even supposed to be able to hold up a human body. The chances that Jill could have pulled it off were something akin to one in six hundred and seventy thousand.

Sometimes magic looked like that.

Maybe the story would have ended differently if—if—if—

But it hadn't.

The story read the way it read and it ended the way it ended.

(*you will never be free of this*)

Zoe pushed herself up, wavering on whiskey-legs. "It isn't that we've gotten old," she muttered to herself. "It's that the world stays young." She snorted and took a slug of whiskey from a paper-bagged bottle. A group of people half her age passed her on the crosswalk. One of the men glanced at her overshoulder and she glared back. *Say something*, she thought. *Go ahead.*

He turned away a half-second later, talking to one of his friends.

Zoe headed east. Why?—hell with it, why not?

The walk felt right-now familiar but the landscape had transformed.

Everything became something else, eventually.

Passing Tompkins Square Park, she saw a ragged, chewed-up man pacing frenetically around the playground. Every few steps he stopped and turned toward the buildings crowding around the park's fence. "Fuckin' yuppies!" he shouted. "Fuckin' yuppies pulled the rug right out from under me. Pieces of shit. Pieces of fucking shit yuppies. Hey, fuck you! Fuck you! Fuck you!"

He howled at the brownstones, at the apartments, at the pedestrians. His voice had the feral quality Zoe associated with people who had suffered homelessness so long that they'd forgotten civilization entirely.

Taking another slug of whiskey, she watched him scream for a while. Where else was she going, anyway? She wondered how many addicts roved the surface of the Earth searching for thread to keep themselves stitched together even as reality razored them apart.

She kept walking. A dozen college-aged kids wearing outfits that could never be mistaken for rags muttered to each other by phone light, standing outside of a bar.

Beyond the bar, Alphabet City reasserted its crusted heritage. Beyond Avenue D, the indigent reigned. Would she drift into that heavy darkness? Would she seek out the trouble so easily found in the crevices of its dilapidation?

She didn't see why not.

Until she saw a row of phone booths.

It shocked her, this bygone monument. Three phone banks waited, garbed in graffiti and reeking of piss, like the statued legs of Ozymandias. Zoe stood for a long time, weight wavering from one leg to another, brown-bagged bottle hanging loosely from her fingers. Taking another gulp of whiskey, she walked over. She tried not to breathe through her nose.

She fed the machine some quarters and dialed a number. The number lived inside her head. She'd thought about punching it into a keypad so many times she'd memorized it. Setting the brown bag and its contents aside, she put the grimy handset to her ear.

"Hello?" Shoshanna Winters mumbled, sleep-voiced.

Zoe felt like her mouth was a loaded gun and she had to empty the mag all at once. "My sister is dead. Nobody set her up, nobody did anything besides follow SOP and she's *dead*."

A pause.

"This is Zoe, by the way. Zoe Briar."

"I know. I only gave this number to three people. And you...you know how stupid it would be to look for revenge, right?"

"I'm not."

"Or justice."

Zoe snorted. "I'd have as much luck hunting the fucking Easter Bunny."

Another pause.

"What is it you want, then?" Shoshanna asked.

"I want in."

"In on what?"

"Whatever you're doing. Whatever you're doing while the world thinks your brother is still in charge."

"There is no 'in.' I'm sorry."

"Don't hang up on me," Zoe snapped.

"Tell me what you want. If it's not justice or revenge, then what?"

"Come on. You know."

"Tell me."

Zoe peered behind her. A scarecrow vagrant shuffled down the sidewalk.

"I have to be up early tomorrow," Shoshanna said. "I'm sorry, Zoe. Goodb—"

"I want to change the world," Zoe confessed.

(*look at me*)

(*and he did*)

(*I don't c—*)

"Call me when you're sober." She could almost hear Shoshanna's grin. "Use a different payphone—but use a payphone, not a burner. Maybe we can set up a meeting."

Zoe opened her mouth to reply but couldn't think of anything to say.

"Good night, Zoe Briar."

Shoshanna hung up.

Zoe put the gross handset back on the receiver and picked her whiskey up from the ground. Turning around, she saw the scarecrow vagrant again only a couple yards away. "Hey," she upnodded to the lanky man, approaching. "Free whiskey."

"Huh? Wha—oh, shit, thanks."

He said something else but she'd already continued walking.

Acknowledgments

First of all: thank you for reading. The whole point of publishing something is to have people read it—by being one of those people, you've given this thing a purpose. There's nothing I appreciate more.

Of course, if you'd like to leave a review somewhere, that would also represent a monumental boon for me. Reviews of any variety are treasured artifacts among author-kin. I would hold such a trophy in high esteem, indeed...

Anyway, onward to the other acknowledgments!

A special thanks Pam Benjamin, Beau Groff, Sarah Kewin, Taronté Veneble, William Arthur Maurici, and Jake VanBortel-Buckley for serving as beta readers and providing such excellent critique on earlier drafts. Questions, commentary, and critique are the three primary avenues of improvement, and I think this version is significantly improved thanks to you. In return, I offer significant love. Thanks to Patrick Tsao, who designed the original serial cover, and to Tania at GetCovers for the final novelization cover.

And a very special thanks to my love Ashley Clark.

Thanks to everyone who helped me out with research, people and sources too numerous to name.

About the Author

Greetings, squidlings, 'tis I : a madman.

I exist primarily in digital and imaginary landscapes but, physically, I live in the dozy suburb of Fairport, NY, licking wounds and yearning for the twelve years I spent in NYC. I write horror fiction, dark fantasy, and diet sci-fi. My previous book, also placed in the Oceanrest setting, was *The War Beneath*, published by Permuted Press.

If you liked one (or both) of my novels, you'll probably like what I'm cooking up next. I have a working draft for *A Kingdom Without End* and a somewhat *less* working draft of *When They Wear the Mask* — though I'm hoping to release *When They Wear the Mask* first. Timetables remain difficult to nail down due to ongoing scheduling and financial issues but do trust, fellow weirdo, that I am working to advance the situation.

If you're interested in peering behind the curtain, or just supporting a small-time author, please feel free to join my budding Patreon community at https://www.patreon.com/thesrhughes. As a Patreon patron, you'll receive access to all previously-published short/flash fiction, early novel drafts released in serial format (including a serialized version of *A Kingdom Without End* coming up), behind-the-scenes posts, and craft/genre essays. I'm hoping to expand those offerings as the community grows.

You can also find me on certain social media platforms, primarily Instagram and Facebook.

Author Site : https://thesrhughes.com

Instagram : https://www.instagram.com/thesrhughes/
Facebook : https://www.facebook.com/thesrhughes
Patreon : https://www.patreon.com/thesrhughes

Discussion Questions

1. Is Zoe Briar a good person? Why or why not?

2. Is Jill Briar a good person? Why or why not?

3. Are you a good person? Why or why not?

4. Who (or what) serves as the primary antagonist for each timeline?

5. Do the events of later timelines negate the events of the earliest timeline? Why or why not?

6. What would you have done?

7. What do you think happened to Frank?

...Coming Soon from S. R. Hughes...

Excerpt From

A Kingdom Without End

...The Present...
(as the fallow soil offers up one living thing)

Hyun-jung dug nails into Rashid's shoulders. Below them, a blanket they'd bought in Cuzco and the cracked dust of the Andean desert. Above them, an infinity of stars.

Rashid bit his lower lip, his hands iron around her hips. "Hyun-jung," he groaned, pressing up as she ground down, "Hyun..."

A full moon glistened his sweat into pearls. Cool desert breeze stroked his pores to gooseflesh. His neck curling, his back arching, he gripped her. She bent over him, hands on his shoulders, her body rocking serpentine. Breaths escaped them in delightful gasps and awe-struck curses. "Fuck yes, oh, fuck yes, fuck yes, fuckyesfuckyesf—"

"Slow down!"

"—uckyesfuckohmygod—"

"Hyunnnn—"

She felt it like magic. The climax rose through the conceptual and into the material; it pressed itself against the surface of reality ready to become everything. It pushed, liminal, being and not being. Rashid thrust up, she bore down. Nails bit skin. His voice pitched high, grasp so tight on her hips that their molecules met, and the world split open. She shivered and shook, speaking tongues, euphorically out of control.

He groaned, still plunging, his grip rocking her even as she lost the mental wherewithal to do it herself. As his moans dissipated into pants, she collapsed on top of him in a hungry swarm of kisses. They laughed, hands wandering, until she rolled off of him with a sigh.

"Accidental vacation," she muttered, staring up at the blazing gallery of night.

Intel-Analytics had reported the decent probability of an active and dangerous *pishtaco* in the region. Since the South American field operatives were already all booked on assignments, Malleus North American's ASOD caught the case—and Rashid and Hyun-jung caught it from there. They'd landed in Peru less than sixty hours later.

Except Intel-Analytics had gotten it wrong. The *pishtaco* turned out not to be a *pishtaco* at all, but a small group of mundane men and women with a willingness, if not a taste, for violence. Rashid and Hyun-jung filed reports with local authorities as anonymously as they could and received the rest of the week off. Since the Advanced and Specialized Operations Division required ten business days of Decompression/Recovery anyway, and since they didn't have anything to decompress or recover from, they'd turned the entire situation into an impromptu vacation.

Such things were among the very few perks of the job, the byproduct of a field where intelligence and analysis were simultaneously required and, by the nature of their world, essentially dubious.

She kissed sweat from his collarbone, her head on his chest.

"Hyun-jung," he said, staring up, his chin slanted against her crown. "I…"

"Uh-huh?"

"I…" he swallowed, gulped, and took a deep, sucking breath. Grabbed for his throat with his free arm.

"What's wrong? Can you breathe?" she jerked up, kneeling, scanning his body for clues.

The liquid on her lips wasn't sweat. The drying slick on his chest wasn't sweat, either. His heart jumped, pumping hard. His Adam's apple bobbed and spasmed. His jaw clenched. "I--I--I wanted..." his eyes bulged.

Hyun-jung pushed away from him, reaching for--for what? They were on vacation.

"Hyun-junggggg...." the sound stretched as he ground his teeth together. His stomach bulbed, something pushing up against the skin from inside. His lower ribs popped one by one, breaking. She scrambled through their picnic for something to do. Veins bulged down Rashid's arms and up his neck. He spat, gagging. "I lo—I l—I lo—"

His skin ripped apart, shreds of stomach and liver and unspooling intestine spilling out of him. Twin mantid appendages reached up from the ragged cavity, tearing him open from throat to groin. A skull tried to force its way through his skull. His teeth shattered. His tongue lolled.

The monster crawled out of his empty skin laughing.

Hyun-jung shouted herself awake behind the cashier's counter. Faint music jingled through the empty gas station. The clock on the register couldn't tell her when she'd passed out or how long she'd stayed under, but it told her the current time, 8:41 PM. She wiped nightmare sweat from her brow and ran a hand through fear-greased hair.

The Peru vacation had happened over five years ago. Rashid's death, three years ago.

Her court martial from ASOD and subsequent burn notice from Malleus came only months after that.

Now she worked at a gas station in the middle of southwestern U.S. nowhere. After nine years as a monster hunter, after over a decade of military and ASOD training, after a lifetime spent in the secret shadows of a hidden world...now she worked at a gas station. The burn notice saw to that. The burn notice and a lack of alternative skill sets.

But something was coming, now, she knew.

She'd first felt the magic a couple weeks earlier, the hairs on her arms and the back of her neck all standing static-straight as she drove to work one evening. The car clock had read 3:00 PM and the song on the radio had switched over mid-track. It played 'Sixteen Tons' by Tennessee Ernie Ford, not a song that usually appeared on radios anymore. Not long after, she'd found three dead crows on her apartment balcony, causes of death uncertain. Other flares of mystical synchronicity had unfolded from there, warning signs of some major ritual or powerful entity putting its sights on her.

She pushed herself off of the stool and excused herself to the employee bathroom. She excused herself for her own sake, her work-buddy Trey having neither shown up for work nor called with justification for his absence. On the toilet, she puffed on her vape pen, trying to bury her nightmare in THC. She clicked the pen four times to turn it on, took four hits, and clicked it four more times to turn it off again. She coughed after the last hit, hacking until something gunky formed at the back of her throat. She hocked it into the toilet on her way out.

Back behind the counter, she checked the cashier-clock again. 3:33 ??, it told her.

She blinked, recoiling from the wrongness. 3:33 ?? it repeated. She blinked again, rubbing at her face this time.

8:58 PM, the clock corrected.

Nine and three were important numbers cross-culturally. People in the know paid attention to cross-cultural patterns, to the coincidences that suggested so much more than coincidence. Ramadan happened during the ninth month of the Islamic calendar; in Christian myth there were nine choirs of angels. Nine looked like Bahá'í completeness, like divinity in Hinduism, like a body curled up, head bowed, asleep or maybe dead. Odin hung himself from an ash tree for nine days and an average human pregnancy lasted nine months. Etc. Or three: father, son, holy ghost; maiden, mother, crone; Brahma, Vishnu, Shiva; *neshamah*, *ruach*, *nefesh*; the three treasures, the three jewels, the trinity. And, of course, nine was a triune of trinities.

Coincidence? Maybe. Sometimes the strongest magic looked like coincidence.

Sometimes that was the whole point.

The hex laid on her during her court martial, for instance: if she ever successfully convinced someone who didn't believe in the para-normative to start believing in the para-normative, black cancer would eat her alive within weeks. If she spilled the wrong information to the wrong people, she'd rapidly develop brain and bone cancer. It would be terminal, impossibly terminal. Doctors would shake their heads at lab reports that didn't make sense to them, anymore; they'd try every treatment in the book and every treatment would fail. Sometimes cancer won. Statistically, it happened.

Magic hid in such places.

Hyun-jung reached into her uniform pocket and found her charm ring. Dozens of cross-cultural symbols hung from it. She ticked them off like rosary beads. A spell formed in her mind, a defense against harm. Before the court martial and the burn notice, people had considered her among the best ward witches in the organization. Now, few people considered her at all.

The cashier-clock said 9:00 PM.

Tennessee Ernie Ford crooned from the speakers. Hyun-jung figured one of two things was about to happen, and she hoped for the one that meant she lived a little longer. She held her breath. The prepared cantrip floated in her mind, ready.

The gas station door swung open, mounted brass bell dinging.

The woman who walked in was, in many ways, Hyun-jung's opposite. Five foot eight to Hyun-jung's five-three, slender and toned to Hyun-jung's more muscular stockiness, middle-aged to Hyun-jung's…well, nearly-middle-aged. A white forty-something woman wearing a leather jacket, jeans with subtle armor plating sewed inside, and motorcycle boots approached the counter. She lifted her eyebrows expectantly.

"Holy shit…" Hyun-jung whispered, finally recognizing her.

Zoe had commonly visited Hyun-jung's father back when Hyun-jung's father was still alive and working for Malleus/ASOD. The two had had something of a mentor-mentee relationship before Hyun-jung was old enough to pledge. Zoe, Leo, and Shreya had all spent a lot of time in that apartment. But after Hyun-jung's dad transferred from field work to a desk assignment, Zoe appeared less and less frequently. After his retirement, especially. Hyun-jung remembered seeing her only three or four times between her dad's retirement and his funeral.

"Long time no see," Zoe said.

Hyun-jung nodded.

"Leo sent me."

Hyun-jung nodded again. Tennessee Ernie Ford told Saint Peter not to call him. He couldn't go.

"We should get drinks," Zoe continued. "Have a chat."

"What kind?"

"Well…how would you like to be reinstated?"

(*I owe my soul to the company*—)

Hyun-jung's head swam, memories of Rashid screaming into memories of what she'd done to avenge him. She'd killed four people in Florida, left them cold-cased in Missing Persons. It had seemed fair. They'd killed the love of her life, after all. The Arbiters hadn't seen it the same way. Thus the court martial. Thus the burn notice. Thus, a gas station surrounded by silence and dark. "Wh-what?"

"First, I need some Zippo fluid," Zoe scanned the wall behind Hyun-jung. "And do you know a place I could get a pack of Djarum this late at night?"

"Uh, no. Not legally. We have some—"

"No, thanks. I'll just take the fluid."

"You said…they want to reinstate me?"

Zoe smirked. "There's a catch. We'll have to talk about it somewhere more private."

Hyun-jung closed the gas station early.

Excerpt From

When They Wear the Mask

...Six Months Earlier...
(where the story starts but not the start of the story)

Robert Robertson, Jr., recently divorced and more recently unemployed, sifted through his late Uncle's estate mostly on autopilot. Bob had loved Uncle Nick more than any other member of his family, mother and father included, and the vice versa seemed equally true. Nick had always called him "Mikey," which Bob preferred to his own name despite the cereal connotations. It beat out "Have you met Bob, y'know, Bob's son?"

Ha ha.

He'd always hated his father for that. The name. Who lived their lives with such an embarrassing name and then handed it down to their children? But to Uncle Nick he'd always been "Mikey," never Bob-Bob's-son, many-faceted disappointment.

Few other people had harbored such affection for Uncle Nick. Bob's late Aunt attested to that.

In the basement of a dead man's house, recently divorced and more recently unemployed, Bob-Bob's-son, multi-faceted disappointment, discovered a box, lock-garlanded and patina'd in a layer of white-out painted sigils and glyphs beyond his recognition. Breaking it open without quite knowing why (had he heard something whispering inside?), Bob found a mask.

What did it look like?

What an unimportant detail.